DARK IMPERIUM

More Warhammer 40,000 from Black Library

• DARK IMPERIUM •
Guy Haley
BOOK 1: Dark Imperium
BOOK 2: Plague War
BOOK 3: Godblight

• DAWN OF FIRE •
BOOK 1: Avenging Son
Guy Haley
BOOK 2: The Gate of Bones
Andy Clark
BOOK 3: The Wolftime
Gav Thorpe

INDOMITUS
Gav Thorpe

BELISARIUS CAWL: THE GREAT WORK
Guy Haley

• WATCHERS OF THE THRONE •
Chris Wraight
BOOK 1: The Emperor's Legion
BOOK 2: The Regent's Shadow

RITES OF PASSAGE
Mike Brooks

KNIGHTS OF MACRAGGE
Nick Kyme

CADIA STANDS
Justin D Hill

CADIAN HONOUR
Justin D Hill

• VAULTS OF TERRA •
Chris Wraight
BOOK 1: The Carrion Throne
BOOK 2: The Hollow Mountain

MARK OF FAITH
Rachel Harrison

EPHRAEL STERN: THE HERETIC SAINT
David Annandale

DARK IMPERIUM

AN ERA INDOMITUS NOVEL

GUY HALEY

BLACK LIBRARY

A BLACK LIBRARY PUBLICATION

First published in 2017.
This edition published in Great Britain in 2022 by
Black Library, Games Workshop Ltd., Willow Road,
Nottingham, NG7 2WS, UK.

Represented by: Games Workshop Limited – Irish branch,
Unit 3, Lower Liffey Street, Dublin 1,
D01 K199, Ireland.

10 9 8 7 6

Produced by Games Workshop in Nottingham.
Cover illustration by Vladimir Krisetskiy.

A CIP record for this book is available from the British Library.

ISBN 13: 978-1-80026-124-2

See Black Library on the internet at

blacklibrary.com

Find out more about Games Workshop
and the world of Warhammer 40,000 at

games-workshop.com

Printed and bound by CPI Group (UK) Ltd, Croydon, CR0 4YY

It is the 41st millennium.

Ten thousand years have passed since the Primarch Horus turned to Chaos and betrayed his father, the Emperor of Mankind, plunging the galaxy into ruinous civil war.

For one hundred centuries the Imperium has endured xenos invasion, internal dissent, and the perfidious attentions of the dark gods of the warp. The Emperor sits immobile upon the Golden Throne of Terra, a psychic bastion against infernal powers. It is His will alone that lights the Astronomican, binding together the Imperium, yet not one word has He uttered in all that time. Without His guidance, mankind has strayed far from the path of enlightenment.

The bright ideals of the Age of Wonder have withered and died. To be alive in this time is a terrible fate, where an existence of grinding servitude is the best that can be hoped for, and a quick death is seen as the kindest mercy.

As the Imperium continues its inevitable decline, Abaddon, last true son of the Primarch Horus, and now Warmaster in his stead, has reached the climax of a plan millennia in the making, tearing reality open across the width of the galaxy and unleashing forces unheard of. At last it seems, after centuries of valiant struggle, mankind's doom is at hand.

Into this darkness a pale shaft of light penetrates. The Primarch Roboute Guilliman has been wakened from deathly slumber by alien sorcery and arcane science. Returning to Terra, he has resolved to set right this dire imbalance, to defeat Chaos once and for all, and to restart the Emperor's grand plan for humanity.

But first, the Imperium must be saved. The galaxy is split in twain. On one side, Imperium Sanctus, beleaguered but defiant. On the other, Imperium Nihilus, thought lost to the night. A mighty crusade has been called to take back the Imperium and restore its glory. All mankind stands ready for the greatest conflict of the age. Failure means extinction, and the path to victory leads only to war.

This is the era Indomitus.

This is the second edition of *Dark Imperium*, and has been revised for this publication. Originally, this story took place following the conclusion of the Indomitus Crusade, a century after the opening of the Great Rift. To better integrate the events depicted herein into the ongoing story of the Era Indomitus, they now take place around twelve years after the crusade left Terra.

The first part of the Indomitus Crusade is over. Imperium Sanctus enjoys some stability. Imperium Nihilus remains in grave danger.

Guilliman returns to Ultramar to save his kingdom from his fallen brother, Mortarion.

War ravages the galaxy from end to end.

The fate of mankind hangs in the balance...

PART ONE

THE DEATH
OF A PRIMARCH

10,000 YEARS AGO

CHAPTER ONE

THESSALA

The void is impossible for the human mind to encompass.

Within the galaxy mankind calls home there are three hundred billion stars. Around these revolve hundreds of billions of worlds, and the spaces between are crowded by a diversity of objects that defy enumeration. Mankind's galaxy is but one of trillions of galaxies in a universe of unguessable size. The distances between even proximate astronomical bodies are inconceivable to creatures evolved to walk a single, small world.

This is why the void cannot be understood. Not by men, nor by their machines.

And when one considers the warp, that nightmare realm skulking behind that of touch, sound and sight, well... any being who claims comprehension of that is either deluded or insane.

Among the higher races there are those that grasp their limitations better than mankind. They understand that the cosmos is ultimately unknowable; they accept their lack of insight. By comparison, the creatures of Terra are so crude in thought that – in the opinion of these more enlightened civilisations – it is a wonder humanity can understand anything at all.

Humans are beings of short reach. Give them voidships, change their shape by gene-forge and augmetic, provide them with weapons of sufficient power to break a star, and the children of Old Earth are still but apes removed from the savannah. Just as an ape's mind cannot hold an ocean, and the notion of a whole world is inexplicable to it, so a man's mind cannot hold the void, and the layered infinities of the warp are beyond him entirely.

The Imperium claims a million worlds as its own. It is an empire spread gossamer-thin across the run of stars, its worlds so far removed from one another that it requires the bloody effort of countless men and women to sustain. In the grand flow of history, the Imperium is the greatest galactic empire of its day. To the people that populate it, it is the most powerful ever to have existed.

To the uncaring universe, it is nothing – the latest in a line of such realms that stretches back to the days of the first thinking beings, when the stars were young and the warp was calm and horror had yet to uncoil its tendrils into the material realm.

There are philosophers that argue war is man's natural state, and to the inhabitants of this era of blood it is a proven hypothesis. War is everywhere. Peace is the dream of a silent Emperor, broken by His treacherous sons.

Those sons continued to fight.

Over the green gas giant of Thessala, two battlefleets engaged. Titanic energies snapped and blinked in the eternal night of space.

The total efforts of star systems went into the construction of these fleets. Neither was free of the taint of blood: not in their construction, nor in their usage. The resources of planets had been poured entire into the forging of their frames; tens of thousands of lives had been expended in their making, and the secrets of ancient sciences plundered to bring them to life. Both had been responsible for the levelling of civilisations.

The fleets differed in only two regards. First was in their appearance. One was a gaudy assault on the senses, the other a motley collection of sober liveries. The more fundamental difference was in their allegiance. The sober fleet fought for the continuation of humanity's great stellar empire; the gaudy one was dedicated to its extinction.

The battlefleets pursued each other in a slow dance through Thessala's rings, hundreds of vessels ploughing gaps in the dust that would take centuries to close. The voiceless lightning of their guns filled the skies of Thessala's inhabited moons. The lives of millions below depended on the outcome of the battle, but the consequences would ripple much further.

At the centre of this iron storm there was no calm, no eye in which respite might be found. Instead, there was a pair of leviathans: the Ultramarines battle-barge *Gauntlet of Power* and the Emperor's Children battleship *Pride of the Emperor*. Two vessels, forged in a common cause but now implacable enemies, locked together in mortal combat only thirty miles apart – no distance at all in void war.

Each was the flagship of a primarch, genetically engineered demigods crafted by the Emperor of Mankind. Aboard the *Gauntlet of Power* stood Roboute Guilliman, the foundling of Ultramar, the Avenging Son. The *Pride of the Emperor* was home to Fulgrim – the traitor, the fallen exemplar, the blighted phoenix. Once covered in his Emperor's blessings, Fulgrim had followed the arch-traitor Horus and pledged his allegiance to dark gods.

In fighting for their father, both primarchs were made fathers themselves. Through the application of arcane science, they were the sires of two of the Space Marine Legions, mankind's greatest warriors. The Space Marines were lords of the galaxy, designed to reunite the human race and shepherd it to a glorious future. They had failed and turned upon one another, and their war had nearly destroyed the galaxy. They fought still.

Such fury a battlefleet can unleash!

It can cow a world without a shot. It can extinguish the life of a species. Battlefleets are the tools of tyrants, whomever they fight for. Whether their admirals espouse salvation or damnation matters not to the execution of their purpose. Death follows in their wake.

To those participating, a void war is a terrifying, roiling chaos of violence. It is the pinnacle of mankind's destructive ingenuity, a whirl of gigantic explosions where lives are snuffed out by the hundred. In such combat, a single person is nothing; they are but part of the machine of the ship they serve, only as essential as a steel cog or an indicator lumen. They can do nothing but work their appointed task and pray their life will not end, or if it must end, that it does so in painless disintegration. A single crewman's task dominates everything, even their fear of death. There is no escape from service. War and their part in it are the totality of their existence.

Yet what is a void war to the timeless blackness that envelops the footling motes of inhabited worlds? A void war is twinkles in the distance. It is silence. It is infinitesimals of matter sparking and dying, scintillas of metal and flesh consumed by transient fires. The detonation of a battleship miles long is insignificant to a cosmos where the deaths of suns are mere blinks. On a galactic scale, the loss of a warship is a nugatory flash, outshone by the billion-year candles of the stars.

The inverse is true to a single person. Their life is all that matters, for one life is all a human being has, and they fear to lose it. Yet they must blindly serve in terror. The universe gives meagre gifts, and it does not care how they are spent.

Over Thessala, mankind fought a civil war already centuries old. The Emperor of Mankind had tried and failed to unite humanity's scattered worlds so that the species might survive the supernatural threat of Chaos. His sons, the primarchs, who He had created to complete this task, had themselves been corrupted, and half had turned against Him. The Horus Heresy, that war was called. It had ended the Emperor's dream.

To the beings of the galaxy, the war was everything; to the blank gaze of time, it was nothing. And yet, for all humanity's seeming inconsequence, the children of its greatest son held the fates of two realities in their grasp.

Roboute Guilliman remained loyal to Terra. His ship was sternly decorated in gold, so much so that it rivalled Fulgrim's vessel in ornamentation, but whereas the *Gauntlet of Power* was ornate, the *Pride of the Emperor* was vulgar. Its decoration had been applied with abandon – everything that could be adorned had been adorned. Back when the two ships had fought side by side, its extravagance had not been to the taste of the Ultramarines, who were born of more solemn worlds. Now it was an affront to decency, added to and added to again until the tawdry obscured all trace of art. Neglect went hand in hand with this ostentation, and it made the *Pride of the Emperor* appear ugly. It was a decayed relic, like a theatre from a decadent age left to rot in the rain.

The *Pride of the Emperor*'s ability to mete out destruction remained undiminished. At point-blank range, it traded blows with the *Gauntlet of Power* as the ships passed slowly alongside each other. Huge cannons flared, exchanging projectiles the size of transit containers. The space between was a deadly thicket of lance beams and laser light. Void shields blurred and sparked with the dissipation of mighty energies. Multi-hued lightning silenced communications and burst sub-systems with their feedback for thousands of miles around. Weaponry capable of levelling cities blinked and flashed.

Around these metal behemoths, dozens of other ships struggled in cosmic silence, some approaching the size and power of the flagships in their own right. Without exception, those on Fulgrim's side were the damned ships of the Emperor's Children. Though Fulgrim had lost his war and his humanity, his Legion yet held some cohesion. On Guilliman's side fought half a dozen successor Chapters of the proud XIII Legion, the Ultramarines. Dissolution had been the price of fidelity for the Legion of Ultramar, and though there were strengths in the smaller formations Guilliman had forced upon them, there were weaknesses also.

For all Roboute Guilliman's strategical genius, the loyalists had been outmanoeuvred and caught. Their pursuit of the fallen primarch had become a fight for survival. Three fleet elements of Emperor's Children had pinned the loyalists into place above Thessala; Fulgrim had turned his flight from Xolco into a devastating trap.

Once, Roboute Guilliman would not have made such an error. Perhaps the situation over emerald Thessala was simple misfortune. Fulgrim was no ordinary opponent, after all. Should Guilliman fail, history would surely be forgiving, if there were any good men left to write it.

Or perhaps the truth was that rage had clouded the Avenging Son's judgement. Perhaps, some dared whisper, Roboute Guilliman had allowed his desire for revenge to overtake his reason.

Roboute Guilliman was stretched. Although several other

primarchs still stood as champions of humanity, the wounded Imperium looked to Guilliman to save it. Every human has a limit, demigod or peasant, and Guilliman's burden was the heaviest of all.

The *Pride of the Emperor* heeled over, bringing its portside weapons batteries into better firing arcs. In response, the *Gauntlet of Power* intensified its barrage, and the void shield covering the *Pride of the Emperor*'s ventral towers winked out.

Explosions bloomed suddenly across hull plating encrusted with gold and filth.

An opening had been made.

On board the *Gauntlet of Power*, one hundred of Ultramar's finest warriors waited on teleport blocks, surrounded by buzzing machinery. They comprised fifty of the First Company and fifty of the Second, all garbed in the deep blue of the Ultramarines Chapter. The white helmets of the First Company's veteran Space Marines, recessed under the cowls of Terminator armour, looked out at hundreds of tech-adepts and mortal crewmen labouring to prepare the Ultramarines' way through the warp.

The Space Marines of the Second Company were in standard power armour, and were being equipped with tall breaching shields by the arming servitors. Their battleplate lacked the thickness of Terminator armour, and the shields, though bulky, would increase their survivability in the close-quarters fighting of boarding.

Ammunition trains rumbled across the deck. Smartly uniformed Ultramarines Chapter menials handed out munitions to their masters while the enhanced warriors performed last-minute checks on themselves and their brothers. Chaplains strode from platform to platform, hearing oaths and affixing papers to armour with wax seals that hissed as they were impressed with sacred irons. Whether human or transhuman, every member of the Chapter worked with perfect efficiency. Even so, as invested as they were in their preparations, all of them had half an eye on the grand archway leading onto the deck.

The ship shook violently. Alarms blared. Lumens spat sparks and went dark over part of the deck. A section of gantry clanged down from the tangle of struts and pipes that clogged the high ceiling. The crew continued upon their business with unhurried purpose. Orders were given to reroute power. Emergency teams of armoured voidsmen and specialised servitors began clearing the wreckage. All was restored to order.

Such calm made it easy to forget the punishing fire the ship was under. But there was no doubt they were losing.

This was not how the battle was supposed to have gone.

From voxmitters studded into the columns and walls, a clipped voice sounded.

'*Shields down on the* Pride of the Emperor. *Prepare for assault.*' The words were swallowed by the clatter of preparation and tumult of war beating at the ship, yet they were not repeated, for the superior hearing of the Space Marines caught them all.

A clarion followed shortly, sharp and loud enough to be heard by mortal and transhuman alike. The servants of Ultramar stopped what they were doing and stood to attention.

A towering figure clad in the famous Armour of Reason strode through the archway. On his left hand he wore the Hand of Dominion. Belted at his waist was the Sword of the Emperor Himself. The bearer of these weapons was taller by far than the Invictarus Suzerain guard escorting him. He exuded a power and purpose that halted the breath of mortals in their throats.

'First Captain Andos! Second Captain Thiel! Are your companies ready?' the giant called.

The two captains crossed the floor to meet their lord. Second Captain Thiel was helmetless in power armour heavy with honours, while First Captain Andos was completely enclosed in a hulking suit of Terminator battleplate. They saluted their father the Ultramarian way, one fist across their chests – the old symbol of Unity.

'My lord Guilliman! Your veterans await your command,' said Andos, his voice ringing from the voxmitter set below his helm.

'We stand prepared, my primarch,' said Aeonid Thiel. His voice, rich and soft, was unmoderated by machinery. It was not so very long after the Heresy and Thiel was still young for a Space Marine, though his face was lined with cares.

Guilliman looked down upon his captains resolutely. The primarch overtopped even Andos in his massive Terminator armour. He was a demigod, humanity's might captured and moulded in flesh.

Thiel gazed back, unable to take his eyes from the face of his gene-sire. Thiel was a good warrior, tested in battle many times, unafraid to voice his mind and modest enough to hide the love he had for his lord, but it shone in his face like a light.

Such devotion they bear me, thought Guilliman, *even as I fail them.*

There were so few of his original Legion left alive, and their replacements were born of a different, less certain era. Thiel's regard was tempered by long friendship, though he had never lost his rebellious streak. The younger Space Marines were another matter. Guilliman remembered when his warriors had been less reverent. They had been better times.

'We depart immediately,' he said, his voice uncompromising. 'The traitor will not escape again. The warriors of six Chapters stand ready to aid us. We shall not fail. To your stations – prepare for mass teleport.'

'My lord, we are prepared,' said Andos carefully. 'But the enemy will outnumber us greatly. I am concerned for our chances of success. What is the practical action should resistance prove overwhelming? It is Second Captain Thiel's and my opinion that you should remain here. We shall occupy the enemy, while the *Gauntlet of Power* withdraws. We cannot–'

The Avenging Son cut Andos dead with a look.

'Too much blood has been shed on my behalf. I will not shy from this fight,' Guilliman said, and his tone would brook no disagreement. 'There can be no retreat until the *Pride of the Emperor* is crippled. I must face my brother and occupy him while these tasks are done. And if I must fight him, I will kill him, or I will die in the attempt. I cannot let him escape unpunished again. My sons,' he added, his tone softening, 'it is the only way to escape this trap.'

Andos bowed his head. Thiel paused a moment, uncertain, before doing the same. Sure of their agreement, Guilliman took his helm from a grav-platform pushed by two mortal men. He mounted the teleport platform – stepping directly onto it with no need of the steps that led from the deck – and turned to address his sons.

'Now, my warriors, let us show my brother the consequences of turning upon the Imperium of Terra!'

'We march for Macragge!' they bellowed, and their combined voices were enough to drown out the thunder of battle.

Guilliman's Invictarus Suzerain guard followed him onto the pad. They formed a protective shield wall around him, axes ready for combat teleport.

To his men, Guilliman was an infallible leader, his abilities supernatural. Even to the rational Ultramarines, who believed the Emperor of Mankind to be a man and not a god, and likewise His primarch sons, a sense of near-religious awe had crept into their attitude towards him. It had only become more pronounced since the last days of the Heresy.

But Roboute Guilliman was not infallible.

He knew this course of action to be fraught with risk. Andos had been right to raise the possibility of defeat. The primarch only wished he could praise his son for his insight rather than dismissing his concerns. His campaign against the Emperor's Children had, to all purposes, failed. Fulgrim had the initiative. Guilliman's choices had been made for him. The pieces were set on the board, there was only one real option. They should withdraw.

Currently, withdrawal was impossible. If the *Gauntlet of Power* broke off from the fight, then the *Pride of the Emperor* would inflict massive damage upon the battle-barge. Fulgrim would then most likely attempt a boarding assault of his own once their defences were shattered. Guilliman could not allow his brother to do that at a time of his choosing.

The primarch's powerful mind had examined all possibilities. His own strategic treatises would have him retreat quickly, forming a fighting rearguard so that he might withdraw those of his ships that he could, minimising the damage to his flagship by sacrificing many of his others. Spending the lives of other men to save his own was not to Guilliman's liking when he saw a chance for true victory. He could not ignore this opportunity to slay his treacherous sibling. Guilliman had come to the conclusion that by defying his own tactical orthodoxies, he might surprise Fulgrim.

It was a risk. Fulgrim might well have dropped his ship's shields on purpose, a mocking re-enactment of Horus' last gambit to lure the Emperor aboard his ship at the end of the Siege of Terra.

But Guilliman had his own plans. Other boarding forces drawn from multiple Chapters would teleport in simultaneously, tasked with mutually supportive objectives at the enginarium, the command deck, the navigatorium, the magazine, the subsidiary command deck and the main gunnery control. If only half of Guilliman's strike teams were successful, they had a good chance of crippling the *Pride of the Emperor* from within. His warriors had orders to retreat immediately once their objectives had been achieved. He would make sure as many survived as possible; he would not let his sons pay the price for his mistakes.

He had to settle the reckoning for his errors.

Guilliman could not deny he had been hooked and played like a fish. All he could do was struggle free and bite the one who had snared him.

'Make ready! We go to war!' he called.

At his signal, the machines of the teleport deck hummed into life. Giant reaction columns crackled with power, feeding the focusing arrays that would tear open the veil between real space and the warp. They glowed with painful light. As they shone brighter, wisps of corposant were leached from initiation prongs and fed into containment flasks, where it twisted as if alive.

So many of my brothers are dead, fallen to Chaos or lost, thought Guilliman. *We assumed we were immortal. We are not. My time must come, but not today. Not at the hands of Fulgrim.*

The arcane machineries of teleportation whooped and hummed, the deck vibrating with their activity, and built to a crescendo.

A booming crack and flash of actinic light whited out the teleport deck. Suppressant vapours gushed from tubes in anticipation of fires in the overstressed machinery. Human armsmen raised their shotguns in case of warp breach and daemonic incursion.

None came. Signal strobes blinked: red, red, red, then blue.

'Teleport success, teleport success,' droned a mechanical voice.

The lumens came back on. Corposant flasks emptied to the

sounds of half-formed screams. Atmospheric vents drew smoke away, revealing empty pads. Adepts consulted vid-screens and paper cogitator strips, and relief crossed their faces at the read-outs.

Roboute Guilliman and his warriors were aboard the *Pride of the Emperor*.

CHAPTER TWO

THE PRIDE OF THE EMPEROR

There was always a moment of enlightenment for Guilliman during teleportation, when he hung in a state that was neither life nor death.

In those moments, when his soul straddled two worlds, he knew himself for what he truly was: not a being of matter alone, but a creature of both realities. In those moments, he was convinced – no, he *knew* – that he was spun from warp stuff and matter both. Though the feeling faded and became absurd after his deliverance to his destination, at the time it was profound, as if an understanding of the mysteries of creation awaited his discovery if he had but the courage to look a little deeper.

He had the courage, but he never looked. Damnation lay that way.

Temptation passed. The sense of enlightenment fled. A blaze of light delivered him and his warriors back into ignorance and to their target. The afterlight was slow in dispersing, putting them at risk of attack while they were half blind. Guilliman tensed, ready to fight, but no challenge came. Greasy tendrils of warp energy contorted themselves out of existence, leaving the boarding party in darkness.

It was darker than a terrestrial night, but systems in Guilliman's helmet aided his superior eyes in creating a grainy image of the voidship's interior. For a second, Guilliman thought himself lost, cast into the empyrean itself, for he looked upon a scene drawn from nightmare. In the century since the end of the Heresy, Guilliman had fought daemons, he had trodden the surface of worlds changed by the unclean touch of Chaos, he had seen through windows of flesh conjured by sorcerers into depthless dimensions of evil. The interior of the *Pride of the Emperor* was of similar ilk.

As intended, the boarding party had emerged within the Triumphal Way, the great corridor running the length of the *Pride of the Emperor*. Once, the massed Chapters of the Legions had marched its length in celebration of Fulgrim's victories for the Imperium, but those days were lifetimes dead, and the derelict avenue was now empty.

Guilliman's Invictarus Suzerains scanned their surroundings, shields and Legatine power axes held in anticipation of an attack that did not come. Handheld auspexes whined and chimed the all-clear. Lamps stabbed out from suit mountings, their pools of bright illumination dancing over vile shapes.

Cogitator systems built into the Armour of Reason highlighted points of interest and threat for Guilliman. He examined them all cursorily. His engineered brain was capable of processing a phenomenal amount of information; that had always been his special talent. He listened in to the battle chatter of the fleets and the quiet order exchanges of his squads as they spread out. He scanned the frequencies for notification from his other strike teams, all while reading data-screed read-outs scrolling down his faceplate display. He formulated plans, gave brief orders via vox and data-burst, but it was the ship that absorbed him most.

The Triumphal Way had changed beyond all recognition. Where once was splendour, darkness held court. The little light that the Ultramarines brought was swallowed quickly, reduced to a dismal silver that took the edges from everything, smearing all features into an uncertain blur where distance was difficult to judge and the darkest areas could prove to be anything but shadows. The warriors of Ultramar were a lonely island of blue in the dark.

Thiel was first to break the silence.

'The Triumphal Way,' he said. 'It has changed.'

'A century of years is more than enough time for evil to do its work,' said Guilliman.

'The Emperor's Children have fallen far,' said Andos.

The primarch remembered the Triumphal Way as it had been, when it was a showcase for all that was fine in human art. Gone were the bronze heroic statues that had lined its broad path, as were the masterpieces painted by the artists of the 28th Expeditionary Fleet that had hung between them. In their stead were hideous abominations, contorted sculptures of a shocking nature and artworks that depicted the profane and the obscene. The latter had been rendered in pigments derived from unclean fluids, which, left alone, had sprouted thick mats of mould.

No attempt had been made to place these new adornments carefully, or to clear away the old. Shattered frames were heaped like driftwood. The bronze scrap scattered across the floors was obscured by a clotting of filth. The marble cladding of the walls was pitted all over, and black liquid oozed from wide cracks. Onyx columns had been wrenched from their settings and lay broken, their engraved lists of victories reduced to jumbles of letters. The paving was cracked in many places, and where the metal of the deck should have been visible there were only black, watchful pits.

Worst of all was the silence. Sound was unnaturally muted. Battle raged outside and the ship was under heavy bombardment, but unlike the *Gauntlet of Power*, whose halls rang to explosions and the howls of overworked machines, the *Pride of the Emperor* did little but shiver from time to time, like a giant stirring in its sleep. No light flashed through the high armaglass windows at the avenue's apex. Discordant music drifted from somewhere. Three screams issued from another direction, shockingly close.

Guilliman had seen more overt horrors wrought by the minions of Chaos, often on a stupefying scale, but there was a pregnant doom to the Triumphal Way that overtook even the goriest displays.

'Be on your guard,' he said. 'Things are not as they seem. The *Pride of the Emperor* no longer wholly occupies real space.'

'Yes,' voxed Thiel. 'This place stinks of the warp.'

A Space Marine's mind is robust, altered during his apotheosis from human to superhuman, and hardened against fear by years of training. Guilliman's veterans took the disquiet in their stride. They arrayed themselves for battle: shield-bearing breacher teams taking up station near ingress points; Terminators forming up into squads; the primarch's own Invictarus Suzerains assuming positions that maximised the protection their shields could provide their lord. The disruption fields around their axes shone in the gloom.

Guilliman set his vox to encrypted wideband. 'We have arrived. Task forces, inform me of your status.'

Static laced with laughter and screaming burst into his ear. Half a minute went by before a voice resolved itself from the cacophony.

'*My lord primarch, can you hear me?*'

'I have contact with you, Master Ludon,' said Guilliman.

'*I have been attempting to reach you for several minutes, my lord. The Aurora Chapter stands firm. We are meeting minimal resistance. There are–*' The Chapter Master's voice blurred out for a moment, replaced by wild shrieks. '*–only fourteen. Mostly bodies. All of them mutilated. We are proceeding towards our objective.*'

'*Strike Group Vengeance, my lord,*' said another voice. A rune blinked in Guilliman's display marking out a position on his cartograph twenty decks below. The report came with a background of banging bolters and the roaring sound of atmosphere flash-heated by melta weapons.

'Master Corvo,' said Guilliman with a smile. There were too few veterans left from the times before.

'*The Novamarines are engaged on three fronts, my lord,*' the Chapter Master shouted. '*Enemy numbers are higher than expected. Estimated arrival at target zone twelve minutes after intention.*'

'Keep me informed,' said Guilliman. His own group remained unharried. He contacted the other task forces; all but that of the Aurora Chapter had been engaged by large numbers of the enemy. There were Emperor's Children everywhere, but not on the Triumphal Way.

'Advance!' Guilliman ordered. His guard broke into a swift stride as he set out, heading into the night that had hold of the *Pride of the Emperor.* 'We will meet no enemy here.'

'We cannot be undetected. This is another trap,' said Andos.

'Of course it is a trap. My brother is challenging me,' said Guilliman. 'Fulgrim was always too enamoured of theatrics.'

'We must be on guard for ambush,' said Andos.

'Do not expect it, brother,' said Thiel. 'This dismal corridor would not suit Fulgrim. Where else would he be but on his greatest stage? We will find him in the Heliopolis.'

Combat reports came through with relentless efficiency. Guilliman cycled through each of his sub-commander's vox-feeds one after the other. The *Pride of the Emperor* continued to shiver minimally from the bombardment it suffered from Guilliman's fleet. Reports from the *Gauntlet of Power* said their foe was taking heavy damage, but there was scant evidence of any of that inside Fulgrim's ship. The two flagships had passed, and their escorts fought rapid duels to clear the way so they could lumber about and make another run at each other. Lesser ships succumbed to concentrated firepower as other vessels lent their might to the struggle. Guilliman's fleet was fighting well, but it remained heavily outnumbered. He did not have much time, and quickened his pace.

The Second and First companies ascended stairs as tall as hills. The atmosphere became cloying with the scents of sweat, perfume and blood. An overpowering musk that derived from no mundane body penetrated the Space Marines' respirator grilles, though they had sealed them tightly enough to defy hard vacuum.

The last time Roboute Guilliman had walked the Triumphal Way it had been as an honoured guest. The Emperor's Children had lined the stairs and landings in their hundreds, and bright light had sparked from their artistry as they saluted him. His brother had greeted him warmly.

Guilliman felt a pang of sadness for what might have been. Now, in the murk, he returned like a thief in the night.

The atrium to the Heliopolis emerged from the unnatural dark. From its rear, the Phoenix Gate came at them like an ogre striding out of its cave in challenge. Guilliman had his men halt and spread out. The reports from the other strike groups crackled in his helmet, interrupted by hellish screams and moans, as – with sorrowful eyes – Guilliman took in what Fulgrim had done to the Phoenix Gate.

In the days before the war, the Phoenix Gate had been a masterpiece of the sculptor's art. Together, the closed bronze gates had depicted the crowning moment of Fulgrim's life. The Emperor still stood there, holding out the palatine aquila to Fulgrim, whose figure also remained. The giving of this honour was the ultimate display of respect from their father, and the gate had been a reciprocal show of devotion from His son. Behind the two figures, a crowd looked worshipfully on.

In all other respects, the gate had changed.

The rich artwork was much abused. All over, the soft bronze had been cut with profane symbols. The figures behind the two principal actors had been reworked into cavorting, lewd things. The work was of variable quality. Some of it was executed with skill, other parts crude, and its inconsistency destroyed the careful illusion of depth the sculptor had created. Originally, the lesser figures had subtly drawn the eye to the principal actors of the piece; now these background characters clamoured for the eye's attention, overwhelming the Emperor and His son.

Only Fulgrim's Legion had been permitted to display the personal symbol of the Emperor. The irony of the honour weighed heavily on Guilliman's heart. Fulgrim had been pompous, vainglorious, boastful and proud, but his better qualities had outshone these foibles.

Examining the wreck of the door hardened Guilliman's heart. The aquila's eyes had been hacked out. The head of the Emperor had been gouged from the relief and replaced with a mess of bones lashed together with blackened sinew. Fulgrim's face was a mask of silver that shifted almost imperceptibly through a range of expressions, all of which were variations on sneering arrogance. His body too had been changed, made multi-limbed and serpentine. It depicted him as a savage god, rich with potency, though it could not match the truth of his new form.

'He will be within, waiting,' said Guilliman, running his gaze over the vandalism one more time. He turned from the gates to address Thiel and Andos. 'Await me here.'

'My lord,' said Thiel. 'All this showmanship appears childish, but Fulgrim is dangerous. I remember how he was. By entering, you are playing into his hands. We should not indulge him. We should go on in force and slay him.'

'I go alone,' said Guilliman firmly. 'If we attack en masse, he will respond in kind and we will be driven back or destroyed before our brothers can complete their tasks. Let me occupy him. His arrogance will demand he gloat awhile. While he is engaged in pointless display, his attention is away from the others, and we will have the opportunity to disable the ship.'

'He will want to fight you,' said Thiel.

'He will,' agreed Guilliman.

'He may ambush you,' said Andos.

'That is unlikely,' said Guilliman. 'He will want to prove he is better by feat of arms, face to face. It is not enough to kill me. He will want to beat me.'

'Either way, he will kill you, my lord. Do not do this,' said Thiel.

Guilliman stared back, his expression hidden by the muzzle of his helmet.

'I must fight him.'

'Do you truly believe you can win?' asked Thiel.

'I do not know,' answered Guilliman after a pause.

Thiel looked away and sighed. His helm rendered it as a growl. 'I fear there is more to your desire to face your brother than practicality, my lord.'

'What do you mean by that?'

The ship trembled as a heavy hit burst its way inwards, perturbing the unnatural serenity of the craft.

'Pride doomed your brother,' said Thiel simply. 'Pride undoes the mightiest. Do not be proud, my lord.'

'Are you not proud, my son?'

'I am proud,' said Thiel. 'To be an Ultramarine, to have you as my gene-sire, to have fought with you for so long. But I am not proud enough to let it kill me.'

Guilliman smiled. 'You have not changed, Aeonid. Fear not – I will not let pride doom me. Stand aside but for the moment. Guard my back. If I cannot best Fulgrim alone in combat, come when I call and we shall give him the honourless death he deserves.'

'My lord,' said Thiel, relieved.

'It will be so,' added Andos.

Reluctantly, the sons of Roboute Guilliman stood away from the doors. The primarch placed his palms flat upon their defiled metal and pushed. He expected them to creak and squeal, but they opened soundlessly, emitting a gust of foul-smelling air as they parted. Nothing but darkness was beyond, closer still than that in the Triumphal Way.

Guilliman entered the Heliopolis, and the gates swung closed behind him.

CHAPTER THREE

THE FALLEN PHOENIX

The Heliopolis was in a ruinous state. Shattered tiers of marble seats crowded the dark. In times past, the followers of Fulgrim had gathered upon them to hear their primarch speak, before he fell to darkness and took his Legion with him. Now, pageantry and light had been cast out by decay and dereliction. The great windows in the dome were shuttered. A thick layer of dust coated everything, and the air reeked of sweat and stale musk.

Bones were scattered about amid toppled fire bowls. They were mostly baseline human, but here and there were the skeletons of Space Marines, identifiable by their greater size, the solidly fused bones of their ribcage and the tattered remains of black carapace clinging to them. Shell holes in the marble told of a battle long ago. The craters had the signature blast patterns of bolt detonations in soft stone. Space Marine had fought Space Marine here, though when and why, Guilliman could not guess. Perhaps there had been a last stand of Emperor's Children loyal to Terra, though it could just as easily have been a clash between rival warbands decades later. It was impossible to tell.

The mosaics on the ceiling were full of holes, the faces all smashed in. Hooks between the figures held bent banner poles. Shreds of triumphal silk standards moved in the ship's breath. When whole, these flags had proudly commemorated thousands of triumphs in the Emperor's name, but now they were as spoilt as the oaths of the warriors who had won them. A rare complete example stood out amid the rags. The devices on it were smirched with filth. That was worse, in a way.

Silence made the Heliopolis its domain. Vox reports chattered in Guilliman's helm, telling of goals almost accomplished, and bringing the clamour of war into the dead auditorium, but the racket was contained by his helmet. The silence was stronger, pressing in hard upon his ceramite faceplate and distancing Guilliman from the men fighting in his name.

At the centre of the Heliopolis was a ring dominated by a black throne. Guilliman recalled standing there beside his brother and speaking in the days when all this madness was inconceivable. A cone of soft light ignited and fell onto it, casting shadows from chunks of rubble and bringing an eerie shine from the black terrazzo floor. Guilliman descended the steps slowly from the Phoenix Gate, down the main stairs whose once shining finish had been scratched dull.

The battle cries of the Aurora Chapter, the war oaths of the Novamarines and the howling of the Doom Eagles all echoed in his helmet. A burst of loud static signalled an explosion. A signifier rune in Guilliman's helm blinked green – the Aurora Chapter had knocked out the ship's navigatorium. Garbled reports from their captains competed with the other incoming traffic, ecstatic with hard-won victory, signalling their withdrawal. He overheard jubilant calls for teleport lock, and then they were gone.

Other signifiers glowed dull red around the top of his helm-plate display, representing his strike teams' remaining targets. Two more critical systems, two more green runes, and they might escape this yet, but his men needed more time.

'Continue with your objectives, my sons,' he told them. 'Fall back upon their completion. The Emperor watch over you.'

He cut his vox. The Heliopolis' malevolent silence rushed into his helmet.

Guilliman reached the final step and paused at the edge of the inner circle. The last of his heavy footsteps echoed to nothing. The light was unclean, some warp effect obscuring the far side of the Heliopolis from his vision. He was vulnerable here. This was the stage his fallen brother had chosen for their confrontation, the derelict site of Fulgrim's lost glories.

'Fulgrim! I am here. Fulgrim! Your brother, Roboute Guilliman, stands in the Heliopolis again. Will you not greet me?'

Guilliman's vox-amplified voice echoed, each repeat growing with sadness until it became a sobbing caricature.

The effect disappointed Guilliman. 'My brother, your cheap sorcery cannot upset me. Come out and face me, if you dare, or have you become as cowardly as you are debauched?'

There was a metallic rattle, and a rasping of scaled skin over stone that wound around the outer row of seats. Guilliman squinted, but the light before him cheated his vision, allowing him to see only into the circle.

'I hear you, Fulgrim!' he cried. 'Come out into the light!'

This time, Fulgrim replied. His voice was as mellifluous as it always had been, but the neediness that had lurked at the back of his words had come to the fore, a poison masquerading as confidence.

'Why are you in such a hurry?' he said, his whisper filling the hall. *'Your strategy is to play for time, is it not? To allow your*

sons in their fine new paints to cripple this ship. They look so colourful now, Guilliman, so much less dull than blue, blue, blue. How was it to break up your Legion, Guilliman? Did it hurt?'

'Come and face me. Let us settle our differences honourably.'

'Do you want to talk?' Fulgrim, still unseen, tittered. *'About what? A little family reunion? You and I have nothing in common. We never did, and now we have even less. I serve the true powers of this universe, while you languish under the dead hand of our father. You are so predictable, Roboute.'* He laughed. *'So dull, so stolid. Boring old Roboute! You were the unloved child, while the brighter stars got all of father's attention. Overlooked, until the end, and then when you were needed you were not there. It must have stung, brother, to be so outshone. Perturabo did not enjoy it, I know. Did you?'*

Guilliman peered hard through the light and caught a hint of sinuous movement on the far side of the circle.

'Our father honoured me always,' said Guilliman.

Fulgrim laughed, louder and louder until the Heliopolis filled with wild mirth that seemed to issue from a thousand throats. *'Oh, forgive me! That is so precious. Do you not remember my eagle, dear Roboute? It was I who was honoured, not you.'*

The rasping of scales drew closer. Luminous green eyes glinted. Guilliman set himself and stood tall.

'My Legion may not have won your plaudits, Fulgrim, but I chose the slow and steady road, and that was the better way. You were always racing towards perfection, away from your fear of failure. Your fear made you run right into the arms of damnation.'

'Failure?' Fulgrim scoffed. *'Damnation? I have not failed! I am not damned!'* Fulgrim slithered into the light. *'I am saved.'*

'For the love of Terra…' whispered Guilliman.

Guilliman had seen pict-captures of his brother from the siege of the Imperial Palace. He had viewed them many times, noting the changes wrought upon his sibling as dispassionately as he could, fighting back the revulsion he felt at the sight. Reports and the occasional image of his sibling had surfaced from his reavings since. The image on the Phoenix Gate had been no surprise, he knew what to expect, but faced with Fulgrim in the flesh, Guilliman struggled to contain his dismay.

The Phoenician's legs were gone, replaced with a long serpent's tail. His torso and face had become elongated, his chest altered to accommodate an additional pair of arms. Despite his obscene form, everything was weirdly perfect. The muscles in his bare chest were exquisitely defined. His skin was a gorgeous shade of lilac. The snakeskin of his lower half shone with jewelled colour, and he moved with grace to shame the aeldari. But all this was a perversion of his former beauty, if not of the very idea of beauty itself. It was too much, so perfect in its awful twisting of the human form that it went beyond the ability of the mind to process. Fulgrim's new shape provoked revulsion by its very nature, while awing with the artfulness by which it had been done. By design, he was made to arouse and repulse equally.

His head in particular was changed, long and crowned with horns that rose crimson from his shock of white hair. His face remained his own, a sickening joke to crown his dark transcendence. Seeing the features of his brother melded to this monster brought tears to Guilliman's eyes.

Finely wrought ornaments jangled on Fulgrim's limbs. Soft leather straps held long gloves in place on his right arms. The left arms were painted with delicate patterns, his fingers hung with chains and their nails stained clashing shades. Sigils decorated the buckles of his harness. More were tattooed upon his skin.

Fulgrim rose up on his banded tail, holding his four arms wide in the insipid light of the inner circle.

'Behold, my brother. See! What the Emperor made, the Prince of Pleasure has improved upon. Am I not perfection? I was made to be a slave, but now I am free, and the companion to a greater god than our father can ever be.'

'The Emperor is not a god,' said Guilliman.

The ship quaked. A signifier in Guilliman's helmet turned from red to green. The portside void generators had been disabled. Data-screed informed him the Fourth Company of the Iron Snakes was fighting its way out.

'Do you still believe that?' said Fulgrim. He came forwards, swaying hypnotically. *'He always did protest too much about that. You think I am a traitor, I know. You think I am selfish, and deluded, but no more so than dear, dear father. He gave me so much, not least a taste for treachery.'*

Fulgrim leaned closer, close enough for his hot, perfumed breath to caress Guilliman's armoured face. The cloying stink of it penetrated his breathing grille. There was a scent of something rotten beneath the melange of spices, one note of decay in a bouquet of opulence.

There is the truth, thought Guilliman. *The miasma of corruption, a corpse hidden in a bed of flowers.*

'Join with me,' said Fulgrim seductively. *'You must be tired of all this strife. We can bring an end to war, and revel together in sweet excess for all eternity. I can show you things, pleasures, you would never have dreamed existed. You think of the warp as a hell, but it can be a heaven, also. Together, we can usher in an age of delight for all mankind that will never end.'*

'Never,' said Guilliman. 'You have been deceived. I will not follow you into darkness.' He stepped backwards, his hand going to the hilt of the Emperor's Sword. The primarchs were mighty beings and great in stature, but swollen with the power of Chaos, Fulgrim overtopped Guilliman by several feet.

'It is you who has been deceived, Roboute,' said Fulgrim.

'Look at what you have become, and you will see the wages of disloyalty.'

'You speak to me of loyalty?' Fulgrim tutted and shook his long, warped head. *'And where do your loyalties lie, lord commander? You were late to the Palace, were you not? Delayed. Always, your love for your own kingdom trumps your so-called loyalty to our father. Like a little Emperor, playing at being father in the sand, making tiny empires. You would have saved the Five Hundred Worlds and lost a million. Pathetic.'* A long, forked tongue flitted over his painted lips. *'How are your Five Hundred Worlds now, brother? How many are left? Four hundred? Three? I hear Angron and Lorgar had a rare time bringing down the bastions of your realm and slitting the throats of your people.'*

Guilliman's anger ran hot. 'I will not bend my knee to your masters. These gods you and the others profess to worship are monsters, nothing more. There can be no rapprochement between us. No reconciliation. You have become the tool of the enemy, and so I must kill you.'

'You have come to kill me? Really? How amusing, because I have come to kill you!' said Fulgrim with mocking surprise. He clapped his upper pair of hands. *'What a coincidence. You do realise, I need no starship to travel the void.'* He gestured at his body, his four hands moving with obscene, suggestive precision. *'I am no longer a thing of this realm of ash and dust, but a radiant creature of the warp.'* He pulled a moue of sympathy. *'Oh, I am so sorry, but this was a trap for you, Roboute – the whole thing, from my first raids to your supposed victory at Xolco, and you have fallen into it.'*

Since the first indication of Fulgrim turning to fight here, Guilliman had known he had been outplayed, but he would not give his brother the satisfaction of knowing this. He steeled his heart and prepared to fight.

'I will not be turned.'

'I never thought you would,' said Fulgrim sweetly.

Another shudder passed up the *Pride of the Emperor*. The rune denoting the strike against the enginarium turned green. Corvo would be pulling his Chapter back.

'You can run now, if you want,' said Fulgrim. *'I believe your warriors have accomplished what you sent them to do. You have done sufficient damage. This vessel cannot pursue you. Some of you might even live. I do not care. All of you will bow before Slaanesh before the end.'*

'Enough!' said Guilliman. He drew the Sword of the Emperor in his right hand, and it burst into flames.

'Father's sword! Maybe you are honoured after all, dear brother.'

The Hand of Dominion sparked into life, an oily field of blue light encasing its massive robotic fingers and underslung bolt-gun. Raising the flat of his blade to the muzzle of his helm, Guilliman saluted his brother. He thumbed a switch, and a sheath of energy covered the blade to match that of his fist.

'You are staying?' said Fulgrim. *'No dramatic teleportation? No strategic withdrawal? You actually want to fight someone you cannot hope to beat? Well, well, well, you are beginning to surprise me, Roboute. I never thought you had it in you. Perhaps you are not so boring as I thought.'*

'Honour demands I slay you.'

Fulgrim stretched out his arms. Blades rose from nothing, sprouting from his clenched fists, black vapours boiling off their metal as they were forced into being. The swords were mismatched in form, and every one a different pastel hue. Bright poisons dripped from their edges.

'Honour will get you killed.' Fulgrim raised his own blades to his face, the edges ringing off one another. There was no mockery to the salute. *'So it is, brother. We come to the end. With*

you dead, our other brothers will follow, one by one. The Impe-
rium cannot last without your guidance. It is you who holds the
whole crumbling thing together.' He smiled sadly. *'Dull as you*
are, you were among the best of us. I almost feel sorry to kill you,
if only because you will not see the triumph of the true powers of
the universe, and know the liberation they bring.'

Swift as a striking viper, Fulgrim attacked, all four blades driving down at his brother primarch so quickly that they did not
seem to pass through the intervening air. Guilliman caught them
on the edge of the Sword of the Emperor. Fire blazed, scorching
Fulgrim's face and making him snarl. The eruption of energy
threw both primarchs backwards.

Fulgrim attacked again. Guilliman cried out as one blade
found its way past his parries and left a smoking groove in
the ceramite around his left arm. He would not win this fight.

'Thiel, Andos,' voxed Guilliman. 'Now.'

There was a sound like sigh that turned into a rumbling groan.
The Heliopolis boomed with conflicting resonances, and the Phoenix Gate exploded inwards, showering the room with gobbets of
molten bronze. The Ultramarines of the First and Second companies came charging in, bolters firing at the daemon primarch
battling their lord.

'At last! Your true colours,' said Fulgrim. *'For all your talk of*
honour, you will not face me alone.'

Angered, Fulgrim rained blows down on Guilliman, driving
the primarch back up one step, then two. The bolts aimed at
the daemon primarch were turned aside by diabolical art, and
he stood unharmed in the full face of the Ultramarines' attack.

'My sons are here to greet yours,' he said. *'Let them join the*
revel.' Parrying Guilliman's attacks with insolent ease, Fulgrim
threw back his head. His jaws opened wide enough to swallow
a man whole, and he let out a shrieking ululation.

From the far side of the Heliopolis, a harrowing, discordant noise answered the call of the daemon primarch. From the upper tiers of the Heliopolis marched the warriors of the Emperor's Children, many bearing sonic weapons from which came the thrumming of destructive music.

'Now, we shall see whose children will survive!' snarled Fulgrim, and he came at his brother. Guilliman countered, his mighty gauntlet batting aside Fulgrim's swords as his own hunted through the cage of steel Fulgrim wove with his four blades, seeking out the tainted flesh behind.

Fulgrim snarled as the tip of Guilliman's blade nicked his skin, the fires upon it turning his pastel skin black. Rising up on his tail, he swept down with his swords in quick succession. Guilliman's weapons found them all, turning them aside with economical movements. Nevertheless, he was sorely pressed. He had fought daemons of every kind on many worlds and bested them all. Fulgrim, however, was an unholy blend of primarch and daemon. In him the energy of the warp was married to the wisdom of ancient sciences. He was part material god, part immaterial daemon lord, and his power was great.

Guilliman cut and feinted, using the Hand of Dominion to catch the sword wielded by Fulgrim's lower-left arm. The unholy metal of the blade cut into the thick ceramite of the gauntlet, and corrosive poison spattered the Armour of Reason, eating into it with smoking ferocity.

Pain somehow afflicted Guilliman through his armour, as if his war-plate itself were hurt. A spicy agony burned up his arm from his interface sockets. He gritted his teeth and twisted the gauntlet. Energy crackled and banged, and the sword snapped in two. Ichor pumped from its hollow innards. Strings of flesh tore free as Guilliman cast the broken blade aside. Fulgrim screamed as if his limb had been ripped off, and he recoiled. Guilliman fought against his own pain to slash hard with the Sword of the Emperor, cutting deeply into Fulgrim's swordless arm.

'How dare you!' Fulgrim screamed, rearing back. He lunged at his brother and crashed bodily into him, knocking Guilliman from his feet. The Invictarus Suzerains thundered down the steps to join their lord, forming a shield about him as he scrambled up, but Fulgrim slithered into them, barging them over and slaughtering them contemptuously, his swords lopping limbs off with every strike.

'You will die!' shouted Guilliman, and he surged past his last bodyguard as Fulgrim's swords punched through the Space Marine's shield, armour and body. He swung hard with his gauntlet, but Fulgrim was too quick and weaved to the side; the Hand of Dominion punched down and into the marble steps, pulverising three of them.

Guilliman spun around, anticipating Fulgrim's next strike, but the daemon had gone.

He searched for his brother in the conflict. Their two armies had met, and their struggles filled the Heliopolis side to side. His warriors and the Emperor's Children were intermingled, the blue armour of the Ultramarines dotted within a sea of clashing colours and battleplate decorated with the stretched skins of the dead. Cones of sound visibly tortured the air, blasting Guilliman's warriors from their feet. Blood fountained from breathing grilles as dying Space Marines coughed up shattered internal organs. A knot of white-helmed Terminators stood back to back, dealing death to any traitor that strayed near, while a wall of Ultramarines Second Company brothers advanced, guns booming, pushing back insane warriors.

Battle was everywhere, desperate and wild. The situation in the void was now mirrored within the Heliopolis. His men were outnumbered. They would die.

First theoretical, Guilliman thought. *Fulgrim is a prime evil in this world. First practical, I will kill him.*

Second theoretical, he countered, *you are angry. Second practical, you will throw your own life and those of your men away for nothing. You have failed in this campaign. Retreat.*

A memory of King Konor, his adoptive father, flashed in his mind.

'Control your humours,' Konor had told him. 'You are mightier in every regard than any man, and that includes your passions. Master them, or you will fail.'

Temper. There was always his temper. For most of his life, Roboute Guilliman had kept his emotions in check, but there had been occasions when he had lost his head. At Calth, and when Sotha was attacked. Or when he had arrived late to Terra. Or the early days of the Scouring... He would add this day to that record. Beneath his commanding exterior, Guilliman was tight with wrath.

'Fulgrim!' he bellowed. 'Face me!'

A whip-fast motion flickered to his side. Fulgrim sped through the melee, coming from the left. Guilliman barely had time to raise his sword before Fulgrim crashed into him, snarling incoherently, knocking him backwards.

'You hurt me, you corpse-master's lapdog.' The last vestiges of Fulgrim's humanity melted from his face as it transformed into a mask of pure hatred. *'No one hurts me. No one beats me!'*

He wrapped his tail around his brother primarch, constricting him with such force that his armour plate began to crack. Casting aside one sword, Fulgrim reached down and grasped Guilliman's head.

'You wanted to face me, so face me!' he said, throwing aside his swords and wrenching free Guilliman's helmet, exposing his naked flesh to the air.

The stink of his corrupted brother made Guilliman gag. His head swam as the daemon primarch's scent invaded his nose and throat, unmoderated by his battlehelm's systems.

'*Pathetic!*' cried Fulgrim. He uncurled, flinging Guilliman aside. His wounded arm was already healing, crackling warp energies working in tandem with his primarch's physiology to make him whole again. He conjured swords from poisoned mists to fill his empty hands and flew at the Master of Ultramar.

Guilliman staggered upright, gasping. Every breath poured more of Fulgrim's lethal perfume into his lungs, a poison so potent that it taxed his superhuman body. He parried, and parried again, but he could land no counterstrike and was forced back up the stairs.

A blow flung his arm wide. He never saw the blade that cut him coming.

A cold kiss across his throat, followed by agony. Arterial blood sprayed from his ruined neck. He clamped his hand to the wound, but it gaped beneath armoured fingers, and the blood would not stop. Poison crawled in where his blood flooded out. Already it affected him, numbing his lips and making his eyes heavy. With supreme effort, Roboute Guilliman raised the Sword of the Emperor for the last time.

'How?' he mouthed. His vocal cords were severed. Blood spilled from his mouth in place of words.

'*I see the mark of Kor Phaeron's athame.*' Fulgrim swayed as he approached. '*He could never turn you, but the cut he inflicted is a scar on the warp that will never heal. It is as great a weakness as your rectitude.*' Fulgrim smiled with lips coated in poison paint. '*Or, I should say, was. Here the Avenging Son meets his end.*'

He smashed Guilliman's blade aside. Fulgrim raised his swords for the killing strike. '*Say hello to father for me.*'

A storm of fire blasted down the stairs, bolt-rounds streaking by, followed by burning streams of plasma. Fulgrim screeched. The unearthly field that shielded him shrieked and flickered, splitting his image. He screamed as a blaze of incandescent gas pierced his protection and burned his side.

'The primarch! To the primarch!' roared Captain Andos.

Guilliman sank to his knees, unable to speak. His perceptions became fragmentary. Warriors in blue threw themselves at the reeling daemon prince, only to be carved up into red chunks in mid-air.

Guilliman's sons tossed their lives away to spare a few drops of his blood.

Names and faces flashed through his mind, so many bold and honourable men cast down by betrayal. His brothers unwittingly corrupted or undone by personal failing. Others slain. His sons, dying in battle. So many of his sons…

A roaring blackness encroached. He fell, but he hit nothing. It felt like floating. A perfumed ocean lapped at him. Joy rode upon its waves.

Lies, he thought. *Lies! I cannot die!*

Guilliman forced open his eyes. He was on his back, looking up at the ceiling, his limbs deliciously numb. A treacherous pleasure thrilled his mind as the poison worked on him.

Captain Andos was at his side. A wall of warriors in blue ceramite surrounded him.

'Now, damn you all! Now! Emergency teleport! Emergency teleport!' shouted Andos, his bolter barking.

He is panicking, Guilliman thought. *Andos is panicking.*

The howling thrum of sonic weaponry tore away the last of Andos' words, and his head vanished in a mist of red. Chained explosions boomed around Guilliman. Part of the wall of men guarding him was knocked down. A body sailed through the air, the Ultramarines blue of its power armour cracked open and stained red. A dozen bolters fired near his feet as desperate hands dragged and pulled, hauling him up the steps towards the ruined Phoenix Gate. His armour caught on the corpses of his sons, each knock a spike of agony in his ruined neck. Blood poured down his windpipe into his lungs, making him splutter feebly. He was going to drown on it.

'Retreat! Retreat!' called a voice. 'The day is lost!'

Thiel? thought Guilliman. *Is that you?*

He could hear Fulgrim's silken, daemonic laughter drawing nearer.

How many Ultramarines have died to save me?

An instrument chimed, louder than the bleating alarms of Guilliman's battered armour.

'They have locus lock, my lord,' someone else said, close enough that Guilliman felt their breath on his ear, though he could not turn his head to see him. 'We will have you safe soon.'

Guilliman tried to place a face to the voice. He knew many of his sons, but this one eluded him. His mind was filling with black fog.

'We're losing him!' said the voice, rising in panic. 'Where's the teleport? Get us out of here. Get us–'

Thiel, thought Guilliman. *Definitely Thiel.*

A flash of blinding light and the bang of air displacement stole Roboute Guilliman away from the blades of his brother. Time hung, caught between an instant and an eternity. Guilliman ceased to be. For a moment, there was peace.

'–out of here!'

Another roar, and the needling discomfort of materialisation. Guilliman was thrust back through the veil into the world of men, and he fell to the teleport deck, jarring his wound. Fiery poison sketched out his circulatory system, thrusting the realisation of his own mortality upon him.

He was going to die.

In his final moments, Guilliman began to panic. He did not fear his death, but what it meant for the Imperium.

Andos had been right. And now Andos was dead.

I cannot die, he thought. *I cannot die! I will not!*

He exerted his formidable will to keep his body alive.

A fruitless effort.

His dispassionate nature did not desert him, not even at the very end. As he railed against his fate, he noted the failure of his organs, the dark ring thickening about his sight and the numb bliss creeping towards his hearts, as calmly as if he were reviewing progress on new public buildings.

Faces crowded the narrowing well of his vision. Helmets were cast aside to reveal anguished expressions.

They mourn me already, he realised. *I am dead. I cannot die now, not now. There is too much to do. Too much, too much. What will Russ do without me, or the Khan? Too much...*

Ultramarines shouted for their Apothecaries. Something tugged at his ruined breastplate. A white gauntlet flashed past his dimming eyes. The cool relief of drugs pushed back the exquisite burn of Fulgrim's poison for a breath, but they could not stop it and it surged back. His pulse slowed. Coloured spots whirled before his eyes.

'Father,' he mouthed. Poisoned blood frothed at the gash in his neck. 'Father, who will guide them now?'

'What is he saying?' cried an anguished voice. 'What does he say?'

Father, thought Guilliman. *Save me.*

His hearts quivered one last time, drawing themselves in for a further beat that would not come. The voices of his sons sounded far away.

Darkness enveloped him. His hearts relaxed. The flow of blood ceased.

He stood upon a precipice. A roaring, terrifying sea of souls, haunted by the laughing of mad gods, churned all around, red and ugly.

'Father!' Guilliman shouted, his voice free from the prison of his flesh. His sons could not hear him now, but he was heard.

There was a cold, golden light, and an end to pain. The roaring sea vanished. Sorrow engulfed his soul.

Roboute Guilliman was no more.

The immensity of the void is impossible to understand; the layered infinities of the empyrean even more so.

Only death can encompass them both.

PART TWO

CRUSADE

THE 41ST MILLENNIUM

CHAPTER FOUR

GUILLIMAN LIVES

Roboute Guilliman drew in a deep breath, then another.

He lived.

Blood rushed around his massive frame. Air passed in and out of lungs four times the size of a baseline human's, inhalations and exhalations that moved with the power of tides.

Death had come. For ten thousand years he had slept, his body preserved in stasis upon his home world of Macragge, until Archmagos Belisarius Cawl, aided by the alien aeldari and a saint said to be the personification of the Emperor's will, had awoken him to a galaxy tormented by war.

Traitors from Horus' time had emerged from the Eye of Terror, a wound in reality where the warp bled into real space. By destroying ancient alien technology, their leader – Abaddon the Despoiler, one-time lieutenant of Horus – had caused the Eye of Terror to spread across the galaxy as the Cicatrix Maledictum, a great warp rift that had cut the Imperium in two.

To Guilliman, the dire state of the Imperium was a horrifying surprise. He awoke from death to find himself fighting a war he thought he had won a hundred centuries before. There was no hope in this world. There was no promise. The Emperor's plans had failed completely, and suffering was the lot of all men. Only during the long, dark times of Old Night had humanity stood so close to the brink. He was all that remained of the old dream, the last feeble light in the descending dark.

Since then he had led. He had fought. He had bled. But he had not slept. He could not, even had he the desire to – the Imperium was dying. In sleep's place, he retreated to his private quarters, to the Chamber of Reflection, and meditated there when he was weary.

Death had disturbed his being in several ways. Sleep was one casualty.

Since his resurrection, he did not feel the need to sleep often. His personal physicians could not tell him if this was a genuine physical change or a psychological effect of his traumatic awakening. Both the mind and body of a primarch were so far beyond understanding that any medicae was next to useless. Only Archmagos Cawl, that insane polymath, might begin to comprehend how his body functioned.

It could simply have been that after ten thousand years, Roboute Guilliman thought he had slept enough.

Fulgrim's poisoned blade had come close to ending him. Were it not for the actions of his men, Guilliman would have died. As it was, his absence had been costly to the Imperium. So much had been lost because of his miscalculation. He had vowed never to underestimate his fallen brothers again.

What happened in the aftermath of Thessala had become myth. Like so much of Guilliman's life history, the truth of his death was shrouded in the embellishment of repeated telling; he had found no less than twenty-six divergent versions of the event in the Ultramarines libraria alone.

What was certain was that he had been as good as dead. Most of his fleet had been destroyed, and the moons of Thessala were wastelands to this day. He did not know what had become of his sons who had fought alongside him. In most cases, their names had been lost to time. Aeonid Thiel, for example – Guilliman could not discern what had happened to him. Back on Macragge, he had discovered the Second Captain's name on worn honour plaques in a chapel buried deep under the Fortress of Hera. These suggested that Thiel had survived the battle, but Guilliman did not know for how long. He did not know how Thiel had borne the loss of his primarch. Did he rise above it, or was his life one tormented by guilt?

Guilliman did not know which Apothecary had saved him, or who was in command of the Chapter when the *Gauntlet of Power* broke free of Fulgrim's trap, or how he had come to be placed in stasis in the Temple of Correction. In the archives of the Aurora Chapter and the Novamarines there were fragmentary accounts of what had happened to their lords and captains at Thessala, but little concerning the Ultramarines.

It was certain that he had been saved, just as it was certain that his sons had paid a heavy price for his blundering into Fulgrim's web. He had woken nearly ten thousand years later to another battle in the same war.

He had been given a chance to put things right.

He ran through those first moments of awakening again. He had come to in the Temple of Correction, clad in unfamiliar armour, the Emperor's Sword in his hand, surrounded on all sides by his sons battling the servants of the Great Enemy. Wrenched from one conflict to another, there had been a moment when he could have fallen, when his confusion threatened to leave him vulnerable to the Traitor Astartes of the Black Legion.

The Black Legion – even the names of the enemy were unfamiliar.

Everything had changed, and war was everywhere. Yet war he knew, and he prosecuted it with greater zeal than ever before. It was a constant in a universe thrown out of true. In his darkest moments, Guilliman thought he could well have died and been condemned to the hell of some primitive cult. But he did not believe such things, and he did not believe he deserved such punishment.

Serene within his own expansive mind, Roboute Guilliman took stock. Today, a hammer blow would fall. The war was far from done, but after twelve years of hard campaigning, the Indomitus Crusade neared a crucial juncture. He had battled to reach Terra. He had spoken with his father. He had made his decision as to what must be done.

He had turned the Imperium over to a state of complete and total war. New fleets had been constructed and whole populations recruited into the armed forces. Archmagos Belisarius Cawl had been good to the oaths he had made before the primarch's death, and he had spent the millennia of Guilliman's long sleep fashioning legions of new, improved warriors: the Primaris Space Marines. From their ranks, dozens of new Space Marine Chapters had been founded. All across Imperium Sanctus, Guilliman's crusade fought, speeding from one crisis to another. Everywhere they went, the fleets of the Indomitus Crusade brought relief and reinforcements to the beleaguered worlds of mankind. More than that, the crusade brought hope, and the impossible truth that a son of the Emperor strode the stars again.

The first phase was over. Several traitor fleets had been shattered and daemonic legions banished back to the warp. Many worlds had been taken back, and many others purged of corruption. With Imperium Sanctus shored up, the days of the great armies of Primaris Space Marines were done. A change in strategy was called for.

So much had to fall into place for victory to be assured. Guilliman revised plans long in the making, thinking through countermoves to multiple potential enemy actions. He found it hard to find time to think when he was not in his Chamber of Reflection. There had been so many demands on his attention since he had been revived. This small, cubic room – four yards by four yards by four yards – was the only place he might bring all his prodigious powers to bear on a single issue.

But time was precious, and hard to find. A metallic voice broke his concentration.

'My lord, we are approaching 108/Beta-Kalapus-9.2.'

Guilliman's eyes opened upon a plain space lit in a soothing blue light. The gothic extravagance that typified human art in this era was absent. He filled his lungs with blood-warm air, held his breath, then let it out in a long, controlled exhalation, sending a little of his tension with it.

He stood and rotated his neck, wincing at the awkward stretch of skin at his throat.

The wound still hurt. Primarchs did not scar easily, but Fulgrim had left him a fine one. A thick rope of tissue crossed his throat from side to side, angled just enough for the raised side to catch on his armour seals, no matter how many times he had them adjusted.

'Give me an exact time of arrival,' asked Guilliman.

There was a short wait while the pickled brains of dead men searched for the answer.

'Four hours, thirty-six minutes, nine seconds, primarch.'

'Inform my equerry Felix and Captain Sicarius of the Victrix Guard that I am rested. Tell the command deck to expect my presence shortly. Alert my arming servitors and master of arms. I will go to them now.'

'As you wish, primarch,' said the voice.

Guilliman reached out. The meditation chamber was small enough for him to be able to touch the door mechanism without taking a step. His fingers brushed a blank steel sheet. The embedded sensors recognised his unique energy signature, and the door swung open.

Guilliman stepped out of the room into his private chambers. A whole spire upon the *Macragge's Honour* was his, as it had been long ago, for the Gloriana-class battleship had been his flagship throughout the Great Crusade. At the beginning of the Heresy, he had ordered it to pursue the *Infidus Imperator*, the flagship of his traitor brother Lorgar. Guilliman had thought the *Macragge's Honour* lost in this pursuit, but it was not, the battleship finally limping home long after the primarch had died.

A Gloriana-class battleship was designed for a Legion, a formation a hundred times the size of a contemporary Space Marine Chapter. The maximum complement was thousands of Adeptus Astartes, but it had been rare for so many to be aboard the *Macragge's Honour* at once before Guilliman's return. Under the reborn primarch, the Ultramarines flagship had again rung to the march of armoured superhumans as it had in ages past, but for the ten millennia before that, the halls of the *Macragge's Honour* had been underused, and there had been no need to employ the primarch's old chambers.

The Ultramarines ever were a practical breed, but sentimentality was in their make-up too, and reverence added invisible locks to their father's quarters. Not one of the Chapter Masters that followed Guilliman had ever taken up residence there, though they had every right to, and the primarch's palace had become a shrine. Beyond ceremonies commemorating their primarch's life, the rooms had remained sealed, warded by means arcane and mundane. Not even the Red Corsairs, who had taken the ship on Guilliman's hard road to Terra and held it for a while, had managed to breach this sanctum.

In the main, Guilliman's palace had been expertly preserved, but entropy had wormed its fingers into the complex's fabric nonetheless, dulling metal and rotting cloth. Even now they were restored, Roboute Guilliman still caught the scent of neglect beneath the oily smell of ship's air.

He passed through staterooms and down corridors whose doors opened on opulent guest chambers. This area was currently unoccupied, and he passed no one save for a scattering of maintenance servitors. His household servants had little business on these levels if he had no guests, and Guilliman demanded solitude when not attending to his many duties.

By grand staircase and express lift, he made his way to his arming chambers.

There were but a handful alive now who remembered the Great Heresy War. The teeming multitudes of the Imperium had no inkling of the dream Horus' betrayal had killed. Few beings lived that would have noted the changes the Avenging Son of Ultramar had undergone. His patrician's face was lined, more with cares than with years, and sunken in on itself a touch, especially around the cheeks. He was still handsome, if not beautiful, for all the Emperor's sons had been made to be perfect in thought and form. But though his features had a fineness a sculptor would struggle to capture, his was an eroded handsomeness, worn at the edges like a mountain's crags. His golden hair had thinned a little, and at the temples were a few strands of grey. Pale brown circles gathered under his eyes when he grew tired, and there was tightness in his jaw, a legacy of the internal pain he had borne since his resurrection.

Part of this discomfort was physical, an ineradicable effect of Fulgrim's poisons. But there was also a sense of an absence in his gene-forged body that made itself known as a dull ache. Guilliman called it emotional pain. After all he had seen in this new age, he remained loath to name it spiritual in nature. He was too enamoured of reason to truly believe his soul had been injured.

The discomfort had grown worse since he had first removed the Armour of Fate. He could wear the armour constantly for it dulled the pain greatly; indeed, he had been advised never to take it off by Yvraine of the aeldari, but he refused to be beholden to anyone or anything but the Emperor, and so he first chose the risk of taking it off, then to suffer without it.

In contrast to the upper levels, the lower decks of the palace spire were full of activity. Human servants bustled to and fro. Servitors clumped by, bearing heavy burdens. A pair of tech-priests broke off their conversations and bowed as he strode past them. Men clad in a variation of Ultramar's Praecental Guard uniform stood to attention as he approached his arming chamber doors. The doors hissed open, and he passed within.

'Arming chamber' did no justice to Guilliman's collection of weaponry. Part museum, part armoury, it was a complex in its own right. The Grand Hall of Armament was its centrepiece, housing not only his personal wargear but also xenos trophies and ancient designs of human weaponry. A huge window filled one wall. The central panels were taken up by a glassaic map of the old Five Hundred Worlds of Ultramar, commissioned by the primarch himself after the vessel was returned to him. A mezzanine crammed with more devices of war ran around the three sides of the room not occupied by the window.

An honour guard of empty suits lined the central aisle, examples of every sort of power armour worn by the Ultramarines in their long history. There were three dozen of them all told, with many variants of every mark, from lightweight Scout armours to enormous prototype Terminator suits constructed at the height of the Great Crusade.

Guilliman passed the last podiums, where stood numerous iterations of Belisarius Cawl's new Mark X power armour, all designed for differing tactical situations. Between them stood more men from the Praecental Guard's Naval Division, their energy pikes dipping in salute as he passed.

From the Grand Hall of Armament, Guilliman went into his personal armourium. Serfs and servitors stood waiting for him, a pair of tech-priests at their head. The pieces of the Armour of Fate were neatly arrayed upon a slab covered with blue velvet. The suit was of Archmagos Cawl's design, like so much else, and superior to the Armour of Reason Guilliman had worn in his previous life, and which now resided in the reliquaries of Macragge.

The Victrix Guard were there to greet him. Captain Cato Sicarius led them.

'My lord,' said Sicarius. The Victrix Guard got down on bended knee.

'Rise,' commanded the primarch. He entered an outsized arming frame and took off his robe. The man he handed it to was almost lost in its folds.

Under the robes, Guilliman wore a dark grey bodyglove, its surface marked with the dull silver of inactive circuits. These gathered in complicated whorls where the interface ports studding his body poked through the material.

'You are ready, my lord?' asked the senior of the tech-priests, his voice emanating from voxmitters embedded in his back.

'Arm me,' commanded the primarch.

Guilliman held out his hands. At the terse orders of the Adeptus Mechanicus, the arming team began to assemble the armour around their lord. It was so massive that dedicated servitors equipped with industrial-grade augmetics were required to move each piece. The boots were brought forward first in soft-gripped cargo pincers. They alone weighed hundreds of pounds.

'Captain Sicarius, report to me,' said Guilliman.

Sicarius approached the arming cage. When Guilliman had first met him, he'd had the swagger of a master swordsman. He was captain of the Second Company, Master of the Watch, Grand Duke of Talassar, Knight Champion of Macragge and High Suzerain of Ultramar – proud titles, but his arrogance had since been blunted somewhat by a period lost in the warp.

As always, he rested his hand on the pommel of his sheathed broadsword. Guilliman only recalled seeing Sicarius' right hand off the blade a couple of times. Despite his recent change in character, the captain remained headstrong, and in that he reminded Guilliman a little of Thiel.

'My lord,' said Sicarius. 'The enemy is gathering in strength around the third planet of the system. Elements of the Word Bearers, Black Legion, Iron Warriors and various renegade forces act in concert. They noted our presence as soon as we departed the Mandeville point, but have not moved from the planet to intercept. The Word Bearers are the greatest contingent.'

'Good,' said Guilliman. There were ancient grudges between the Ultramarines and the Word Bearers, and the fallen Legion had mounted strong resistance against the Indomitus Crusade. 'A chance to spill the blood of Lorgar's sons is always welcome. Their presence is unsurprising. Only those fanatics would undertake the construction of something like this orbital. How is the enemy's disposition?'

'They are fragmented, and lack our organisation, my lord,' said Sicarius. 'There are enough to put up a creditable defence. It depends whether they have a strong leader, as always. If not, they will be easily dealt with.'

Guilliman winced as an interface spike buried itself in a neural socket. 'We must be swift, before their sorcerers bring forth daemons to aid them.'

'By our strategos' calculations, this flotilla represents a significant proportion of the enemy's strength in this sector,' said Sicarius. 'It is their interpretation that this group have assembled to protect the orbital fane. If they gather here so that we may destroy them more easily, we should not complain.'

'I admire your optimism.'

Servants with powerdrivers for hands bolted Guilliman's greaves to his legs while the tech-priests muttered benedictions of protection and smooth operation.

'Order Battle Group Cerastus to turn about,' said Guilliman. 'Tell Groupmaster Diameos to lead them in reinforcing our rearguard. The rearguard will hold position three million miles rearwards. I want picket groups on regular sweeps around the edge of the system, and full deep-void augur scans every five minutes looking for warp-exit signatures. Check the Mandeville points, the gravipause and every area in this system where gravitic interplay might allow an emergency ingress. The traitors are becoming desperate. We must be wary of reinforcements.'

'As you command, Lord Guilliman.'

'This system is critical, Sicarius. I will not lose it. Send word to Dominus GiFellivo that I want him and the higher-tier command of his battle congregation, together with Prime Hermeticon Cordus-Rho, to attend upon me the moment the battle is over.' He avoided the term 'Taghmata'. The military organisation of the Adeptus Mechanicus had changed radically since the days of the old Mechanicum. 'Together. Make that absolutely clear. I will entertain their petty rivalries no longer. The dominus is to aid the prime hermeticon or they will answer to me directly. Make that understood. We must work quickly once the fourth world is taken, with no dissension.'

'Yes, my lord.'

'Have there been any developments while I rested?'

Sicarius smiled slightly. Guilliman's attention to detail was exacting. He had been meditating for thirty-two minutes only.

'All relevant information has been inputted to your personal data-feeds, my lord. There is nothing of note to report, either from within this system or elsewhere, though proximity to the Pit of Raukos makes astrotelepathy problematic.'

'Nothing relayed from the other crusade fleets?'

'Nothing significant, my lord.'

'Then all is well,' said Guilliman. His armourers had clad him as far as his waist. Their activity lessened a moment as diagnostic handsets were plugged into his armour's ports to check the function of the lower assembly. The legs tensed as their fibre bundles contracted. The handsets chirruped, and the arming recommenced.

'Leave Macullus and Dibus here,' said Guilliman, nodding at two of the Ultramarines. 'I wish to speak with them about their plans for redevelopment of the Veridian System. Take the rest of the Victrix Guard with you to the command deck. I will join you shortly.'

'As you command,' said Sicarius.

'And where is Felix?' said Guilliman.

'He is delayed, my lord. He sends his apologies.'

'Very well,' said Guilliman. 'See he is with us at the opening of the battle. I will have representatives of all arms of Fleet Primus present. This is an important day, Sicarius.'

The backplate of Guilliman's armour was lowered into position by a crane and held steady by the velvet-gloved hands of four mortal servants. Two massively augmented servitors manoeuvred the Armour of Fate's breastplate from the table. Moving it into perfect alignment with tiny whinings of their servomotors, they slammed the breastplate home. Small clicks sounded as it locked to the backplate, and two men worked quickly to tighten the hex screws, making the seal good.

'My lord,' said Sicarius. With one last bow, he departed, leaving the two Victrix Guard behind.

'Praise the Omnissiah for the Armour of Fate!' proclaimed the tech-priest. 'Praise the Emperor for His wisdom! Praise the motive force for the activation of the primarch's shield.'

Guilliman hid a wince at the tech-priest's fervour. He had little time for religion.

At least they are not singing, thought Guilliman. He had put a stop to that.

'Dibus, Macullus – come here,' Guilliman said. He settled back into the arming frame as the rest of his armour was assembled around him. 'Tell me more about this water-conservation regime you wish to impose on Calth's feed worlds. I understand you have been suffering disagreement. We will resolve this now, or I will decry you as worse than the archmagi.'

The two warriors glanced at each other and approached. They set out their plans, and where they did not accord. The primarch listened and gave his advice.

So matters of peace were discussed as Guilliman's armada sped on towards the Pit of Raukos, and the enemy awaiting them there.

CHAPTER FIVE

GUILLIMAN'S MERCY

The Indomitus Crusade had taken Guilliman away from the star-realm of Ultramar, but still he found time to govern his home from afar.

War raged in Ultramar as it did everywhere else. The followers of the Plague God, Nurgle, assailed the worlds of the Ultramarines, and the diseases of the enemy claimed far more lives than their bullets.

At Roboute Guilliman's direct command, sick and injured soldiers were brought to the planet Iax from across Ultramar. Iax was tithed as an agri-world, but such was its beauty, it was informally referred to as the Garden Planet. That was before the war. The empire of the Ultramarines was bleeding manpower at a terrifying rate, and so Guilliman had redesignated Iax as a hospital world for the duration of the conflict – that is to say, most likely forever.

Landing the sick and wounded at Iax's Hortusia space port took an amount of time congruent with the complexity of the task. The diseases spread by the enemy were supernaturally vigorous, so quarantine procedures had to be stringent. Like everything in Ultramar, if a job were deemed of enough importance to be done, then it would be done correctly.

A fresh shipment of patients was coming in by shuttle. The decontamination crew returned to the landing field and its surrounding mushroom patch of white dome tents for the seventeenth time that day. Between each trip, the shuttles were cleaned on the ward-ships in orbit, for that was the responsibility of their medicae-captains, but ensuring the purity of the landing fields fell to the chirurgeon-general's office on Iax.

Though Caradomus, the chirurgeon-general of Iax, would have preferred to decontaminate the shuttles after their journey from anchor to the surface as well, speed had to be given some consideration – cleaning the landing aprons was faster than cleaning the exterior of the landers. His concerns were allayed a little by the Adeptus Mechanicus biologians attached to the Officio Medicae upon Iax, who calculated atmospheric re-entry paths for each shuttle designed to burn the worst of any contamination away. Magos Kromek had suggested the landing field cleaning procedure could be omitted altogether, but Chirurgeon-General Caradomus was diligent, and if he could avoid risks he would.

Besides, propaganda had its role to play. The ships were not serious vectors of infection – the soldiers they carried to Iax from the war's multiple fronts were. But they couldn't be turned away. The outgassings of high-pressure cleansing hoses at the aprons could be seen for miles. They were reassuring. So the landing aprons were cleaned, and often.

Upon Iax, the lesser sick recuperated alongside the injured. Some of the diseases unleashed into Ultramar could be treated under median-range quarantine conditions with standard medicines. Others required specialist care, up to and including Adeptus

Ministorum-approved exorcism. Those suffering from the more aggressive, spiritually corrupting illnesses were held in specially commissioned stations in orbit. As few as possible were euthanised. If they could be helped, they were.

This, it was said in Ultramar, was the difference between Roboute Guilliman's and the Emperor's mercies, and the beleaguered people of that realm took heart in their lord's concern for their wellbeing.

In typical Ultramarian style, multiple Imperial ordos and officios were brought together to tend to the war's casualties, and they were made to cooperate by members of the new Officio Logisticarum embedded in Ultramar's government. Regarding the screening of the injured and sick, the Officio Medicae was given free rein. Much of the processing went on in orbit. As the hospital ward-ships arrived from Ultramar's warzones, the wounded soldiers on board were tested for infectious agents. Those passing the first round were transferred to smaller void-ships, most commandeered for this purpose from the chartist merchant fleets or taken from among Naval vessels too badly damaged to be made combat-ready quickly. The smaller the better, in the chirurgeon-general's view, for smaller ships could be more thoroughly isolated.

During transit from the front back to Iax, the soldiers were kept in solitary confinement to prevent the spread of disease, their physical needs attended to by servitors of only the highest classes of biological sanctity. There were not enough ships left to separate the sick from the injured before transit, not that it would have prevented cross-infection; so many of those wounded in battle and now bound for Iax harboured disease unawares.

Around Iax, troops exhibiting symptoms were divided by type. The first appraised were those suffering purely from injury, be it physical or mental. They were also rigorously tested for disease. Those who proved free of secondary infectious conditions were separated from the rest and taken to the surface via decontamination protocols at the star fort Korsteel, which had taken up anchor over Iax for the purpose. The remainder of the casualties adjudged sick, injured or not, were returned to the main group.

The sick were split into known and unknown pathogen groups, then further into physical, mental and spiritual afflictions, then by grade of severity, and finally all these groups were divided between the wounded sick and the merely sick.

After all this, groups were subdivided into numbered cohorts and relocated to holding vessels in permanent orbit. There, further anti-biological procedures were undertaken. Second and third rounds of testing virtually eliminated any possibility of transmission. Those that passed the third test were deemed safe and transferred to the surface of Iax, bound for facilities that treated all ailments.

Those who failed the second or third tests were kept aboard the isolation ships, where they were treated and repeatedly tested for pestilence. Those that improved were transferred in time; those that did not were given their final blessings and their corpses incinerated in psi-warded plasma pyres.

Thus it was that – with breathtaking efficiency – huge numbers of Ultramarian casualties were broken down in stages into manageable groups. Hundreds of thousands of men became thousands, then hundreds, then tens. And all were thoroughly, relentlessly catalogued by the Officio Medicae's Divisio Descriptor. Elsewhere in the Imperium, such work would have been unimaginable. On most worlds it would never have been undertaken – the sick would have been exterminated; the wounded would have been left to their fate.

Not in Ultramar. The white-and-blue-clad human auxiliaries

each represented a significant investment in training, and most had accrued substantial combat experience. By treating and returning its casualties to the war, the realm of Ultramar kept its armies fighting without loss of effectiveness.

'By the preservation of life do we maintain our capability to mete out death.' So the primarch had said. Or, at least, so the records indicated. Now Guilliman was among the living once more, it was possible to ask him if all the words attributed to him were truly his. For the first few years, Guilliman had been in the habit of correcting his subordinates, insisting many of his supposed sayings were apocryphal, until he had given up in exasperation. He was simply not believed by most, for whom the primarch remained an ideal. They valued their preconceptions of him over the living evidence.

No one could argue that the efforts to save the troops' lives were undertaken in a manner at odds with the primarch's own beliefs. Though diminished in efficacy, something of Guilliman's methodology had survived the ages.

Iax had become the hub for all counter-plague efforts, a laboratorium and sanatorium both, where treatments for the war's ever-evolving sicknesses were concocted and disseminated to the fronts of Ultramar.

The processing of casualties was labour intensive, no matter how efficient. Ensuring the purity of bulk landers was difficult, so they were forbidden from the surface, but smaller lighters or shuttles meant more trips. As a result, landing all the troops from a single medicae ward-ship took days, and there were always plenty more waiting.

To the untrained eye, the cleansing of the landing aprons was an impressive sign of the diligence with which the screening procedures were undertaken. In reality, it was the least important and easiest, entrusted to low-ranking ground crew and mono-task servitors whose biologic components were sealed deep within inorganic frames.

Iax had a pronounced axial tilt, and the southern hemisphere's autumn was coming to an end. It was evening and growing cold as the cleansing team climbed down from their transports. They unspooled their lines and passed through a spray gate, the only gap in the complex of bubble tents around the field. Drenched in strong antibiologics, they paced to and fro, the huge hoses leading from the tankers looped over their backs and pointed at the ground. Their human forms were lost in the bulk of their protective suits, so that servitor and true man were hard to tell apart. Blasts of boiling water were followed by sheeting sprays of antivirals. Bio-killers swept across the rockcrete. The water sent up huge columns of condensing vapour into the chill air. Appearances were maintained.

When the cleansing had been done, priests in biohazard surplices marched out from the interconnected domed tents crowding the apron. They trailed back and forth over the antiseptic ground, flicking aspergillums full of sanctified oils to banish psychic corruption that chemicals could not purge.

Finally, the quarantine masters – the mid-ranking medicae officials, the Frater Hospitaller Majoris Inferior of the local Adeptus Ministorum and purity officers from the Commissariat – came out from the tents, inspected the work, gave their approval and affixed their seals to the relevant order parchments. Only then was a lighter given clearance to land.

The whole process took half an hour, every single time.

The ground crew were kept on hand in case the cleansing had not been performed satisfactorily. With relief, they watched their superiors march back into the bubble tents around the field. As the last closure zipped shut, the crew wearily rolled up their disinfectant hoses, retreated back through the spray gate to their service vehicles and sped across the landing fields for forty minutes of rest, one cleansing closer to the end of their eighteen-hour shift.

The field was now yielded to several medicae equipped with bulky auspexes attached to their suits with sealed, flexible pipes. Angry red lights flickered condemnatory patterns on the instruments' upper surfaces.

Bright points shimmered against the evening, thousands of feet into the sky. The lighter came in fast. When it had grown to a growling, angular shape black against the low sun, the medicae set off cleansing bombs around the landing apron that belched plumes of astringent white smoke. The lighter touched down in a mist of anti-biological agents, dropped its ramps without powering down its engines, and was away as soon as the last injured soldier was out of its hold.

In this way, Tullius Varens of the Talassar 30th Ultramar Auxiliary Regiment came to Iax. He shuffled onto the apron with a hundred others like him, blinking against daylight after a week inside a voidship cell. He carried nothing but his lasrifle, his flak armour and the uniform on his back. Everything else he owned had been incinerated.

'Stay close, Bolus,' he said to the man beside him. 'Don't wander off.'

Bolus, an older man with rough salt-and-pepper stubble, stared ahead with the eyes of the profoundly disturbed.

The medicae came out of the chemical fog, shoving the exhausted troopers into a line. Varens was too weak to resist as rubber-gloved hands grabbed him, but he growled out a challenge when his wounded back was roughly pawed.

'Careful,' he said. The medicae manhandling him went on to the next man without comment. Varens shuffled along with the queue of men. He turned when he realised Bolus wasn't following him, but was still standing where the ramp of the ship had deposited him. Sighing, Varens went back to Bolus' side.

'Come on, Bolus,' he whispered. He took his friend by the elbow.

Bolus had not been the same since the last assault at Konor's Reach. Once voluble and confident, he now went meekly where Varens led.

'Weapons in a pile in the red circle. Armour and webbing in the green,' a medicae barked through voxmitters set into his thick armaglass visor. He pointed at painted circles offset from the entrance to the bubble-tent complex. 'Uniforms in the blue.'

'Everything?' said one of the other soldiers. He was stupid with exhaustion. One of the medicae waved his burbling medical auspex up and down his body.

'Everything,' the medicae said.

Wearily, the auxiliaries stripped. Emaciated bodies shivered in the cool evening.

Varens reached for Bolus' gun. His own lasrifle slipped on a shoulder gone scrawny from months of poor rations, grazing his wound. The gun felt like it weighed as much as a heavy bolter, but he gritted his teeth against the pain, unslung it and took hold of Bolus' weapon as well, gently unhooking the strap from his friend's limp fingers.

'Best get undressed,' he said to Bolus.

Bolus looked at him wildly. 'Fifteen! Fifteen!' he said. He jabbed a finger on his good hand at one of the other troopers, a man by the name of Gideon.

Gideon was one of the few others Varens knew in the group. He was a braggart. Varens did not think much of him.

'Fifteen!' Bolus said, urgently gesturing at Gideon.

'Hey! Hey!' Varens snapped his fingers before Bolus' face. The older man quieted and stared at the weapons in Varens' hands with red-rimmed eyes, as if they affronted him.

'What, the guns?' said Varens. 'I'll deal with those. Get undressed, old man, I'll pile everything up for you. Don't draw attention to yourself. You got that?'

Bolus nodded. Varens squeezed his shoulder. Reluctantly he left him alone and trudged to the coloured circles. Guns and equipment made fragile-sounding clatters as they were tossed into piles on the rockcrete.

It didn't seem right to Varens, disrespecting their weapons like that, and he scowled at his fellows. Most of them were from worlds far away from his. They were too tired and too sick to notice his disapproval. He elbowed his way forward and carefully laid his and Bolus' guns down at the circle's edge.

'You've served me well,' he said quietly, resting his hand on the stock of his rifle. 'I pray your spirit finds rest, if you are not to return to the war.'

Leaving his gun was like leaving his heart on the floor, but when he stood and let out a shaky breath, he realised it was a release to be free of it.

His hands went to the buckles fastening his webbing and armour. He was still clothed, but he was cold and shivering already, and his numb fingers struggled with the catches. It wasn't just the chill; his injuries troubled him. There was a core of flesh missing from his back, just below his shoulder blade. It was still raw around the edges, unnaturally hot. He had not even noticed receiving the wound. In one moment, what had been simple became fraught with pain. Try as he might, he could not refuse to acknowledge the frailty of his own flesh. The evidence was there in his weak fingers slipping on the catch, and the burn of the mark on his back.

After half a minute of fumbling, the catch cooperated and

undid. His shoulder plates slid from his body, taking a good portion of his bodily warmth with them. He wasn't looking forward to taking his uniform off.

Bolus' shouts had him looking up.

'Fifteen!' Bolus was struggling in the restraining arms of a medicae. He was trying to get at Gideon, his hands outstretched. Shouted orders from the medicae team ripped across the throng, augmitters harsh. In a minute, there would be armed men emerging from the tents.

'Don't know what's got into you, old man!' said Gideon as Bolus lunged towards him. He smiled widely. 'You should calm down. Easy street for a month or so, before we're back to the front.'

'Fifteen!' shouted Bolus. He pawed at the medicae's faceplate.

'Stand down!' shouted the man. His colleague was reaching for a compact webber. It looked to Varens like the medicae were used to this kind of thing. He wasn't surprised. The sights they'd seen were enough to drive anyone insane.

'Hey!' called Varens. He dropped his armour where it was and shoved his way back through the soldiers. A gaggle had stopped to watch, and it made the going tough. He carved a path with his elbows.

Bolus had made no move to disrobe or remove his armour.

'Put your armour and webbing in the green circle, uniforms in the blue!' one medicae shouted. The webber was out now. Varens was afraid how Bolus would react if he were trapped again.

They grabbed at Bolus hard, making the man twitch and wail.

'Leave him be!' shouted Varens. 'He's not in his right mind. He's suffering combat stress. Emperor's teeth, I thought you were healers! Can't you see? He'll be all right soon, if you let him alone. Bolus, Bolus, hey!'

The medicae parted enough to let him near.

'V-v-varens?' spluttered Bolus.

'Yes, my friend, it's me. Do as the medicae say, do you understand?'
Bolus looked at the medical staff suspiciously.

'Bolus! Come on, do you understand?'

The medicae still had his webber out. Bolus was oblivious
to the device.

Hesitantly, Bolus nodded.

'Strip,' said the medicae. 'Armour in the–'

'Yeah, we get it,' snapped Varens. 'I heard you four times already.
I'll help him.' He interposed himself between his friend and the
medic. 'We've been together for the last two years, fighting on
Espandor. Where've you been?'

'I don't have to answer you,' said the medicae with the webber.

'Here,' said the other one. 'Only here.'

'Then you don't know what we've been through. Give him his
due. If it weren't for men like him, you and all this would be
nothing but ashes and slime. Plague warriors, Heretic Astartes, the
walking Emperor-damned dead – Bolus and I have faced them
all, while you've been having a fine old time in your rubber suits.'

'We're saving lives here,' said the first medicae. 'By the grace of
the Emperor. We all have our roles to play. We are here to help
you, but you both need to be processed. If he won't cooperate,
he won't make it.'

Varens grabbed Bolus by the shoulder a little too fiercely,
making him flinch. 'This man's saved my life five times. You
have a lot of catching up to do if you think I'll let him die.'

'Your choice, trooper.' The webber came up.

Bolus calmed. Some of what had been said must have sunk
in, because he was unclipping his combat webbing. 'No, no,'
he said. 'No, Varens, no.' His head jerked, barely under control. His armour slithered to the ground in a mess of straps.

Mechanically, Bolus undressed. Varens did the same, watching his friend warily, but no more outbursts came.

Bolus handed over his grubby white uniform. Varens bundled it up with his own. Their bodies, grimy and pale, were exposed to the unkindness of the autumn air.

The medicae finally holstered his webber and passed his auspex over Bolus. It burred to itself, and clunked. A green lumen shone from the top.

'He's clean, but keep him calm. This process takes time.'

'He'll be all right,' said the kinder medicae.

'I understand,' said Varens. His anger drained away. He was on a hair trigger. Aggression had kept him alive, able to react quickly, effectively. Such an intense state of readiness didn't suit a place like this. The whole thing felt surreal to him. How could the medicae understand?

The medicae waved his auspex over Varens' bandaged wound. 'What happened to you?'

'Flesh wound. Got it fighting Heretic Astartes,' he said flatly. 'Don't know how.'

The medicae wasn't impressed by Varens' claim. 'If you got wounded by Traitor Space Marines, you should be dead.'

'Are you calling me a liar?' said Varens.

'I'm calling you lucky.' The auspex made an angry bleat. 'The wound is infected.'

'You don't say,' said Varens. 'If a dozen screening processes hadn't told me that, the burn in the skin does.'

'The wound looks nastier than it is. It is not serious. The infection can be treated.' The green light shone, and the medicae took the auspex away. 'Main tent.'

'Emperor, we know. We could do with a little empathy here. Get us inside out of the cold, or we'll catch our deaths. We're men, not munitions pallets.'

'You're not a man until you've been checked and triple cleansed, trooper. Until then you're a vector of infection that endangers this whole world. Now keep your friend under control or we'll have to give him the ultimate cure.'

'We're here for Guilliman's mercy,' said Varens.

The medicae laughed behind his mask. 'Mercy's in short supply. Dump your kit, and proceed to decontamination.'

The man was already waving his auspex over the next trooper.

'A disease vector, is that right?' called Varens after the medicae. 'I'd check out Trooper Gideon, then.' He pointed out the other man to the medicae. 'Bolus and I have been fighting the plague lords for so long, he's developed a nose for disease.'

Varens helped Bolus put his uniform and equipment onto the right piles, then they joined the line of shivering men heading into the tents. None of the auxiliaries were in a good way. Without exception, the naked bodies around Varens bore traces of disease and trauma. A lot of them had passed this way before, as shown by the way they were lining up and doing what was required without being told, stoic throughout. Varens was cold, strung out and exhausted. Only the discipline instilled in him by the auxilia kept him from snapping, and that was close to wearing out.

He still had space for a smile when he heard Gideon cursing and the auspex beeping angrily.

'Ship lice,' the medicae said. 'External parasites, nothing serious, get him into tent three, triple-plus sterilisation protocols.'

Varens' turn came. He pushed his way through three sets of plastek strip doors and into the fuggy air of a decontamination chamber. Chemical steam filled his nose and made his eyes water. His wound stung under its dressings. Whatever awaited Gideon in tent three, Varens hoped it was less fun than this. He deserved it.

'Fifteen!' cackled Bolus, as if sharing a special joke. 'F-f-fifteen!'

Varens' brief humour blew away like the steam billowing from the pipes. The counting thing was new, and he didn't like it. Varens hoped a respite from the war would help Bolus' mind heal, but he wasn't confident. He had seen battle shock before. The only cure that was sure to work was a mercy bullet. He had never thought Bolus would fall prey to it, and that made him angry. Bolus had been so brave, so unshakeable. If he could lose his mind, then anyone could.

'Come on, old man,' Varens said. He took hold of Bolus' arm again. His skin was damp and loose on wasted muscle, his regimental tattoos distorted by the sag. 'Time for a bath.'

Under Bolus' armpit, there was a brief squirming, maggoty motion. If Varens had seen that, he would have known that battle shock was the least of what ailed his friend.

The thing turned and vanished into the cage of Bolus' ribs, undetected.

CHAPTER SIX

THE BATTLE OF RAUKOS

The high officers of Fleet Primus gathered on the command deck of the *Macragge's Honour* around the dais occupied by the primarch, crowding the command throne of Fleetmaster Khestrin, which was set before it.

Astra Militarum generals rubbed shoulders with the Sisters Superior of battle convents. Adeptus Mechanicus archmagi stood in clusters of orange, rust and blood-red robes. Space Marine lords waited with commissars, inquisitors and the barons of knightly courts. Princeps had come down from their Titans' steel skulls, ill at ease to be surrounded by so many people. There were Naval wing commanders and captains of capital ships. Sisters of Silence stood aside from everyone else, their disquieting auras eliciting shudders. The augments of skitarii clade commanders buzzed. Departmento Munitorum and Officio Logisticarum officials talked in low voices. Historitors recorded the occasion discreetly.

Every branch of the Imperium's forces and those who supplied, directed and supported them were represented there, whether in person or as one of the ghostly hololiths projected by the servo-skulls swarming above the throng.

Through the grand oculus, the plough-blade prow of the *Macragge's Honour* pointed in challenge at the Pit of Raukos. A huge, lazily turning interface between the warp and real space, the Pit of Raukos was set apart from the Great Rift, but although an isolated wound, it was a deep one, punching a hole through space-time into the heart of the warp. It was an area of bruised void millions of miles across. Purple around the periphery, towards the middle its colouration tended to putrid yellow-white, and at the very centre a vast, dark orb like the pupil of an eye rotated with the ferocity of a pulsar.

At the edge of the Pit languished a system around a medium red star. It had never been settled or given a name by mankind, but bore the Adeptus Astra Cartographica designation of 108/Beta-Kalapus-9. Gravitic shear drew long plumes of incandescent gas from the star towards the anomaly, which was slowly consuming it. In the years since the Great Rift had opened, the sun had dimmed considerably, and the planets that orbited it were going dark.

Tendrils of glowing matter twisted out from the fringes of the Pit, merging with the surrounding star gas and bending it into loops that reached for the greater slash of the Cicatrix Maledictum like parasitic worms migrating from their host.

Such breaches between dimensions were once terrifying anomalies. In these dark times, they had become commonplace. The Great Rift split the galaxy side to side, and a thousand places like the Pit of Raukos pierced reality.

Nature's iron grip was weak there. From its churning depths came half-mad vessels crewed by children's nightmares. Impossible monsters crept gibbering out of the shadows on worlds for light years around it. Most of these things had only a brief foothold in reality, and the more esoteric types died as soon as they were birthed, smeared to glowing corposant by the laws of material physics. Disturbing as they were, such minor Never-born were not the real threat. The Pit of Raukos was an open gate to the daemonic legions of the greater powers. Given form by the wills of their dark gods, and sustained by the unnatural energies of the rift, they did survive, and armies of them peri-odically emerged from Raukos. The terror they generated fed them further, and so the cycle of horror continued.

Guilliman stared unflinchingly into the unclean cyst of the Pit.

'Another lost system.' Stratarchis Tribune Actuarius Maldovar Colquan of the Adeptus Custodes spoke angrily. Five others of his order stood guard behind the primarch. When he spoke, and it was not often, it was as if every affront to the Imperium he saw compounded his shame. Guilliman was well aware that for ten millennia the Emperor's bodyguard had done little. All Colquan had to offer in recompense was gall.

When Guilliman had returned to Terra, he had discovered a warrior brotherhood blinded by grief and duty, uninterested in anything that happened beyond the walls of the Imperial Palace. Crisis after crisis had battered the foundations of the Imperium, and the Adeptus Custodes had retreated further from view with each one.

They had finally come out from behind the Palace walls in large numbers, and now the pendulum had swung too far the other way. The golden warriors of Terra were in danger of being blinded by rage.

'It was not lost, because it never belonged to the Imperium,' said Guilliman. 'This target is nevertheless worthy, and we shall claim it as our own. See how the enemy gather around it. Their temple nears completion.'

A hololithic strategic display showed the system and its monstrous parasite as a series of neutral graphics. The Pit looked so bland rendered that way, an innocuous nebula. The Chaos fleet was gathered at the world of 108/Beta-Kalapus-9.2, invisible to the unaided eye, but clear enough to the augurs of the *Macragge's Honour*, and bright dots of light tagged with data-screed swarmed at high anchor around a single point, the orbital fane of the Word Bearers.

The primarch's voice needed no amplification to reach all of his commanders. His words carried into the furthest reaches of the command deck. When he spoke, all stopped to listen.

'A temple is under construction here. It must be destroyed. This is a staging post for our enemies, but it is for no mundane resupply that they come to the Pit of Raukos.' He pointed at the black eye in the anomaly. 'They come here to make blood sacrifice, and call upon their diabolical gods to favour them with aid from their servants. From this rift, daemons walk and lend their power to the traitors. Such doorways must be closed.

'The ability to do so eludes us for now, but they will be closed, all of them. I swear this in the Emperor's name. Until then, the monsters that come from within them will be beaten back, and the thresholds guarded by the mightiest warriors the Imperium can spare. So we shall divide the mortal servants of Chaos from their unnatural allies. The Indomitus Crusade has swept from one end of Imperium Sanctus to the other, bringing retribution to our foes. I propose we add one further victory to our tally!'

The crowd cheered loudly. Booming transhuman voices joined with mortal shouts and chittering data augmitters.

The Pit grew in the oculus as the fleet accelerated. A large part of Fleet Primus had been gathered for this victory. Dozens of capital ships led the battle groups Alphus, Cerastus, Dominus and Gamma. The artificial stars of their engine stacks flared brightly as they manoeuvred into attack positions. Guilliman had the armada arranged in a five-fingered claw. The long talons were arrayed in lines to pound the enemy as they passed. The palm was a wall of ships, with the *Macragge's Honour* at its centre. The primarch intended to trap the foe against the mobile fortress of the palm as the fingers of the claw slowed and closed, as surely as a clenching fist, around the rear of the enemy fleets.

An entire battle group ran outwards from the main line of advance, towards the Pit. Within the knot of vessels at its centre, the Null Ships of the Sisters of Silence flew protected by three battleships. Miles long, the battleships were cathedrums of war, unused to escort duty, but the move was justified. For the foe they faced, these mighty vessels were not the battle group's deadliest weapon. The ships of the Sisters – large, black and swift – were the key to success.

The command crew of the *Macragge's Honour* were a mixture of standard humans and Space Marines. Mortals predominated. They had been gathered to the Indomitus Crusade from all across the Imperium. Their diverse origins had been no barrier to Guilliman forging them into an effective unit.

Above the vox-pits, the master divulgatus swung his command pulpit around. Tall banks of organ pipes, each one a powerful voxmitter, hid him from the neck down. His head was encased in a bulky communications unit. Only his mouth was visible. 'The Null Ships will be in position in an hour, my lord.'

'Seconded,' said the master augurum from his own station high up on the stepped walls, a sub-kingdom of screens and hardwired servitors. Runic icons blinked on the hololithic tacticarium orb, dotted lines flickering into being, describing their trajectory and ultimate position.

Before being returned to Guilliman, the *Macragge's Honour* had undergone an extensive refit in the shipyards of Metalica, and the command deck had been entirely rebuilt. Cawl's stamp was on everything. New machines and unheard-of configurations of old devices replaced equipment that had been in use for tens of centuries. The tech-priests had been outraged, but Guilliman had silenced them, and Cawl had had his way.

The result was worth upsetting the Adeptus Mechanicus' religious sensibilities. The machinery still had the ugly look of 41st millennium technology, but Guilliman reckoned there was a ten per cent increase in tactical responsiveness alone. Multiple redundancies and newly integrated systems allowed for better survivability. Dozens of tech-priests from Cawl's faction laboured to keep the archmagos' finely balanced design working, but it did work, and excellently so.

'My lords and ladies,' said Guilliman, 'today will be a great day for the Imperium. I commend you to the protection of the Emperor. Now go to your vessels and war machines! To your transports! To war!'

'War! War! War!' they responded.

The majority of the commanders left. Hololiths blinked out. Soon the command deck was empty but for Guilliman's core command staff and the ship's bridge officers, though that still amounted to almost four hundred people.

About the graphic of 108/Beta-Kalapus-9.2, the dull red signifiers of enemy craft began to move.

'The enemy responds,' said Guilliman. 'All fleet to engage full thrust. We fall upon them without mercy.'

Fleetmaster Khestrin stood from his throne.

'*Macragge's Honour* to full thrust,' he said. 'All fleet to full thrust.'

'All fleet to full thrust!' repeated the master divulgatus, sending the order across the fleets. A ripple of activity spread out across the tiered work banks and station pits of the deck. Field-integrity technicians adjusted the matrices that stabilised the ship's frame, compensating for the coming acceleration. Tech-priests passed on minute adjustments to their counterparts deep in the ship's engine halls.

'Reactor ready,' reported a metal-faced tech-adept.

'Enginarium ready,' said a man in a smart ensign's uniform.

A coterie of electro-priests began the hymn 'Body Electric'. Tech-priests muttered their prayers over their desks.

The master motivatum gripped the rail of his podium. Around him in a circular array a dozen servitors sat, the calculations required to move the *Macragge's Honour* from its current position into its attack run flickering through their butchered brains. Cogitators bleeped out rapid beats of binary data transfer.

'Compliance. Engines operating at maximum efficiency,' the servitors said with one voice.

'Full thrust in three, two, one. Mark,' said the master motivatum.

'Mark. Engaging.'

A rumbling sounded aft, drawing closer like the approach of a great engine. A tremor passed up the ship, growing stronger. Machines burbled as it passed through their fabric. It joined with the never-ending thrum of the ship's systems, became one with it, and passed from the crew's notice.

Acceleration was a gentle push in the chest, a trailing heaviness that dragged at the heels.

The *Macragge's Honour* built up to one hundredth of the speed of light. Around it, the fleet's engines blinked into life as all the vessels began their acceleration, holding formation with the flagship.

108/Beta-Kalapus-9.2 grew rapidly.

The first round of projectiles came at them not long after. Destroyers escorting the larger cruisers and battleships fired anti-munitions weapons in response. A series of pinprick explosions started up and soon became a constant accompaniment to the advance. A handful of torpedoes got through, dangerous for their kinetic energy more than the payloads they carried, but they exploded upon the void shields of the ships, thousands of feet short of the hulls. The shields blinked and flashed as they shunted destructive energies into the warp.

Guilliman watched without concern. Such long-range exchanges were never decisive, nor particularly damaging. On the main tacticarium, the fingers of Guilliman's claw formation expanded. He tapped out a few orders on a data-slate to adjust the positioning, but for the moment the most important part of his plan was being performed correctly. The Null Ships were moving between the Pit of Raukos and the planet. Their presence would disrupt any daemonic incursion that might come through, while Sisters of Silence and Grey Knights Adeptus Astartes stationed across the fleet were ready to deal with any onboard manifestations. There would be no supernatural aid for the enemy.

They approached 108/Beta-Kalapus-9.2, now showing itself to be a dull, orange ball with ice caps of frozen water. Miserable patches of green covered its equatorial regions, but in the main it was desert. Another low-grade world too remote to settle. They were close enough now that the engine flares of the enemy were visible to the naked eye. The Chaos ships were spreading out, attempting to intercept the fingers of the claw head-on. Guilliman watched their manoeuvring. There was no single warlord in control; he could see that by the way the ships were operating. They moved in close groups, each warband sticking to its own.

Chaos resisted authority. It was a weakness the primarch had exploited time and again.

Four smaller groups struck out on their own, poorly coordinated with each other and with the fifth, largest group. This last formation made up the majority of the fleet, and its ships moved in good order, fanning out in a standard interception pattern towards the leftmost of the two leading Imperial groups.

The challenge was there, in the Word Bearers fleet. Something of the scale of the orbital fane was rarely undertaken by others. The Word Bearers were better organised than most of the fallen Legions. Fanatical in their devotion, they raised giant temples on the worlds they conquered, and would fight to the last to defend them.

The leading elements of Guilliman's fleet started firing as soon as they came within half a million miles. Broad spreads of torpedoes fanned out in intersecting patterns. Cannons hurled multi-ton anti-ship shells at the enemy. Such munitions would take minutes to arrive, and most would not hit their targets, but they were not intended to. Guilliman was closing off avenues of manoeuvre for the traitors with streams of explosives, forcing them into the positions he wanted.

The second finger of his claw was intercepted by one of the smaller enemy battle groups. Both were travelling at such speed that only a brief flurry of broadsides was exchanged before their respective velocities tore them apart. The discharge of powerful nova cannons obscured the combat. A brighter light suggested a reactor death had consumed a vessel. When the augurs cleared and the light died away, the Imperial formation was speeding on, leaving one of its cruisers wallowing afire. The traitor fleet had come off worse, being badly mauled. Two of its four grand cruisers had been hit hard; one listed off the flight path of its fellows, engines out, while fires burned all along the side of the other, and it was falling behind. The remaining two cruisers were coming straight for the claw's palm.

Guilliman's hands tapped out targeting data on his instruments. 'Wall grouping gamma, target and annihilate traitor battle group,' he said. The master divulgatus relayed his orders to the relevant ships.

'They are rash' said Tribune Colquan. 'They cannot get by us.'

'Perhaps,' said Guilliman. 'They may be attempting to disrupt our formation.'

'To damage one battle group? We have four, and the wall of the claw-palm is impassable.'

'Then to distract us, or perhaps there has been a falling out between their warlords. Or maybe they are running.' Guilliman took his eyes from his displays and the tacticarium to spare the Custodian a glance. 'I make no assumptions. Neither should you.' As he spoke, his scar itched, reminding him of the last time he had been in error, a situation the primarch had sworn never to repeat.

Colquan's lip curled. He disliked being lectured on tactics. Guilliman did not relent. Though they remained superlative individual warriors, the Adeptus Custodes had rarely served as generals since the old times, and centuries of isolationism had dulled what command abilities they had once possessed.

'Never underestimate the enemy, Colquan. Nine times out of ten, a mixed group of traitors will be disorganised and internally divisive, but the tenth time they will surprise and destroy you. Their greatest lords can forge the most antagonistic warbands into a devastating fighting force. Their intentions here are counter-envelopment and delay. Their sorcerers will be attempting to summon daemonic allies while their battlefleet keeps us occupied.'

He glanced at his Concilia Psykana, several Space Marine and Primaris Librarians stationed close at hand. The mortal humans looked pained by the nearby Sisters of Silence.

'It is so,' confirmed their leader, Codicier Donas Maxim of the Aurora Chapter. 'There is a weakening in the veil. The warp is unquiet.'

'Warp-spawned aid will not help them.' Guilliman put from his mind the unspeakable things the sorcerers would be doing; the creatures of the gods would only come to offerings of blood, souls and pain.

'My lord,' said the master augurum. 'Primary target will be within range in ten minutes, nine seconds.'

'He's fifty seconds off in his estimation,' said Colquan.

'If you prefer, you can take his place, tribune.'

Colquan made a dismissive noise.

The main body of the Chaos fleet was coming into range of the Imperial battle groups. The various signifiers for each enemy vessel acquired screeds of data as the augurs of the fleet gathered more information. Five battleships formed the core of the chief grouping. Three were of the Word Bearers Traitor Legion, as Guilliman had expected; the remaining two belonged to the Iron Warriors. Ancient beacons in their corrupted hulls broadcast codes dating back to the Great Crusade. Guilliman recognised the names of two of the ships. The fleets of Chaos often differed to those of the Imperium, incorporating many classes of vessel no longer produced. Their battleships were spear-headed things, sleek and deadly – superior patterns from a more enlightened time.

The remaining three subgroups of Chaos vessels were speeding past the outstretched fingers of the claw to get behind the Imperial fleet and engage their vulnerable rear. One flotilla bore the markings of the Lords of Pain, a once loyal Chapter whose full strength had turned to Chaos during the Noctis Aeterna; the rest were motley collections of pirate vessels and other renegades.

The lesser battle groups could be ignored, for now. The Lords of Pain had a significant presence, but Space Marine ships were planetary assault vessels, intended for bombardment and delivery of warriors to the surface. They were less effective in void combat.

The battleships were a bigger problem. They had arrayed themselves into a stepped arrowhead. A formation like that could do serious damage to the wall as the two fleets passed through each other.

As one, the enemy opened fire with their prow weapons. Lance beams slashed across the void, splashing in blinding displays of displacement energies on the void shields. A glancing blow off the *Macragge's Honour*'s forward shield lit up the deck with lilac discharge. Energy waves from an off-target nova cannon sent ripples of sparks over the flagship's escorts.

'They are targeting our position,' said the master augurum.

'Any fool can see that,' muttered Colquan.

The tribune's contempt for baseline humanity troubled Guilliman.

'You have spent your life guarding the Emperor, yet you forget who the Emperor guards in His turn,' said Guilliman. 'Be more forgiving.'

'As you wish,' said Colquan. Traditionally, the Adeptus Custodes had taken orders only from their own officers and the Emperor. That was until Guilliman had been declared Imperial Regent, the Emperor's living voice.

'Hold course,' Guilliman ordered. 'All power to forward void shields. Task forces Three and Five, break off and engage outflanking enemy elements. Target all Lords of Pain Chapter assets. All fleet to fire on targets of opportunity as subsidiary enemy groupings pass. All batteries load for close-range combat. Prepare prow weapons for forward fire. Charge lance batteries to maximum. Nova cannons to draw firing solutions ready for my order.'

Various stations reported their understanding of Guilliman's order. Activity on the command deck intensified.

On the forward oculus, the ships grew from flecks to objects the size of models, then bigger, swelling as the crusade fleet swept in at high speed. Perspective in the void lies. When the ships seemed close enough to touch, they continued to grow. Their spear prows went from scalpel sharp to giant, blunt cliffs bristling with sensor spikes and weapons cupolas.

'My lord?' asked Khestrin questioningly.

'No order to fire,' said Guilliman.

A storm of laser and solid-shot fire blasted from the forward batteries of the Chaos ships. Guilliman ignored it, instead examining the enemy disposition, seeking weak points no augurs could see. Another barrage of lance strikes sparked off the forward shields. The majority of fire was coming at the *Macragge's Honour*, the Chaos battleships adjusting position to track its approach.

'Forward void shields failing!' called out the master scutum.

'We have multiple target locks on the flagship,' reported the master augurum.

'My lord?' said Khestrin again. He was remarkably calm, curious to see what the primarch would do rather than concerned. Men like Khestrin were rare.

'A moment,' said Guilliman. His fingers danced along the gel screen, the giving material distorting as he touched it. Schematics and augur data flashed up on phosphor displays and minor hololiths. Guilliman read each page quicker than a man could blink, processing volumes' worth of data in seconds.

There.

A void-shield flicker, out of syncopation with its pulse modulators, the suggestion of an unstable core reactor.

A weak spot.

'That vessel, the *Steel Lord*,' he said decisively. 'Target these positions.' His hands moved over his instruments, depressing keys and activating holomarks in a blur. An image of the *Steel Lord* materialised upon a secondary hololith in front of

Khestrin's throne. Targeting orders for a score of Imperial ships appeared almost as quickly.

The data was disseminated via data-squirt across the fleet. A rush of affirmations were returned via the master divulgatus.

'All vessels confirm targets acquired.'

'Then open fire,' said Guilliman.

The reserved fire of twenty great ships of the line flared out at once, all aimed at the *Steel Lord*.

Battleships could withstand hours of pounding. Layered void shields protected their hulls, and the hulls themselves were yards thick, their vital cores hidden deep inside. Even gutted, a battleship might be salvaged and fight again, for their frames were forged from adamantium.

But a primarch was in command of the Imperial fleet. And as a master knapper knows how to strike a flint just so to cause it to split, Roboute Guilliman knew how to slay a starship.

The *Steel Lord*'s void shields were overwhelmed instantly, undone by the frequency flicker in their generators. Lance beams spread themselves as golden pools before the shields gave out with a guttering brandy fire. Thousands of tons of solid and explosive ordnance followed. The *Steel Lord* weathered the impacts for a good twenty seconds before the fires on its hull gathered into one giant eructation of flame that broke its spine. A second later, the reactor blew. A miniature sun engulfed the ship in a perfect yellow sphere. The oculus of the *Macragge's Honour* dimmed in response. The edges of the reactor nova touched the shields of the *Steel Lord*'s sister ships, bringing them down in storms of squirming purple lightning.

The Imperial fleet had not slowed, and the enemy ships were large in their oculi.

'All ships, engagement manoeuvres!' commanded Guilliman. 'Fire at will!'

Expertly, the formation of the palm broke apart, passing between the enemy vessels. The *Macragge's Honour* punched through the boiling cloud left behind by the *Steel Lord*. Wreckage flashed to nothing on its void shields and then the Imperial flagship was through, its guns raking down the sides of the exposed Chaos vessels.

As the others passed, they fired with their broadsides. The Chaos ships fired back, but most were shieldless, and they peeled away, venting flaming atmosphere. As the palm wall went through the enemy formation, the three fingers of the claw not engaged with the lesser fleets had turned and were coming back, firing directly at the vulnerable engines of the Chaos vessels. A titanic explosion rocked one into an uncontrollable spin as its stacks went up. It rolled away, missing its stern.

There were no cheers on the deck of the *Macragge's Honour*. All worked to ensure victory. Celebration could wait.

The Chaos formation was disrupted. The fingers of the claw harried the remaining three battleships and their escorts as the palm raced on towards the orbital platform under construction at 108/Beta-Kalapus-9.2's highest orbital anchor.

The fane was far from finished, but its basic framework was in place, an eight-pointed star like a compass wheel, the symbol the priests of the Dark Gods called the octed. Strange lights played about its centre.

As fire flashed behind them, the ships of the palm approached unopposed. The light about the hub of the wheel of Chaos shone brighter.

'Ninety degrees to starboard,' ordered Khestrin. 'Show it our big guns. Target enemy battle group with the portside batteries.'

The ship rumbled around as torpedoes from the smaller craft accompanying it raced towards the fane. The move was performed in the face of decelerative force, and the vessel moaned as its engines pushed it into the turn, but it was done quickly. The orbital moved out of view of the forward oculus. Side views were brought onto the main tacticarium.

'Open fire!' roared Guilliman as the ship lined up. 'Bring it down!'

Banks of macrocannons boomed in series along the side of the battleship, their recoil making the command deck shudder. Energy had to be diverted to the integrity fields, so great was the stress of the guns combined with that of the turn. Giant munitions slammed into the incomplete temple-station, pruning it of spear-tipped arms and breaking its hub. Bombs designed to kill whole worlds were deployed to ensure its demise. After two volleys, all that remained of the octed was an area of spinning orbital debris a thousand miles across and still expanding.

'And so they see, no fane to their dark gods will they raise that I shall not cast down!' said Guilliman. 'These traitors oppose the will of the Emperor's last faithful son. They will learn the error of their ways. Ten thousand years some of them have defied the Emperor. Their lives end now!'

There was no vessel powerful enough to best the *Macragge's Honour*. There were a few remaining Chaos battleships, and under different stars they might have been a match for the venerable flagship alone, but the Imperial fleet outnumbered the traitors and Guilliman wielded his armada expertly. The traitors were disunited. The last battleships were quickly isolated. Unwilling to act in concert at first, then rapidly made unable to do so, the Chaos fleet could do nothing to halt the *Macragge's Honour* as it powered through the debris field of the temple-station and towards the world beyond. As the Imperial fleet swung into orbit, the stratosphere flashed with the discharge of ground-based defence lasers.

The *Macragge's Honour* rocked to the impact of multiple hits.

'Master divulgatus, send my words to the fleet,' said Guilliman.

'My lord,' the master divulgatus replied.

'The station is destroyed!' said the primarch. 'The way is open. All landing ships forward. Begin deployment of main ground attack. In the face of their fire, put down your armies and your legions. Generals of the Imperium, it is time to scour this world clean.'

CHAPTER SEVEN

LAST FLIGHT OF THE GREYSHIELDS

A furious shaking gripped the *Rudense*. The wailing of alarms filled the ship, accompanied by the dull, edge-of-hearing crackle of void-shield generators working to capacity. Then the insertion craft broke through the enemy line, and the racket was done. Aboard, the Greyshields readied themselves to go to war one final time.

'Brothers, we are approaching the insertion point,' voxed Lieutenant Sarkis. 'Assault in two minutes. Begin drop preparations. Imperator victoriam!'

'Victoriam!' his warriors replied.

Of the many tens of thousands of Primaris Space Marines created by Belisarius Cawl, only half were initially formed into new Chapters. The rest had been gathered into great armies, each of one gene-line. They wore the livery of their founding primarchs, their badges crossed with pale grey chevrons, and within their gene-groupings they were then further organised into Chapter-sized formations.

There agreement with the Codex Astartes ended.

Officially, the Primaris formations were designated the Unnumbered Sons of the Primarchs, but they called themselves the Greyshields. They were the new sons of old science, and they had no fraternity but their own. Guilliman deployed his new weapons in every way imaginable. The Primaris Space Marines sometimes fought as the Legions of old had, in huge formations of one type, but as time wore on they also fought in mixed groups of every size, from strike teams of five up to double Chapter strength. They knew the strengths of their gene-cousins, and their preferences. Brotherhood crossed the lines of primarch and gene-seed.

As the first phase of the Indomitus Crusade progressed, the Unnumbered Sons dwindled. All across the many fronts of the war, Roboute Guilliman took the Primaris Marines from their companies and their squads, and he assigned them to under-strength Space Marine Chapters encountered on the way. Whole companies might be hived off, or only a few units. Where he saw the need, the primarch took them by the thousand to create new Chapters. Warrior by warrior, the Unnumbered Sons were scattered across the galaxy, taking with them the secrets of their creation to their new homes. Unnumbered Sons of Guilliman became Aurora Marines or Doom Eagles; Unnumbered Sons of Dorn joined the Black Templars or the Imperial Fists; Unnumbered Sons of Corax became Raven Guard or Revilers. By the time Guilliman reached Raukos, only a few thousand of the Unnumbered Sons' original strength remained in Fleet Primus, a situation repeated across all the groupings of the crusade.

Sergeant Justinian and his Inceptor squad hung from robotic drop-arms. There were three warriors in each unit and six units in their bay, along with their leader, Lieutenant Sarkis. Cordus, scion of the line of Guilliman, flew with Justinian, as did Aldred of Dorn's breed. In the ship's other two drop-bays, thirty-six more

Primaris Space Marines awaited battle. They were giants clad in drop armour – Inceptor battleplate reinforced for solo atmospheric insertion – and equipped with heavy jump packs for sustained flight. For armament, they carried paired assault bolters. Like their armour, these guns were one of Belisarius Cawl's heretical marvels, massive pistols with the stopping power of heavy bolters.

In the bay, lit only by the winking lights of machines at their work, Justinian's comrades were outlines edged in green and red. His view was restricted by the massive jump pack of the warrior before him. It belonged to Solus, his friend, only the Baalite red of his plate – blood-dark in the drop-hold – giving his identity away. His back was high and round like that of a monstrous beetle, the backward-pointing nozzles a pair of steel-toothed maws. Solus was so still, and his suit so large, that from the rear he appeared wholly robotic. No trace of the man inside the layered ceramite was apparent.

'Exloading mission data. Prepare armour cogitators for cant reception,' said Sarkis. 'Awaken drop-overlays. Mission active.'

Justinian's earpiece chimed with data-inload. Pulsed lasers flickered at the edge of his eye-lenses, projecting a false-world display directly upon his retinas. The overlay obstructed more of his view. The giant reticle of a drop-pelorus blinked in front of him – two stationary circles contained by cross hairs, all divided by fine rules of measurement. The mission count glowed a dull orange, all eight digits at zero.

'Program drop coordinates. Beta-7987-3872, Kappa-0031-4822. Confirm,' said Sarkis.

Though the overlay existed only in the witch-world of the squad's noosphere, the pelorus seemed to hang solidly in the air before Justinian. Using the neural links connecting his nervous system to his cogitator, he brought the coordinates onto the grid. The display's larger wheel turned within the smaller, his positional tracker shifting through three dimensions as the *Rudense* ploughed its way towards their drop-point. A faint roar came from the ship's engines, the vibrations conducted to Justinian's armour by way of the drop-claw. The gentle pushback of oppositional forces grew as the craft accelerated. The *Rudense* always came in fast.

'Confirmed,' said Justinian. Indicators on his display blinked green as he homed in his suit's auto-senses and cogitator on the drop-zone. Paired runes flickered to the same colour in the top left. His squad was locked on. 'Squad confirmed.'

The other sergeants acknowledged mission readiness as their own battleplate processed the data.

'Thirty seconds to planetary drop,' said Sarkis. 'Final weapons check.'

Justinian went through the procedure automatically. Runic indicators flickered, half obscured by the drop-pelorus dominating his view. Drum magazines on his assault bolters spun around once, ammo feeds clicking. Chimes informed him all was well. The machine-spirit of his Inceptor armour performed a number of automatic adjustments. Hissing atmosphere lines increased the internal pressure. The reactor beneath his jump engines whined into high-output mode then back again, and his jets gave a single hollow huff that jolted him in his harness. In front of him, Solus' jets ignited, metal teeth spinning around a trapped vortex of blue fire, then went out.

A schematic of his armour blinked in the upper right of Justinian's view, segments switching from amber to green. He was only half watching all this. He trusted his battleplate's spirit to ready itself. The ship shook hard. The engines' voice changed timbre. The push of acceleration shifted around his body as the ship curved away from an unseen threat. Several more jarring shakes followed as the *Rudense* came under fire.

'There is a firestorm out there,' said Sarkis. 'The enemy are displeased to see us.'

'Was that a joke, Sarkis?' said Bjarni Arvisson, sergeant of the second squad.

'I do not joke,' replied the lieutenant.

'A wry comment then,' said Bjarni. The son of Russ was hanging from the drop-line next to Justinian. He tapped him on the arm with the butt of his assault bolter. 'Wish me luck, brother,' he said quietly. Vox-beads fed his voice into Justinian's ears.

'Why do you need luck more than the rest of us?' Solus interrupted.

'It's my thirteenth planetfall,' grumbled Bjarni. 'An ill-favoured number.'

'The primarch's Legion was the thirteenth! Do you not remember?' said Justinian.

'Why would I forget?' replied Bjarni. 'But where is the Thirteenth Legion now?'

'Made into Chapters ten thousand years ago, for the greater good of the Imperium,' said Cordus.

'Broken into pieces you mean,' said Bjarni. 'I do not want to be broken into pieces.'

Red lumens flashed. The air was sucked out by powerful fans. The noise in the bay went with it.

'*Doors opening, doors opening, doors opening,*' droned a machine voice over the vox.

The narrow bay doors slid back, letting in a corridor of bright sunlight unsoftened by atmosphere. Residual ship air froze upon the Space Marines, bringing a diamond sheen to their battle-plate. The drop-arms went into action, pushing them out from the side of the ship and into the fury of void war.

The *Rudense* was a small ship of a class designed specifically for the Indomitus Crusade. Its Adeptus Astartes complement was set at fifty – not even a full company. But the warriors aboard had an important role, one never seen in the armies of the Space Marines before the Ultima Founding. Slender as a dart, two thousand feet long and as fast as its shape suggested, the *Rudense* was heavily armed for its size class, and strengthened to withstand brushes with planetary atmospheres. It was a rapid insertion craft, intended to fight its way through the maelstrom of close-range orbital combat and deliver its payload to the surface directly from the edge of a planet's atmosphere.

It only had small hangars and no drop-pod tubes. The *Rudense* was something new, and it had taken the enemy by surprise many times.

Explosions burst around the *Rudense*. Justinian's helm-lenses darkened against the dazzle. Las-beams stabbed from the ship's side out to infinity. The wide rays of defence lasers flashed from the planet below, but the *Rudense* was fast, and it was never where the lasers fired.

A massive explosion ahead sent shivers along the ship. The Space Marines swung below their drop-arms. Flaming debris spun past, wreathed in dying sparks and glittering ices. An escort of interdiction fighters accelerated and fell in alongside the *Rudense*, weaving through the turmoil and then off ahead, guns blazing. Justinian's view of the battle was limited by the projecting shields sheltering the Primaris Space Marines from the deadly impacts of shrapnel. The ship's iron immensity blocked off everything. Somewhere beyond that great metal cliff, larger ships would be fighting.

For all the fury of the anti-ship fire streaking up from the surface, beneath Justinian's feet the world floated peacefully, its ochre surface hazed by the blue of a thin atmosphere and mottled with clouds. He had seen many worlds from this vantage point. He had thought he would grow jaded at the sight eventually, but he never had. Every world was different, and when viewed from this height, every world – whether hell or paradise – had been beautiful in its own way.

'The calm before the storm, brother,' said Solus, as if reading his thoughts.

'These places we fight for,' said Kalael, his armour the green of the Dark Angels. 'How small they are. We hold that to ourselves as a secret truth. From space, every world is but a fragile ornament against the infinite black.'

'*Ten seconds. Nine seconds. Eight seconds…*' The machine counted down.

Justinian kept his eyes on the planet. Flashes of light burst further along its curve, drawing closer as the ship raced towards the battle site. Ground combat from orbit looked deceptively celebratory, a display of multi-hued explosions and storms of light that appeared too artistic to be destructive. Shock waves burst clouds apart, and Justinian spied Titans lumbering away from their coffin ships. Beneath the sheath of air, the giant war machines were like aquatic insects that had never learnt how to swim, doomed to laboriously plod along the pond floor.

'Battleground fifty miles and closing!' said Sarkis, his excitement revealing itself as a slight rise in his voice. 'Prepare for drop! Emperor preserve us in our flight and grant might to our fists!'

'*Four seconds. Mark,*' said the machine voice. '*Three, two, one. Drop. Unit 10-5011/32A away.*'

The drop-arm disengaged from Sarkis' back. The claw that held him dangling over the planet's sky opened silently. A disposable thruster burned on top of his pack, shooting him towards the target zone, and the black-clad son of Ferrus Manus fell away. The booster exhausted its fuel supply quickly and detached. Sarkis fell without a word, plummeting towards the world as surely as a cogitator-guided munition. There was a flaring burst of jets as he corrected his course, and he was gone. Half a second later, the machine intoned Bjarni's Primaris number. The Wolf's son fell with a whoop, a grey streak, his squad going one, two after him, swift as heartbeats, their impeller jets burning and detaching.

Then it was Justinian's turn.

'Unit 13-10889/189E away,' said the machine, and let him fall.

The claw's release was gentle as a kiss, the firing of the impeller hard as a punch. It ceased after a second's burn. Justinian felt it come off his jump pack as a bump in his otherwise smooth flight.

Justinian plummeted. The long, slender shape of the *Rudense* vanished overhead, becoming a blade of light in the sky surrounded by the starbursts of orbital combat. The ship drew away, trailing a wake of false lightning through the world's magnetosphere and chased by the stabbing beams of enemy lances. Enemy fighters sped after it, drawing their own lines in the sky. Naval interceptors approached obliquely. They made marvellous patterns about the cruiser.

Justinian fixed the sight in his memory, and ordered his armour to capture a series of images at fifty millisecond intervals. Maybe if he survived this, he would paint the war in space. Justinian liked to paint.

The pelorus' nested reticles shifted slightly, and he looked down. The circles tilted within one another, providing him with a false horizon and a vertical gauge to set his descent by. Cordus and Aldred were bright orange teardrops drifting across the circles, the members of the other squads yellow dots spread above and below.

A blue line rose up the display towards him. For minutes he fell in silence. The surface was so far away he appeared to be making no progress.

There is no sharp delineation between a world's air envelope and the void, but instead a region of increasing attenuation where, atom by atom, air gives way to vacuum. But there does exist a point where the air becomes thick enough to support atmospheric flight. Justinian hit it with a jolt. Heat followed almost immediately, as friction, imperceptible only moments before, quickly built around his armour. A plasma-torch roar filled his ears.

The coming moments were critical. Gaining a good angle of descent at this stage would ensure mission success – a colourless statement that meant only that he would not die before the enemy got a chance to shoot at him.

An alarm sounded in his ear. Cordus' signifier flashed.

'Cordus, correct course two points vertical, you are drifting,' said Justinian.

'Yes, brother-sergeant,' Cordus responded. His signifier dot and its accompanying rune moved across Justinian's display, and the graphic ceased blinking.

The others spread out into a wide dispersion pattern. Three targets awaited the demi-company's attention, a series of closely bunched bastions joined by a wall, each one bristling with ordnance.

A bright corona of heat streamed around Justinian, most intense about the reinforced ceramite of his boots. It became uncomfortable, but not dangerous. Provided there was no breach in his Inceptor battleplate, he would be safe.

The curve of the world grew quickly. The ground spread beneath him. Space retreated to the periphery of his vision and vanished. When the last of the black was gone, Justinian finally felt like he was falling. Individual surface features resolved themselves, details popping into sharp definition, though all were flattened by his relative height, so that mountains appeared as painted flourishes upon a round canvas. Soon after, he reached terminal velocity and stopped accelerating.

Below him, fighting raged upon a plain bordered by a range of hills pierced by a wide valley. Across the valley mouth was the great wall, and a strong fortress not far behind. Two battle lines became visible. Their exchanges of fire were startling weaves of light. A vast phalanx of Astra Militarum tanks, supported by Adeptus Mechanicus cyborg troops and war machines, advanced on the wall from the drop zone.

The wall looked like a ribbon, but in truth it was almost one hundred yards tall, and forty wide. The Titans of the Legio Metalica swelled, their carapace insignia taking on form. They were now the size of men, and the warriors milling about their feet became the insects as the scene unfolded like a fractal tapestry before Justinian's eyes.

Aircraft sped below, swift as avians, duelling with draconic daemon engines for control of the sky.

'Demi-company, split,' ordered Sarkis. 'Squads to target designated mission objectives in three, two, one. Fire jets. Formation disperse.'

'Fire jets!' ordered Justinian. A smaller reticle ignited in the centre of his pelorus and settled over his own squad's landing zone on the middle tower of the wall – the tallest one.

His jets roared furiously against the drag of the planet. Justinian slowed only a little, but his course altered, and he was sent hurtling laterally towards the tower.

They avoided firing their jets until the last second of a drop. When the Inceptors had first been deployed, the enemy had mistaken their squads for falling debris or stray munitions. In the chaos of battle, they had been paid little attention until it was too late. Lately, the foes of the Imperium had become wise to Inceptor drop tactics. The sky filled with a storm of flak moments after their jets finished burning.

Justinian fell through a wash of fire. Shrapnel pinged off his armour. The thunder of atmosphere lessened. The demi-company's attack spread widened, the dots that denoted each warrior perfectly positioned in three clusters, one for each defence tower.

The target went from a toy to a towering edifice in a matter of seconds.

'Fire jets, prolonged burst,' he ordered. 'Decelerate to engagement speed. Rouse the spirits of your weapons.'

He hefted his own guns, eager to unleash them upon the enemy. His jets ignited again, and this time they stayed burning. The fuel gauge in his display rapidly fell from full to a third as he braked. He was no longer falling but flying, and that ate up his fuel quickly. In a graceful arc, he and his squad thundered towards the upper battlements of the tower. The bastion was ludicrously embellished with screaming daemonic faces, its crenellations tall and fashioned into unnecessary spikes, but it was well armoured, and four quad flak cannons squatted in heavy turrets at each corner, banging off shots at the attacking Space Marines. Traitor Astartes opened up as the Inceptors approached, and their fire was more worrisome than the flak cannons. A bolt-round spanked off the cowling of Justinian's left jet nozzle, staggering his flight. More bolts came, then a blizzard of them.

Cordus' ident signifier blinked to red and fell away from Justinian's display. Justinian risked a glance back. Smoke and explosions hid Cordus' fate, and he did not see his comrade die.

Another bolt smacked into his breastplate, cracking the outer casing and fracturing the power cabling beneath. Smoke blew from the crack and his jump-pack engines coughed. A lurching drop made his stomach flip. Icons blinked, alarms squealed. At his urging, the cogitator in his suit rerouted power. The jets roared again, and he surged on with renewed speed. Sealant foam bubbled up to plug the breach in his armour.

The enemy would have to try harder than that to stop him.

Justinian dropped down then burst upwards and over the battlements, Aldred beside him. Half a dozen members of the Iron Warriors lined the parapet. Boltgun flash revealed horned helms and faceplates cast with daemonic visages. They were terrifying foes, made Adeptus Astartes by the Emperor and granted greater vigour by their dark gods. Once, they had been among the mightiest warriors in the galaxy.

They were the mightiest no longer.

'Your death has been too long coming!' Justinian roared, his voxed shout blasting from his helm as he descended on pillars of fiery smoke. 'Prepare yourselves for the Emperor's judgement!'

He came down with a bone-jarring thump hard enough to crack the ferrocrete of the tower, guns already blazing. Assault bolters were powerful weapons, but if used unwisely they would run through their ammunition stores in seconds. Justinian checked his fury. The resupply pods had yet to land.

Even utilised with care, the assault bolters fired at a terrifying rate. Flames roared from the weapons' exhaust slots. Explosions smashed the Iron Warriors from their feet, hurling them backwards with a force that a standard bolter could not hope to match.

Bjarni came over the side, howling joyously, his warriors following him. Then came Sergeant Rusticus' squad, of which Solus was a part. The Primaris Space Marines looked almost as daemonic as their foes, with their varicoloured liveries scorched and smoking from the heat of their descent. Caught between the murderous crossfire of eight Inceptors, the Iron Warriors were cut to pieces. One of them came at Justinian through the firestorm, a chainaxe raised. Justinian leapt back from him with a controlled burst of his jets, retargeting one of his guns on the warrior as he flew. He could not let the enemy get close.

The Inceptor loadout's only real weakness was a lack of melee weaponry. The guns he held in his gauntlets meant it wasn't much of a weakness at all.

Justinian's bolts hit the traitor square in the chest. The Iron Warrior's antique armour burst apart, spraying his ancient innards in a red slick across the ramparts, and his chainaxe fell to the ground. Its teeth bit on the ferrocrete, and it spun madly before the motor cut out.

'For the Emperor! For Guilliman! For mankind!' Justinian shouted, stamping across the bastion's roof. He was taller than the Heretic Astartes. Shock-absorbent calipers around the lower part of his legs and feet granted him more height, and he fired down at his enemy.

The last of the traitors fell. They had not been caught by surprise; they had seen the Inceptors coming. It did not matter. None could stand before the Primaris Space Marines, the new sons of the Emperor.

Sergeant Rusticus' warriors went to the flak cannons, raised their assault bolters and riddled the firing mechanisms. Bolts exploded inside the guns, setting off their shells. The cannon barrels fell away from popping detonations, clanging from the ornate tower sides and falling down to the wall ramparts far below. Soon all four cannons were smoking wrecks.

'Primary objective achieved. Anti-air guns are silent,' voxed Justinian, his feed going to Lieutenant Sarkis and the command cadre of his Primaris Chapter simultaneously. 'Pursuing secondary objective.'

With Aldred's garish Imperial Fists yellow at his side, Justinian stormed down the stairs into the lower levels. His guns banged out death to everything he encountered. There were an insignificant number of Traitor Space Marines within. That had been the pattern these last few years. The armies of Chaos were legion and everywhere, but it was arguable that they were losing their best to Guilliman's relentless crusading. Most of the tower's defenders were born thralls, or deluded mortals from conquered worlds who had thrown in their lot with evil for the chance at a few more weeks' life. They came at him in hordes, dirty faces branded and tattooed, twisted into desperate snarls. Justinian cut them down without mercy.

'Death to the traitor, who in weakness denies the supremacy of the Emperor,' he said emotionlessly.

They died messily, their frail bodies blown to pieces by his assault bolters' mass-reactive shells. More took their place, coming so quickly that Justinian ceased firing to conserve his ammunition and commenced clubbing them down. The tower soon ran with blood, and his armour's colours were obscured.

Justinian and Aldred fought their way further down the stairwell, passing through several levels. Bjarni's squad was close behind them. At the sixteenth level they parted ways, Bjarni singing loudly as he led his squadmates towards the power core. Justinian and Aldred headed for the bastion's fire-control centre, whose machine banks and slave minds directed the vast array of artillery projecting from the lower reaches of the building. The occasional vox-blurt came through to Justinian: status updates, or requests for reports from Lieutenant Sarkis or from his line commander. Nothing higher tier than that. Sarkis and others like him bore that responsibility.

Their guns spoke less often. The bravest of the thralls were dead. A few still threw themselves hopelessly at the Space Marines. Most sank to their knees and begged for forgiveness. All died.

'There is no forgiveness. Better to die twice than betray the Emperor. You made the wrong choice.' And Justinian's assault bolters would bark, or his fists would swing, leaving red ruin where men had knelt.

Battle was replaced by a fragile calm. The building evinced little of the touch of Chaos, being fairly made of plasteel plating upon a ferrocrete core. The sheer mass of it dulled the thunder of battle outside upon the plains, so that the worst of it was felt only as gentle tremors, and the rest they did not notice at all. Machines hummed in the fabric of the building. Although the decoration was barbarous and the grisly trophies nailed to walls told of the Iron Warriors' bloodier proclivities, the warp was absent.

When they reached fire control that changed. A large room of three inverted tiers, the tower's fire-control centre was similar in design to those in Imperial fortifications, but what occupied the space there would never be found in any Imperial facility.

Where ranks of tech-thralls and servitors should have sat guiding the weapons of the fortress, there was instead a thick organic mess. Spreads of noisome matter linked wall to wall. This filthy mass grew thicker in the middle, somehow coming together to make a living thing, though at its edges it was nothing more than a set of flimsy, folded membranes. At its thickest part, pulsing veins made it quiver. A soft keening sounded from somewhere, and an intolerable sense of suffering pressed at the Space Marines' minds.

'Emperor preserve us,' said Justinian.

Exposure to warp-born horror did nothing to lessen his revulsion. Countless times he had seen creatures made of the pressed flesh of men, mutant weavings of corrupted genes, and daemons trapped in machine and mortal form. No matter how often he encountered these things, they never failed to disgust him.

'If any pure machine exists here, then I commend your spirit to the god of Mars,' he said loudly. He meant it sincerely. Though he had no belief in the Emperor-as-Omnissiah, he respected the machines' own beliefs.

He raised his gun and opened fire. Aldred joined him, raising both guns and filling the rotten mass with explosive rounds. The keening became a scream. Gunfire blew huge holes in the organism, opening its innards to the smoking air. Hot yellow liquid slopped from it in amounts the thing could not possibly contain. The scream grew so loud it made the aural dampers of the Space Marines' helmets thrum. When it abruptly cut out, their equipment squealed with relief. The oppressive nature of the room disappeared along with the creature's death cry.

'Whatever that was, it is dead,' said Aldred. Fyceline smoke drifted from his guns. Heat bloom discoloured their muzzles.

A moment later, the lumens died, and the few machines in the room relying on more natural forms of power flickered off.

'Bjarni has fulfilled his role,' said Justinian. He switched to a direct vox-link to Lieutenant Sarkis. 'Tower Beta is neutralised. Flak batteries are down. Central fire control destroyed.'

'Affirmative. Notification heard,' replied Sarkis. *'We are done here. Rendezvous with the others. Await further instruction.'*

'Come on,' said Justinian to Aldred. 'We shall wait upon the roof. We can jump free if the enemy decide to bring the building down around us.'

By the time they rejoined Bjarni's and Rusticus' squads on the parapet, drop pods were plummeting down from the sky like fiery rain. They touched down behind the wall, untroubled by flak thanks to the Inceptor squads. Similarly, the army outside now advanced free from the attentions of artillery fire.

Bjarni peered down over the parapet, then turned his grey helmet towards Justinian and Rusticus.

'It is boring up here.'

'We are awaiting orders,' said Rusticus.

'We are awaiting orders,' parroted Bjarni dismissively, mocking Rusticus' grave voice. 'Well, fine for you. I am not missing the battle. Are you two honestly going to stand here and watch?' He ignited his jump pack, its throaty roar deafening in such proximity. Heat wash battered Justinian as Bjarni's squadmates followed suit.

Rusticus cursed. 'Savage,' he said, but meant it fondly, more or less.

Justinian laughed drily.

'*I would hurry if I were you,*' voxed Bjarni. His assault bolters made long pealing reports under his voice. '*I will save you some, but there are not that many left.*'

'He is right,' said Justinian.

'He is not following protocol,' said Rusticus.

'Lieutenant Sarkis, this is Sergeant Justinian, notifying immediate re-engagement in combat. Tower is clear, we move to aid landing forces.' Justinian activated his jets slowly – slamming them into action like Bjarni had done shortened the lifespan of the rotors. 'There, brother-sergeant,' he said to Rusticus. 'Protocol satisfied.'

Justinian opened up his throttle. Aldred followed him over the parapet. His fuel indicator was blinking madly, the tank close to exhaustion. It added to the exhilaration of dropping into combat. The ground rushed up at him so fast in comparison to his stately freefall from orbit, he barely had time to process the sprinting figures and explosions before he was in the thick of it.

He shut his jets off thirty feet above the ground, letting his impact dampeners take the jolt of landing. He came down in a crouch, stood with the grumbling purr of his armour soothing his ears and strode into battle.

The fighting was ahead of him, the lee of the tower quiet. No drop pod or gunship could land close by it, and no foes remained to pour from the bastion's armoured gates. The sun was on the other side of the building, and cast a shadow over this minor domain of calm. As soon as Justinian and Aldred were out into full light, the battle noticed them and gathered them enthusiastically to itself.

Drop pods filled the space behind the wall, doors blowing open with violent bangs to allow out their cargoes of power-armoured angels. Several pods had been hit close to the ground, and listed, blazing, hazing the air with thick towers of black smoke. More numerous were the shattered wrecks of traitor fighting vehicles. What had been a wide-open killing space had become a tightly packed maze of broken armour. Within it, age-old foes hunted one another, intent on hatreds born at the dawn of the Imperium.

Loosing off tightly controlled shots, Justinian walked through the broil of war. The traitors had become fragmented. Many were trapped on the wall parapet. There they made their last stand, assailed by Space Marines coming at them from the towers either side and by the greater forces arrayed outside the walls. Others were falling back, using their armoured vehicles to cover their retreat to their great castle of steel, which loomed in the near distance, more brutal and overdecorated than the wall towers, its guns still firing.

'Where is Bjarni?' asked Justinian.

'We will never find him in this,' said Aldred.

'Then we shall count those we kill and shame the wolf brother when we return to the *Rudense*.'

'There is Rusticus,' said Aldred, pointing to the sky as the other squad hurtled down from above, and disappeared into the cauldron of battle.

'More rivals for the battle tally, as our Fenrisian friend would have it,' said Justinian.

'You spend too much time with him. Warfare should be more considered.'

'You sound like Rusticus.'

Justinian and Aldred were so massive in their heavy drop armour that they had no chance of stealth, and so they pounded through the tangled wrecks relying on speed to shield them.

'Rusticus speaks sense,' said Aldred. 'But I concede Bjarni's manner of war can be entertaining.'

They rounded the canted hulk of a heavy drop pod, its paint scorched to bare metal and the lower thruster assembly pushed up into the passenger compartment by impact. The main stanchions were rumpled, and the lower parts of the doors buckled like card. A precise cluster of las-burns had drilled the side. Fire roared from the top, and a whiff of cooking flesh penetrated Justinian's breathing filters. The maze of wreckage thinned out there and the field opened up again. Only a few destroyed tanks, all blazing ferociously, stood between them and the foe.

There were more of the enemy than Justinian had expected, and they were well supported with armour.

'Brother!' Justinian voxed on their closed net. He held up one of his hands, almost encased by the assault bolter's bulky firing mechanisms. 'A chance to aid our cousins.'

Close to their position, five enemy Predator battle tanks were rolling backwards, firing as they withdrew, their thicker frontal armour presented towards the main press of the Imperial forces. Their heavy bolters had pinned a squad of Space Marines from the Silver Skulls Chapter behind a burning wreck, and a squad of Heretic Astartes was moving in to flank their position.

'There. To the left,' said Justinian, his cogitator canting over his intended target to Aldred.

'A good choice,' said the yellow-clad son of Dorn. They fired their jets.

Together the Primaris Space Marines jumped, sailing over the heads of the embattled Silver Skulls. Bullets whined past, bolt-shells roaring by on the hot blades of rocket motors, and las-beams cracked the air with miniature thunderclaps. While airborne, the two Inceptors became a favoured target. Death of various kinds knocked upon the thick plating of their armour, but none could gain entry to the soft meat within.

Justinian heeded a rising shriek from his inbuilt tacticarium, swerving out of the way to allow the rocket it had detected to pass between him and Aldred. Then they were down, and their would-be killers found other things to fire at.

They landed off to the right of the Iron Warriors skulking in the piles of wrecked machines. Justinian and Aldred had not been seen by their prey, and they took shelter behind a broken-backed Knight carcass. Blasphemous sigils covered its carapace, and its cockpit was cracked open, revealing an ossified melding of man and machine where a pilot should have sat.

'They have not seen us,' said Aldred.

'They will,' said Justinian.

He stepped out, both arms at full extension, and opened fire.

The Iron Warriors' armour was sufficiently thick that they weathered the first of the mass-reactive bolts. They therefore had time to register the two Space Marines flanking them, but several fell before they could return fire.

Justinian's left assault bolter clicked dry. A red warning sigil shone angrily near the centre of his vision, and he ducked back behind the Knight. The ammo indicator for his second gun flickered.

'I am down to seven rounds,' he informed Aldred.

Aldred laughed drily. Seven rounds was a half-second burst.

'I have only a few more.'

'We need to resupply.' Justinian pulled up another tactical overlay. 'I have the location of a resupply pod, three hundred feet east. Not far.'

The Silver Skulls were still under pressure from the Predators, but thanks to the Inceptors they were now aware of the Iron Warriors flanking them. A fierce firefight had commenced between the loyalist Space Marines and the remaining Heretic Astartes.

'A shame we cannot do more,' said Aldred.

An explosion ripped up one of the Predators, flinging its burning remains end over end.

'We do not have to,' said Justinian.

Three Repulsor grav-tanks fell from the sky like stones, slowing rapidly and coming to a gentle halt a few feet above the ground, right by the Iron Warriors. Their pulsing, aggressive grav-impellers knocked the traitors sideways. One of the Iron Warriors yanked a melta bomb from his side and dived under one of the tanks, seeking to attach the charge and destroy the armour.

The traitor had evidently never faced a Repulsor before.

The tank's pounding grav-engines squashed him flat, leaving a silver, blurred human outline pressed into the ground, leaking blood. The grav-tanks' anti-infantry weapons made short work of his fellow traitors, and the Repulsors flew onwards, the sand crushed to a glassy shine beneath them. The enemy Predators redirected their fire, increasing their rate of retreat as they volleyed lascannon shots at the grav-tanks, but the Repulsors were swift as well as heavily armed, and they chased down their traitorous tracked cousins, blasting them apart with pinpoint accuracy. They flew over their vanquished foes, buckling the wrecks with gravitic backwash. The Silver Skulls ran after them, the jewels on their pauldrons sparkling.

A terrific roaring rent the sky, so loud that it even drowned out the pounding of the Titans approaching the wall. Hundreds more drop pods and gunships were coming down from orbit, many racing off to attack the fortress. Explosive door bolts blew in miniature, rippling cannonades as the petals of the pods slammed down.

Thousands of Space Marines disgorged from their landing craft as the Astra Militarum forces reached the foot of the wall on the other side. Stern-faced Titans loomed over the fortifications, raking the ramparts free of the enemy with gigantic power fists wreathed in the lightning of a hundred storms. The crackling of disruption fields powerful enough to crush a small voidship harshened the battle's sound. A part of the wall came crashing down beneath a Titan's ponderous blow. As the debris settled, the Titan was already turning, its carapace-mounted cannon roaring fire at some other target Justinian could not see.

'It is over,' said Justinian. 'The wall is taken.'

To the howling of Legio Metalica war-horns, the traitors upon the wall were surrounded and destroyed.

The fortress fell five hours later.

CHAPTER EIGHT

RESPITE ON IAX

The weeks went by quietly on Iax. As Varens' wound healed, he took to coming out on the medicae facility balcony every evening.

The facility was set on a rise overlooking the Hythian wetlands. From the foot of the ridge marshes stretched as far as the horizon. Like everything in Ultramar, the wetlands were well managed and thoroughly exploited, dotted with aquaculture facilities and helical turbines that chopped at the wind soothingly, and yet despite its tended nature, the area retained a hint of wildness. A healthy ecosystem thrived there.

The hospital was well sited. The brutality of the era had eroded much of humanity's gentler qualities, but the medicae of Ultramar had enough insight remaining to appreciate the healing potential of natural spaces.

Autumn night drew in, fragrant with the smell of falling leaves. Out over the marshes, birds wailed shrill laments for their summer homes as they wheeled away towards the equator.

Meadows fringed the reed beds and children ran through them waving switches, driving bovids home for the night, their shrieks as piercing as the birds'. The hot breath of the cattle snorted out in miniature, short-lived storm fronts.

Peace reigned. It was bizarre to behold. Varens had thought never to see peace again.

Varens leaned on the parapet, letting himself relax. His fear was lessening. He no longer expected death to come at any moment, though he wasn't sleeping well. But if nightmares still had him screaming himself awake in the late watches, his days were calm.

The balcony sat atop the hospital portico before a recessed entablature, an unusual arrangement that did not, to Varens' eye, quite work. Although the site was well chosen, the architecture of the hospital did not respect Iax's garden beauty, and the somewhat clumsy hard lines stood out jarringly. The marble's cold luminosity added to the chill of the evening, further setting the building apart from the soft landscape.

Varens shivered in his hospital shift, but he didn't want to go back in, not yet. The cold of the tiles through his thin slippers reminded him he was still alive, and the itchy tightness in his wound, until recently so hot and sore, told him he would soon be whole again. Out on the balcony he felt like a man, not like a patient as he did when he was in the healing halls, or worse, like a number. To the logisticians of the Departmento Munitorum, all men were numbers, as dispassionately expended as bullets. Varens relished these rare moments when the war and the needs of the Imperium retreated from the forefront of his mind, those times when he might simply be.

Once healed, the men had a few days of peace before they were returned to the war and became numbers again. Numbers transferred from one column on the balance sheet to another, from sick to well, from resource drain to asset.

Few had many months of life left beyond their return to battle. No one lived long in these awful times. Upon the fringes of Ultramar, monsters stalked. Worst of all were the Heretic Astartes and their lords, the traitor sons of the Emperor Himself. A mortal man cannot triumph against beings nourished for millennia by hatred. Miraculously, Varens had faced them and lived. The chances were that his next encounter would see him dead.

He was fully aware of the brevity of his life, so Varens enjoyed the view and the cold in a way that a man from a more peaceful age would not. Someone whose life was full of pettier concerns would take far less from the experience. Had he considered this, Varens might have taken comfort in how rich every moment was for him, but he lacked the individualism of men from less troubled times, and he did not think much about himself. He took pride in Ultramar and what he fought for. He looked at the view and was prepared to die for what it represented. It was enough for him.

'Humanity finds a way to live, even in the face of death,' he whispered to himself.

'What was that, my friend?' said a gruff voice close behind.

Varens started from the balcony rail. The speaker was a barrel-chested man, with a thatch of greying red hair sticking up from his shift front. An unruly beard covered his chin, matching the band of hair circling his bald scalp.

'Didn't hear you coming,' said Varens. He looked at the man's thick gut. 'That is a surprise.'

'Don't be fooled by this.' The man slapped his ample belly with both hands. 'No one ever hears me coming – it's a knack I have. What were you saying there?'

'Something our priest says a lot,' Varens said. The newcomer looked at him for elaboration, but Varens was embarrassed to be caught in so personal a moment, though the sentiment was an approved one, and offered nothing more.

'I am Varens,' he said, 'of Talassar.'

The man grunted his disappointment at Varens' reticence, but he was friendly enough.

'Garstand is the name, Four Hundred and Fifty-Fifth Calth.'

He extended a beefy hand, its back also thick with hair. Varens shook it. Garstand's palm was warm in the cool evening.

'Like the view?' Varens asked.

Garstand pulled a face.

'Do you not?'

'Can't say I care for all this open space,' said Garstand. 'I grew up in the arcologies, way underground. A view like this gives me agoraphobia. No roof!'

'Then why come out?' asked Varens.

'I need a break from the groaning of unhealthy men,' said Garstand ruefully.

Varens nodded. 'It's quiet out here.'

'Too quiet.'

'It's better than the war.'

'Maybe for you,' said Garstand. 'I want to get back to the fighting. I don't like kicking my heels while good men are dying. It doesn't seem right to be taking in the view when my lasgun could be burning hot in my hand. All this looks pretty enough, but nothing's right here. Nothing's been right anywhere since that.' Garstand jerked the crown of his head skywards without looking up.

'The Rift?' Varens glanced at the sky. The Great Rift was visible as a purple smudge across the gathering dark. It was light years away from Iax, but its baleful influence was felt everywhere across Ultramar.

'Don't look at it, boy!' said Garstand. 'No one should willingly look.'

Varens frowned. 'It doesn't make any difference,' he said. 'It'll be there whether we look at it or not. War goes on like it always has. We're still fighting. The primarch leads us. I don't see the Rift makes much difference. I barely remember the time before.'

'Been a soldier long?'

'Since I was old enough to join up. I blame my father's stories. He was an auxiliary. He served all over the segmentum with the Astra Militarum.'

'When we still sent regiments out, you mean. We don't do that so much any more, do we? A shame. It'd be a fine thing to be picked for the crusade,' said Garstand, and Varens caught tension beneath his friendliness. 'But there's too much going on here in Ultramar for us to spare many men.' He scowled. 'Just don't look at the Rift. It's forbidden.' Garstand made the sign of the aquila over his heart.

'Everything's forbidden,' said Varens. 'Who's to see whether I look at it or not?' He peered pointedly up and down the balcony.

'It's not the sanction of the commissars you should be afraid of. Look at it too often you'll have nightmares – bad dreams.'

'Everyone has nightmares,' said Varens with a shrug. 'I do every night.'

'Not like the ones you'll get here if you stay too long,' said Garstand nervously. 'I've heard things, talk of bad dreams that have whole wards of this place waking up screaming. Things aren't right. The eye of evil is upon this place.'

Varens had not wanted company, especially not of this sort. His mood was spoilt. He had nightmares enough to contend with, without hearing talk of more.

'Goodnight, Garstand,' he said.

'Wait!' said Garstand. His friendly air slipped away, and his eyes took on a wildness Varens did not like. He caught Varens by the upper arm. 'I've fought them, you know, the Heretic Astartes.

They have some plan – they always do. The warp looks here, and hungers. We should not look back. Never!'

'You fought the plague lords?' said Varens.

Garstand nodded. 'I did! Believe me. Awful things I've seen. Out near Tartella, before that fell...'

'I fought them too.'

'Did you now? Did you.' Garstand calmed. He let go of Varens and smoothed his shirt down. Some of his previous bonhomie returned. 'Then you're a member of a select group. They do not show themselves often, you know. There's not so many of them. They prefer the dead or those whose minds they have turned to do their work for them.'

'I have seen that too. The walking dead. But after a time on Espandor, the plague lords came more frequently. Small groups at first, then in greater numbers. The last time there were twenty or more. I thought they would kill us all, but when they got into the trench they... well, they disappeared.'

Garstand nodded along with Varens' words in agreement. How could he know? Varens felt a stab of annoyance at him.

'The same happened to us. There were only seven of them. They attacked, they slew, then they vanished.' His eyes widened. In the lumen light spilling from inside, Varens saw the whites had an unhealthy yellow cast.

'Just like on Espandor,' Varens said uneasily.

'Were there any Adeptus Astartes near your unit? Space Marines?'

'None.'

'The same!' said Garstand. 'You'd think they'd go where the Angels of Death are, wouldn't you? I hear they hate each other. And I met another man, Rusen, with a similar story. He was on Efor. He said the plague lords came at his position, and they fought, and just before they killed everyone in his building, they just disappeared. Why do you think they did that?'

'What?' said Varens. Thinking about it made him feel sick. His peaceful mood was completely spoiled. He wanted to be left alone, but Garstand was oblivious to his quickening breath and shaking limbs.

'Why did they come in such small numbers. Why did they vanish? Did you kill any?'

'Some,' said Varens. 'I think. I don't know.'

'There's something to it, don't you think?'

'A soldier sees coincidences in everything,' said Varens. 'Death makes us suspicious.'

Garstand's beard bristled. 'There are no such things as coincidences. Do you want to meet him? I think it would be a good idea. We could compare our experiences. There's something going on here. How can the plague lords raise the dead so easily? Sorcery, Varens, sorcery! And it is everywhere.'

Garstand looked conspiratorially about.

'Up there,' he said, pointing at the Great Rift without looking at it. 'All through Ultramar,' he added, waving his hand vaguely at the sky. 'And here.' He slapped his hand on the balcony's balustrade. 'Rusen's got a theory. Darkness on many worlds. Things slithering through the warp. This is no war of ships and men, though they make it look that way. He knows! They can, he says… They can get in your head. They can *use* us somehow.' Garstand went pale, and once more his eyes became crazed. 'Come and meet him.'

Varens was light-headed, like he wasn't getting enough oxygen. Garstand wasn't making any sense. 'Meet who?' he said quietly.

'Rusen!' said Garstand. 'Meet Rusen! Perhaps there are more like us, those who have faced the plague lords and lived. Perhaps we can find them. Perhaps we can figure out what's going on.'

Varens wanted nothing to do with the idea. There were plague lords everywhere. The Death Guard, a hatred from ancient days.

They had ships. They sailed the void and the warp. That was how it worked.

A memory overtook him, of a monstrous man, corrupt with disease that should have killed him many times over, his face covered by a rotting respirator, his armour leaking pus. Varens had fought him, and others, others that had vanished into thin air.

'No!' he said, far more loudly than he had intended. He didn't want to think about it. He wanted to enjoy this brief quiet. Time would come soon enough to face the enemy again. He had no desire to revisit his memories. Any more of this and he would end up like Bolus, or, he was beginning to suspect, like Garstand.

He could not articulate his fear. His throat wouldn't let him.

'Goodnight, Garstand,' he managed. The words were hard.

The last vestiges of friendliness vanished from Garstand's expression.

'Suit yourself,' he said quietly, and there was something absent in his slack face. For all his dislike of the view, he tucked his bearded chin into his chest and looked away from Varens out over the marsh.

Varens hurried back inside, suddenly weak.

CHAPTER NINE

IMPERATOR GLORIANA

When the demands of war retreated, Roboute Guilliman was not idle. He worked like he always had, ceaselessly toiling for humanity, even if now he struggled for the species' survival rather than its advancement.

At the heart of the primarch's palace upon the *Macragge's Honour* was his scriptorium. Roboute Guilliman's chambers were better stocked than most libraries, and far better ordered, full of texts taken from all over Imperium Sanctus during the first decade of the crusade. Beneath the scriptorium's dome, at a desk surrounded by circular walls of shelves that stretched a hundred feet up, was where Guilliman spent what little free time he had.

Old paper made the air tart. Mouldering scrolls lay next to data crystals and magnetic tape. Runic inscriptions on crumbling bark lay on top of hololith cylinders containing tri-D representations of forgotten wars. Graven copper cubes, wherein languished thoughts captured from living brains, shared desk space with yellowed cardboard boxes full of images on simple chemical film that was brittle with time.

Thousands of years of history recorded upon every device employed by mankind surrounded the primarch, and this was but the smallest part of his collection. Much more he had studied, digested, processed and recorded onto more permanent data-capture systems.

Guilliman had not yet grasped all the events of the ten millennia since he fell. Belisarius Cawl had provided the primarch with painful but necessary machine-moderated engrammatic updates, but Cawl had always been a secretive creature, detached from the wider galaxy while he pursued the creation of the Primaris Space Marines. His records were incomplete, fragmentary, and all of them were low on detail.

As happened too often, Guilliman found his own efforts were required to make up for the shortcomings of others.

The discipline of history, like so much else based on reason, had fallen foul of superstition, fanaticism and the High Lords of Terra's need for iron control. Comparative and corroborative analytical techniques had given way to the recording of gossip, hearsay and folklore. All was liberally mixed with complete fabrication. Imperial interference in redacting chronicles, misguidedly or not, had further destroyed much of the past. War had eradicated the histories of entire worlds. Precious records had been burned by zealous inquisitors, often in order to eradicate a single uncomfortable truth. If anything, the state of man's knowledge was worse than it had been back after the Unification Wars, when the Emperor had united Terra before the Great Crusade. Much of Terra's ancient history, painstakingly pieced together by the remembrancers of Guilliman's own era, had been lost again.

Knowledge of the warp's true nature had been suppressed,

but patchily so. The great deception the Emperor had practised had become impossible to sustain, though that had not
stopped the Inquisition from trying. Knowledge of daemons
or the Dark Gods was forbidden. Many innocents had paid the
ultimate price for accidentally learning the truth.

Even Guilliman, the Imperial Regent himself, faced opposition from the Inquisition in his quest for enlightenment. To
oppose puritanical redactionism, he had trained his own corps
of historitors. Between campaigns he sought out inquisitive
minds, exactly the sort that had long been frowned upon, res-
cuing them from penal servitude and impending brain wipe. The
first handful he had tutored himself, when time allowed. They
in turn taught more, and more still. Each one was assessed by
the primarch personally. Those that passed were given the rank
of historitor-investigatus. Those that failed to meet his exacting
standards were given less taxing roles within the new organisation, as librarians, servants and assistants. Guilliman had learnt
that the machinery of Imperial government was unkind to failures, yet another thing that saddened him about the present
age. The primarch had enough blood upon his conscience, and
a much finer grasp of how to get the most out of his subjects.
No life was wasted.

As the decade since his rebirth rolled on, the numbers of
historitors grew from four, to eight, to sixteen, until now the
Logos Historica Verita numbered over a hundred operatives
and thousands of support staff. Utilising long-dead academic
arts, they attempted the impossible – the construction of a reli-
able history of the Imperium. Against great odds, small cells
of the Logos searched out ancient records. At their presentation of the primarch's seal, forbidden vaults were opened and
emptied, their contents copied and dispatched to Guilliman's
flagship, wherever it was.

The Logos' work was a torturous, dangerous affair. Warzones engulfed half the galaxy, and his historitor teams sometimes disappeared into them without trace. Often, they were opposed. Still Guilliman would not be stopped.

Every man needed a pastime. Even a primarch.

He was reading a book new to his collection. Ancient leather, friable to the point of disintegration, bound a partisan work on the Chronostrife of Terra. As he read, he worked. Flickering screed passed over multiple data-slates mounted around his desk. Dust motes danced in the light of two small hololiths either side of him. The primarch appeared to be ignoring them, but every iota of data that passed over them was processed. He absorbed everything, annotating reports and answering a shifting stream of queries with quick scratches of a quill on an autotablet set at his right hand. The movements were so deft that they would be easily missed, had anyone been watching him. His superior mind organised the actions of a thousand groups working towards different aims, all while translating the book's obscure dialect.

Guilliman digested the work with a frowning countenance. What he read made him despair. One of thousands of secret conflicts conducted by rival factions in the Imperium, the Chronostrife was a bitter, ongoing internal war within the Ordo Chronos over the Imperium's dating system. Not even his father's calendar had survived the millennia intact.

During the Great Crusade and the Heresy, the standard dating system had provided some idea of the order of events over time, but like everything else the Emperor had created, the calendar had become degraded by both dogmatic adherence and thoughtless revisionism. Various rival dating systems had evolved from the Imperial Standard, making a true chronicle of the galaxy almost impossible to construct. By the five main factional variants,

Guilliman calculated the current year to be anywhere between early M41 and a millennium later, and that was leaving out the numerous lesser, more heretical interpretations.

The current book was of the latter tendency. There was much useful information in its pages, but the viewpoint of the writer transcended fanaticism.

'Who is not a fanatic in these benighted times?' he said to himself. Guilliman pushed away the crumbling tome, his patience tested by the author's endless calls for the public immolation of his opponents. 'Emperor save me from faith,' he said, and rose from his seat. He was annoyed he still had not found a satisfactory solution to the dating system.

He washed paper mould from his fingers in a silver salver set on its own table, and he checked the endless run of reports again. There was nothing that could not wait. He required a moment's respite, and he went to find it in the armoured cloister encircling the library's ground floor.

Outside the shelves, the tower's base was a series of arches. In every archway a blast door waited to slam down. On the other side of the arches, a long gallery of armaglass looked out in every direction over the *Macragge's Honour*. If Guilliman walked around the circumference of his library, he could see all the way to the massive prow and its adamantium ram. Either side on the flanks, stubby wings swept out, covered in sensor arrays and auguries. Almost directly below his spire were the main hangar decks of the vessel, while to the aft the sun-bright glow of the engines reflected around the cloister.

Off to starboard, the Pit of Raukos turned. Guilliman had a notion the warp was angered by the traitors' defeat, and so the eye of Raukos glared the harder at him. Once upon a time, he would have dismissed such feelings as fancy, an artefact of the way the Terran mind processed visual information. Now he knew they were not. The galaxy was a far stranger place than either of his fathers had taught him.

At the thought of his fathers, the memory of the sights he had witnessed in the Imperial Palace rose powerfully within him. Against the odds, something lingered on the Golden Throne. His last encounter with his true father had been a spear of light and pain whose psychic aftershocks troubled him still. The Emperor had lost His subtlety.

Guilliman pushed the memory aside before he began dwelling on it. Such ruminations never ended well. He wished he could speak with one of his brothers about what had transpired there on Terra, but they were all gone, lost to death or madness.

He sighed morosely. Seeking solitude, he reminded himself of how alone he was. He let his eyes drift over the void, emptied his mind and urged his sorrow to slip away.

Debris fields occluded some of Raukos' violent depths. Sparkling showers of metal, clouds of frozen gas and shattered hulls drifted across the sun. Work proceeded to salvage wrecked Imperial vessels. Great Adeptus Mechanicus Salvator Arks stood off at nexus points between the wrecks calculated for maximum distance efficiency. Ships flew between them and the broken vessels in precisely spaced streams. Scavenger scows crawled back and forth across space, their articulated limbs and swarms of attendant drones working together with insectile efficiency. The more intact wrecks had many small salvage pods anchored to them like limpets, blue flashes sparkling all around these viable craft as they were made fit for warp transit to shipyards.

The adamantium frames of Imperial ships were practically indestructible. As long as the reactors did not explode, they would survive to be refitted again, and some had been a hundred times over.

Some changes had been made to Imperial salvaging policies

within the fleet. Guilliman had ordered the wrecks of the traitors' ships to be utterly destroyed. It had been the habit of
the Adeptus Mechanicus and the Navy to recover enemy ships.
Chaos vessels were of Imperial make, and were often of older,
superior patterns. The primarch stamped hard on the practice.
Build new ships, he had said. Leave the past where it is. The corruption of the warp buried itself deeply into whatever it touched.

The Martians had not been happy with that. They had looked
upon the older marques of vessel with greedy eyes. They had
pointed to his own ship, the *Macragge's Honour*, returned from
the Red Corsairs in the Maelstrom. Guilliman had been firm.
Examples had been made.

The rest of the fleet hung against the raging Pit in a box defence
pattern. Thin lines of lights passing between the battleships
marked out the flight paths of inter-ship traffic, as officers and
repair crews shuttled back and forth. Every craft bore some sign of
damage, from this or prior engagements, and over them all flickered plasma torches. They were strong still, even wounded, and
Guilliman took an immense pride in the scale of Fleet Primus.

Behind the wall of vessels nearest to the Pit of Raukos, the
Null Ships of the Sisters of Silence waited, their arcane weap-
ons ready to obliterate any uncanny foe that dared entry to
the material realm. Guilliman did not expect any. The Concilia
Psykana told him the rift was dormant. The fane was gone.
The system's sole viable world belonged to the Imperium now.

Beyond Raukos the Cicatrix Maledictum shone, a broad band
of energies stretched across space from one side of the galaxy to
the other. It divided the Imperium in two, shrouding the dense
yolk of stars at the heart of the galaxy completely. The light was
painful to observe. Though it appeared to be a natural stellar
phenomenon, to look into it for any length of time showed a
man things that he would rather not see.

What Guilliman saw when he looked at it was a tragedy, the latest play in a war millions of years in the fighting. The last ten millennia, though an age in the lifetime of mankind, was a heartbeat of time, a single summer's campaign. The magnitude of the war against Chaos, the empires lost and the peoples damned, awed the primarch. He had learned these things from the aeldari, though they were unwilling to tell him the complete story. Even so, he knew far more than he had, of the War in Heaven, and of the conflicts between the ancient races.

Against this all-devouring cosmic evil that had consumed species after species and brought man's first stellar empire low, Guilliman's father had set Himself. The scale of His self-appointed task was yet another thing the Emperor had not deigned to share with His sons.

We constantly battle the sins of the fathers, thought Guilliman. *That is no less true on an eternal scale than it is within the history of a single world. We suffer because of those that have gone before.*

Guilliman looked upon the ruins of the Emperor's dream in despondency. He would never give in to his feelings, and he would never show them to another, but they were there nonetheless. Even after the Emperor had fallen silent following the Heresy, there had been the promise of something better, the possibility of realising His dream for Him. But Guilliman had pursued the wrong path. He had not grasped that the Imperium had been the means to an end, not the end in itself. If he allowed himself some forgiveness, he could say that was because his father had not told him. He had told them nothing.

He could never have foreseen this future, where pain and ignorance were the universal lot of ordinary citizens. Superstition had overtaken reason. There was no hope, only blind faith in the Emperor, trillions of souls united in frantic pleas for salvation, and now the lion's share of that desperate expectation was Guilliman's to bear. The eyes of all mankind looked to him.

He would never complain. But in these moments when he stopped, when the need for strategy and planning slackened for a second, the despair was there, waiting to drown him.

'I will not give in.' He spoke to the Pit of Raukos through gritted teeth. 'I will never, ever stop until this is set right. I defy you, as my father defied you.'

Father. The word caught on his lips. After the throne room, he used the word rarely now. Still the habit of ten thousand years was hard to break.

He unclenched his jaw. His hands had formed themselves into tight fists without him noticing. Rage. Good – that kept him on the correct course. That would see him through.

He uncurled his fingers, and let out a long, calming breath.

A soft fanfare sounded. A cyber cherub clattered in a clumsy search pattern around the scriptorium on metal wings. Such things were grotesque, techno-alchemy far removed from the purer machinery of his day. The madness of Mars had infected everything. Guilliman let it flap about pathetically, its under-powered ocular senses gridding the scriptorium as it searched for him.

The pallid flesh of the cherub's torso and arms was sore where steel cables plunged into the skin. The rest of it was mechanical, with metal wings and legs. A naked child's skull made in perfect silver capped a neck of woven copper. Hateful art for a hateful time.

It weaved jerkily under one of the arches into the cloister, and found him, halting in a noisy hover.

'*My lord, Guilliman.*' The thing's skeletal jaw was cast shut, and Captain Felix's voice crackled out of a brass trumpet stitched into a dead hand. The cherub's emerald eyes flashed at each word.

'I am sorry to disturb your work,' continued Felix, 'but the priest is here.'

'He is early,' said Guilliman.

'He apologises, my lord – he merely wished to be on time.' Behind the tinniness imparted by the cherub's augmitter, Felix's voice was unnaturally deep, a mark of his transhumanism. 'He says he is happy to wait, my lord, but I thought it best to inform you.'

'There are many vices, Felix. Earliness is not one that troubles me,' said Guilliman. 'I will see him now.' Guilliman looked into the eyes of the cherub. 'I need a respite from the tedium of other men's ramblings. Send him in. I will be glad of the change that conversation will bring.'

'Even with a priest?' It was a rare wry comment from the equerry. Captain Felix was a serious creature who never made light.

'Even with a priest,' said Guilliman.

'As you wish, my lord.'

The light went from the cherub's eyes. It flew off, motor buzzing. The primarch watched it go back to its roost with critical eyes. The wings were more than adornment; from the sound of it, there was not enough lift in the gravity impeller to keep it aloft. The machines of this millennium were crude. The engineers among his brothers would probably have caught the thing and rebuilt the motor; he was close to doing so himself. Either that, or tossing it out of an airlock into the void and replacing it with something less ghoulish.

He refrained from acting out his thoughts. Consideration, evaluation, action. That was his way. Roboute Guilliman was not a slave to impulse.

Thinking on the cherub brought another unwelcome flash of what he had seen behind the Eternity Gate. He saw clearly the corpse in the ungentle embrace of Mechanicus technology, part meat, part machine, and the terrible screaming of the soul syphons...

He shook his head to quash the memory. He could not fix everything. Not all at once. Guilliman deliberately put the device from his mind and returned to his desk. He did not sit, but pulled out a new book and stood flicking through it. He was unwilling to continue reading the chronolog's ranting today. The man was a thousand years dead. His words could stand another day's wait.

Three minutes later and he had absorbed half the book's contents. Nothing interesting, another small world of small deeds and small men.

The door to the library opened with a soft whoosh of equalising pressure. Voices too low for even Guilliman to catch blunted themselves on his books. The primarch looked up. He resolved to avoid judging the priest until he saw him in person, but previous experience had coloured his perceptions of the adepts deeply. Would the man start to wail like the last one, or collapse into religious ecstasy? The possibilities were as irksome as they were limited.

Lorgar, thought Guilliman. *He would have enjoyed crowing about this.*

The soft slap of sandals on marble echoed around the library. By this humble sound was the next militant-apostolic to the primarch announced. It was far better than the herald cherub's synthesised warbling.

Frater Mathieu was a slight man. His crossed arms were buried in the sleeves of the plain cream robes of the Acronite Mendicants. Guilliman doubted he would have recognised the habit without the information he had gathered on the priest. The sub-orders of the Adeptus Ministorum were so numerous even he had no hope of memorising them all.

Mathieu wore a quiff that clung to the forefront of his skull. The rest of his thick hair was shaved down to stubble-blued scalp.

He appeared healthy. If anything surprised the primarch about Mathieu, it was his youthfulness. Guilliman had, of course, extensive files on those who had made his shortlist for the role, but his natural prejudices assumed the priesthood to fall into a small number of categories: old, mad, dissolute, fanatical or a painful combination of the same.

Guilliman made a mental note to adjust his thinking. He was falling into dangerous patterns.

Mathieu was not a bullet-headed rabble-rouser, nor a wan, black-toothed extremist. Nor was he an aged primate, thick with the brocade of office and the dust of inactivity. A peaceful air radiated from him, and though Guilliman had encountered this religious serenity before, Mathieu's was without the accompanying self-satisfaction that invariably suffused men of faith.

His movements suggested someone used to fighting. A red rope belt cinched his waist. On one side was a simple pouch purse, on the other a battered leather holster for a long-barrelled laspistol. The gun had been taken from him. Felix's diligence amused Guilliman. The priest posed no threat to him whatsoever.

A servo-skull trailed behind Mathieu at head height, as modest as its owner. A large 'HV' was engraved into its forehead, but otherwise it was unadorned. The motor cowling, manipulators and frame for the single sensor were plain plasteel, and there was no plating of precious metals upon the bone.

Mathieu approached confidently, without outward signs of pious joy at being so close to a son of the Emperor. He did not quake or sing, or burst into tears. He was not afraid. He smiled instead, with an edge of sly humour Guilliman instantly liked. It was a smile that acknowledged the uncomfortableness of the situation, and the uneven power dynamic. It was a smile that said its wearer understood those things, and found them amusing.

There was a wide rug near Guilliman's desk. The priest stopped on it, spread his arms wide, and bowed low.

'My lord Roboute Guilliman,' he said. 'It is an honour to meet you.' The priest's long sleeves brushed the carpet.

'Please, Frater Mathieu, sit.' Guilliman gestured to a stool built for mortals tucked away under a table. Guilliman had balanced a pile of books on it. Mathieu removed them, and they both sat, Guilliman in his oversized chair, Mathieu on his stool like a child at a scholam before the master. 'Do you know why I have called you here?'

Mathieu nodded. 'I think so.'

'Then say why.'

Mathieu pursed his lips, raised one knee and clasped his hands around it. 'It sounds like arrogance when voiced, but to borrow the parlance of your sons, it is the only practical that fits the theoretical. However, I fear I am being tested, and am wary of looking foolish.'

Guilliman appreciated the man's honesty. He nodded in open approval. 'Nothing will happen to you if you are wrong. I am not in the habit of burning people I disagree with.' An undiplomatic statement given the Adeptus Ministorum's love of fire, but calculated. If the priest was to serve him, he must accede to Guilliman's thoughts and beliefs. Too many in the Church reacted badly at any indictment of their practices.

Mathieu ignored the comment but paused for thought before speaking.

Good, thought Guilliman.

'Militant-Apostolic Geestan is dead,' said Mathieu, 'passing shortly before the glorious victory at Raukos. You seek a new militant-apostolic for your crusade. The Adeptus Ministorum would appoint one itself if you allowed it, but you would prefer to recruit one of your own. I think you'd prefer one from the lower ranks of the priesthood, though I am surprised you have gone so low as mine. I am no stranger to war, which I am sure appeals to you. I am honest. I speak my mind, another quality you favour. I am well known aboard this ship, having ministered to its people during their captivity in the Maelstrom, and I have served faithfully in the crusade since it was brought home.'

'You believe that this qualifies you?'

'No, but I think you might. The Emperor moves us on a crooked path, my lord, but He does move us. To give me this appointment as your holy mouthpiece is the only reason I can think of for you to call me here, unless I have offended you personally in some way and you wish to punish me. Forgive me if I have, but I do not believe that is so. Nor do I think you have called me here to gather intelligence, for there is little I could tell you you would not already know.'

'Mouthpiece?' said Guilliman.

Mathieu nodded. 'A tool in priestly garb. That is what the office of militant-apostolic is. I have heard it said you do not hold the Emperor to be a god, or believe in your own divinity. You require someone to allay the fears this belief raises. Therefore, a mouthpiece – a priest to reassure the masses that you are not a terrible heretic.'

Mathieu smiled again.

Guilliman made a noise in his throat. 'I need free-willed men to serve me, not mouthpieces. But that aside, you are correct.' He plucked up a large sheet of illuminated vellum. 'Your certification of office.'

Mathieu raised an eyebrow. His raised leg thumped to the floor, and he scratched the back of his head.

'That's it? No ceremony?'

'Not today, no,' said Guilliman. 'I will of course formally invest you soon, but I need you to begin work now.'

Mathieu did not take the vellum. 'This is a great honour.'

'It is,' said Guilliman. 'You do not take the certification.'

'I am not sure I am worthy. I must be careful before I accept. Perhaps I should not accept.'

Guilliman shrugged his mountainous shoulders. 'You are wise to hesitate.' He put the sheet aside. 'You have questions. Ask them. You are entitled to.'

'I was afraid questions would be unwelcome.'

'I make my methods and tempers well known. Am I such a stranger to my own people?'

'You are surrounded by legend, my lord.' Mathieu looked about the room, craning his neck to take in the shelves. 'What is it exactly that you are doing here, my lord?'

Guilliman followed the priest's gaze around the high stacks. 'Knowledge is power, and my own is lacking. I have a great deal to understand before I can rebuild the Imperium. To that end, I am collecting as many histories of as many worlds as I can. I will use them to model the last ten millennia so that I might study it, and from it make a true history, the like of which has not been written for thousands of years. By doing so, I will understand what went wrong with the Emperor's plans, and with my plans, and be able to formulate a corrective.'

'You speak plainly.'

'Nothing is gained through obfuscation,' said Guilliman. 'Time is short. Why would I lie?'

'I see.' Mathieu paused again. 'I beg your pardon for my impertinence, my lord–'

'You are aware enough to recognise impertinence, yet still you proceed,' interrupted Guilliman testily. 'Ask me, or do not. There can be no secrets between you and I if you are to serve me effectively.'

'My apologies,' the priest said smoothly. Frater Mathieu's

peaceful face showed the barest sign of strain, but a tick under one eye betrayed his nerves.

Guilliman noticed it. Irritated with himself for putting the man on edge, he leaned back in his chair, adopting a remarkably human posture for one so inhuman. He folded his hands in his lap.

'Let us start anew,' Guilliman said. 'It is I who should apologise. A man may hold a different point of view to another. It is no excuse for ill manners. Once, I was more even-tempered. But now...' Guilliman trailed off, his eyes straying over the mounded remains of ten millennia of history. 'Things are not what they were. I am not who I was. I am pressed on all sides. I let my temper get the better of me. It is late, and there is so much to do.' He shook his head and attempted to smile. 'Please, priest, your impertinence – voice it openly.'

Frater Mathieu relaxed, a change in posture imperceptible to a normal man, but clear to the primarch. The flicker of a decision being made passed over his face. Again, the priest considered his next words carefully.

'There is an element of hypocrisy to your activities, my lord. You ordered the doors to the Library of Ptolemy on Macragge barred, pronouncing the time of learning done, but here you devote yourself to the pursuit of history.'

Guilliman made a reasonable face, conceding the point. 'I stand by my actions. One day those doors will be unbarred. What I did there was symbolic. Who even in my own realm read and understood what the library contained? I sealed the doors not against the truth, but against the superstition that has taken truth's place.'

Guilliman did not lie often but he did then. There was one book in the Library of Ptolemy that told a history he would rather no one read. He could not afford the shadow of the Imperium Secundus to hang over his latest ventures.

'All eyes must be on the future,' Guilliman continued. 'One version of the past is in that library, another is in the heads of men. The closing of the doors was symbolic, but powerful. It seals both versions of the future away for now. I prepare, Mathieu. When this crisis is passed, perhaps something of my father's dream might be reborn, though we have a long way to climb. If we are lucky, when I reopen the doors to the Library of Ptolemy, those who enter in might finally understand what they read.' He frowned a little before going on. 'I will be honest with you. I will make you privy to matters I do not readily share, so listen. I see that in the period following the Great Heresy War I was too focused upon the reformation of the Legions, trusting to the council my father created to govern wisely. My optimism was misguided. This terrible future I find myself in is my fault as much as anyone else's. Now I have concluded my revisions of the Codex Astartes, I have begun work upon a new book. This book I shall call the Codex Imperialis. In it I shall set down the principles of good governance long denied our species. Compiling an accurate history is only the start of the process.'

'You do this while conducting this war?' said Mathieu in disbelief.

'I have few of the powers your priesthood ascribes to me, Mathieu, but I do have some abilities. I was made to accomplish many goals at once.'

'Truly the Emperor was wise in creating one such as you.' The unwelcome signs of awe stole across the priest's face.

'Not as wise as you think,' said Guilliman, unable to keep the bitterness from his voice. 'I was one of twenty. Two failed. Half the rest turned on my father. The Emperor is not infallible, nor am I.' The blasphemy was intended to provoke the priest. A cheap tactic. Mathieu was thankfully unmoved.

'Twenty?' The priest arched an eyebrow.

'Yes,' said Guilliman.

'Not eighteen? Nine holy primarchs, nine fallen devils? That is what the scriptures say.'

'No. Twenty. Your Church is ignorant of many things.' As most people weren't aware that Horus and his followers had been loyal once, that his two failed siblings were not known of in the 41st millennium was hardly surprising. More information deliberately hidden. More myths.

'I see.' Mathieu looked thoughtful, stowing away the information for later. He smiled serenely. 'But in your holiness, you did not turn.'

'I am not holy,' said Guilliman. 'Worship the Emperor, if you must, but I am not deserving of your praise, nor will I accept it.'

'I have heard some of your beliefs,' said Mathieu. 'When first awoken, you insisted upon something called the Imperial Truth?'

Guilliman looked away, irritated, reminded of old lies. He had been rash to so stridently voice his objections to the Ecclesiarchy in those early days after his awakening. It had taken him time to recover the full measure of his wits, and he had been alarmed by what he found.

His feelings on the Imperial Truth remained conflicted. He had not forgiven the Emperor for hiding the true nature of the warp from them all. He did not know if he ever could. That one great lie undermined everything else the Emperor had done. If He had not lied, then history might have been very different.

Theoretical, thought Guilliman, slipping into Macraggian dialectic. *What if He were lying about more than the gods of the warp?*

Once, he would never have entertained such thoughts. This living hell had challenged everything he had once believed. There was a great change coming to humanity for which Guilliman was ill-prepared, because of the Emperor's lies. There were other threats abroad now, more players from distant aeons, whose presence competed with Chaos in their danger to mankind. Had the Emperor known about them too?

What he had seen behind the gate...

Focus.

'A modified version of it, yes,' he said. 'Reason still has a place amid all this madness.'

'Some may disagree with that,' said Mathieu amicably. His eyes glinted shrewdly. 'As I understand it, my lord, this truth denies not only your divinity, but that of your father.'

'The Emperor denied His own divinity,' said Guilliman flatly.

The priest shrugged. Guilliman had seen the look on the priest's face too many times on other holy men. It was the look of the blindly faithful.

If the Emperor Himself stood up, thought Guilliman, *came down off His Golden Throne and proclaimed 'I am not a god!' then they would burn Him as a heretic.*

Mathieu exhibited few signs of fanaticism, but the primarch would give it time. The more serene the priest on the outside, the deeper his faith was on the inside, and the deeper the faith, the hotter the fires of righteousness. It was a risk, but there was a balance of humours Guilliman required. His militant-apostolic needed some of that zeal.

Be careful there is not too much fire, Roboute, he chided himself, *or you will be burnt.*

'If you do not hold with the teachings of our glorious Church,' said Mathieu, 'then why did you treat with us at all?'

'Because the Adeptus Ministorum has power, and though it has used that power unwisely on occasion, once the balance sheet is reckoned, I see it is and has been a force for good.' Guilliman looked the priest squarely in the eyes. The priest tried and failed to return his gaze. 'I need the Adeptus Ministorum. I need their support. The turning of the galaxy depends on their approval, though I may wish it were not so…' He paused. 'The first phase of the Indomitus Crusade is over, yet there remains much to be done. I would have the blessing of the Ecclesiarchy – both for my men's morale, and to present a united front to those who would sow division within the Imperium. Of whom, in case you are not aware, there are a great many.'

'You do not need to ask for the Adeptus Ministorum's blessing, my lord. Any of my peers, any cardinal or episcope, would have leapt at the chance to proclaim your divine will.'

'I suppose I do not need to ask,' said Guilliman, reaching for a slender, leather-bound volume. 'But if I do, then in time you will see me for what I am, and not what you believe me to be. A god has no need for manners. There are other factors.'

Guilliman held out the book.

'Let us leave your certification for now, if you wish, but take these notes of mine. These are the topics I would like the blessing to cover. You claim to represent the Emperor's word. You are better placed to speak His will and obey my orders, and resolve neatly any contradictions there might be between the twain. A delicate time lies ahead. I cannot rule by diktat alone. Every institution does as I ask, for I am the Imperial Regent. I am the Emperor's living agent. But I am no tyrant, and I will not become one. I will have all the Imperium at my back willingly, or we will fail. I cannot become my brother Horus.'

'Nobody said you were a usurper, my lord,' said the priest, and he took the slim book from the primarch's hands. His fingers shook. In terms of paper and leather, it weighed hardly anything, but there was responsibility enough to crush a horde of saints.

'The most dangerous thoughts go unsaid,' said Guilliman. 'Many think it, even within the fleet. On Terra, it is openly spoken.'

He turned back to his datasplays and hololiths, and opened

up the book on the Chronostrife. The conversation was over, but the priest remained. A moment later, Guilliman looked over his shoulder.

'Still here, priest?'

'I have one more question, if you might indulge me,' said Mathieu.

Guilliman picked up a stylus and began marking a data-slate, where a list of new finds for his library glowed. He began ticking off the books he desired to see soonest. 'You want to know why I chose you. Why not a cardinal, or the Ecclesiarch himself? It is only natural.'

The priest nodded. 'I am the lowliest sort of priest, my lord,' Mathieu said. 'Even in the Missionarus Galaxia, I am beneath notice. My ministry is with the poor, and the sick. It carries no prestige and not a little disdain. I have never craved power or influence. I simply desire to do your father's work. That is reward enough for me.'

'Well said. That is exactly why I have chosen you, and not some princely demi-pope. You *care*. You fight alongside my armies, and you care for the meanest serf.' Guilliman's noble face became more solemn. 'And I have heard your sermons.'

'You have?' said Mathieu. He was surprised and honoured, but still he did not fall to his knees and start wailing. Guilliman was satisfied he had chosen well.

'Take the book. My equerry shall present you with my seal and your identification as militant-apostolic. As far as I am concerned, you are he. We shall treat it as a temporary appointment, if you like. You have one week to decide whether or not you will take the post permanently. Regardless of your decision, I would like you to do this one service for me. Write the sermon for the triumph I am planning, and deliver it.'

'Are you commanding me?'

'I am asking you. You do not have to do it.'

Guilliman looked searchingly at the priest. Mathieu gripped the book.

'Good,' said the primarch. 'Now go – anything you require will be made available to you.'

'You could deliver the words yourself, my lord.'

'Frater Mathieu.' Guilliman rested his hand on a pile of files, all in rough binders marked with the barred 'I' of the Inquisition. 'I have looked carefully at many possible candidates for this office. I chose you as all the intelligence I have on your life suggests you are an honest man, fervent but reasonable, kind yet bold. As you said, you help the needy, and you have no ambition other than to do good. As far as I can tell. I have been wrong before.'

'I have my own work.'

'And I have greater for you,' said Guilliman. He lowered his voice, and looked out through the cloisters to the floating wrack of void combat. 'If I say I am not a god, I damn myself in the eyes of the Emperor's worshippers. If I say I am, I damn myself again in the eyes of those who are suspicious of me. Not every man regards my return as fortuitous. Some suspect fell powers at work. I have my detractors in the Church. I require someone who can handle the Adeptus Ministorum gently. Most dangerous of all to me is to have a man in this position of a worshipful character. I need someone who can get things done, who will not go into paroxysms whenever I speak, and one who will question what I say should it need questioning. In short, I need someone who can see the man behind the god.

'You came to me freely. You have not cast yourself upon your knees. You may be surprised to learn that you are one of the very few members of your organisation that I have been able to hold a proper conversation with. In the first few minutes of our exchange, you called me a hypocrite. The fundamental of it is, you are not overawed. You are therefore perfect for the role. You may not believe in me completely. I see that as an advantage.'

The priest hugged the book close to his chest as if it were a precious child. 'I believe in you, my lord.'

'Because you have faith, priest?' said Guilliman, and this time he could not mask his feelings.

His scorn slid off Frater Mathieu like water.

'No, my lord. It is because I have met you, and I see you are sincere, if misguided.' He bowed again. 'I shall do as you ask and write the sermon, and I shall speak its words, and in one week I shall give you my answer as to whether I will accept the appointment.'

CHAPTER TEN

NEWS FROM ULTRAMAR

As ships underwent repairs and resupply, vessels flew in from across the sector to provision Fleet Primus, and work was begun on the surface of 108/Beta-Kalapus-9.2. Battlefield scrap was taken away. The bodies of the traitors were burnt. When all trace of the fighting was removed, the site of victory was prepared for the Triumph of Raukos.

Flocks of auto-praisers flew over the bare earth, singing hymns, while priests in floating pulpits shouted out blessings to cleanse the ground. Staggered lines of giant machines scraped the terrain flat under dozer blades. Behind them came large tankers with fanned nozzles that sprayed liquid rockcrete. Following the tankers, an army of men with rakes and brushes laboured to spread the rockcrete before it could set. Dozens of artisans watched over them, their servo-skulls and slaved cyber-beasts measuring the level with pulsed laser light. As the screed set, servitors followed, laying coloured stones brought from all over the sector. Finally came trucks fitted with brushes and polishing limbs. In this way the rocky plain was replaced by a martial square three miles across, decorated with a giant mosaic.

The square at the valley mouth was just the beginning. Demolition walkers tore down the wall of the Iron Warriors to make way for a giant, triumphal building that would cross the plain side to side, joining its bordering hills. Before they had dismantled half of it, work started at the site of the wall's central gate. Already huge pillars loomed, each topped with a pediment from which the statues of Imperial heroes gazed. The noise of industry was tremendous, echoing across the planet for hundreds of miles. The activity continued up into orbit, and lines of freighters came down constantly from the sky, bearing workers and materials.

Guilliman watched his plans being put into action from the viewing deck of a bulky construction crawler. Felix had done his job well. The machines outside were not the great geo-planers of old, but they were adequate to the task. The captain had learned much.

Guilliman was waiting while nervy architects and artists fussed over their plans, preparing them for the primarch's inspection. A pile of blueprints held in place with carved stone weights had already accumulated on a deactivated chart table. Rather more collected were the military engineers awaiting their turn. Upon their devices the complexities of the new Chapter fortress to be raised over the Iron Warriors stronghold were stored.

'My lord.' A sculptor with a fixed, terrified smile approached Guilliman. The primarch turned from the angled crawler windows to view a hololith of a frieze for the main structure. The man stuttered and mumbled his way through the presentation. His talents in design were great, those in interpersonal communication less so, and Guilliman was glad when Captain Felix came onto the viewing deck. The artists were almost as scared of Felix as they were of Guilliman, and scattered before him. Felix coughed, beck-oned, and whispered into the primarch's ear when he bent his head. Guilliman frowned, and nodded.

'Gentlemen, this will have to wait a few moments, though I will see all your plans today, I promise. Please, while you wait, Captain Felix will arrange some refreshments for you.'

Felix's brows drew together in consternation. The crawler's provisions amounted to tepid recycled water and emergency biscuit rations. Guilliman trusted him to organise something. If anyone could source suitable victuals from nowhere, Felix could. The expression on Felix's face was almost comical. Guilliman resisted the urge to reassure him. The Primaris captain had to learn to trust himself. Felix was too unsure of his own abilities and he would need them all, soon enough.

'This way,' Felix said, herding the artisans into the crawler's small stateroom. 'I shall see if we can find some wine.'

The men and women filtered through the door with unsure glances behind them. When they were all through, Guilliman addressed Felix.

'Thank you, captain. I shall not be long.'

'He is outside, my lord.'

Guilliman left the crawler deck. Comfort had not been a high priority in the vehicle's design. It was cramped enough for a standard human, but Guilliman had to stoop to negotiate its corridors, bending almost double to squeeze his way through the doors.

Outside the sound-screened command level, the thunder of the machine's workings made itself known. Guilliman's ears buzzed to the sound of thumping pistons. The crawler was idling at that moment. The din it made while it was in motion was astounding in volume.

Guilliman stopped outside the crawler master's cabin and

knocked on the door. The master was made of sterner material than the architects, and looked only mildly surprised to see the Imperial Regent standing outside his private chamber.

'Be at ease, Master Fulpin. I have come only to tell you we have not yet finished,' said Guilliman. 'I have received a visitor. We will need to impose on your hospitality a while longer.'

'My command deck is yours as long as you require it, my lord,' said Fulpin with a smart bow. 'I welcome the rest.'

Guilliman peered past the man's shoulder. His room was crammed with papers and data-slates.

'Your idea of rest accords with mine,' said Guilliman. 'No rest.'

'Service to the Emperor never finishes, my lord,' said Fulpin. 'There is always more to do.'

Guilliman nodded. 'I will send word when we are done.'

He left the master and continued down the corridor. The crew were taking their unscheduled break from work more in earnest than their leader. Loud conversation came from the crawler's common room as he passed it, the men inside laughing and playing musical instruments, ignorant that the master of the Imperium was only a few feet from them.

He followed steps downwards, emerging from a double gate set behind the crawler's dozer blade. He picked his way over massive hydraulic systems, and emerged onto the plain.

An Ultramarine stood waiting for him, his crested helm held under one arm. His armour had already acquired a layer of dust, but the green trim of the Fourth Company shone beneath, and his honours were so numerous that his rank was without doubt.

'Captain Ventris,' said Guilliman, walking to stand beside him. 'My apologies for keeping you waiting. You have come a long way to see me.'

Ventris turned and dropped to his knee. 'My lord primarch.' He bowed his head, and kept his eyes on the floor.

'Please, my son,' said Guilliman, 'you need not bow before me.'

Ventris remained kneeling. 'My lord, forgive me. I have not had the honour of meeting you. My duties kept me away from Macragge when you returned.'

'Performing your duty is not an error, captain. I do not accept your apology, for there is no need for one.'

'It feels important that I should have been there.'

'You are here now,' said Guilliman. He took a step towards Ventris, his hand out. 'Please.'

The captain did not rise. 'I have spoken with my brothers about you, listened to everything they had to report. Not a word of it does justice to actually being here. I have wished with all my being to stand in your living presence, but I did not expect this. I expected to feel something. To see a primarch is something from a tale, I thought, but this is no fiction, and I am confounded.'

'You may stand.'

'But… but, my lord, I cannot stand.' Ventris looked up at Guilliman, his battle-worn face made young by wonder.

'Then I command you to stand,' said Guilliman. Ventris' reaction touched and irritated him equally. 'Look upon me as a father, not as a lord. You are of my line, and a son to me.'

'As you command.' Uriel Ventris stood slowly, his armour's motive systems growling loudly, as if they too were awestruck. The captain searched the face of his gene-father. Guilliman looked down on him. For all the captain's meek reaction, the primarch could sense the defiance in him, the rage, the desire to serve.

The spell broke. Ventris smiled a little sheepishly. 'Severus warned me about this,' he said, shaking his head. 'He warned me, and I did not believe him. "I will not lose my head," I told him. I can see his face now when I tell him that I did.'

Ventris stood tall and saluted. 'My apologies. Captain Agemman was right.'

'It is nothing,' said Guilliman. He held out his hand. Ventris reached out and grasped it firmly, unhesitant now. 'I am pleased to make your acquaintance finally. Your reputation precedes you.'

'Not all of it is good, my lord,' said Ventris.

'If rules and customs remain unbroken, Uriel, then they become meaningless – either redundant from misuse, or so strong and overwhelming that they become walls to the mind, blocking out the truth of what they were intended to protect. I assume you have been sent to represent First Captain Agemman at the triumph. You must also have a message for me if you interrupt my work with the architects.'

Ventris dipped his head in a bow. 'I have. The war in Ultramar has entered a new phase. Three large forces have issued forth from the Scourge Stars. The *Endurance*, the ship of Mortarion, lord of the Death Guard, leads a fleet towards Ultramar.'

Guilliman nodded thoughtfully. 'So he comes out at last, as I expected. It was only a matter of time. With Magnus abroad in the Imperium again, I expected more of my brothers to leave their fortresses behind and venture forth once more.' Guilliman paused. 'Has Mortarion actually been seen? Deception was not favoured by him when last we met, but he has had long years to learn new tricks.'

'He appeared in person at the sacking of Daedallos. An astropathic message was sent with pict encoding. Once the metaphors were processed, we had a good image of him.'

'Daedallos? What was the fate of that world?'

'High casualties, and large amounts of toxicity. Disease is rife where Mortarion's dogs go. They poison the earth, though once they move on, their influence dies somewhat – the pollution they bring is not entirely natural and requires the presence of the traitors to remain virulent, or so Chief Librarian Tigurius says.' Ventris shrugged. 'It is psychic in nature, Librarius business. That being said, they bring mundane pestilence with them also. Daedallos will take years to recover.'

'He did not destroy the world?'

'No, my lord – he attacked, slaughtered the auxilia there and withdrew before we could respond.'

'Then he shows himself deliberately,' said Guilliman. 'Daedallos has little strategic importance. Mortarion is seeking to draw you out and put you on guard.'

'He has done more than that. We have reports of his presence in four of the core systems. Wherever he goes, rebellion follows. Lately he has changed his approach, and gathered a large fleet to himself. He is holding position in the Macragge System. His fleet is too large for defence fleets to engage head-on, but too small to attack Macragge itself. Ardium is blockaded, and two of its hives under attack. His presence has led to a wave of unrest across all six planets of the home system. Our people are not immune to the draw of Chaos. We spend much of our time putting down death cults, or dealing with outbreaks of disease. Under the cover of these distractions, he sends in small strike teams to attack crucial infrastructure. I would not say that Macragge is under siege, but it is close to being so.'

'What is his game, I wonder?' mused Guilliman to himself. 'These attacks,' he said firmly. 'They appear random, but they will not be.'

'Severus assumes so. He is yet to determine their intent.'

Guilliman appeared displeased. 'These are poor tidings,' he said. 'Espandor is not yet taken?'

'Espandor stands,' said Ventris. 'The enemy has been escalating their attacks on Espandor Prime, but Fifth Captain Phelian has thwarted them all, and they have not been able to make sufficient gains elsewhere that would allow the traitors to concentrate their assets and overwhelm the system. While its supply lines are open, Espandor will not fall.'

'That is at least something.'

'My lord, I do not mean to dampen your mood, but Espandor cannot hold out for long. All the system worlds besides the prime are in the hands of the foe, and their ships resupply freely there.'

'Perhaps I have delayed too long,' said Guilliman, once more lapsing into thought. 'Come with me,' he said abruptly. 'I have been closeted all day. I need to move.' The primarch set off alongside the crawler. Sixteen giant wheels lined the side, twice Guilliman's height, their hard plastek treads caked with sand. 'What is the composition of the other forces?'

'A smaller fleet of Death Guard ships terrorises the outer regions,' replied Ventris. 'The lead vessel appears to be the *Terminus Est*. This is the ship of–'

'Callas Typhon, First Captain of the Death Guard.'

'That was once his name, so the legends go. He is known as Typhus to us.'

'Yes, of course,' said Guilliman.

'Typhus' fleet is of lesser concern,' continued Ventris, 'though he has already taken the star fortress of Eumenice, and is concentrating his attacks against the others. We can be thankful that where he goes, Mortarion does not. Most of the Death Guard congregate around their traitor primarch. The larger danger is posed by the third force, a daemonic horde. They are slipping in and out of real space at will, and we do not know how. Lord Tigurius has undertaken a mission to the outer reaches to determine the reason. The daemons have returned to the empyrean for the moment, but the warp grows turbulent around

Ultramar, and the Librarius and our astropaths are certain that they will return. The enemy is planning something, the First Captain is sure. Tartella was ravaged recently by the daemons. The governor survived, but reports casualty rates of over ninety-eight per cent. The daemon leading this force has been identified as Ku'Gath, that calls itself the Plaguefather. Further sightings have been made in three other systems, always fleeting, but verifiable. Furthermore their appearances come close after, or simultaneously with, those of Mortarion.'

Ventris stopped, and looked at his gene-sire earnestly.

'My lord, Mortarion and his daemonic allies are engaged in something ill-favoured. Ultramar is in peril. When I departed, there were one hundred and six active war fronts across the realm. Of course, this number changes all the time. Fourteen days have passed in Ultramar since we left, at my best calculation. That is long enough for the situation to have altered, and I fear for the worse.'

'Your report gives me an adequate picture of the challenges faced by the First Captain,' said Guilliman. 'You were entrusted to deliver this to me personally to prevent the information falling into enemy hands, I take it?'

'There have been too many instances of the enemy anticipating our moves, my lord,' replied Ventris. 'We do not know how, but they are intercepting and accurately interpreting our astropathic sendings. For the most delicate messages, we have come to rely on messenger ships.'

'Mortarion wants to force my return to Ultramar,' said Guilliman. 'He chooses his moment perfectly. He knows I will have no choice but to respond.'

They continued, passing out of the shadow of the command crawler, and came to where the square of triumph began. The plain ended at a low wall. Above the level of the sand the gleaming plaza stretched away, perfectly level, to where the great machines continued their work a mile off. The sunlight of 108/Beta-Kalapus-9 made feeble attempts to penetrate the pall of dust thrown up by their remodelling of the world. The air was thin but breathable, and through it a cold, soft wind blew, scattering sand over the freshly polished mosaic.

'Nothing lasts,' said Guilliman, watching the gleam of the tesserae dulling under the falling dust. 'Our efforts are too often temporary.'

He was quiet a moment. Ventris waited expectantly.

'Tell me, Captain Ventris, what is the progress of the reconsolidation of Greater Ultramar?'

'That is another poor story,' said the captain reluctantly. 'Agemman is being obstructed in his efforts. Disputes as to what was in Ultramar and what was not are delaying plans to reconstitute the Five Hundred Worlds as it was in your day. Recalcitrant governors are exploiting our ignorance. Our historical record is incomplete, my lord. We do not have a definitive map of Ultramar during your time. The Mappa Guillimanus in the Library of Ptolemy was damaged millennia ago. The surviving complete maps show the realm at various stages of expansion, or after your division of it, but not at Ultramar's height. Many of the documents you drew up to grant sovereignty to local planetary commanders are lost. But things progress. We believe three-quarters of the ancient realm of Ultramar is back under the direct stewardship of Macragge.'

'Agemman has a list and a map I drew from memory,' said Guilliman. 'It carries my seal, and the full weight of Imperial authority. I have that map depicted in the window of my Hall of Armaments. There is nothing to argue about.'

'Some of the worlds dispute the proof. They are more than glad to welcome our warriors, but the Imperial governors in two dozen systems quibble over reaffirming their oaths of loyalty. In one case, we have had an outbreak of intra-system civil war over the issue, where one lord has declared for you and three against. Some lie outright, telling us they were never part of Ultramar. Perhaps some of them sincerely believe it. A few are braver and insist the ancient treaties cannot be revoked, even by you, my lord, and are determined to retain their independence.'

'They are wrong,' said Guilliman.

Ventris watched a small wheeled transport speed across the plaza towards the construction line, throwing up a plume of settled dust that drifted back down as it passed. 'They are... disquieted by the fate of some of their peers.'

'Only those who rule poorly have anything to fear,' said Guilliman.

'It is, naturally, the more autocratic rulers who oppose your rescinding of their independence.'

'Then they only delay the inevitable,' said Guilliman. 'They will fall into line and ask politely for mercy, or they will be executed.' He watched a giant earthshaper grind an outcropping of rock flat in an instant, belching out a fine spray of pulverised stone. A furnace on its trailer puffed smoke as it baked the harvested material into rockcrete powder. The stone would soon be returned to the plain in this new form by the foundation teams.

'I should never have set the Five Hundred free,' he said.

'My lord?' said Ventris.

'I should not have done it,' repeated Guilliman. 'I thought I was doing the right thing. I thought I was following the Emperor's wishes, letting men rule the affairs of men.' He gave a rueful smile. 'After I implemented the Codex Astartes and split the Legion, I thought it impossible for a force of one thousand battle-brothers to effectively govern such a large realm and perform their primary duty as guardians of the Imperium. My

Legion was gone, and I did not want the Chapter that continued their traditions to become insular. They would have been distracted, perhaps never left Ultramar, had they Five Hundred Worlds to govern.'

'Maybe,' said Ventris. 'Perhaps we could have managed, my lord. I think your decision was wise.'

'Was it wise?' said Guilliman. He began walking again, turning around the rear of the crawler to where the untouched plains began.

In that direction there was little evidence of the battle or of construction. Away from the industry of change, 108/Beta-Kalapus-9.2 looked as it probably had done for millions of years: cold, flat and mostly lifeless. Like Mars in the time before man. The temperature had dropped a few degrees in the last century. What did that mean to a place like this? A little more frost, a little less light. Without intervention, the sun would eventually be swallowed by the Pit and 108/Beta-Kalapus-9.2 would freeze completely. There would be no one to care. The world was so barren. Guilliman pitied the Space Marines he would station here, but places like the Pit of Raukos needed guarding. Countless baseline humans and transhumans suffered to maintain the watch upon the Imperium's new, terrifying borders. Such was service to the Emperor.

'I am no longer convinced,' continued Guilliman. 'One of my sons, a man much like you as it happens, once warned me against pride. I thought I had avoided its vices, but there are many kinds of pride, and it had a part to play in my decision to shrink Ultramar. You see, I wanted the Ultramarines to be out there, among the stars. I wanted their legacy to continue.' He stopped again, sweeping his gaze across the desert's low, arid hills. 'Does that make me selfish, my son?'

Ventris did not know what to say. The primarch continued.

'There was a more practical consideration. I did not wish

to set the precedent of Chapters of Space Marines ruling large portions of the Imperium. What good would it have been to remove the use of Legions from potential tyrants, only to turn the legionaries into tyrants themselves? The Emperor made it clear that governorship of the Imperium was to be undertaken by mortal men, not by the Legiones Astartes, or we primarchs. If the Ultramarines were left masters of the Five Hundred Worlds, it opened a potential avenue of corruption. I would not have the existence of Ultramar be the spur to the creation of a thousand small empires, because I could not trust others to replicate what we have at home. Warriors make poor lords. The likes of the Empire of Iron was the more likely outcome than a crop of new Ultramars.'

The reference to the Iron Warriors' short-lived, Heresy-era realm was lost on Ventris, but he kept his silence while the primarch continued to speak.

Guilliman looked to the sky. Past the veils of dust, the atmosphere was so thin that the brightest stars shone in the day and the lights of ships in orbit were visible. 'And yet I return to life and find the entire Imperium a prison for its people. By avoiding one problem, I created another. If I had left Ultramar intact, more worlds would have been havens from such pain and remained centres of reason. A bigger beacon burns brighter. I should have left it whole, as an example of what can be.'

The primarch turned to his son. 'You are so many generations removed from the original founding. You remain true to the Imperium. The dedication of the Ultramarines is a testament to the spirit of Ultramar and the will of the Emperor. It would have been better had more worlds been in your keeping. You must understand why I did what I did. I watched half my brothers fall to Chaos, and became determined that no one should ever hold the power of a Legion again. I became obsessed with the potential misuse of a few hundred thousand Space Marines, and in doing so I forgot about the petty self-interest of lesser men. This is I, whose preoccupation was to hurry the Great Crusade to an end so that I could get on with the business of peace!' He laughed at himself. 'Perhaps I would have failed, even if I had lived longer. These rulers who deny my seal and my right to revoke our treaties, they are not evil, they are not stupid, they are simply limited as all men are limited.'

Guilliman fell silent, then smiled sadly. 'Does it shock you, my son, to learn a primarch can err?'

Ventris looked uncomfortable. 'My heart says yes, but that primarchs can be mistaken is an obvious conclusion when the argument is reasoned through, my lord,' he said. 'Your admission does nothing to lessen my respect for you. We of the Ultramarines remain human, despite our transformation. We make mistakes. As a son grows, he learns that his father is not infallible, whether he is glorious or humble.'

'Sometimes I wonder if I am human at all,' said Guilliman thoughtfully. 'In any meaningful sense.'

'If you were not, you would not care for the fate of other men.'

'Many of my brothers did not. Maybe it is an affectation?'

'Humanity is not measured on form alone, but by deeds, my lord,' said Ventris. 'A mortal man may be inhuman towards other men, yet I have seen xenos behave with honour and fairness when we offer them nothing but hate.'

Guilliman appraised the Fourth Captain carefully. 'You impress me, Captain Ventris. I have heard much about your deeds. I did not expect you to be so thoughtful.'

'Your principles persist, my lord,' said Ventris modestly. 'You are right to say warriors make poor rulers, so we strive to be more, to be wise men who would govern fairly, for the good of the greatest number, as you taught in the great days.'

'Yet the day when my sons shall set aside their weapons seems impossible now,' the primarch replied. 'That was always my intention. After the Great Crusade, you were all to become administrators and statesmen. It seems so naive. Look at this.' He gestured to the baleful light of the Pit smeared by the dusty air.

An explosion rumbled out from the hills where the walls had closed the valley. A slope collapsed, leaving a blank stone cliff. Before the detritus had finished rolling out from the base, excavators were clearing the rubble, and scaffolds being wheeled into position for the artisans who would carve the bedrock into statues.

'Have heart, my lord, we are statesmen still. We talk. We reason. Some of the first generation of Primaris brothers remember the days when you walked among us – to hear some of their stories is remarkable. Their presence has helped with some cases of dissension. They speak so eloquently of the ancient times, and of the unity of the old Ultramar, that several governments saw that their opposition to reunification was not to the taste of their peoples. Peaceful means do not elude us in all disputes.'

'This is a war. All weapons are valid, Captain Ventris. Propaganda is one, and what I have done is still propaganda, even if it is the truth.'

'Your frankness is a credit.'

'There have been too many lies,' said Guilliman.

'And this work here, my lord, this is also a weapon?'

'A triumph is a statement. I ape the exultation of Horus at Ullanor, maybe, but such displays are important. The last of the Unnumbered Sons are to be assigned to their Chapters. I have kept the formations in service as long as I dare. I was accused of recreating the Legions I disbanded right at the start of the crusade. That talk has only grown. I have to make a show of doing it properly and thoroughly. The order has gone out to the other fleets. The Greyshields will be no more.'

'A shame.'

'Necessary,' said Guilliman. 'I am not the only power in the Imperium. This is a criticism I cannot stop any other way. Internal division will kill the Imperium as surely as Abaddon would. My situation is precarious, politically. Our success in stabilising the situation in Imperium Sanctus breeds complacency. Those fools on Terra see our victories and begin to scheme again. They forget that the forces of Chaos and xenos alike run rampant. They forget that Imperium Nihilus still waits for us. If I could, I would return to Terra and make them see sense, but I cannot. Preparations for the crossing into Nihilus proceed. There is the war in Ultramar. We have no lasting victory – the Imperium teeters on the brink still – but I will make this last hurrah of the Greyshields here at Raukos seem like one.'

Guilliman turned back to the plain.

'I know why you have come to me, captain. I cannot return home, not yet. I must make a statement of intent, and it must be made carefully. The last of the brotherhoods have to be divided and commanded well, and the process must be coordinated across all the crusade fleets. I cannot hasten through. Just as much as they must see me disband these so-called legions, the people of the galaxy cannot see me running home the moment Ultramar is in danger.

'Soon I will ask so much of them. For generations they have oiled the machines of war with their blood. They have wet the harvest ground with their tears. They have sent their children away to die. This is but the least I shall be forced to ask of them in the coming years. What I have won here is just the beginning. To conclude this endless war will require sacrifice from everyone – man, woman and child. I need to show them we can win, that I am in control, that I am no tyrant. I cannot do that if I leave now.'

'Mortarion is abroad, my lord,' said Ventris. 'He threatens Ultramar itself.'

'Ultramar is not the Imperium,' said Guilliman softly. 'If it were, perhaps none of this would ever have happened. But it has. Ultramar is crucial to my plans, but I cannot be seen to favour my own home over the worlds of every other sector. Fear not, captain. We will return as soon as the business here is done. I will drive my brother away from Ultramar, and I swear that when I leave to free the rest of the Imperium, the realm will be better organised, better fortified and better able to deal with whatever may come in the future. But that time is not yet. Tell Agemman to hold the line. I trust him to ensure Macragge will still be there when I come home.'

Ventris bowed. 'I shall have your response sent immediately–'

Guilliman held up his hand. His earpiece was buzzing.

'Captain Felix,' he said, 'can you not encourage our guests to wait a little longer?'

It is not for their sake that I interrupt you, my lord, voxed Felix. *There is a priority request from the palace. Master-Astropath Losenti has received a message from Archmagos Cawl.*

'I will attend immediately. Make my apologies to the architects. Have the plans of the Chapter fortress sent to my scriptorium. I will examine them tonight.' He turned to the Fourth Captain. 'Forgive me, but I must leave. It appears I am in demand today.'

Roboute Guilliman sent a message to his personal shuttle, commanding the crew to make ready for flight, and departed, leaving Captain Ventris alone to watch a battleground transformed into a symbol of Imperial might.

CHAPTER ELEVEN

ESPANDOR REMEMBERED

Varens dreamed. He was back in the trenches of Espandor, as he had been every time he had slept on his journey to Iax on the ward-ship, and every night since.

Espandor was always so real in these dreams that it felt like he was there again. The ankle-deep water stank just as bad. The sky was just as dark. The rising and falling drone of flies was just as monotonous. The fear was just as real.

He and Bolus were on the line. The broken city of Konor's Reach was behind them and miles of shattered trees were in front of them, mist wrapped tight about them like a funeral shroud. Death was everywhere. This was the War of the Flies, the Creeping Doom offensive. The campaign on Espandor was but one of many plaguing Ultramar. To Varens it was the only one that mattered.

Greasy rain pelted them, not sufficiently acidic to burn the skin, but over time it degraded a uniform's fabric and caused boots to disintegrate. Feet exposed to the mud rotted. Compromised bioseals let in disease. The enemy had myriad ways to kill a man; the rain was only one. The mist, laced with infection and chemical poison, was another, though it was thin enough today that Varens and Bolus risked leaving their respirators and goggles off for a while. Intense claustrophobia afflicted many of the troops on the line.

Varens twitched at a tickling sensation on his back. A moment later he felt it again, coming up over his shoulder and onto his neck, then brushing his ear. His skin crawled and he swatted at his head without thinking, mashing a fat fly against his helmet. With a grimace, he wiped the mess off onto his filthy uniform, adding pale, pus-streaked smears to the crust covering his gloves.

'Even in the damn rain the flies don't let up,' said Bolus. 'If there's one thing I hate about this war, it's the bloody flies.' He waved more of them away from his face. 'Suppose that's why they call it the War of the Flies.' He grinned.

The warriors either side of Bolus and Varens had tight faces, white with fear. One of them attempted to smile; the rest of them remained glazed.

'Cheerful bunch,' muttered Bolus.

'Go easy on them, acting sergeant,' said Varens. Another fly buzzed too close to his face. He blew out at it, disrupting its lazy flight.

'I'll go easy on you before I go easy on them.'

'They're in for a hard ride, then,' said Varens. 'I'd rather face the enemy than another scolding from you.'

Their exchange was purposefully inflated with bravado, but what they intended to be wry and sardonic came across as forced, and it had little effect on the morale of the recruits. All their other squad members were new. Casualties were high. Of Varens' last squad, only six were left, and they'd been split and incorporated into fresh units to stiffen the resolve of the newcomers.

'Fresh meat goes off quick in this war.' That's what Bolus had said about them. That didn't make the rookies smile either.

This had happened so many times, Varens was close to losing count. He didn't bother to repaint his unit markings any more, not that they could be seen under the filth of Espandor's battle-fields anyway.

He rotated his shoulder. The tickle returned with the hint of a sting. Another fly, probably, looking for weaknesses in his double-thickness uniform. The damn things were bloodsuckers, all of them.

A civilised cardinal world with broad expanses of wilderness, Espandor had been a place of cool forests. With human settlement restricted to the cities of the western continent and the lesser agri-complexes scattered across its warmer zones, the planet's woods and oceans had been left in a near pristine state. Or so the pre-mission edifications had said when Varens arrived, two interminable years ago now. He had only ever known it as a sea of mud, a moribund place plagued by the dead who came shambling from the wastelands every seven hours, regular as manufactorum shift changes.

Several of the larger civitae were gone. Trench lines surrounded the remaining three. Their hinterlands were seas of mud, the patchwork of forests and agricolae levelled to provide fields of fire. The assaults of the dead were therefore severely hampered. The dead were slow, and the Ultramar Auxilia's guns many. The enemy's diseases were rife, the population was a shadow of what it had been and the planet had ceased to be a productive part of Ultramar in any way, but though Espandor was sick, it was still alive.

'Still Imperial, still Ultramarian, still living. Fight for it with every breath in the primarch's name, for that is the will of the Emperor,' Varens whispered to himself. After that, he had no more time for prayer, for the seventh-hour klaxon blared, and the enemy came lurching out of the mist.

'Here comes today's batch!' shouted their lieutenant, his amplified voice distorted by the voxmitters attached to his comms-operator's pack. 'Hold the line. Prepare to fire on my mark.'

'Respirators on, men. Goggles down,' said Bolus. He snapped his equipment into place over his mouth and eyes by way of example. His next words were muffled. 'Make sure the seal's tight on your body suit. Don't get their filth on you.'

Varens got down off the firing step to help a panicking young soldier who was failing to get his gear set right on his face.

'Your clip's twisted, that's all,' said Varens. He tugged off one dirty glove – not with his teeth, never that – adjusted the hood around the soldier's face and untwisted his strapping.

'With goggles and respirator on, there should be no exposed skin, and so the Emperor protects,' he said, setting the youth's mask in place, and then his own. 'Whisper your thanks to your battlegear, trooper. It will keep you alive.'

The young man nodded too hard. His eyes were wide with fear behind the yellow plastek of his combat goggles. Varens slapped his shoulder plate and moved on. The mortal warriors of Ultramar were better protected than most Astra Militarum regiments. Without this equipment they would lose half their number to sickness after every fight.

Varens checked his part of the squad over, patting backs and steadying nerves. When he was satisfied, he climbed out of the quagmire of the trench and took up position on the firing step again, resting his lasgun on the sodden wood of the parapet. The sting in his back became an annoying itch, but he barely noticed it. The time had come to fight.

Slowly, the enemy emerged from the driving rain. Their

silhouettes were human, their gait anything but, a shambling, jerky walk that betrayed their nature from afar.

The dead of Espandor came to war.

One of the recruits gasped, the humanity strangled out of his exhalation by his respirator. A sharp las-crack had Varens turning; a shocked, boyish face looked back at him. Rain steamed off the muzzle of the recruit's lasgun.

'Hold fire.' Lieutenant Attinus' voice crackled over the squad vox.

Bolus rested his hand on the body of the gun. His damp glove hissed as it brushed the barrel. Heat radiated off the power pack. 'Wait, son, you need to be precise. Shooting at this distance is a waste of charge. Rain and fog disperses the light. You don't want to be swapping out your pack while those things are clawing at your face. Every shot saved is another to fire when you need it. Save it until the command comes. Aim for the heads. Always the heads,' he added, looking meaningfully up and down the line.

Those of the young soldiers who had grasp of their wits nodded and leaned into their gunstocks. A couple stared tearfully out, gazes fixed. The auxilia ordinarily had excellent training, but the needs of the war meant these recruits had been hurried through. They were conscripts, and they were raw.

The shapes of the dead solidified. Their torn and dirty clothes were whole enough to give hints as to their origins. They had been civilians, mostly. There were a few Astra Militarum uniforms among them. If a position fell, it wasn't always possible to behead and burn the bodies.

'We're fighting ourselves,' a trooper said. Unease rippled down the line.

Varens cursed the boy inwardly for speaking the truth. 'Quiet there. Guns up. Take aim.'

A soft tattoo of clicks and rattles undercut the drumming of the rain as his order was obeyed. Other sergeants and veterans gave their own commands, and the parapet grew a leafless hedge of las-barrels pointing into the blasted forest.

There was no bombardment. Too many times the dead had clawed their way back up from the earth, taking the defenders by surprise, and shells for the big guns were running low. Espandor was remote, always had been, right at the edge of Ultramar. Supply had become increasingly difficult as the Plague Fleets stepped up their activities. Even back in the days of the Five Hundred Worlds, it had been isolated, though when so many other worlds had been cut loose from the Ultramarines' realm, Espandor had remained within the fold.

The dead staggered onwards, slack expressions on their faces. They did not speak or make any sound. Only the sucking of the mud at their feet and the drumming of the rain accompanied their march. Their flesh was rent, innards hanging from split stomachs, greening muscles exposed in ragged skin. There was no way an organism like that could function. All the men stationed on Espandor knew the dead were born of warpcraft. The commissars ruthlessly dealt with any soldier found speaking of such things, but they were facing unnatural monsters. Sorcery. It could not be denied.

Varens let out a tense sigh. His breath was sour in his mask.

From away down the line one of the last regimental priests bellowed prayers. The dead turned away from that quadrant as if ordered. Varens wished there were more holy men. Cardinals ruled Espandor in the name of the Adeptus Ministorum, though it was subordinate to Macragge, and so there were many men who claimed to be holy in its cities. But the priests of the world rarely came to the front. They were busy beseeching the Emperor to turn away the clouds of flies from the cities, they said, and tending to the many sick, and overseeing the disposal of the dead before they could reawaken. They said they had their hands full.

Varens thought them cowards.

He had been terrified at the sight of plague zombies in the beginning, but Varens' fear lessened with each exposure. For all the horror of their being, the dead were clumsy. They were only dangerous in large numbers, and these assaults, though unpleasant, were easily dealt with.

Once a theatre of war like Espandor would have attracted the attentions of the Ultramarines themselves, but there were worse things attacking their empire, and they were needed elsewhere. There were supposedly Space Marines on Espandor somewhere. Varens couldn't say if that were true. He had never seen them.

The dead drew closer, lips smacking wordlessly together in a parody of living speech.

'*Fire!*' roared Lieutenant Attinus.

Ruby las-lights stabbed out from the trench. The air cracked. Rain hissed loudly into steam, generating rank, warm clouds that settled on the line and thickened the fog.

'*Fire!*' ordered the lieutenant again.

Multiple las-beams riddled the corpse walkers. The dead began their dance, jigging as beams of coherent light blasted divots from their ruined bodies, but still they did not fall.

'Aim for the heads!' shouted Bolus at the recruits. He snapped off a shot at a lurching shape, pierced already with half a dozen black holes. Though the flesh was cauterised, the wounds leaked black fluid. Bolus cursed as his shot tore off the thing's ear, and he adjusted his aim.

Varens felled the one behind Bolus' mark, trusting the acting sergeant to make his next shot count. He had a glimpse of a filthy officer's uniform on the dead man, a priceless power sword scabbarded at his side.

'Men! They are dead, but they will die anew. Hit them in the heads!' shouted Varens.

Bolus' second shot was true, taking the approaching plague walker full in the face. Its head disintegrated and it died its second death.

It got darker. The fog thickened in front of their line. Scattered silhouettes became a shadowy mass.

'Damn it, there's a knot of them coming this way.' Bolus spoke into his respirator's integrated vox-bead. 'This is Acting Sergeant Bolus, Fourth Squad, Second Platoon, requesting fire support on my quadrant immediately.'

The veterans of Espandor reacted quickly. A heavy bolter dug into a projecting bunker fifty yards away banged loudly. Compact, self-propelled munitions burned through the mist on streaks of flame numerous enough to light it up. The bolts cut the dead to pieces, burying themselves in their flesh and exploding, scattering gobbets of rancid corpse meat.

The men on the line let out a premature cheer. But the dead were not done with them. Many remained. More hauled their broken bodies across the mire with crippled limbs, immune to pain. Las-beams snapped out at them, but too many of the recruits fired wildly, and things that should have died in the kill-zone reached the trench line. There they simply toppled forwards, landing with bone-cracking force in the mud at the bottom of the trench, or fell onto hapless troopers. Those that didn't land upon a target flopped about, stiff arms and legs twisting as they struggled to right them- selves, teeth snapping at the legs of the living. Most of the recruits remembered the drill and moved out of the way, but not all.

'Quick! Don't let them bite you! Kill them!' ordered Varens. He drew his pistol and put a shot into the head of a foe struggling with a new recruit. 'One bite and you'll be like them. The heads, the heads! Aim for the heads!'

A scream had him whirling around as another dead man fell on top of a recruit. Teeth, unnaturally white in the ruin of a face, clashed at the soldier's neck. The plague zombie bore the soldier down off the step. The creature was naked but for a helmet still snugly strapped about its chin. Blurred regimental tattoos marked its upper arms. Varens' first shot was deflected by the helmet, the second cored it through. The reanimated corpse died, head dripping molten plasteel and rotten brains. Varens was at the youth's side before the corpse had collapsed, dragging him from the muck and shaking the shock out of him.

'Are you all right?'

The recruit stared mutely back. Varens checked the seals around his mouth and eyes and shoved him back against the wall. The last few dead were being permanently put down, and no more had reached the trench line. Out over the wasteland others were falling, speared through the head by ruby light. The fresh soldiers seemed to have finally caught on.

'Varens!' Bolus called, motioning him over.

'We didn't lose anyone,' said Varens.

Bolus shook his head grimly. 'It's not over yet. This is something new. Listen!'

Varens struggled to see anything. The fog had thickened further with steam from las-fire, and the rain was coming down harder, reducing visibility to a hundred feet.

A dirge came out from the murk.

'All is ash, all is ash, all is ash.'

The words were wet and thick, carried on breath from lungs full of fluid up throats clogged with phlegm, and uttered by swollen lips.

'All is ash, all is ash, all is ash,' they droned.

The words were laden with loss and sorrow, and the inevitability of the end. They sent a chill down Varens' spine. Hysterical giggles and guffaws of mirth interrupted the chant, as if the chanters performed some sacred duty they could not take entirely seriously. That made it worse. The new recruits wavered.

Behind the last few staggering dead stalked bloated giants. The grinding of ancient motors sounded out their every step. Though spikes and unholy adornments had changed their shapes from their intended form, there was no mistaking what they were.

'Guilliman save us,' said Bolus. 'Heretic Astartes.' Behind his visor, his eyes shone with fear. 'Keep the lads in line,' he whispered. 'These aren't going to fall as easily as the dead.'

Varens' stomach tightened. He teetered on the brink of utter panic, but his training took over, and he nodded.

'All is ash, all is ash, all is ash,' chanted the enemy.

'Stand firm!' shouted Varens. 'Have faith in the Emperor! Trust to His protection and to your guns, and you will live!' He looked at the soldiers to his right. They gripped their guns tighter. All down the line, other veterans shouted similar encouragements and threats, or cursed the new men for cowards – whatever it took to keep them from breaking. Screamed orders to halt came from close by, followed by the single bang of a bolt pistol. They all knew what that meant. The recruits stilled. The certainty of death for those who fled versus the probability of death for those who stood firm steadied them. Silence filled the trench as surely as water.

'All is ash, all is ash, all is ash.' The drone persisted.

A quiet voice gibbered out of the mist. 'I don't like it, I don't like it, I don't like it.'

Bolus spoke into his vox-bead.

'Lieutenant Attinus, please advise actions regarding new foe,' he said. 'Lieutenant?' He looked at Varens. 'Not answering, damn him.'

One of their squad sank down to his knees to pray, his lasgun sliding from the saturated trench wall and landing in the slop at the bottom.

Bolus was on him in an instant, dragging him up.

'Get back on your feet!' he screamed in the young man's face. 'If you want to die on your knees, I'll shoot you myself and save the enemy the bother.'

A second later, the heavy guns opened up. This time there was no holding back. Shells rained down from artillery to the rear. Disgusting mud heaved skywards, cascading down over the trench lines. Man-portable heavy weapons added their fury to the storm descending on the traitors. Through the blizzard of earth, metal and fire, Varens saw a Plague Marine bisected by a lascannon blast. That one had the decency to die. The rest walked on as if the Medusa rockets, the heavy bolter shells and the rest of the Imperium's martial rage was of no more concern to them than the rain.

The barrage crept near to the lip of the trench, pelting the defenders with debris. A last whistling descent, a final explosion, and the shelling ceased, leaving fyceline smoke to wisp into the greater body of the fog.

The enemy was in range.

'*Give fire,*' ordered Attinus over the vox.

'Fire!' yelled Bolus, his voice raw-edged in panic.

A hundred lasguns blazed, their bright red light illuminating the mud and the visored faces lining the trench. It was a vision of some primitive netherworld, raw and bloody with punishment. Varens counted no more than twenty or so of the enemy giants, but their boldness in assaulting the position was justified. He watched as one was riddled with shots that would have blown apart any other target. The Plague Marine didn't even slow, but trudged onwards with his fellows as if nothing had happened, his armour smoking. All the while they chanted.

'All is ash, all is ash.'

The nearer the traitors came, the more awful details emerged. They were no longer fit to be called men. Space Marines once, they had sold themselves to fell powers for reasons no rational mind could comprehend. Diseases of every kind afflicted them. Their stomachs were distended, straining the capacity of their swollen wargear to contain them. Where exposed, their skin was inflamed or outright necrotic. Their innards dangled from corroded gaps in their armour. Mucus, urine, faeces, blood – every humour of the body dripped from them, all of it stinking and tainted with the hues of illness. Parasites wriggled freely into and out of their never-healing wounds. Their droning spoke of great misery, but on helmetless faces smiles shone. There was a joke they all knew, and they were eager to share it with the rest of the universe.

Though the wind blew away from the trenches, and though the auxilia's respirators were manufactured to strain out all atmospheric pollutants, the stink of the foe was overpowering, a charnel smell of rot that made Varens retch into his mask.

'All is ash, all is ash.'

Nonchalantly almost, the traitors levelled their weapons. Rusting boltguns and plasma guns whose cracked containment chambers sent out hissing jets of steam pointed at the line of heads exposed at the lip of the trench.

'All is ash, all is ash.'

As one, they opened fire. The boltguns banged as they ejected their munitions. A second louder bang sounded as the bolt-shells' jets ignited and accelerated them well past the sound barrier. The final noise, the one that had the boltgun rightly feared as a weapon, was a flat banging as the rounds slammed into soil and flesh, and there detonated with deadly force.

Varens' visor spattered with gore as the head of the soldier at his side was obliterated. He'd been with the unit two days. There had not been time to learn his name.

'Keep firing! Keep firing!' he shouted, over and over, until he was hoarse, but the blare and clatter of battle was so great he could not hear his own voice.

Then the flies came, despite the rain and the gunfire, and everything collapsed into confusion. They buzzed in swarms so thick they turned the air solid. Varens lost sight of the man nearest him. For a long second, he saw nothing, then the swarm was away and over him, and Varens looked death in the face.

The traitors had made their way to within yards of the trench. Directly opposite him, a giant in armour stained the violent turquoise of ocean-corroded iron turned his weapon upon Varens. He thought then he would surely die. Then the emplacements at either end of their section opened up, raking the traitors with fire. He watched in amazement as the Plague Marine's obese frame absorbed four heavy bolt-rounds, the explosions of their detonations in his massive body sending squirts of ichor out of the holes in his armour. The traitor shook, but did not fall. He only succumbed to the impact of the fifth, and keeled over like a rotten tree into the quagmire.

A new wave of flies battered against Varens' helmet, hard as death-world hail, obscuring his vision with swirling curtains of pale, furry bodies. Then they were gone once more, and the traitors were at the defences.

Three Heretic Astartes attacked Varens' section, tossing wizened heads before them that exploded like grenades. A choking gas filled the trench, and several men fell to the poisons within as the smoke ate through their respirators.

'All is ash, all is ash,' the traitors sang.

The Plague Marine nearest Varens stepped onto the edge of the trench. Dozens of las-beams found him. His corroded armour turned the light aside, or else the beams were absorbed by his monstrously bloated body. Pulsing, rotting organs hung through the ancient ceramite. Oil dribbled from the armour's ailing systems, and the reactor unit on his back hitched and coughed with the maladies of machines.

The plasteel facing gave way under the traitor's immense weight, and he rode the collapsing wall down, bringing a wave of sloppy mud and flesh with him.

He rose over Varens. Half his helmet had corroded away, exposing rotten teeth and a single yellowed eye. The remains of the helm looked like it had melted somehow into the warrior, becoming one with him, but incompletely so – the bottom still moved as a separate artefact, whereas at the top, rippled green skin melded with the metal into a semi-living mass dotted with suppurating boils. A grey horn sprouted sideways from the warrior's temple, the cracked mess at its root bleeding plasma.

Behind the giant, others fought with stolid efficiency, bludgeoning their way through the dozens of mortals who opposed them. There was shouting, and much weapons fire, and the crack of disruption fields as auxilia officers brought their power weapons to bear, but Varens saw only a little of it past the steaming, diseased bulk of the Plague Marine bearing down upon him.

The visible portion of the Heretic Astartes' face was bloated and pallid, the face of a man close to death, but a fevered mirth lit up his eye. Scabbed lips quivered with an avuncular chortle. He held up a clubbed hand whose little finger was a limp tentacle. A greening nail pointed at Varens.

'You first!' he said.

The Plague Marine raised a bolter flaking with rust. Such a thing should not have functioned, but the servants of Chaos were not bound by natural law. The heretic roared with laughter and the gun slammed out bolt-rounds. Varens threw himself aside as men were cut down all around him. Mass-reactive shells pierced bodies and detonated, tearing them into red scraps that were quickly lost to the mud.

'I said you first!' Mumbling annoyance, the Plague Marine stomped forwards, crushing the ribcage of a wounded auxiliary. Red-tinged water filled his bootprints.

He was monstrous, a blasphemy against mankind and his proper place in the universe, and he was unstoppable. Las-beams pattered off his armoured hide. Expanses of exposed, leathery skin hissed as they burned. The Plague Marine acted as if nothing were amiss.

'Father Nurgle waits for you in his garden, little man,' he said as he racked a final bolt into his gun and levelled it at Varens. 'Be glad, you go to a better place than this. When your joy has subsided at the sight of your new home, be sure to tell him Odricus of the Death Guard's Fifth Sept sent you.'

From nowhere Bolus appeared, ducking in under the Plague Marine's arm. The traitor moved to react, but his only weakness, or so it seemed, was that he was as slow as the dead he shepherded.

Bolus was not. He jammed his gun up and under the Heretic Astartes' helm. The creature growled as the weapon forced the helm's metal away from the conjoined flesh.

'So you can be hurt,' said Bolus. 'Good.'

The traitor wrapped his diseased hand around Bolus' throat. Bolus pulled the trigger.

Devised by the high sciences of the Emperor to withstand great damage, and made more resilient yet by the magics of Chaos, the Plague Marines of Nurgle were nigh on immune to harm. But they were not unkillable. Even they suffered from a point-blank lasgun shot to the face.

The traitor's head cracked open with a squelch. Smoky threads of atomised flesh rose from his helmet. From the ruins of his throat came a last, bubbling breath, and then he toppled forwards, landing squarely on top of Bolus and pushing him into the mud.

Bolus was buried by his dead foe; only his arm protruded from under the traitor's cracked battleplate.

Varens threw himself forwards and dug. Bolus' hand scrabbled madly. 'Hang on, Bolus! Hang on, my friend!'

As fast as Varens tried to hollow out a space so that he could drag Bolus free, it filled up with dirty water. Rank fluids from the dead Heretic Astartes seeped into the muck.

Bolus was drowning in that filth.

In desperation, Varens hooked his hands under the shoulder plates of the dead traitor and heaved. Corroded ceramite flaked to pieces in his grasp, and though the plate shifted on its joints, he could not move the bloated Space Marine. A tearing pain stabbed beneath his shoulder. He did not remember being hit, but that did not matter. He could not exert his full strength. It wouldn't be enough if he could. He might as well have pushed at Espandor and tried to move it as shift the dead traitor.

It seemed a long, desperate time, but perhaps only seconds passed.

Hands shoved him away, making space for others to join him. The new recruits were there. Two of them jammed retaining poles taken from the trench facing under the traitor's armour.

'Heave!' they shouted, using the beams as levers. 'Heave!' The poles slipped in the filth. Bolus' movements were lessening. His respirator had limited rebreathing capacity. He only had moments left.

'Dig deeper!' shouted Varens, scrambling up and grabbing one of the poles. 'Find solid ground to push against!'

He helped shove the plasteel down until it would go no

further, then he leapt for the top, hung off it and leaned backwards, ignoring the hot pain in his back.

'Heave!' shouted the young soldiers. Teeth gritted, they shifted the giant's shoulders enough to expose Bolus.

Two of the youths pulled the acting sergeant out the instant before the poles slipped and the traitor fell back into the mud. Varens grabbed Bolus' face.

'Bolus!' he shouted. He scraped mud off his friend's visor. Bolus stared back at him with wide eyes. He was silent, but alive.

The rain hammered down on a sudden quiet. The traitors were gone; whether dead or in retreat, Varens could not tell.

He had no time for relief. He suddenly felt very cold. A slow pulsing in his back told him he was hurt. Bolus stared up at him, his expression empty.

When this had happened back on Espandor, Bolus had been unharmed in body but something had gone in his mind. Varens had the wound on his back. They had been through triage and had been taken away from the front line on medical transports back to Konor's Reach. At the space port began the endless rounds of processing that had resulted in their evacuation to Iax.

That was then. Now, in the dream, nightmare departed from memory.

A movement within Bolus' flesh had Varens recoil in horror, but his hands would not obey him and he could not release his friend.

'Forty-nine! Forty-nine!' Bolus giggled. His mask filled with writhing maggots that burst from his shrivelling eyes. But he laughed on and on. 'All is ash!'

Varens awoke screaming into the silence of the medicae ward. Feeble hands shook him. Varens screamed again, and lashed out.

'Ouch!' The hands were removed. 'Shut up, Varens, we're trying to get some sleep,' groused Mukai, the man who had the cot next to his. He stood over Varens looking grumpy.

Consciousness came, displacing sleep just as rushing water sweeps away sand. The horror remained. Varens clamped his mouth shut to stifle the last of his screams.

Mutters from the beds nearby spoke of a lack of sympathy.

Varens fumbled for the water by his cot. His shaking hands knocked the plastek cup onto the floor.

'For the sake of the Emperor! Keep it down!' Hammadsen, the man on the other side, grumbled into his pillow.

'Sorry,' Varens said. He was awake now. He still needed a drink, so he slipped out from under the thin blanket and picked up his cup. His back twinged, but it was a good, healing pain.

Rubbing at his wound, he padded between the beds. The ward was a wide hall, with eight long rows of low cots. The men here were all injured in ways serious enough to warrant their evacuation, but not likely to be invalided. Nearly all of them would be sent back to the war, unlike the men on some of the other wards. There were halls in the hospital for whose occupants a hard life of poverty awaited, doing whatever work their disfigurements allowed. The very brave might be given augmetics and sent back to the front as morale-boosting examples. The rest would do what they could.

'For Ultramar, for the Imperium, for the grace of the Emperor,' he whispered under his breath. He made the sign of the aquila obsessively over his chest.

The lights in the small rest area calmed him down. Varens poured himself a cup of water that tasted of disinfectants. He drained it, pulling a face at the aftertaste. It was better than the water on Espandor, though, and in plentiful supply.

He had another cup, then started towards bed, but a

superstitious unease halted his steps, and before he knew it he was turning around and heading towards the ward where Bolus was.

A medicae in low-ranking grey sat in the chair outside, head bowed over a devotional pamphlet. He wore a small lamp over one eye that shone through the cheap paper, each splinter of wood in the pulp a strong detail against livid yellow. The hands holding it were just as blotted, and blunted by hard work.

'What do you want?' The medicae looked up, the lamp shining into Varens' face.

Varens held up his hand to shield his eyes. 'I came to see my friend, Bolus. He's in there. Patient 900018/43A?' He waved at the scratched glass partition. A large 'XVI' was stencilled onto it.

'What do you think you are doing? No visitors,' said the orderly. He looked back at his pamphlet.

'Please,' said Varens. 'It's not for him so much as for me. I... I have these nightmares. If I could see he's all right then I'll sleep better. If I sleep better, then I'll get out of here quicker, and be back to the fight.'

The orderly sighed and set his pamphlet aside, and looked up and down the corridor. He was the only man on duty. Unoccupied chairs sat outside the other wards.

'All right – just this once. No one's looking. But if I see you around here again, I'm reporting you. Do you understand?'

Varens nodded gratefully. 'Yes. Yes, thank you.'

The orderly took a ring of keys from his belt and unlocked the door. Checking they were unobserved again, he held it wide and ushered Varens in.

'One minute. Any disturbance, I'll see you shot.'

The halls for the psych cases were much smaller than those where the physically injured rested. During the day they were bedlams, but at night drugs brought merciful sleep. Machines pumped soporifics into arms chained to the sides of sturdy beds, keeping dreams at bay. Varens came to Bolus in eerie silence.

Varens looked down. Bolus wore a scowl that made him look like the hard man he had been. He was peaceful. Varens let out a sigh of relief.

On the way back to the door, he heard Bolus speaking. He should not have been able to, not with the drugs, but he was.

'Forty-nine,' Bolus mumbled. 'Forty-nine.'

CHAPTER TWELVE

THE CAWL INFERIOR

There was a place upon the *Macragge's Honour* where none were allowed to go but Roboute Guilliman, and he went by invitation only.

Guilliman's shuttle landed in his personal hangar bay. From there, the primarch went straight to the depths of his quarters. Located in a hidden space was a gene-locked elevator whose inbuilt weapons were primed to kill any other who attempted to access it. A simple retinal scan allowed him inside, but once he was within the elevator, the security protocols Guilliman underwent were extensive. Arcane devices extended from the walls to test his body, mental state and spiritual aura. One by one the machines croaked their approval, and the last withdrew into its recess. The elevator activated smoothly, descending two hundred decks in a matter of seconds. It stopped nowhere else. At the bottom, rear doors opened onto a chamber lit by rubicund light. His primarch's eyes struggled with the illumination. A mortal man would have been virtually blind.

The chamber was hot, loud with the chatter of hidden machinery and heavy with a sense of foreboding. Once through the doors on the far side of the chamber, that sensation would grow worse as Guilliman was exposed to Cawl's blasphemous device. But first he must undergo another series of tests. Again, he passed each one, and the chamber's inner doors opened into a second and much larger circular space, lit the same bloody colour. The doors were complex, three interleaving sets of yard-thick bonded hexsteel whose toothed edges clunked ominously as they unlocked from each other. The chamber's walls were similarly armoured. Cawl's machine would survive the death of the *Macragge's Honour* itself.

Guilliman readied himself for the greater psychic pressure and stepped inside.

His head throbbed. The air smelt of ozone, sanctified oil, curdled milk and old blood.

At sixty feet across, the interior space of the machine was modest by voidship standards. A grilled floor was suspended over a pit full of humming machines, dividing the interior space horizontally into two. Quieter than virtually every device Guilliman had seen in this era, the machines nevertheless made the room vibrate at a high frequency with the turning of their parts. Through the floor grille came the majority of the red light, confusing shadow and highlight and breaking down any visual sense of the space.

'Lumens!' barked Guilliman.

The machinery's high whine dropped to a grumble. The red crept down the walls, like fire dying. The metal of the room groaned in relief, as if the touch of the light had a physical effect upon it. Hard-white lumens snapped on above, banishing the sanguine glow beneath the flooring and bringing the room into sharp focus.

The chamber seemed smaller in the cleaner light, and its features were clearly resolved. A small door was set opposite the main gate. Closed panels at a man's eye level lined the walls between the two doors, ten on the left and ten on the right. Pipes bound tightly by metal staples hung in bundles from the ceiling. It was pure of form, if not of function. The Machina Opus glaring down from a rondel set into the domed ceiling was the sole decoration; even Belisarius Cawl was not radical enough to omit that symbol.

The room's other access slid upwards. It too comprised three massively thick doors that opened in sequence. On the far side were the quarters of Guidus Losenti. They were totally black, for Losenti had no need of light of any kind.

'My lord.' Losenti appeared in the doorway and came into the room. As he detached himself from the blackness, pools of it came with him in his eye sockets. His body appeared old and frail, but as he drew near the primarch, the inner strength that allowed Losenti to withstand the psychic pressure of the machine became palpable. There was great power clinging to him.

'I came as quickly as I could, master astropath,' said Guilliman.

Losenti smiled, the skin wrinkling around the darkness in his eyes, which, when one was close enough, revealed themselves to be shiny orbs of jet. Losenti paced across the floor to the Imperial Regent. As he walked, he placed his staff with utmost surety, the ferrule that capped the black wood never once slipping into the holes of the grating.

'To speak with my lord pleases me,' he said, stopping before Guilliman. Losenti had the voice of a much younger man.

'Are you well?'

'I am well.' With one blue-veined, pale hand, Losenti pulled back the green hood of his robes. His scalp was hairless, and his skull clearly defined under its covering of parchment-thin skin.

'I trust your duty remains onerous but bearable.'

'I thank you for your concern. I do not enjoy my duty, lord commander. By nature Cawl's sendings are exceptionally tedious, and lack the vitality one experiences when minds touch across the immensity of the void. I think he might use a machine, although once I would have said such a thing was impossible.' Losenti paused, waiting for Guilliman to confirm or refute this notion.

'Perhaps he does,' said Guilliman. 'Having witnessed what I have of his works, nothing would surprise me.'

'Be assured, I do not wish to change my life. Cawl's missives are so simple they suffer no corruption of the like that has plagued astrotelepathy since the opening of the Great Rift. There is no interference, no unwelcome intrusion. I am alone here, and isolated from my own kind, and that is hard to bear. The times I must be within the machine pain me greatly, but I am free from insanity, and as much as we all wish to serve the Imperium above all things, I admit to a certain sentimental attachment to my own life and soul.'

'If you ever crave release, Losenti, I can provide it.'

Losenti had a clear, youthful laugh to match his voice. Its brightness angered whatever skulked in the machine's depths, and the spiritual pressure grew. 'My lord, forgive me. We both are aware of what "release" means. I assure you, I am content. You may keep the mercy of your boltgun for the time being. Now, shall we begin?'

'If you would, master astropath.'

Losenti worked alone as his mission dictated. He had been selected from the strongest astropaths Guilliman could find. Among his many gifts, Losenti required no translator for his visions, but was able to recall the images from his fugues and explain them himself. Not a particularly unusual skill in an astropath, but a crucial one to the running of a machine that secrecy demanded have a sole operator, and when found in conjunction with his fortitude, rare indeed.

'By the will of the Omnissiah,' he said in his crystal voice. 'Engage initiation sequence.'

A crunching sounded from the curved walls. A harsh machine voice boomed out.

'Provide identity.'

'Astropath Prime Ultra Guidus Losenti.'

'Ident confirmed. Secondary unlock necessary.'

'Primarch Roboute Guilliman,' spoke the primarch. 'Lord Commander of the High Lords of the Imperium of Man, and Imperial Regent.'

'Secondary unlock ident confirmed. Stand by for gene scan. Gene scan.'

A flat, striated band of green light fanned out from the wall. It washed up and down the primarch and the astropath.

'Gene scan confirmed. Ident confirmed. Code required.'

A noise damper projected a privacy field around Guilliman. He heard nothing; even the vibrations of the machines under his feet were robbed of auditory expression. From Guilliman's position, Losenti's lips moved wordlessly. Guilliman looked away. He could lip-read. Cawl knew that. The first and only time he had idly let his gaze rest on the astropath's face while he spoke his code, Guilliman had been temporarily blinded by a las-strobe.

Guilliman could not fault Cawl's dedication to security. The archmagos' attention to detail bordered on pathological, and for ten thousand years Cawl had kept Roboute Guilliman's secrets for him. He had no grounds for criticism there.

The privacy field snapped off. Guilliman spoke out his own code, a string of nonsensical words that changed depending on the date.

'Codes accepted,' said the voice. 'Commencing main series activation sequence.'

The twenty small doors in the walls opened downwards. Behind each was a lit armaglass tank containing a severed human head bathed in clear yellow nutrient fluids. Metal neatly capped each severed neck. From these issued small bundles of tidy cables and pipes that curled downwards under the heads, then up into the machines above them.

'Activation code required,' said the voice.

This time, there was no privacy field. The code sent astropathically to Losenti by Cawl to turn on his abominable machine was different every time, and there was no need to rob the primarch of his hearing. Cawl made a virtue of economy in all things he did.

'Charnibel crow, white crow, white crow, white crow, charnibel crow, black crow,' said Losenti.

'Code accepted. Code accepted. Code accepted,' said the machine. 'Stand by for communion. Cawl Inferior awakening rite underway. Stand by for communion.'

Machines hidden behind the panelling surged into life. The chug of the devices below them grew more muted, ceding space to the waking voices of the others. Thin lines in the metal walls, invisible before, glowed with sluggish, golden energies. Circuitry engraved into the tanks' glass glimmered similarly, and the faces of the heads twitched. Guilliman was absorbed by the jerking of their muscles. The weight pressing onto his psyche grew.

Losenti grimaced at the primarch. 'I ask your leave to depart, my lord,' he said. 'The awakened machine's presence is uncomfortable for me.'

'Yes, yes, of course,' said Guilliman. He tore his eyes away from the severed heads. 'Please. You do not need to ask my permission. We have done this many times. I know how much the Cawl Inferior pains you when active.'

Losenti gave a slight, grateful bow, tugged up his hood and walked back towards his perpetually dark quarters.

'Losenti!' called Guilliman on a whim, raising his voice over the smooth thumping of the machine. Losenti paused at the threshold of his door. 'What do you do down here, when you are not needed, when you are alone?'

Losenti turned his head. His wrinkled face was bathed in the warm light of Cawl's device. 'I write poetry,' he said. 'And I dream of better times.'

The doors slid shut behind him, leaving Guilliman alone in the chamber of the Cawl Inferior.

Guilliman lacked the psychic potential that his father had granted to several of his brothers, but he was a child of the Emperor's making, and he was sensitive to psychic energies of which a true non-psyker would be ignorant. Some hidden part of the world changed. Energy ran more freely around the channels engraved into the walls, extending its web outwards from the heads until the whole room was a tracery of gold. The yellow light outshone the ruddy light under the floor and the bright lumens overhead. As the energy network expanded, warding runes in the secret techno-arcana tongue of Magi Psykana blazed brightly, along with others of obvious alien origin. Cawl was a magpie magos, taking what he needed no matter its ancestry. His freethinking made Guilliman profoundly uneasy, but a labour ten thousand years long, delivered perfectly, attested to the archmagos' efficacy. He had been instrumental in restoring Guilliman to life in this terrible age. And, most amazingly, in creating the Primaris Space Marines, Cawl had improved upon the Emperor's own designs.

I have no choice but to trust him, thought Guilliman. *That's the only practical I need consider here.*

As the light grew, the constant, hollow pain in Guilliman's chest intensified, as if the two were inextricably linked. He gritted his teeth as the gnawing in his gut outdid the pressure in his head. The muscle twitches in the tanks became a frenzy of gurning. The heads jerked and jiggled, mouths gaping in silent, drowned screams. Bubbles streamed over clay flesh, agitating the surface of the fluids that nourished them. Eyelids fluttered over eyes that appeared to contain shreds of intelligence, and they looked out from their watery prisons with absolute horror.

Pressure built at the back of Guilliman's mind until his eyes throbbed. The air smelled of hot steel, and his saliva took on a metallic flavour. The emptiness his soul contained expanded beyond the physical confines of his body.

There was a definite pop, not generated by the machines, he was certain, and suddenly all was still. The thumping of the hidden devices levelled out to a quiet whir. The faces ceased their pained contortions. Their eyes went blank and closed. The bubbling ceased.

Guilliman waited. The pains the machine brought did not decrease, but familiarity made them bearable. There was a clunk, a hiss, then the eyes opened again, and a fresh machine voice spoke – an emotionless facsimile of Archmagos Belisarius Cawl.

'Greetings, lord primarch, Lord Commander, Lord Imperial Regent. The Lord Guilliman of the High Twelve.'

The mouths of the heads gaped clumsily, silently parroting the machine voice's words.

'That last title has no meaning,' said Guilliman.

'For a millennium, your name was an honorific for weaker men. By the conventions of those times, you are the Lord Guilliman,' said the Cawl Inferior. Guilliman had no idea whether the machine was mocking him or working its way down some dead-end logic path. 'Redundant repetition. Your resumption of the original title is illogical. The position of lord commander was banned in the wake of the great War of the Beast.'

Guilliman knew little of that conflict or of the infamous Beheading that followed. The near destruction of the Imperium had passed Cawl by. The archmagos had been deep in his studies of the Emperor's fragmentary research, and therefore his records of the time were maddeningly brief. Most of the histories appertaining to it had been deliberately destroyed.

'Your recreation of the position lacks wisdom. The position of lord commander is similar in title to that of Lord Commander Militant of the Astra Militarum. It has a fifty per cent match with that of Lord Commander of the Segmentum Solar. Inefficiency can arise by duplication of titles. Confusion is inevitable. I prefer Imperial Regent. No other can lay claim to the wording of this honour.'

'I am more than a title,' said Guilliman. 'Every time we speak, Cawl, you bring this up.'

'I am not Cawl. I simulate Cawl. Familiar complaints act as social bonds between members of the human species. I seek to emulate this interaction to make you comfortable with my existence. This preamble is to ease tension and re-establish empathy between Belisarius Cawl and Roboute Guilliman.'

'You make poor conversation, machine. Deliver your report.'

Cawl had lived more than ten thousand years. Such a great span of time would wear out all but the greatest of souls. The changes he had wrought upon his body to support his mind had stripped most of his humanity away. His emotions had become ghosts in the mechanism his mind now inhabited, and here, mediated through the Cawl Inferior, they should have been practically absent. But Guilliman could never shake the feeling of intense superiority hidden in Cawl's pronouncements, nor ignore the touch of sardonic humour that revealed itself from time to time, even in this soulless copy.

'It is not the report of the Cawl Inferior. It is Archmagos Belisarius Cawl's report.'

'It is easy to forget,' said Guilliman, 'that you are a mechanism, and that such large amounts of information can be conveyed by such simple encoded messages.'

'The information does not come from the message. The information is innate to my construction. The code unlocks the appropriate response. My creator supplied me multiple likely scenarios that he, in his great wisdom and genius, mathematically extrapolated. The messages I receive merely modify these prognostications to fit the actuality of current circumstances. My programming is preloaded. These linked brains and the logic engines in the greater portion of this chamber contain all eventualities relevant to the tasks undertaken by Lord Roboute Guilliman and Archmagos Belisarius Cawl. All probable futures are within me.'

Guilliman looked around at the heads. They were too individual to have come from vat-born slaves, and there was no sign of the penal coding tattoos worn by servitors drawn from criminal stock. He did not want to know where Cawl had sourced his grisly collection.

'I am impressed, as always, Cawl Inferior,' he said. This was also a conversation they had had many times before.

The machine's voice changed, becoming hectoring. 'Then my master repeats his request that you install him as Fabricator General of Mars. You replaced five of the High Twelve upon assumption of the regency of the Imperium, and hundreds of the lesser high lords. In light of the treachery after you left, you did it again. What is one more?'

'For the hundredth time, I will not do this. The Imperium

does not exert so much control over Mars that I may appoint my own Fabricator General, and they would never accept you even if I could. The tenets of your creed forbid such artificial consciousnesses as this. Your experiments–'

'Archmagos Belisarius Cawl's experiments, not my experiments,' said the machine pedantically.

'Very well,' conceded Guilliman. 'Cawl's experiments have made him many enemies.'

'The detail is open to interpretation,' said the machine. 'Take this unit, for example. I am no abominable intelligence as your attitude implies you believe me to be. My responses are not spontaneously generated, but predetermined. The servitors that make up my being are sanctioned for use. They are not machines, and what they generate – me, the Cawl Inferior – is not a unique creation but a limited expression of Archmagos Belisarius Cawl's mind. By these means, I am free of the wickedness of forbidden sentience.

'Archmagos Belisarius Cawl is a genius. Consider this unit further. The hexidecimal encoding that he projects to this unit is immune to decryption, for it is incomplete. My responses are inherent to this unit. An astropathic message can be intercepted, no matter how many locks are put upon it. Anything that uses the electromagnetic spectrum is worse. Not only can it degrade, or be captured, or be lost, but the journey of a message from where Cawl is now to where you are would take three thousand Terran years. Expediency is the enemy of dogma. You have asked him to be expeditious. He alone has been able to unlock, understand and improve upon the work of the Emperor. He alone is the master of a hundred fields of technology. He alone is unafraid of innovation. He is the best candidate to rule Mars. I present his petition to you. Give Archmagos Belisarius Cawl Mars, and he will hand you the galaxy.'

Guilliman had considered doing exactly this, but he did not

lie to the Cawl Inferior. The result would be outright civil war in the Adeptus Mechanicus' sub-empire of forge worlds.

'Your colleagues would disagree with your evaluation,' he said. 'It cannot be done.'

'I have no colleagues.'

'*His* colleagues then.'

'His colleagues are limited. Their beliefs have become a faith that they dare not challenge. The Adeptus Mechanicus is far more trammelled in its thinking than the Mechanicum of your time was, my lord Guilliman, and the archmagos was a radical in those distant centuries. You would not have come to him if he were not. Already you have asked him to perform many forbidden duties. You are as culpable as he in any crime that may or may not have taken place.'

'I am no adherent of the Machine-God's creed,' said Guilliman.

'You have asked the archmagos to interfere with technologies expressly forbidden by your own creator, the Emperor of Mankind.'

The machine waited expectantly, far too lifelike for a supposedly lifeless machine.

Guilliman did not believe it was free of will. There had been in Guilliman's youth a device called the Thracian Automaton. Fashioned in the semblance of a man, the machine had played at regicide with any who would challenge it, and won every game. Questions could be put to it on matters of science and history, and the answers it gave were unerringly accurate. Konor, Guilliman's adoptive father, had taken the boy primarch to see this marvel. Guilliman had seen through it immediately, and challenged its creator. The man had insisted that it worked from the old sciences, showing the consul and his adopted son complicated workings within the figure, but Guilliman would not be convinced, and he had leapt forwards and torn loose the mannequin. Inside the stool it sat upon was a very real, if rather short, man.

The man had proved to be a gifted polymath, if a cheat, and he had spent many years serving Guilliman's foster father.

The Thracian Automaton had been a powerful lesson. It was probable that the Cawl Inferior was an inverse of that device, a real machine masquerading as a pretence. Guilliman was no technologist of the ability his brothers Perturabo, Vulkan or Ferrus Manus had been, but he doubted that the archmagos was telling him the complete truth about how the machinery worked. It was clearly partly psychic in nature, and its blend of xenos and Imperial technologies made it entirely heretical by the tenets of the Adeptus Mechanicus whether it could think or not.

'The final answer is no, as it is every time,' said Guilliman.

The machine clicked deep in its cybernetic innards, filing the response for later broadcast to Cawl.

'Give me Cawl's report,' commanded Guilliman.

'The Conclave Acquisitorius proceeds through the galaxy. Cawl has recently finished war operations on Cadmus Phosp. Unfortunately, the pylons discovered there are too degraded to be reactivated, and so he must begin his quest anew.'

'So he cannot yet reproduce the technology.'

'Regrettably, not yet. Not on the scale necessary for your ends, my lord.' The slack mouths of the heads continued their jerky aping of the machine's voice. 'However, Archmagos Cawl has formulated a number of smaller experimental devices that project a similar effect to the xenos originals, albeit to a lesser degree. He has provided several to seal the Pit of Raukos. They will arrive soon.'

'I am aware of this. That is why we are here. That is why the battle for Raukos was fought.'

'Forgive me, my lord, I can say only what my cogitators select as the most appropriate response according to Cawl's code,' said the machine. Was this a lie, or a genuine artefact of how the machine worked? Cawl obfuscated everything.

'Will the devices work?'

'They will be staples in a wound. Cawl does not yet completely understand how the pylons function, but the actions of the test devices here will further his research. Eventually, he will be able to replicate the technology, and he shall bring the Great Rift under control, parsec by parsec, until it is at last sealed. This he swears, my lord. He shall dedicate the remainder of his life to it.'

Guilliman scratched his face thoughtfully. His chin was stubbly. He had neglected his personal grooming these last few days. 'Encouraging words.'

'I am instructed to offer a cautionary note, my lord,' replied the machine. 'The culmination of this research is a long way off. Nevertheless, now Archmagos Belisarius Cawl has fulfilled his oaths to you and delivered the Primaris Space Marines as commanded, and now he is free of the crusade, he has more available cogitation power to put to this task. The principle of the pylons is sound. The technology is proven. With what little remained of the pylon network around Cadia, he came close to sealing the Eye of Terror. He will not give up now.

'The devices that are en route to 108/Beta-Kalapus-9.2 are untested. They may be unstable. They may work for a while before failing. They may not work at all. They are inferior to the technologies of the necrons in every way. Our understanding of metaphysical science is hopeless compared to theirs. The Pariah Nexus has shown us that.' The Cawl Inferior uttered the blasphemy as easily as it might bid him good day. The idea that alien technology was in any way superior to that of humanity was anathema to the machine cult. 'Without testing, Archmagos Belisarius Cawl cannot be sure of the efficacy of their design. With time, and should the Conclave Acquisitorius be successful in its quest to find an intact planetary pylon network, he will be able to refine the design.'

'If these designs do work, surely we can make use of them now,' said Guilliman. 'Assuming Cawl's pylons are functional, how long will it be before we can establish stable corridors to the Imperium Nihilus? That is a matter of pressing concern.'

'Years, at least,' said the machine. 'Possibly decades. This trial will better inform Archmagos Belisarius Cawl, and he will better inform you, my lord Guilliman. But Belisarius Cawl will triumph. The ancient races held the answers. The Old Ones, the necrons, the aeldari. Soon we shall hold all the pieces to the puzzle that they held only in part. We shall fit them together. We shall succeed where they failed, and overcome the monsters spawned by our own minds.'

Again, there was a flash of emotion in the Cawl Inferior's words, that of determination and anger. The technologies that sustained it hummed.

'Trafficking with xenos. The usage of forbidden technology. Your peers in the Cult Mechanicus will not take kindly to this.'

'I predict their response will be nothing short of furious, my lord regent. They hate Belisarius Cawl, but it is chiefly envy that motivates them. If they knew the extent to which his knowledge outreaches theirs, some would move to destroy him and his creations. I trust you will shelter me should the time come.'

Guilliman laughed. He did not laugh often now, and when he did it was sorrowful. 'The Cawl Inferior, you betray your disguise. You wish for protection as a living being would.'

'I require it. I do not desire or not desire it. My continued existence is necessary. If Cawl dies, the key to his knowledge will survive in me. That is why I must live. Archmagos Belisarius Cawl can protect himself. I cannot.'

'Archmagos Cawl is the last being I know who needs protection from anybody,' agreed Guilliman. 'And you are safe here in the bowels of the *Macragge's Honour*. Now, the Primaris Space Marines. We have a decade of data. How are they performing?'

'Archmagos Belisarius Cawl repeats that all gene-lines continue to operate at peak efficiency. Tested gene-seed reveals a mutational deviancy of less than zero point zero zero one per cent per generation. All Adeptus Astartes Chapters once again have access to the full suite of additional organs, replacing those zygotes lost through improper treatment or evolutionary variance, along with the addition of the three new implants. All Chapters who have adopted the Primaris paradigm have adapted to the new creation processes with minimal wastage of recruits or mistakes in implantation. As can be expected, those new Primaris-strain Chapters founded by you, my lord, have the lowest error rate. The new equipment functions well. Requests for resupply with the new type of battle-brother and their associated weaponry have increased, suggesting a ninety-four per cent acceptance rate among the Chapters.'

'What of those gene-lines with more deeply ingrained flaws?' asked Guilliman. 'The Blood Angels and the Space Wolves?' Cawl's research, and his own reading, had uncovered dangerous faults that the sons of both gene-lines in question had done their best to hide.

'My standard response remains unchanged. Archmagos Belisarius Cawl understands your reservations. The corrected flaws in the new gene-stocks show no signs of regression to previous unstable states, whether in successor Chapters composed entirely of the new Primaris Space Marine type, or in already established Chapters. Elimination entirely of the more idiosyncratic traits of some gene-lines is, however, not to be recommended. They form part of the Emperor's original vision, and are, in any case, crucial to their proper function. I will restate Archmagos Belisarius

Cawl's position on this matter. The improved gene-seed of Ninth and Sixth Legion stock is operating within acceptable parameters.

'Furthermore, he has continued experimental implantation and monitoring of the thus-far unused gene-seed in experimental test subjects. That of the Second, Third, Fourth, Eighth, Eleventh, Twelfth, Fourteenth, Fifteenth, Sixteenth, Seventeenth and Twentieth Legions all shows no sign of degradation or incidence of unwelcome tendencies within the recipients. All is well, my lord, Archmagos Belisarius Cawl reassures you. He is so satisfied that I am instructed to repeat his request that those gene-lines be put into full production and be allowed to serve the Imperium as the Emperor intended.'

'No,' said Guilliman firmly. 'I cannot allow it.'

'My lord, the characteristics of your brothers are too valuable to discard. The Emperor's original schema of warriors bred to specific purposes is sound, and should be exploited. Under the current circumstances, we are operating with half our weapons unavailable to us. The Omnissiah's plan is unbalanced. Putting the remaining eleven augmented Primaris gene-lines into production would allow far greater tactical and strategic flexibility of Space Marine forces, particularly when working in concert.'

'I say again, no. Do not progress any further with this research.'

'The warriors were not at fault. The science is not at fault. Their primarchs were. Chapters from your gene-line have also fallen in the past millennia, lord regent, and we do not censor them.'

'I said no!' said Guilliman forcefully.

There was a silence full of hums and clicks.

'As you command, my lord,' said the machine eventually. 'Archmagos Belisarius Cawl will comply.'

Can I truly believe that? thought Guilliman. All magi of the Adeptus Mechanicus hungered for knowledge. When they had it, they could rarely refrain from using it. On this particular matter, he did not trust Cawl one whit. There was the existence of Cawl's servant, Primus, for example. Whatever unholy blend of gene-seed that warrior had Cawl remained coy about.

Guilliman's manner betrayed nothing of his thoughts.

'Is there anything else?' he asked.

'That concludes the selection of responses engendered by today's code reception,' said the Cawl Inferior. 'I shall prepare myself for encoding of your orders to Archmagos Belisarius Cawl.'

Things clacked and turned somewhere, awaiting Guilliman's response. Another simple code would be projected to a second ghoulish mind aboard Cawl's Ark ship. In the same way that Cawl's message had been delivered to Guilliman, preset responses would activate within this other unit in response to the code. Or so Cawl insisted.

'Here are my orders.' Guilliman had no time nor any need for the preamble the Cawl Inferior had subjected him to. 'The enemy fleet at Raukos has been crushed. The first phase of the Indomitus Crusade is over. Plans proceed for the crossing of the Rift via the Attillan Gap. I will shortly return to Macragge to face my brother Mortarion, who has come forth from his lair. Once he is dealt with, the reconquest of Imperium Nihilus will begin. You are to continue your efforts to unravel the secrets of the pylons. We will persevere in this war, but the ultimate survival of mankind can only be assured by undoing the damage Abaddon has inflicted on the fabric of reality. Concentrate on this above all else.'

'That is all?'

'That is all.'

'I shall deliver the coding to my brother machine.'

'The next time we speak, I shall provide a time and coordinates for Archmagos Cawl and I to meet, by lithocast if not face to face. It has been too long since our last direct consultation.'

The machine was silent. The flapping mouths of the heads hung still.

'The Cawl Inferior?' said Guilliman. A machine coughed under the floor. The red light shone brighter, tinting the golden light of the circuits orange.

'That may not be possible, my lord.'

'Where exactly are you, Cawl? What are you doing?'

The Cawl Inferior was silent. Cogitator data-wheels chattered behind the walls of the chamber. The red light glowed brighter. The gold faded.

'This unit does not possess that information.'

Guilliman stared at the servitors. Dead eyes in dead heads stared back, oblivious to his suspicions. Could they see him? Could the thing lie?

'I have no more information to impart,' said the Cawl Inferior. 'Good day, my lord Guilliman.'

The machine shut off. The glimmering light in the channels died. With one last spastic jerk, the heads went slack in their tanks. The doors slid shut over each armaglass compartment. Suddenly, the painful pressure of the machine was reduced to its merely uncomfortable background level.

Guilliman breathed hard through his teeth. These consultations made him tense.

For all Belisarius Cawl's usefulness and his desire to save mankind, Guilliman could foresee a time when he would become a problem.

CHAPTER THIRTEEN

THE TRIUMPH AT RAUKOS

Upon the martial square of 108/Beta-Kalapus-9.2, the military of four crusade battle groups was arrayed. Armies faced the August Victorium, the gargantuan structure created for this one single day. Where its wings touched the hills, the slopes had been remade, carved with more symbols of Imperial might. No trace of the enemy remained. In the sky the Pit seemed dimmer, cowed by the power of mankind.

A single cannon boomed. The bell on the highest tower of the August Victorium began to toll – once for each month of the Indomitus Crusade.

At this signal, a bizarre flock burst from the upper galleries. Servo-skulls, cyber-angels, preachers on grav-powered sermon-isers and vat-grown gene-constructs flew out over the square in a fog of incense. A dozen different hymns, sung all at once and with varying degrees of loveliness, competed with shouted exhortations to worship. As the aerial crowd dispersed over the troops, down the steps of the August Victorium came priests of every kind, accompanied by all their attendant devices. There were hundreds of them, from the richest to the poorest, from moderate prelates to firebrand demagogues. Between them, auto-preachers crabbed sideways on clanking legs, the mouldering brains of the martyrs within roaring out religious epithets through primitive augmitters. Unruly hordes of flagellants came with them, beating themselves raw and crying for salvation. Every sect of the Adeptus Ministorum with any pretension to power had members present at the Triumph of Raukos. They followed Roboute Guilliman like flies followed cattle, and no matter how often he swatted them away, they always returned.

The stream of holy men went on for an hour. They filled the avenues between the warriors standing to attention, though they set no foot on the carpet running down the very centre. None dared do that, for that was Guilliman's alone to tread. They sang and mumbled and prayed. A hundred bishops and all their aides, servitors and whispering confidantes stalked after the ecumenical horde in pompous parade, each vying with the others in displays of opulence or contrary poverty. Finally, from the iron gates of the lower levels, there came a train of sacred arks bearing the bones of saints and heroes of the Indomitus Crusade, these also accompanied by immense throngs of the faithful.

In their pageantry, in their sheer number and bombast, the priests almost overshadowed the arrival of the primarch.

Almost, but not quite.

Frater Mathieu was the only priest watching from the August Victorium. He stood upon a wide prominence over steps carved from the flesh of the land earlier that week. There were twenty cardinals up there too, somewhere at the back in the crowd, but they affected a lack of interest in the lower orders of clergy and did not observe. They were closer to the Emperor; they had no need to watch the devotional display of their inferiors, and talked among themselves.

In form, the promontory of the August Victorium was, Mathieu supposed, a sort of balcony, with a balustrade and doors that led to halls within the hill, and sweeping staircases to the colonnade above it. But although it had all the appurtenances of a balcony, it was so immense that the word did it no justice. It ran for over a mile, and was crammed with officials of every kind. There were few warriors upon it. All but the mightiest leaders stood with their soldiers upon the square, many upon raised platforms or standing within the cupolas of enormous command vehicles so that their importance was understood.

Well, thought Frater Mathieu, *perhaps not so few warriors.*

He had counted them as they arrived, before the crowds on the Victorium got too thick. There were thirty-six Chapter Masters, a further eighteen Space Marine lords, all the upper leadership of the remaining Unnumbered Sons, six Adeptus Custodes, three canonesses of the Adepta Sororitas, five generals, various warlords and others of similar rank, Captain Felix, Captain Sicarius, all twenty of Guilliman's Victrix Guard, the commissar-general, Fleetmaster Isaiah Khestrin, the groupmasters of battle groups Alphus, Cerastus, Dominus and Gamma, several admirals and rear-admirals, dozens of commodores, more dozens of shipmasters, and scores of other men and women of war. Hundreds then, if not thousands.

Numbers were relative.

The warriors upon the balcony were islands amid a sea of Imperial officials. Navigators, psykers, astropaths, tech-magi, bureaucrats, High Lords or their representatives from the Council Exterra – although a few hundred of the lesser lords of the Senatorum Imperialis had come in person, hoping for advancement, only three of the High Twelve had dared make the dangerous journey – planetary commanders and other potentates.

Not so long ago, thought Mathieu, *this gathering would have represented the very apex of Imperial power.*

Not any more – not when a primarch walked among them and led them. A son of the Emperor had returned. Everyone else was at best an assistant, at worst an impediment, to the efforts of the Imperial Regent, may the Emperor forever bless him.

Faith suffused Mathieu from the crown of his head to the soles of his feet. It held him upright like a scaffold. Without faith, he thought he might collapse, a boneless man, overwhelmed by the glory of the Imperium ranged before him. Such colours there were, and so many great engines of war. So much power!

He could not imagine himself without faith. It gave him strength, and it gave him purpose. When he was with Roboute Guilliman, that faith burned in him so hot that his skeleton seemed afire like molten iron. Miraculously, the heat did him no harm but instead filled him with great energy. When he felt like that, he would gladly have shot down the entire chattering mass of bureaucrats flocking on the balcony if it would have allowed the Emperor's son a freer hand.

He hid these feeling from the primarch, of course. His role in the Emperor's plan meant he had to. There was no shame in that.

Reason was Frater Mathieu's other gift. He was no stranger to introspection. He knew himself better than most men did. In the scholam missionaris, he had questioned his faith, and it had nearly ended his life. When his teachers saw that he questioned it because he marvelled at it, and not because he doubted it, he was let be, though still discouraged from probing too deeply. He had continued to do so, because to Frater Mathieu the one thing better than faith was its affirmation. In the library, he had learnt lessons that the Frateris did not intend to teach. He kept his thinking to himself, but through his youthful explorations he came to the philosophy that shaped his beliefs. Events in the Maelstrom had only confirmed his hopes.

The Emperor had a plan for him. It was obvious. Guilliman had chosen him because of that plan, whether he knew it or not.

He had tested his faith and found it sound. He could not fault it. The Emperor was real. He was a god. He was a force for good in a galaxy of horrors, and Mathieu had pledged himself fully to His service. Faith was real; faith was salvation.

Long after he had reached this conclusion, he had seen the miracles of the Emperor with his own eyes. The first time, in that glorious moment, he had wept.

But he could fault his hope.

There was no rational explanation for hope. The Emperor was powerful, but the enemy was more powerful still. The galaxy was beset like at no other time. For every miracle Frater Mathieu had witnessed, he had seen ten thousand sorrows. How could the Emperor save them?

Yet still his faith kept his hope alive. Nothing could extinguish it. Not reason, nor experience. It was irrational. He should have been wailing out the cry of the end times, but he did not. Provided he did his part, he had a sincere belief all would be well.

Is hope foolish? he asked himself. He looked upon the serried ranks, and he thought perhaps it was not.

He prayed he could bring the mercy of hope to the primarch also.

A fanfare brayed, brassy and short in the Macraggian way. The horde of priests fell as silent as the assembled soldiery. Roboute Guilliman emerged from the carved face of the hill into stillness. He ascended steps to a pulpit fashioned in the form of a giant crouching aquila, and surveyed the army before him.

The primarch was imperious, commanding, his face an ideal of nobility. Mathieu smiled in the depths of his hood. From Guilliman's expression, no one could guess how much the parade of priests irritated the primarch, but he took no pains to hide that from Mathieu, so the priest had been genuinely surprised when the primarch had accepted Mathieu's idea for the Procession of Faith.

The priest was a fine judge of character. Already, he had formed an opinion of Roboute Guilliman as a man who was guided by principle above all else; but one of those principles was pragmatism, and that often trumped the others.

If the primarch is willing to grit his teeth and allow the Ecclesiarchy to trumpet his divinity, thought Mathieu, *he will change his opinion eventually.*

Mathieu was also a patient creature. He did not care what Guilliman did, nor how he did it. The faithful part of himself deemed whatever the primarch did to be right, even while the reasoning part of him picked apart his motivations. It didn't matter to Mathieu why the primarch did what he did now; what mattered was where his actions led him eventually. The priest knew, absolutely, that one day Roboute Guilliman would see the light and accept his own divinity.

There, faith again. He smiled at the thought.

Mathieu tensed. Guilliman was about to speak.

A score of silvered skulls buzzed about the primarch, recording his image for posterity. From what Guilliman had told him, these recordings were meaningless, as history could be rewritten as easily as the notes for a sermon. The primarch looked at the flying skulls, and his regard made them retreat in dismay. The son of the Emperor did not see his own power. To Guilliman, the skulls were morbid mementos, machines nestled in the hollowed-out heads of the worthy. To Mathieu, they were more. Clinging to the mortal remains were the spirits of the faithful serving the Emperor beyond death. They *felt* the primarch's scorn – that is why they veered from him. Why could he not see that?

It is not my role to convince the son of god that he is the son of god, Mathieu scolded himself. *It is my role to serve him, and to guide him through his own efforts to the truth. I cannot tell him. He must see.*

He resolved to shrive himself, by confession or by whip, for his presumption. Still, he could not extinguish his hope, nor his ambition.

If I am the one to open his eyes… he thought. *If it is me who convinces him openly…*

That was enough pride. He squeezed the button hidden in the flesh of his palm. Sparking pain burst within his groin and behind his eyes. He gritted his teeth and swayed, close to collapse. But the implanted electroflail was not enough to break his immodest ambitions. He would have to punish himself harder later. Only in agony was there atonement.

The aftertones of the last toll of the bell hummed across the gathering. Guilliman addressed the crowd.

'The Indomitus Crusade has lasted twelve years. The first phase is done. Imperium Sanctus is stable enough for us to take stock.' A lesser leader might shout, or posture; Guilliman spoke clearly and calmly, and his words carried the power of a thousand guns out across the martial field. 'I did not do this.' He paused. He looked out over the field. Every man and woman felt the touch of his eyes. 'You look to me, and say "See! He is the son of the Master of Mankind! He has come to save us! He has brought low the lords of Chaos. He has crossed the stars when all ships founder in the storms of the warp!"' Again Guilliman paused for effect.

Mathieu saw his tricks; he was no stranger to addressing crowds.

Knowing the art did little to diminish the impact of Guilliman's rhetoric on him.

'I say to you again, I did not do this. It is not I who has liberated hundreds of star systems. It is not I who has provided reinforcement to dozens of our Chapters, or relieved and resupplied beleaguered armies that they might fight again. It is not I who has driven back the dark. I am but one man, and yes, I say I am a man, though primarch I may be. For my soul is human, and my heart, and my blood.

'The intent of the Emperor was that I be the best that mankind has to offer. I am not. You are. It is you, the humanity of all the worlds and organisations of this great Imperium, who have done these things. You are the muscles of war – its sinews, its heart and its spleen. Without you, what would I have accomplished? I would have accomplished nothing! You, all of you, must hold your heads high with pride. Without your efforts, the Imperium would have surely fallen!'

He shouted now, and his voice rolled out across the square. Banners snapped in the planet's dusty wind. It was eerily quiet. There were thousands upon thousands of humans and transhumans arrayed on the martial square. The ranks alone of the Unnumbered Sons filled a quarter of the space. They were arranged into Chapters, but their armour, coloured in the liveries of their primarchs, formed huge blocks that brought to mind the Legions of old.

There were twenty thousand Primaris Space Marines there, the rosters said, along with forty thousand Adeptus Astartes of the older type, twenty million men and women under arms, and the cybernetic battle congregations of the priesthood of Mars. War constructs of increasing size lined the distant back of the square, from the war robots of the Legio Cybernetica up to the sky-occluding bulk of the Titans.

How can we not win? thought Mathieu.

'The Indomitus Crusade is a success,' continued Guilliman. 'I declare its first tasks complete. By our blood and sacrifice, we have bought the Imperium valuable time to retrench. But we are needed elsewhere. Some of us now must part ways.' He paused again. 'The opening moves of the crusade are over. This Triumph of Raukos marks its great victories. The true work must begin.'

Still no one spoke, but a tension rose off the crowd.

'You Primaris Marines are all to be reassigned. Shortly after this triumph, I shall give out new orders. Your forces will disperse, and shall bring ruin to the enemy wherever they might be found. The Unnumbered Sons have fought with a strength that would shame the Legions of the Great Crusade. The time has come for you to be rewarded for your efforts. New assignments will be given. New Chapters formed. Some of you will go to join the progeny of your gene-sires, who will welcome you as brothers, and provide you with places of honour both on the battlefield and at the feasting table.

'Others of you too, must leave me, for my path takes me into unknowable peril. But hear this, though I send you away from me, I do so not because you have failed me, but because you have won my respect. You have performed impossible feats of arms. Wherever you go, the warriors of mankind will see the honour badges upon your battlegear, and they shall know hope, and righteous fury, and see that victory can be theirs. Inspired by you, they shall rise up with certainty in their hearts and guns in their hands, and with a mighty roar they shall cast back the enemy into the formless warp for all time! You have done this. You *will* do this. I stand before you humbled by the sight of you, the men and women who are the heroes of the Imperium!'

Guilliman held aloft the massive Hand of Dominion, its

robotic fingers clenched in victory salute. The square erupted into a rhythmic chant.

'Guilliman! Guilliman! Guilliman!'

It was deafening, and more. Frater Mathieu felt the crowd's exultation as a physical force. Their cries made his faith shine as bright as a star. Where before he nearly collapsed from application of his electroflail, now he swooned in religious ecstasy. The Pit of Raukos seemed to dim even more, and the blasted, lonely deserts of 108/Beta-Kalapus-9.2 felt a little cleaner.

'My sons! My brothers and sisters!' Guilliman called, halting the chant. 'In a moment, our new militant-apostolic will bless you all, and deliver the words of the Emperor, my father!' Another cheer, so loud it shook the ground. Mathieu looked at the primarch sidelong; he had yet to say yes to the appointment. He was going to, of course. But now he had no choice. He admired the primarch's will. They could not fail with him as their lord.

'But I will say this first. Those of you who are my sons, who bear my genetic heritage and the colours of the Ultramarines, who might hail yourselves from Ultramar, I have news. When we are done here, we have a new war to fight. My brother Mortarion brings pestilence to our home. I will not allow it to fall.'

The primarch paused. Slowly, he once again looked across the field.

'We march for Macragge.'

CHAPTER FOURTEEN

PLAGUEBRINGER

Varens was sleeping, and his dreams were stranger than ever before.

He watched himself from outside, as is sometimes the way in dreams, as if he were two separate people – the actor and the observer. The observer saw himself hiding by the hospital entrance, spying on the sentries, their conversation puffed out into the cold night air like smoke signals. The active Varens watched one of the sentries leave his post and go inside to warm his hands. As the soldier passed him, Varens clubbed him down with a stone urn. Then this Varens stalked the gravelled fore-court of the hospital, a stolen lasgun in his hands.

The second Varens watched.

The first Varens raised his lasgun. The remaining sentry's eyes became shocked round zeroes in the shadow of his helmet. 'Don't shoot!' he said.

Varens squeezed the trigger and blasted a neat hole in the

sentry's chest that steamed as he stepped over the corpse. He dropped the gun.

This act of violence half woke him.

He should have been warm, but his feet were freezing and felt wet. A chill wind made him colder still. He tried to go back to sleep. There was a sharp pain in his wound.

How could this be? he thought in his dream. *I am ready to go back to the war. I am fit enough to die.*

Another stab of pain made him gasp and wake slightly. He tried to go back to sleep, but there was an irritating rattling noise all around him. It sounded like reeds, reeds in the wind.

Varens' eyes snapped open.

He was totally disoriented. Pale strands waved at the height of his nose, filling the world as far as he could see, dividing it into hissing paleness below and darkness above. It took him a moment to see that the strands were reeds, and the darkness was the sky where clouds sped over stars under the urging of the wind.

He was in the marsh.

It took him a moment to get his bearings and locate the hospital. It looked small, the marble a blur in the dark. He had come a long way, well past the edges of the meadows into shallow water.

His dream came back to him. The dead soldiers. Or was this the dream, and what he remembered in the dream the true memory? It couldn't be possible.

He felt dizzy. He reached his hand to his forehead. There was something slimy on his hand, and he wiped it on his gown. His forehead was hot. He had a fever. He should get back; there was something very wrong with him.

He turned to face the hospital. His limbs were shivering, and his muscles ached. His feet were going numb. His skin bumped under his hospital gown. He would die out here if he did not get back.

Definitely a fever.

'I've caught my damned death out here,' he muttered. He sloshed through the mud, heading for the firmer ground of the meadows. He had nearly made it when a familiar voice called out in the marsh.

'Bolus?' he called back.

He strained his ears. The last of the year's insects chirruped in the chilly night. He heard nothing else, and he dismissed the voice as a delusion.

'One! One! One!'

'Bolus?' Varens said again, more loudly. He could see nothing through the reeds, which grew tall where the marsh turned into meadow. Cursing, he struggled his way onto firm soil and looked back. Iax's solitary moon appeared from behind a scudding cloud, lighting everything silver and black.

'One!' Bolus' voice was thin as a distant scream. 'One!'

Varens turned back to look at the hospital. If he went back now for help he'd lose Bolus for sure, and when they found him, they would shoot him.

He scanned the marshes, looking for his friend. Finally, he caught sight of him, a white ghost leaping high to negotiate the mud and water, his nightgown sleeves hanging over his hands and flapping. Behind him, Bolus had left a path of broken reeds. The trail meandered dramatically, but he appeared to be heading towards a thicket of low trees clustering on a hillock at the edge of the marsh's first mere.

'Damn him!' said Varens. Ignoring the chills and hot shivers that gripped his limbs, he plunged back into the water in pursuit of his friend.

He soon reached Bolus' trail. It was so erratic that he decided not to follow it, instead chasing down the sound of his friend's voice. He kept his eyes on the low island and its trees, as it appeared that Bolus was indeed heading towards this point. Whenever Varens was forced to divert around deeper water and lost hearing of Bolus' eerie shouts of 'One! One! One!', he would head towards the island and pick them up again.

Hours seemed to pass before his feet found harder ground. Shivering with cold and sickness, he slogged his way up the rise. The hillock had only a few tens of feet of elevation, but in his current state it felt as big as a mountain. He doubted he had the strength now to return to the hospital. This had been a mistake. He should have gone back.

'Bolus!' he hissed loudly, unwilling to shout. He pushed his way through springy branches and down the overgrown far slope. The open water was on the other side.

'One! One! One!' said Bolus.

There he was, squatting at the lake's edge, staring at his reflection in the black mere. Though he was sick and cold, Varens felt a surge of relief.

'Bolus!' he said angrily. 'What are you doing out here?'

Bolus looked up from the water. He looked terrible, with dark rings under his eyes and his stubble caked with scurf.

'Two, two,' said Bolus sadly, pointing at Varens.

'You had reached forty-nine last time I saw you.' Varens' attempt at levity came out heavy as lead. He put his hand on his friend's shoulder. As he did, the wound on his back twinged, and he grimaced. 'Come on, we have to get back. I'm not well.'

Bolus shook his head and crabbed away from Varens.

'Come on!' Varens said.

There was a crack of wood behind them. A man, also in a hospital gown, staggered out of the reeds. He was covered in scratches, and his eyes were blank.

'Three! Three! Three!' said Bolus, jabbing a clawed hand at the other.

'Oh, that is perfect, just simply perfect,' said Varens. 'Hey, hey you! Soldier! Stop!'

The man blundered towards the water. He walked to its edge and, after staring into it for a few seconds, fell forwards face first.

'Damn it!' said Varens. He was frightened. The man's actions reminded him of the way the dead had fallen into their trenches on Espandor. He hesitated, fearing the chill might kill him, but his sense of duty got the better of his self-preservation, and he floundered into the lake. By then, the man had floated out a little. Swimming even that short distance in the freezing black water drained the strength from Varens.

'Four! Four! Four! Four!' shouted Bolus. 'Five! Five! Five! Five! Five!'

Two more soldiers, one man and a woman, came out of the thicket. The man plunged into the water. The woman stopped a moment, her slack face clearing.

'Where am I?' she said, then fainted into the lake.

'Emperor!' said Varens. He dragged the unresponsive first man back to shore, and hauled the woman out onto the island. The other man fought him when Varens grabbed him, and sank out of sight into the peaty depths.

'Bolus! Bolus! Help me!'

'One, two, three, four, five!' cackled Bolus, touching his fingers like a child learning to count.

Swearing profusely, Varens knelt by the first man and rolled him onto his front. A stream of dirty water welled from the man's mouth. When it slowed to a trickle, Varens rolled him over onto his back and pressed his lips to the man's, breathing for him. After three breaths he pulled back and pumped the man's chest.

'Six! Six! Six! Six! Six! Six!' said Bolus.

A sixth person came out of the thicket. He moaned, then collapsed into a seizure.

By now Varens was terrified. This was too much like what he had seen on Espandor. But there were no walking dead here, no traitors, and none of their terrible allies; the ones the officers insisted were xenos, but that rumour suggested were something else entirely. He pumped at the first man's chest, distracted by the latest arrival. Something tickled his hand, and when he looked back he yelled in horror, and stumbled backwards.

Sickly-coloured insects were crawling from the man's mouth and nose, pouring in wriggling masses onto the soil.

'Bolus?' he said, his voice quiet.

Bubbles erupted out in the mere where the other man had gone down. The water boiled, and aquatic creatures bobbed to the surface dead, already squirming with the life of carrion feeders.

'It can't be... Not here. No, not here!' cried Varens. His own flesh crawled. The wound in his back was agonising.

He still didn't remember how he got the wound, but he remembered the fly he had swatted that last day in the field.

It suddenly seemed horribly significant.

His head pounded, and there was a roaring in his ears.

'Seven! Seven! Seven! Seven! Seven! Seven! Seven!' shouted Bolus. He stood, and pointed with a shaking hand up the slope.

Garstand, the man Varens had met on the hospital balcony weeks ago, came out of the trees, his beard dishevelled and his gown filthy. Varens couldn't see his face.

'Garstand?' he said.

'What's going on? What am I doing here? Varens? I was following Rusen. He told me to come. He said it was important!' Unlike all the others, Garstand seemed to be in full possession of his faculties, but when he lifted his face towards Varens, Varens screamed. 'Is it important, what we're doing out here? I am cold. I should get back to bed.'

Garstand's eyes had gone. Fat leeches hung down his face, their pulsing foreparts buried in his eye sockets. A crop of boils deformed his forehead, swelling even as Varens watched.

'Why can't I see?' said Garstand. 'I itch all over. Have I been bitten again?'

'Throne preserve me!' said Varens. The pain in his back was maddening. He jammed his arm behind his back to scratch at it. His fingertips brushed something hard. There was a lump there, swollen, close to bursting.

'One, two, three,' said Bolus, counting everyone with grave concentration. 'Four, five, six.' He pointed at Varens. 'Seven.'

He patted his chest.

'Seven. Seven. Seven,' he chanted, and as he did so, he pulled out a stolen las-scalpel and thumbed it on. He held it so close to his eyes that his eyebrows crackled in the heat.

'No!' shouted Varens.

'Seven,' said Bolus, and cut open his stomach. His innards fell out, diseased, putrid and crawling with maggots. 'Seven,' he said, and died.

Foul gas belched from the bed of the mere. More dead fish bobbed to the surface. Garstand abruptly started screaming and clawing at his face. Varens felt something moving under his skin. He tore off his gown, only to find the flesh of his chest writhing. Terrible pain lanced through him, and the wound in his back tore open.

'Seven!' an inhuman voice boomed out of the dark, and a phlegmy laugh followed.

Odd light shone from the marsh, then Iax changed forever.

Reality tore with a sound like the edges of a half-healed wound parting. Either side of the tear, reality remained, but between the yellowing edges of the rift a realm of madness was revealed. A huge garden in the middle of steamy day, riotous in its decay, stretched out of sight into mustard fogs. Shy things with moist skin peeped from the foliage at Varens and licked their lips.

There appeared to be a skin of energy over this tear, but it was full of holes that were getting wider. Rotten gases drifted through, and then flies rose up from the diseased plants. They boiled through the holes in fat-bodied multitudes, battering at Varens just like on Espandor. Then they were gone, away over the marshes in buzzing shrouds.

Varens looked to his side at the unconscious woman. He moaned at what he saw.

Her eyes ran to jelly in their sockets. Her tongue went black. Her jaw disarticulated from her softening skull. Her necrotic flesh sloughed off bones that, now revealed, shone pink-white for only an instant before accelerated decay turned them slimy grey, and her exposed capillaries went dead black.

He clenched his eyes tightly. His face turned from the rift. No one who looked into something like that could survive. The movements under his skin grew wilder. He had to stop his hands from ripping at his own flesh to get the things inside him out, for he knew they would kill him.

'Don't look at it! Don't look at it!' he said, but he couldn't help it. He looked up into the garden.

A moment of calm fell. Thunder cracked in the suddenly sweltering air. A ripe scent of putrefaction infiltrated everything. A ripple passed over the marsh – tainting whatever it touched, alive or not – and the grasses blackened. Stones crumbled. The trees contorted into horrific new shapes and grew so large that they collapsed under their own weight into mushy ruin. Water turned thick.

'Seven!' bellowed the daemonic voice. A hot, corrosive wind blasted from the rift. Huge shapes rode it, approaching from the horizon of the hellish landscape on the other side.

Varens was racked with burning pain. Lesions opened on his skin, allowing the vermin breeding inside him to fall softly to the earth. His belly distended. His fingers twisted; his back hunched. His eyes moistened and became soft as part-cooked eggs. His cheeks melted like wax in a fire, reforming his features. His skull felt like it was trying to burst itself in two. Relief came suddenly, when a rotting, stubby horn emerged through his forehead and twisted upwards.

The pain got worse, but it didn't bother him any longer. He giggled.

The thing that had been Varens opened a single eye on a blighted world. With warp-born sight, he perceived a net of befouled spiritual power linking him and the six dead soldiers, stretching between their maggoty hearts and then out into the stars. All of the seven chosen were marked by Nurgle in their own way, by obvious trauma, minor scratch or unnoticed wound. Varens' own gift had been a fly bite, something so glorious dismissed in a moment! How bountiful his new lord was. The thing was pleased at the honour, and the last of Varens died under its pleasure.

'One, two, three. Four, five, six, seven.' Varens the plaguebearer counted the approaching shapes coasting through the warp, and awaited its masters.

CHAPTER FIFTEEN

GREYSHIELD

Captain Felix had considered taking off his armour before he took a ship to see his erstwhile comrades. He disliked the distance the unmarked ultima on his shoulder pad put between him and the others. In the end, he decided to keep his battleplate on. He was an Ultramarine now. He should not dishonour that, even if he did not yet feel fully part of the Chapter.

Being the primarch's equerry was an honour heavy with many burdens. *And they shall know no fear!* The Emperor's commandment to His Space Marines echoed down the millennia to the present day. A Space Marine was afraid of nothing. However, being fearless did not stop Captain Felix from worrying as the lighter flew from the *Macragge's Honour* to the *Rudense*.

The crux of it was that Felix had already been admitted formally into the Ultramarines, while his friends remained in their old formation. He was part of the primarch's own Chapter, something ancient and colossal with cultural weight. Furthermore, his swift induction had been... odd. Not least that he had been made a captain of that Chapter without say from the Chapter Master, even though their complement was full, and even though he had no company of his own to command officially.

It was politics, he knew. Exactly what Guilliman wished to achieve eluded him for the time being, but there were a number of reasons why the primarch had chosen Primaris warriors as equerries over more experienced Space Marines.

The first, Felix surmised, was that the primarch wanted to show that the Primaris Marines represented the new Space Marine paradigm. The second – and this was no theoretical, as the primarch had told him so – was that the Primaris Space Marines lacked political experience. Guilliman placed great import on non-combat skills. Archmagos Cawl's prolonged hypno-indoctrination had given the Primaris Space Marines none of that, so the primarch appointed many of their number into important but non-crucial roles as aides to various adepta, or as assistants to established Space Marine officers, and that included those he took as his own equerry; there had been two before Felix. Guilliman changed the holders of these offices frequently to help disseminate the experience that the Primaris Space Marines gained in their service. He took on only those who showed exceptional promise, and afterwards they were given permanent positions of grave responsibility. Felix was honoured to have been so chosen, and he strove daily to live up to the primarch's faith in him.

Thirdly, Felix reasoned, the primarch had wanted to observe his new warriors at close hand. The Primaris Space Marines had been created at Guilliman's behest, but they were creatures made by Cawl. If he were Roboute Guilliman, Felix would not have trusted the archmagos either.

None of this was what worried Felix. It was logical, rational and completely in line with the primarch's preference for contingency planning. But there was a fourth reason in Felix's hypothesising, and it was this last one that troubled him.

Felix had been born on Laphis not long after the end of the Great Heresy War. He remembered his childhood better than any of his peers appeared to, and that meant he recalled the Imperium as it had been long ago, when there was still hope. He remembered old Ultramar, the Imperial Truth and the rekindling of optimism as the threat of Horus receded. He had been thirteen years old and ready to join the Legion as a neophyte when Cawl's representatives had come calling, bearing the highest seals of all, and Felix had had one future taken away and this nightmare substituted in its stead. But he had kept all of his past, through millennia of stasis. He had forgotten nothing.

Felix thought the past was what Guilliman wanted from him.

The primarch often spoke of those times. Felix struggled to see Guilliman as wistful – he was too matter-of-fact for that – but it was plain that he was nostalgic. The fourth theoretical worried Felix because it suggested that the primarch was perhaps lonely, and if he were lonely, then he was all too human.

Seeing Guilliman as a man perturbed Felix. The Imperium needed someone above humanity to lead them, not a man with a man's faults.

The lonely demigod. The thought made Felix's spine shiver.

His maudlin thoughts passed as the lighter approached the *Rudense*'s small port hangar. The ship passed through the atmospheric field and into a space busy with servitors. Felix was seized by an impatience to disembark before the lighter had even settled into its landing gear.

Felix could recite the *Rudense*'s specifications without thinking. He knew exactly how to use it in battle; it was a ship to fire the heart of any who appreciated the art of void war. But its utility could not explain the deep significance it held for him.

Felix loved the *Rudense* because it had been his home, his to command, and the men aboard it were as close to family as he would ever know.

As soon as the lighter's landing lumens changed to green, Felix was out of the door and heading into the ship towards the barracks. Though Guilliman prized Felix for his memories of the times before, the ones he had of the *Rudense* were most precious. He had not been back to Laphis. If he were honest, he had no desire to. He had heard it had become a shrine world, its wide prairies encrusted with cathedra and temples to the Emperor, who the people of this time worshipped as a god. The thought of seeing his home so changed by a foreign ideology saddened him. Perhaps he was like the primarch, homesick for something that no longer existed.

Everyone needed something stable in their lives, some shared purpose and origin. As the primarch turned to him, Felix would turn to his brothers. He had that, for a few more weeks at least.

The familiar sights and smells of the ship mellowed his sadness into a sweeter melancholy. He let his feet lead him from the portside hangar up towards the spinal way. When he emerged into its avenue, his spirits lifted further. Every part of the ship was familiar to him. The companionways which clung to the sides of the corridor welcomed him. The regularly repeated stamp of the Machina Opus on the bulkheads, the massive blast door housings, the way the starlight slanted in through the spinal way's high armaglass windows, all were signs he was home. The ship was small enough that the footings of its dorsal fortresses projected into the spinal way as large plasteel cubes, their lower levels joined together by catwalks and sealed ammunition tubes. A figure shrunken by perspective was moving across the network up there, like an arachnid in its web.

Small was a relative term regarding Imperial voidcraft. The

spinal way was fifteen yards wide, and almost three times as tall. Although compared to the *Macragge's Honour*, the *Rudense* was a minnow, it was still large enough to get lost in.

Felix laughed at himself. Who was he to fret over Guilliman's yearning for the past, when he was becoming overly sentimental himself? Why else would he be here, on his way to deliver orders that could have been sent by a simple message? What was he doing? Did he crave his brothers' approval? Did he wish to impress them, to remind them he was still part of their fraternity? Did he fear that he was not?

He was no longer a Greyshield. Not any more. He missed that; he missed them. The others would miss it too, now it was over.

The spinal way ended in a steep funnel. The funnel further split into three separate corridors and two flights of stairs that led into the maze of holds, stores and generatoria that sat forward of the enginarium and the thrumming reactor-heart of the ship.

The leftmost corridor led him towards the Space Marines' accommodation. The Primaris armouries were also that way, as were their training rooms and the small apothecarion, sited amidships, safely away from the hull. The equipment required for a demi-company occupied a lot of room. He passed a garage where five Repulsor grav-tanks waited in silence, bolted down to the floor around the gaping shaft of a vehicle elevator.

He rounded a corner and heard voices. There were warriors in the refectorum. He quickened his pace. He heard the gruff laughter of Bjarni Arvisson. There were three others in there with him at least. Justinian Parris spoke, and Bjarni laughed again. Then came the quiet voice of Kalael, gene-kin of the Lion. As he neared, their words became more distinct. There were sounds indicating perhaps six more of his brothers, their low conversation muffled by the hard metallic sounds of weapons being taken apart and cleaned.

As he approached the refectorum, a Primaris Space Marine in a day robe emerged from a side room, carrying a dented vambrace and a tool roll. His eyes rose in surprise.

'Brother-captain!' he said.

'Solus,' said Felix. He halted before his old comrade, and the two of them clasped arms. Felix reached up and disengaged his helm, lifted it over his head and tucked it into the crook of his elbow.

Laphis was further out from Macragge's star than the capital. It was cold, but the skies were thin, and the sun burned easily, so like the majority of the inhabitants native to the world, Felix's skin was light brown. His black hair was long for a Space Marine, with a fringe swept over grey eyes that conveyed an impression of utmost seriousness.

Solus was of Sanguinius' line and was as beautiful as his gene-lord had been. His eyes were a pale blue. Though the Unnumbered Sons' armour bore the livery of the Chapters they were kin with, their robes were grey. Solus, however, had dyed his red when Felix had been aboard, in honour of Sanguinius.

'To what do we owe this pleasure?' asked Solus.

'The pleasure is mine, my brother,' said Felix.

Solus gave him a quizzical look. His lips parted, showing sharp eye teeth.

Felix smiled. 'It is good to see you.'

'You have bad news,' said Solus. 'I can see it, brother.'

'Am I really that transparent?'

'I do not need to be of the Librarius to read your face, Felix. You are not a man who dissembles well.'

Felix reached out and grasped Solus' shoulder.

'The news is both good and bad, my friend. Good and bad. Come, I will share it with all of you. You deserve to hear it from me – it is the least I can do.'

There was a horrendous crash, and a roar of laughter went up from the refectorum, most of it Bjarni's feral bellow.

'Do I have to say that half of them are in there?' said Solus.

'I hear them, though Bjarni Arvisson makes the noise of ten men. It is good. I want to speak with them all.'

'Then I shall fetch the others. I will spread the word, captain.'

'Is Lieutenant Sarkis on board?' asked Felix.

'He is in the armorium.'

'Tinkering with his battleplate again?'

'What else?' said Solus. 'I shall fetch him first.'

Solus hurried away. Felix stalked down the corridor. The refectorum door was closed and he pushed it open stealthily. As he looked inside his mind flooded with memories. Twenty Space Marines were dotted around the long tables filling the room. None of them noticed him. Oil cloths were spread out before them, the components of weapons laid out for cleaning, and they were engrossed in their work. The place smelled of men, gun oil, lapping powder and yesterday's nutrient gruel. Regulations said they should not undertake such work in the eating area, but they gathered there because there was nowhere else of size besides the training ground to congregate. The armorium was out of the question. That was small, and Lieutenant Sarkis' pet projects had overtaken the space even in Felix's time. It had got worse since the son of Ferrus Manus had taken command.

Though the Unnumbered Sons were formed into temporary Chapters of their own kind, after several years of the crusade had passed, Guilliman had decreed that they spend time fighting in mixed squads in order that the differing gene-lines learn each other's strengths, and how to best work together. As more of the Unnumbered Sons had been assigned to their permanent homes and their numbers in the crusade decreased, each rotation had been longer, and Felix's demi-company had been fighting together for some time.

Most of the Primaris Space Marines present were of Roboute Guilliman's line. Five were not. Bjarni's gene-seed obviously came from Leman Russ, and his skin was covered in faded Fenrisian tribal tattoos. Then there was Aldred and Urstan, who were kin to Dorn, Lei Jian of Chogoris, and Kalael, whose gene-father was Lion El'Jonson. But being Primaris Space Marines bound them together when their differing heritages might have set them apart.

After a decade of war, the Primaris Space Marines still seemed new. The Imperium was used to technological stagnancy, and in many ways, the Primaris warriors were shocking: a blasphemy against the holy works of the Emperor-Omnissiah to some, a sure sign of the deity's work in the world to others. It was probable, Felix thought, that only the primarch's presence had prevented the advent of the Primaris Marines sparking yet another internal war between the Imperium's factions.

The less theologically inclined cared only about the Primaris Space Marines' effectiveness in combat. They were bigger and stronger than the firstborn Space Marines, and equipped with potent weapons. There were other less obvious differences between the two types as well, but though the unseen was more essential to the salvation of the Imperium, when one witnessed the Primaris Space Marines in battle, these deeper changes seemed of lesser importance compared to their increased durability and new wargear.

Most of the noise in the room came from Bjarni. It was always Bjarni. He was taking aim with a throwing axe at a stack of empty nutrient cans. The wall behind was scarred by repeated impacts. Kalael was a few feet away, sharpening the teeth of his chainsword, unconcerned by the target practice taking place so close to his face.

The others Felix knew well, but none so well as Justinian Parris, who, along with Solus, was his closest friend.

'I will split the third one from the left, second row,' said Bjarni, weighing his axe in his hand.

'What will you wager?' said a warrior named Ciceron.

'Does it matter? I never miss!' bragged Bjarni.

'You nearly hit me once,' said Kalael. 'That was a miss.'

'It was not. I intended to give you a fright, brooding angel,' said Bjarni wolfishly. His hair was grey and shaved into a tall mohawk. His beard retained some red, but he appeared older than he was. His nose was crooked from an ancient break. Not all the scars that criss-crossed his body had been won in service; several he attributed to the attentions of Fenris' notorious wildlife during his childhood.

'You cannot brag without betting, Bjarni,' said Justinian. 'Come on, put down a bet.'

Justinian was typically Macraggian in appearance, though he hailed from the hive world of Ardium rather than the capital world itself. He was tall and blond, with aristocratic features that could have seemed cold had he not smiled so generously.

'I have only my ration of delicious nutrient gruel to offer,' said Bjarni. 'So who cares?'

'It is the form of the thing,' said Felix, speaking up and stepping over the raised lintel of the door. 'Honour demands a boast carry a wager.'

'Felix!' shouted Bjarni. A huge grin split his beard. He hurled the axe without looking. It slammed into his designated target, cutting it in two and sending the rest of the stack bouncing off the steel tables around the room. Kalael scowled under his hood as he flicked cans off his work.

The men rose from their tables and greeted the captain. Bjarni got there first, flinging his arms around Felix in a bear hug.

'Tell me you have come back to lead us, captain,' said the Fenrisian. 'Just one more time, eh?' He slammed Felix on the shoulder pad with his huge fist.

'If only I could. I wish I had been with you during the drop on Raukos.'

'My brother,' said Justinian, grasping Felix's armoured hand in his own. 'It has been too long.'

'If you are not to fight with us, why are you here, Felix?' asked Bjarni.

Felix moved into the room as other Primaris Space Marines filtered in, brought there by Solus' tidings. They filled up the long benches. Work was cleared away. Sarkis came through, giving his old commander a nod. The Medusan sat down by Justinian, his face neutral. Sarkis would not approve of Felix sharing his news in this way.

When most of the company was assembled, Felix called for quiet. He felt a stranger in his Ultramarines armour, particularly as the majority of those he addressed wore the plain grey robes of the Unnumbered Sons.

There were forty Primaris Space Marines in the room by the time Felix was ready to speak. Nearly all of Felix's old comrades were there. He knew them so well. There were several faces he did not know, transferred in as the dwindling groups of the Unnumbered Sons were merged. Far more numerous were the faces missing, all the warriors he had known and laughed with since his awakening. His eidetic memory would never allow him to forget the dead.

There had been many mistakes. The Primaris Space Marines had excellent training but no real combat experience when the Indomitus Crusade began. Many had fallen in the early days. He imagined he saw the faces of those earliest comrades, smiling or grim according to their character, between the living warriors in the room.

'Captain Felix?' prompted Sarkis.

Felix broke free of his memories. The faces of the dead faded. 'I have decided to bring you your new orders myself, my brothers,' he said. 'Our brotherhood is at an end. I wished to say farewell to you all. When we reach Macragge, we will likely never see each other again.' He paused, unsure of how to go on. 'I asked the primarch's permission to tell you personally. He said that I may. So I have your new assignments here.'

He opened a pouch on his right thigh and drew out a sheaf of parchments.

'Finally!' roared Bjarni. He grinned. 'No offence, brothers.'

'I do not rejoice,' said Justinian quietly.

'Brother,' said Ciceron, 'we have known this was going to happen for a long time. It was inevitable. Times change. We are needed elsewhere so that the fightback might begin.'

Felix nodded. 'The Greyshields have served their purpose. The last few formations of the Unnumbered Sons will be broken up, wherever they are. All of us are to be assigned to other Chapters.'

'I have nothing but the greatest respect for our lord, but he lacks flexibility,' said Kalael dourly. 'He only created our formation to get around his ban on the founding of new Legions. It is clear to me he can no longer continue to defy his own edicts.'

'Brother, you go too far,' snarled Bjarni.

'I do not criticise him,' said Kalael emphatically. He had a narrow face, with a resting expression that radiated suspicion. He was always prying behind the seeming of things, looking for the secret truths beneath. 'What I am saying is that Roboute Guilliman is a general with a penchant for imposing rules, who then has to break them when he finds himself trapped by his own regulations. He is a great hero, but as he is at pains to remind us all, he is no god and is imperfect. That is all I am saying.' He tapped his ear. 'Listen to my words, Brother Bjarni, or does the growling of beasts drown out reason?'

Bjarni ignored the slight, and rocked his head. 'He is no Russ, that is sure. Russ had no care for *rules*.'

'You should not talk that way about the primarch,' said Felix.

'He is not my primarch,' said Kalael.

'He is *the* primarch,' said Felix. Kalael had always antagonised him. 'You will show him respect.'

'Just because you do not like what I say does not make it untrue. Is it untrue, Felix? You should know.'

Felix had no rejoinder to that. 'Legion or not, the Greyshields shall fight together no more.'

Justinian looked at his hands. 'We all knew this day would come, but I cannot believe it.'

'Is it not true that our numbers have dwindled as the fight has gone on?' said Kalael. 'Most of us have new brotherhoods. Those of us remaining in Fleet Primus are, in the main, of Guilliman's line. The gene-lines of the other primarchs are in the minority. There are enough Primaris Adeptus Astartes to replenish the Ultramarines ten times over.' Kalael picked up a chainsword tooth and scrutinised it carefully. 'Perhaps he does not wish to disband his power base, but moves to openly proclaim a new Legion. Ten new Chapters of his own gene-line – I wonder where they might possibly be stationed?'

'The Ultramarines will remain as they have been since the Second Founding,' Felix said firmly. 'One thousand battle-brothers. There are already numerous Chapters derived from his gene-line. Many of the Primaris Space Marines will be dispatched to those. They all need rebuilding.'

'That's all well for you and yours,' said Bjarni, slapping his hands against a table. 'Roboute Guilliman was the architect of the Codex Astartes. My gene-father was against it. So far as I know, the Space Wolves still are. Many of my brothers have gone home to Fenris, but I have not. What fate awaits me?'

'You're an oversight, you barbarian,' said Kalael with a sly smile.

'We shall duel, Brother Kalael, and then we will see who is the oversight!' barked Bjarni joyfully. It had always been thus. Kalael baited the wolf constantly; Bjarni pretended not to notice. Either would gladly die for the other. Felix was baffled why they did not kill each other.

Felix's face set as gravely as a memorial stone. Bjarni's face froze.

'Brother?'

'I...' He held out a script of parchment with Bjarni's name and number upon it. This was hard, but a leader could not shy away from difficult tasks. 'Bjarni, I... I know how much returning to Fenris meant to you.'

Bjarni's skin went white. His faded tattoos stood out clearly on his cheekbones as he reached for the order scrip.

'Very few of you will be going to your home worlds,' said Felix. 'I am sorry. I remember how we all spoke of serving with the founding Chapters.'

'It is easy for you to say,' said Bjarni, reading the parchment. 'Who by the ice jotun are the Wolfspear?'

'They are a new Chapter, brother,' said Felix. 'The remainder of the sons of Russ in Fleet Primus are to remain here, at Raukos. You are to guard the Pit.'

Bjarni stared at the order paper.

'There will be many battles,' said Felix. 'You will be a great hero.'

The others were coming forward and taking their papers, discussing their new brotherhoods in hushed tones.

'You may not be serving with the First Founding, but most of you are bound for the Primogenitor Chapters, and there surely cannot be a greater honour,' said Felix. 'Do you not see how important those of the Unnumbered Sons who remained with the fleet are? You, my brothers, are the very best! Do not take these orders as a rebuke, but as the opposite. The Imperial Regent thinks far ahead. His aim with you Greyshields who remain was to create a warrior corps who, when divided, would foster good relations between the various gene-lines of the Adeptus Astartes. I have come to know the primarch well. He believes that the divisions between the Legions of his brothers contributed to Horus' betrayal and dog the Imperium still. The arch traitor was able to divide the Legions and their primarchs by using their mistrust as a lever. They fought together, but rarely understood one another. We have fought together, and we have bled together.'

'Aye, and we have died together!' shouted Bjarni. 'And this is my payment.'

'Many battles, remember that,' said Kalael. 'New sagas. New tales to be told.' Hearing this from his friend calmed Bjarni somewhat.

'We should be glad no matter our destination. A warrior's function is to die well, in a good cause,' said Aldred.

'True,' said Felix. 'And our cause is the finest of all. We have lived and trained together. We are unlike any brotherhood that has ever been. We have known the glory of combat and the tedium of waiting side by side. We have become close, despite our differences. Each of us is part of a unit of many kindreds, and we will take the friendships we have forged with us to our new Chapters. We will be the sinew that binds the bones of the Imperium together, transcending old boundaries.' Felix turned to the Fenrisian. 'Our bonds can never be sundered. You, Bjarni, are born of Fenris and are enhanced with the essence of the primarch Leman Russ, different and strange to my own heritage, but you will always be my brother, no matter what colours you wear or what name the Chapter you belong to bears.'

'This is troubling, Brother Felix,' Bjarni said thoughtfully. He was quick to rage and quick to laugh, but Bjarni had a deeper side that he hid most of the time. 'When my kin went to the Space Wolves, I thought that my time was only delayed. I yearned to return to Fenris and fight alongside the Rout. Can I ever truly call myself a son of Russ if I do not?'

The last of the Primaris Space Marines were filtering into the room, and quick whispers were exchanged to update the newcomers. Felix handed the remainder of the scrips to Sarkis, who passed them out.

'There are many Primaris Space Marines of Russ' line wearing new colours, brother,' said Felix. 'You will be welcomed by them. And you will always be welcomed by me.'

'How will the lords of ice take it, though? Will I be forever lost without a home, brotherless, unable to return to Fenris?'

'You have too large a personality to ever be without friends,' said Aldred. 'I will fight any warrior who says otherwise.' Bjarni and he slapped hands together and clasped them tightly.

'And you will never be without brothers, either,' said Justinian, getting to his feet. 'Not while one of us still lives.'

Justinian had looked at his own orders with perfect equanimity. He had been assigned to the Novamarines stationed in Ultramar – still the realm of the primarch, but the Novamarines were not the Ultramarines. Felix tried to guess Justinian's thoughts, but he could not. When he chose, the man was a fortress, his feelings hidden behind fair walls.

'These are sad tidings,' said Justinian, 'but they hold the kernel of the future in them. We have our new brothers to meet and fight with. There is opportunity for glory for us, always, wherever we go and no matter the livery we wear. I thank Captain

Felix for letting us know. I am sure the lord commander was curious to know why he wished to do this. It is a sign of how much Felix cares for us, to bear the primarch's scrutiny.' He gestured at the dispensing machine at the rear of the room. 'I wish for something better to toast you with, my brother, but all we have is nutrient gruel.'

'No ale,' said Bjarni sadly.

'No wine,' added Kalael.

'We have each other,' said Justinian, 'for a few months more. If I read this right, many of us will remain together until the primarch returns to Ultramar, and the road to Macragge will not be without its battles. We shall fight all the harder knowing the brothers who are to leave us now wage war elsewhere. This is not the end, but the beginning.'

Felix nodded. This was the response he was hoping for. He should have kept himself above it all, but he needed to say goodbye properly.

'To Captain Felix!' said Justinian. 'To our dear friend and brother, Decimus!'

'Felix! Felix! Felix!' the others shouted, banging their fists on the tables.

They spoke awhile of old times, and gradually the company dispersed back to their duties. Felix tarried too long. Realising he was late to attend the primarch, he made his farewells.

Lieutenant Sarkis caught Felix's arm in his bionic hand before he left. 'Are you sure that was wise, Decimus, performing such a role? Should you have not left it to me?'

'I am sorry that I denied you the opportunity.'

Sarkis' lips crinkled around his metal-toothed smile. 'Oh no, I am glad you did. You did a far better job of mollifying Bjarni than I would have done. Had I given that news, I would be fighting him right now.'

'You exaggerate.'

'Not by much. You have a more human touch than I.'

Felix glanced at the bare metal fingers grasping his armour.

'Does the primarch really know you have done this?' asked Sarkis.

'He did not seem overly concerned. I knew he would accept my request, or I would not have asked.'

Sarkis stared hard at Felix through an eye crafted from living diamond. 'You are bold, to presume the primarch's thoughts.'

'We have become close.'

'I pray your bond does not bring you trouble. To be close to power is to be close to danger.'

'I can hide nothing from him,' replied Felix, 'and there are some things I cannot keep from my brothers either. I had to do this.'

'For them, or for you? There are some things that should be kept secret,' said Sarkis. 'Remember your position, Felix. I would prefer it if, a century from now, when I call upon the Ultramarines it is you I deal with, and not some warrior I do not know who has taken your place owing to your needless emotional attachments.'

They locked eyes for a long moment.

Spoken like a Medusan, thought Felix, but left these words unspoken. 'I thank you for your concern, lieutenant,' he said instead. Sarkis stared at him a moment longer before releasing him.

As Sarkis' bionic grip left his arm, Felix knew for certain that he would never be returning to the *Rudense*. That part of his life was over for good.

'Fight well, my brothers!' he shouted, holding his fist aloft in salute. 'I shall see you again in Ultramar!'

CHAPTER SIXTEEN

KU'GATH'S CAVALCADE

In parody of the voidships of the Imperium, giant plague arks came through the strange sky of the Garden of Nurgle. There were seven of them all told, Nurgle's sacred number, sailing serenely towards Iax as stately as pleasure barques upon a perfect sea.

They had been living things. Perhaps they lived still, held to a hideous existence by the will of the Plague God, for they sang with awful sorrow, though their tails and flukes hung limply and their bodies were decomposed as a corpse too long in the water. Their skin hung in great swags from muscles writhing with frantic life. The blubber underneath had decayed into fur-like expanses playing host to a multiplicity of parasites. Ribs the size of docking spars framed dark, stinking interiors. Open wounds dripped viscid matter, and slurry falls of rotten blood and excrement fell from orifices widened by the relentless efforts of carrion eaters. Encircling these carcass-ships were shifting black veils of flies by the billion, fat-bodied and voracious.

Rot had made the creatures barely recognisable as void whales. Dragged into the Realm of Chaos during the Noctis Aeterna, they'd been hollowed out by disease and infested by super-natural vermin until they were suitable to carry the legions of Nurgle.

The first came to the rift some way ahead of the others. The bony beak of its exposed jawbones pushed at the quivering meniscus separating the material world from the realm of souls. An oil-scum iridescence rippled out from the contact, stretch-ing at first without giving. But Nurgle would not be denied, and the bone pierced the barrier with an audible, wet tearing. This final barrier between real and unreal penetrated, the carcass-ship heaved out like a rotting stillbirth, mobbed by its escort of flies.

Whatever magic held it aloft in Nurgle's kingdom did not work upon Iax yet, and the plague ark fell as soon as it was through. Bloated belly met shallow water, sending up a flat wave of mud. It slithered forwards, carried by momentum over the fringes of the marsh and onto the green meadows of the garden world. Away from the empyrean, the meatship's rotting accelerated. The greening skin of its flanks split, spilling a host of daemons into Ultramar.

The most numerous were the flies, shiny black with the triple ring of Nurgle's blessing blood red upon their backs. The great number who escorted the craft were increased by more issuing from the whale's insides in droning blizzards, bringing with them a stink of rot. Upon leaving their host, they rose up into Iax's quiet night in floods so dense that the moon was blotted out and the promise of day broken, and they set out to the four corners of the world, bearing their cargoes of disease.

Giggling nurglings vied with the flies in number, pouring in tittering avalanches from the flanks of the void whale. Upon the ground, the imps plucked at the mud and drew out the smaller life forms of Iax, those creatures that exist beneath man's notice but which are necessary to a world's survival. With nimble fingers, the nurglings twisted these beasts into terrible forms, then set them free with coos of encouragement to do Nurgle's work.

Gangplanks of rotten timber poked through curtains of flesh and thumped onto the dying earth. Down these bridges walked plaguebearers, the tallymen who were damned for all eternity to enumerate whatever caught their god's attention. One-horned and doleful, they came mumbling their litanies of diseases gifted to the mortal universe by their generous father, or else counting the flies, or the nurglings, or the bacteria that were turning the blades of the grass black. The task of keeping count of Nurgle's bounty was impossible, and for them an eternal torment, yet they were compelled to obey, their heralds leading them in their reckoning with drones of maddening repetitiveness.

The plaguebearers kicked and squelched their way through the nurgling tide, arranging themselves into muttering cohorts. Standards were lifted up and shrill music played, and they began their advance. In a great parade seven thousand, seven hundred and seventy-seven strong the daemons marched, more of them spilling from the carcass-ship onto the clean earth of Iax like maggots from a corpse's belly, dull bells knelling, broken pipes wheezing, all the while counting and counting and counting.

The cavalcade was in high spirits; even the miserable plague-bearers had a lightness in their shuffling. Wooden carts were heaved out and down onto the pristine grasslands, rattling with their contents, their brightly coloured sides smirched with every manner of filth.

The second ship passed through the gap. Like the first, it lost its ability to fly as soon as it was free of the strange non-physics of the empyrean, and it slipped from the air with obese grandeur to skid across the poisoned swamp. It came to rest by the first. Hundreds of daemons perished under the bulk of this second carcass-ship, but once its sides split, it replenished the horde with thousands more, and the soil was turned to a stinking quagmire by the tread of soft daemon feet.

The third meatship came down with the elegance of a decrepit palace collapsing, followed by the fourth, and then the fifth. When the sixth carcass came down, the marsh and meadows were full of daemons, and the land bordering them already turning diseased.

It was then that the first of the daemonic lords emerged, those who would lead Nurgle's efforts upon the mortal world of Iax.

A daemonic herald strutted into the giant cavity of a void whale's eye socket and stood upon the dripping lip. It was a daemon, but it might once have been a man. It lacked the sour countenance of the plaguebearers and their single eyes. It had two, and mirth glinted in them so brightly that the streams of rheum running from them could not hide it.

The herald cleared its throat with some considerable effort, scowled, and then waved behind it. A plaguebearer carrying a rusting horn shuffled to its side and blew into the mouthpiece. Its effort was a wheezing raspberry, but from the gaping funnel a mighty blast sounded, and ten thousand ailing faces turned to the whale-ship's empty eye.

Pleased to have the horde's attention, the herald puffed out its distended belly, straining its filthy silks and adding to their stains with leakage from its sores. It pushed down the goitre at its neck so that it might speak, giggling merrily and shouting out as loudly as the horn.

'Septicus, Septicus! Seventh Lord of the Seventh Manse!' wailed the herald. Greening bells clonked dully in response. The daemons shrugged and turned away to continue their muttering, droning, buzzing egress from the realm of Chaos.

'Septicus comes! Lord of the Seven Hosts! Keeper of the Seven Codes of Life! Untwister of skeins, straightener of mortal coils! Septicus the Mighty! Septicus Seven of the Many Plagues! He comes, he comes, he comes!' bellowed the herald.

In the whale's cheek, a flap of skin was cast aside as dramatically as the curtains in a lyceum, and there came forth a titan of pestilence. A Great Unclean One, huge and jiggly in its ampleness of flesh, beneficent in disease and all morbidities. He smiled and waved and hallooed at his servants, full of bonhomie, even though his guts hung in grey ropes from the open skin of his belly. They dangled so low that the infected nails of his feet snagged in them and tore them into shreds, whence leaked black humours and squirming worms.

His arms were long and disproportionate to his fat frame. The seven fingers on each of his hands were tipped with poisonous talons. On his back hung a long, filthy sword, dull of blade but envenomed with diseases to moulder the soul. Septicus' baldrick of failing leather was lost amid his folds of skin, and he wore no other clothes or harnesses other than his weapon and its gear, but under his left arm he cradled the glistening stomach sac of some unfortunate creature, its top criss-crossed with thick, distended veins that pulsed with life still. Pipes of hollowed antlers had been set into the gut, and they clacked together as he shouldered his way out past the curtain of skin. He stopped at the brink and leapt to the ground, trusting to the bodies of his lesser kin to cushion his fall.

He cackled madly as he dropped, landing with a splattering impact that sprayed daemonic foetor everywhere, then rose up from the mud of Iax with a broad yellow grin. As he adjusted his pipes they slipped around in the crook of his arm, letting out an ungodly wail. The music was of the most dreadful kind and pained the spirits of his daemonic host. They cringed from the racket, and the Great Unclean One laughed uproariously at their reaction.

'*Septicus is arrived!*' he announced. '*I have come to guide you, my little ones. The others will be here soon, so I shall play you a merry song, children of Papa Nurgle, to speed you from your vessels and on your way! Tread with joy, for we do great work here – great work!*' And he set the long mouthpiece to his blistered lips, filled his rancid lungs and began to pump at the stomach pipes with one bent elbow. His rotten fingers danced with marvellous dexterity upon the sounding holes of the instrument, and he smiled as he made his music, but what came forth was as jolly as a dirge, and so redolent of fever pain and toothaches it agonised all who heard it.

The last plague ark touched down. It rolled onto its side as it landed, and its jaws flopped open. Grumbling at the poorness of the landing, the seventh and final cohort came out, their cymbals and bells merging with Septicus' jig. Other daemons joined in with his tune, and soon his playing was swollen by an accompaniment of piercing flutes played by seven hundred lesser pipers.

Such a display was a sight to please Nurgle's sore eyes, and a rare thing it was. The creatures mustering upon the garden world were among his very best. They were his most revolting, his most contagious, his finest warriors and his most skilled accountants of ailment. They were the Plague Guard, and they were the vanguard of the great invasion of Iax. A more dread legion could not be found anywhere in Nurgle's garden or beyond.

Regiments of daemons marched out to the sound of Septicus' pipes. There were plaguebearers, beasts of Nurgle, rot flies, maggots and drooling daemons of every degree. Nurglings continued to tumble like rain from the holes and pores and orifices of the stinking whale-ships, flooding the land long after their larger kin had grumbled their way free.

There were other greater daemons there besides Lord Septicus, the leaders of this filthy host, fragments of Nurgle himself, each given will of their own to go out and do mischief. There were but seven of them in total, one for each of the Plague Guard's cohorts, for they were rare even in the Garden of Nurgle. One by one, they forced their way out from the plague arks. The whale-ships were already liquefying, their putrescent fluids poisoning the world. The greater daemons stepped onto Iax slicked in these juices, grinning widely.

There was Bubondubon the Smiler, jolliest of all, who laughed and joked as he capered past Septicus, receiving a friendly wink in return. Then Pestus Throon emerged, chewing his way through the stomach wall of his whale-ship. He gobbled down strips of slimy meat as he joined the stream of daemons, belching loudly. He looked too fat to move, but he was mighty, very mighty. After all, it was Throon who had brought low the ancient empire of the Dravians so successfully that no mortal history now remembered them, an accomplishment he regaled his fellows with often.

After him came the Gangrel, who was as tall and thin as the others were rotund and squat. He knuckle-walked on stilted arms, dragging useless legs through a trail of his own filth. Then came Squatumous, the Pestifex Maximus, and then the one called only Famine, who in keeping with Nurgle's boundless sense of humour was fatter than all save Pestus. Septicus Seven, their lieutenant, made six.

Their general had yet to emerge.

Septicus took the mouthpiece of his pipes from his lips and cupped a puffy hand to his mouth. *'Oh, Ku'Gath! Oh, Plague-father! Oh, First in Nurgle's favour! The host of sickness is assembled! We are waiting! Come lead us, mighty putrefactor. Bring us the blessings of your filth!'*

Septicus began to tap his foot and shout *'Ku'Gath! Ku'Gath!*

Ku'Gath!' to the beat of the music. He waved his free hand, conducting the others, until the place of manifestation resounded to the chants of all the daemons, calling upon their lord with malodorous breath.

'Ku'Gath! Ku'Gath!' the daemons chanted. Septicus joined the song of his pipes to the orchestra gathered at his side. Bubon-dubon laughed loudly.

'Ku'Gath! Come!' gasped the Gangrel. Every word was that being's last. He lived perpetually on the cusp of death.

An angry roar was their answer. An impact squelched from within the first whale-ship, then another, and a rusty broadsword the length of a battle tank carved down through its rancid hide. An arm emerged holding the sword, then a head crowned with a spread of horns, and out came Ku'Gath the Plaguefather, lord of disease, and most favoured son of Grandfather Nurgle.

'Enough! Enough!' he bellowed as his palanquin forced its way free of the whale-ship. Stacked high upon it behind Ku'Gath were mildew-spotted canvas parcels, tied up with fraying rope. Within the damp boxes alembics, thuribles, burners and tubes of matter clinked, for Ku'Gath carried his laboratory with him wherever he went. Hordes of nurglings bore him up, their mirth annoying Ku'Gath, who was by nature a despondent being.

'No more music! No more laughter!' He leaned violently to the left, causing the nurglings on that side to burst, but there were always more of them to carry his massive body. The palanquin shifted in the direction he flung his weight. Its sodden banners swaying heavily behind Ku'Gath's horned head, the palanquin turned and moved forwards.

'Shut up! Be quiet! This is no laughing matter!' he boomed. His shout was powerful as a pandemic, and reached as far. *'Grandfather Nurgle's business is a serious business!'*

Septicus smiled more broadly and played more merrily, and

the horde of daemons swayed from foot to foot in the slow dance of decay.

Ku'Gath rolled his eyes so violently that one fell out from his skull. He was still pushing it back into place when his palanquin drew level with Septicus. He slapped the mouthpiece of the pipes from his lieutenant's hand. The pipes moaned mournfully.

'No more music,' grumbled Ku'Gath. *'Why must there always be music?'*

'Old Father Nurgle demands joy!' said Septicus, grinning his yellow grin at his king. *'See what bounties are here for us to corrupt! Look at all this hateful organisation. We shall plough it under the soil and nourish it with the decay of this mortal realm. We shall raise high a garden ripe with endless fecundity! Entropy beckons! Growth without limit! Decay without reason!'*

Ku'Gath harrumphed. Septicus' pipes were momentarily silenced, but his orchestra played shrilly on, piping out his tune on the femurs of dead men. The whole army was singing, a buzzing, wheezing lament that was entirely the opposite of joyful.

'Never mind,' grumbled Ku'Gath.

Septicus retrieved his mouthpiece, and raised his scabrous eyebrows in a request for permission. Ku'Gath snorted, an action that sent streamers of mucus blasting from his nose.

Tilting his bloated head ironically, Septicus played anew.

Ku'Gath belched and urged his nurglings on. He bullied his way through his Plague Guard until he reached the edge of the meadows, where he brought his palanquin to a halt by lifting himself up and violently sitting, stunning his nurglings into immobility. A gleaming white building, hatefully clean, stood luminous not far away. It smelled of cleansing unguents and disinfectants. Ku'Gath took a dislike to it immediately.

'Medicine,' he hissed. *'Balms. Cleanliness! Oh, oh, oh, it will not do! That place is the death of Nurgle's gifts!'*

A thought took hold in his rotting brain, and his doleful face almost managed a smile. The hospital was a perfect place to begin his task. He lifted his arm and gestured.

'To the place of healing!' he commanded. *'Make it filthy! Make it stink! Make it fit for Nurgle's work!'*

The shuffling, singing horde of daemons changed course, heading towards the hospital on the hill. Swarms of plague drones swung around in the sky and buzzed through the shifting veils of smaller rot flies towards it. Urging their winged mounts on, the plaguebearers riding the giant flies outpaced the daemons on foot. At their approach, gunshots cracked, cutting through the phlegmy dirge of the host.

Ku'Gath pulled a face of contempt. They could not stop the Plague Guard! Turning around in his throne, he bellowed, *'Poxbearers, bring out the cauldron!'*

Seventy times seventy plaguebearers broke off from their march and walked to the drooling corpse-mouth of the lead ship. The dead void whale convulsed, vomiting up slimy, rotting ropes of twisted hair.

Seeing what Ku'Gath had ordered, Septicus waddled to take command, his pipes honking and squalling under his arm. Squatumous and Bubondubon went with him. The latter uncoiled a filthy whip.

'Get the ropes – pull them hard!' commanded Septicus while Ku'Gath looked on. *'Heave, my pretties! Heave, my little dollops of unctuous gore, my decaying ones, my flaking fleshlings, my diseased darlings, heave!'* Once more he began to play.

To the hooting of Septicus' pipe, the plaguebearers pulled. With gnarled hands and paws made soft by fungal infestation, with limbs wizened and leprous, with fingers knotted with arthritis and lessened in number by gangrene, they dragged upon the ropes, mumbling their count of sicknesses all the while.

'*Heave!*' bellowed Squatumous. Bubondubon cracked his whip, and the dirty glass set into its length chopped flies from the air by the gross.

The plaguebearers slipped in the foul mud; some fell and were trampled. Strands in the rope broke and unwound violently, flinging out acidic juices before the cores gave way and pitched whole lines of daemons into the filth. But enough daemons stood and enough ropes held. Flaking rust and grinding bone, a gigantic iron cauldron came juddering out of the void whale's gullet. It clacked on the jawbones, dislodging the great feeding fans of the dead beast's mouth. Upon the edge of the beak, the cauldron became lodged, and no amount of pulling would set it free.

The flies had blotted out the stars. Greenish clouds rushed across the new dark, and a stinking drizzle began to fall.

'*Heave!*' yelled Squatumous.

'*Pull, you laggards!*' shouted Bubondubon.

Septimus' playing took on a see-saw rhythm, well suited to hauling.

'*You, the Flyblown! You, the Rashgirdled, aid your brothers!*' roared Bubondubon, his whip snapping over the heads of the shambling daemons. More cohorts broke from the legion. Palsied hands dragged up ropes from the mud, and they lent their strength to their fellows. Thunder rumbled.

'*Heave!*' yelled Squatumous.

Bubondubon applied the lash, cutting plaguebearers down. The rain intensified, raindrops pounding onto rotting backs. The daemons pulled and pulled, Septicus' braying music urging them on, until there was a crack of rotting bone louder than a tree giving out in a storm. The cauldron shifted. The daemons stumbled at the sudden release of tension, but none fell.

'*Take up the slack! Heave!*' bellowed Squatumous and Bubondubon together.

A last effort dislodged the cauldron from the whale's mouth. It rolled down onto the mud with deceptive slowness, squashing flat scores of the daemons who had pulled it free, and came to rest. Its red rusty sides turned brown as the rain soaked them. It was fat-bellied and high-lipped, with three stout pegs for legs. It was unremarkable in form, similar to cooking pots from any number of worlds and ages, except for its massive size and the three-ringed device of Nurgle repeated three times around its widest part.

Already lords of the Plague Guard were moving to the cauldron's side, commanding the daemon legions to set it upright. More daemons dragged a sled of bone from a second whale and placed it alongside.

Ku'Gath stared at the cauldron while it was hauled up onto the sled and made fast, remembering his own birth within its rusted interior. This was Nurgle's own pot. Ku'Gath had once been a nurgling like the multitudes who bore him, until he had fallen in and drunk up Nurgle's most promising disease.

So the story went, and so it was true.

The shame of depriving his father of his prize malady dogged Ku'Gath still. Nurgle had been delighted with his new son, and showered Ku'Gath with paternal affection, but Ku'Gath did not feel worthy of it.

The Plaguefather looked skywards, his diseased ears picking up the sound of approaching aircraft. The mortals were reacting quickly. It would not help them. He yawned as bombs fell and blazing mushrooms sprouted from his advancing horde. The mortals used weapons of fire, but the horde's flesh was sodden, and vital with Chaos magic. The promethium gels sent to cleanse them guttered out swiftly.

The greater daemons of the Plague Guard chortled loudly as an attack craft fell hurtling from the sky, blue fire wreathing its jets, its air intakes clogged with insects. It plunged into the marsh, its engine's howl gurgling to a stop as it sank beneath the water's surface.

'*Gangrel! Famine!*' Ku'Gath bellowed. '*Fetch out the mortal sorcerers. Bring me the Cult of Renewal and the Cult of Blessed Protrusion. Begin the ritual to summon the remainder of the Bubonicus Infectus!*'

Ku'Gath scowled as his minions rushed to do his bidding. From one of the whale-ships, human worshippers of the Great Father marched, the final members of his vanguard. It was good they did his work, though there were fewer in the cults than there had been. The Garden of Nurgle was not kind to mortals, and many had been killed by their journey in the meatships.

He sighed. Such was the circle of life. Their bodies were now food for Nurgle's blessed vermin.

Ku'Gath did not smile. He never did. There could be no joy in his life, not until he had proven himself worthy of Papa Nurgle's love. But he did allow himself a tentative hope as his eyes lighted again on the hospital, and then on the great cauldron being dragged that way.

Perhaps, here on Iax, he would redeem himself.

PART THREE

THE SPEAR OF ESPANDOR

CHAPTER SEVENTEEN

DEATH IN ILLYRIA

The Thandian Pass was burning, the smoke partly hiding the Museo Illyricus situated at the brow. From the top of a First Company Land Raider, Marneus Calgar appraised the situation with a sense of irritation.

The rebels held the museum. Amateurish, young, poorly led rebels. But they were there nonetheless. The road was closed, the heavy traffic that used it absent. They had a device they said would kill thousands, though they said all they wished was to talk peacefully.

Calgar would not deal with men who would threaten death while speaking of peace.

There was a haze on the air. Shrubs burned on the steep slopes either side of the road, the wind shaping the fires into U-shaped lines of flame that advanced on the Ultramarines' position from where they'd been set at the summit. The smokescreen curled across the road in blue sheets, washing over the plascrete road-block placed across the carriageway some way in front of the

Land Raider and the line of three armoured Rhino transports waiting a little way behind.

Members of the Ultramar Auxilia crouched behind the barrier, guns ready. The rebels had made poor tactical choices, but they did have a lascannon, stolen from the militia barracks in Illyricon a week ago. The audacious theft had probably spurred the group into this action; success often bred folly. It wouldn't help them. The roadblock was at the extreme end of the effective range of a lascannon, and the fumes from the fires they had set would hinder them, as the beam would refract more easily.

Calgar would not hide. He wished them to feel his contempt. They called themselves 'concerned citizens'. The very phrase sickened him. The fools in the museum rose up against their protectors at the urging of creatures they could not comprehend.

What Marneus Calgar did not understand was why so many would betray the realm, wittingly or otherwise. Ultramar was under attack – the Cicatrix Maledictum spread its warping fire across the sky every night, and stories of the bloodshed and woe of other worlds spilled freely from the lips of weeping refugees. But in the heart of the nation, traitors still crept out of the dark. This band was but the latest.

He had been away from Macragge too long. To be called back by the primarch to find the core world of Ultramar under threat...

He took a calming breath. He should not have to get involved in this. But First Captain Agemman had his own problems, dealing with the invasion of Ardium.

A very long time ago, the pass was the site of genuine warfare. The rebels aped history crudely, occupying a museum meant to commemorate Macragge's unity. Weak action, weak propaganda. Calgar had come personally to send a strong response.

Calgar's bionic eye saw through the smoke as easily as if it were not there, and he saw clearly the massive drum of the main building, with a three-stepped roof and balconies interposed between the layers. There was an attached tower built over the pass itself, almost equal in girth to the main building and slightly taller. A four-lane road passed under this symbolic gatehouse on the way to Illyria.

'A desperate, pointless tactic,' he said to himself.

The walls of the museum were no greater obstacle to his augmetic sight. False-colour thermal silhouettes flashed every time he passed his eye over the position of an insurgent. They skulked behind the walls next to windows, stolen weapons held ready to fire. They hid themselves in the balconies between the overlapping roofs. All the obvious places.

He shook his head in disbelief.

'Julio,' he voxed. 'I have seen enough. It is time to put an end to this.'

He stepped down off the front of the Land Raider and jumped to the ground. If the rebels had any marksmen worthy of the name, they could feasibly have hit him there. Having seen what he had, Calgar judged himself perfectly safe.

He landed as surely as a man a hundred years younger, unimpeded by his battleplate or by the massive Gauntlets of Ultramar that formed part of it, and walked around the back of the tank. The engine muttered low, trembling the space around the vehicle's rear with heat and noise, and adding blue exhaust to the smoke. By the engine block, Sergeant Julio of the Fourth Squad, First Company stood with Calgar's honour guard and the Chapter Ancient, a Primaris Space Marine by the name of Andron Ney. Ney had been among the first of the Primaris recruits sent to the Ultramarines shortly after Cawl's revelation, and he had served with distinction. The new influx of warriors had called themselves the Three Hundred, in honour of their number. They were new, different and apart. Now, they were a valued element of the Ultramarines Chapter. Calgar himself had crossed the Rubicon Primaris years ago, and more had followed. They were all just brothers now.

The warriors stood to attention and saluted Calgar with their fists over their hearts.

'You will not speak with them, my lord?' asked Julio.

'I will not speak with them,' said Calgar.

'How many do you count, my lord?' Julio wore his Terminator plate, as did the rest of his squad waiting back with the Rhinos. Terminator-armoured brothers were ridiculous overkill for the situation, but statements had to be made.

'One hundred and thirty-two. There will be more. You will have no trouble. There could be a thousand. Look at their disposition,' said Calgar. 'Can these men truly be sons of Macragge?'

'They will have had little training, my lord,' said Julio. 'Things have got worse since you left, but levels of dissent within the auxilia are still practically zero, and most are shipped out as soon as they are trained. The men within are the unsuitable. The weak. The failures.'

'The agents of Chaos ever appeal to the weak,' said Calgar. 'Only weak men would threaten the lives of their own families with devices of mass destruction in order to secure peaceful negotiation. You are my reply to their request, Julio. Their demands are ridiculous. There can be no increase in rations. There can be no slowing of recruitment. The privations of the people of Macragge are done with the aim of stopping the enemy they unwittingly invite within.'

'The ringleader is a master of the Juventia,' said Ney. 'He has a whole troop of them in there. He has poisoned their young ears.' Ney spoke like a man who had never been a child. He was dispassionate, rational to a fault, even for an Ultramarine. Julio and Ney looked to the Chapter Master.

'This is not their fault,' said Calgar. 'Spare them, if you can.'

'I look forward to making an example of their leader,' said Julio.

'It disappoints me that our countrymen should put on such a poor showing,' said Calgar. 'No matter their age and whether they are opposed to us or not. When this is over, call the local Juventia troop masters to the capital.'

'They will all be screened thoroughly, my lord,' said Ney.

'For betrayal, yes,' said Calgar. 'But I want them *all* re-educated or replaced. This uprising is shamefully executed. The Juventia syllabus needs revision. More drill, less history. The Juventia are the last line of defence for Macragge, and the first place we go to for recruits. How could they stop an ork with this debacle? They are supposed to be young warriors.'

'My lord,' said Ney.

Calgar tapped his gauntlet fingers against his leg. 'Bring as many of the boys in alive as you can, Julio. Make examples of the adults, these appalling dregs unhappy enough with their lot in life to listen to the whispers of enemy agents, but the youth must be spared and given the chance to redeem themselves. If the lies of the Great Enemy seem more appealing than reality of life in Ultramar, and we are seen to be merciless, then we will encourage more to flock to the same foolish cause. Activists, indeed. Locate the device. Purge the leaders.'

'As you wish, my lord,' said Julio. 'But there remains an issue.' He paused significantly.

'Oh?' said Calgar.

'Vigilator Optimare Calleduus of the Vigil Opertii assures me they can handle this threat without our help. He insists on speaking with you.'

'He is here still?' said Calgar irritably.

'He has been waiting to see you for over an hour,' said Julio. 'I did say he was insistent.'

'I thought if I had him wait an hour, he might take the hint. He is supposed to be overseeing the other incident sites and tracking down the masterminds of this debacle. They will be acting to Mortarion's orders, we can be sure of that. This is a protest movement on the surface only – rot lurks beneath. Calleduus will regret remaining here.'

'Then I should send him away?'

'No, send him to me.'

Julio inclined his head slightly within the cowling of his armour. 'Send the vigilator optimare to us,' he voxed. 'Lord Macragge will speak with him.'

It took seconds for Calleduus to come up from the rear of the position. His hurried walk betrayed his sense of self-importance.

Calleduus was dressed ready for action in pale-cream combat fatigues and blue carapace, the same uniform the Ultramar Auxilia wore, though without their markings. A heavy respirator hung by one fastening from the side of his helmet. Calleduus halted and saluted smartly.

'Vigilator optimare,' said Calgar. 'According to your superiors, you have performed your role well for the five years you have held this office, until today. Today you must stand aside. The Ultramarines will handle this.'

'My lord, with all due respect, the suppression of local unrest is the role of the Vigil Opertii,' said Calleduus. 'We are ready to bring the situation to an end. Do not trouble yourself with the resolution of this event. It is a minor matter, below your attention.'

Calgar looked up the pass.

'From a certain point of view, Calleduus, you are right. Ardium is besieged and our fleet fights daily battles with Mortarion's voidcraft not far from Macragge. The enemy has penetrated to the heart of Ultramar. Every day I lose more Space Marines to the enemy in the capital system alone. But this…' He pointed at the museum. 'This is not beneath my notice. There are fifteen current incidents across Macragge, all involving this group. The enemy is so clearly involved in agitating them that I am dumbfounded the rebels cannot see it themselves. The purpose of your organisation is to prevent these incidents before they happen, not to contain them afterwards. Your eagerness to resolve this stand-off suggests to me that you want to distract from your mistakes, or seek my approval for suppressing it. I assure you, my approval will not be forthcoming.'

'My lord, we cannot catch every dissident. This year we have foiled–'

Calgar's Gravis armour whined as he shifted his position. The movement was enough to silence the vigilator optimare.

'I have read your reports. This year you have foiled twenty-six actions against the state, but you have missed fifteen today. You must admit your error. Illyria is too potent a symbol. I am tired of propaganda likening the cut-throats of old to these so-called freedoms. Worse still, their legacy is coupled with the lies of the enemy. First come the demands for greater freedom, then outright heresy. It will not be long before the enemy's religion takes root, and all that offers is miserable slavery. Their leaders lie and pay their respects to the Chapter while condemning the civilian administration as corrupt and calling me to address their concerns.

'I will not have it. The very finest of my warriors shall remove them from this place. Let the whole of Ultramar see what the Ultramarines think of their demands. The realm will see that my eyes are everywhere, and that no one – no matter their age or their station – is below my attention. Nothing, vigilator, is below my attention. In fact, I am displeased that you think it is so. Do I make myself clear?'

'Yes, my lord defender,' said the vigilator optimare stonily.

'The other incidents?'

'Are being handled by the Vigil Opertii, lord defender.'

'And the agents behind all this?'

'We are chasing several important leads, lord defender.'

Lord Defender of Greater Ultramar. Roboute Guilliman had given Calgar that title in recompense for taking the role of Master of Ultramar from him. The title made little difference to the actualities of Calgar's rule. The Chapter Master had presided over Ultramar for centuries before Roboute Guilliman awoke. Apart from the brief period before Guilliman had set out on his Terran Crusade, Calgar's reign had been unbroken. His word was absolute. Calleduus withered under his attention.

'Then this particular incident here will be dealt with by the Ultramarines personally, and publicly,' continued Calgar. 'And I will demonstrate that mercy remains within the armoury of the Chapter. Chaos turns our children against us. What kind of society are we if we punish youthful folly – serious though it is – with death, when all they believe they are doing is getting more food for the hungry? There will be those guiltier in that place. I will see them separated, and judged according to the relative severity of their error.'

'The dissidents will see this as a victory. You say you will not speak with them, and you should not. But whoever is behind this wants you to be provoked into action, my lord. They want your eyes away from the war. If they decide that these little actions can divert a single member of the Chapter, they will do it again.'

'Then they have succeeded, but it will gain them nothing,' said Calgar. 'I am sending my own message. The lords of Macragge will not allow any dissent upon the capital world or in any other place in Ultramar.'

'My lord defender, mercy will be seen as weakness.'

'Mercy is a strength, because it is harder to forgive than it is to slay,' said Calgar. 'They are children led by demagogues. They will be treated as such.' He turned to his sergeant. 'Julio, advance now. Try not to destroy the artefacts – they are priceless, and an important reminder that the myth of Illyrian independence is indeed a myth.'

'Yes, my lord. Squad Julio!' the sergeant voxed.

'We hear and obey,' his warriors replied. Armour growling, they trudged slowly on up the road from the line of Rhinos, their huge shapes as solid as the boulders of the pass' crags.

Upon reaching their leader, the Terminators fell into formation. Julio drew his power sword and saluted Calgar. 'We march for Macragge.'

'This is overkill,' said Calleduus. 'An aerial insertion from Valkyries would have been sufficient.'

'You have spoken, now be silent, Calleduus,' said Calgar. 'We will advance into the fullness of their fire and we will not fall. They will see the Ultramarines cannot be harmed by such as they. Terrorism is pointless.'

The auxilia by the roadblock drew back the central wheeled segment of plascrete, allowing the giant warriors through. When the last clumped by, they hurriedly replaced the gate and hunkered down behind it once again.

When the Ultramarines were a hundred yards from the museum, the rebels opened fire. A mixture of lasgun beams and solid bullets perturbed the smoke.

Many shots went wide, either from incompetence or from fear – talk of killing an Angel of Death was the sort of bravado that vanished when battle came. Those shots that hit sparked off the thick battleplate. Calleduus may have been right about the waste of using Terminators for this minor action, but had the

Vigil Opertii undertaken the task, several of them would now be dead. The secret police's incompetence in allowing this to happen was irksome, but they were still more use to Calgar alive.

The lascannon fired and missed. There was a long delay before the second shot clipped the shoulder of Julio's lead warrior. The force of the impact threw him off balance a little, but he shrugged off the strike and lumbered back into formation, his pauldron dripping molten ceramite.

A good lascannon team could focus and fire four shots a minute. Calgar's displeasure at the local Juventia leaders grew. Where was their weapons discipline?

Julio's squad plodded on in the unstoppable manner of Terminators. They reached the glass frontage of the museum. One of Julio's veterans smashed the glass with his power fist and walked into the building. Bullets sparked off his armour as he disappeared inside. The sound of shattering glass tinkled down the pass as the rest of the squad forced their way in. More gunfire blasted at the squad. A grenade went off in the middle of their formation. They strode through the explosion and the bullets without hindrance, and the rest of them vanished from sight.

The shooting stopped. There was shouting, both of young men and that of the Ultramarines loudly amplified by voxmitter. Shooting broke out anew. Now the hard banging of bolters was intermingled with the pathetic popping of stubbers and autoguns. There were screams, more shouting, and then a final stutter of bolt explosions.

Similar exchanges were repeated as the unit went room to room. The rebels put up no coherent defence. They were easily overcome.

Half an hour later, a line of young rebels came out of the museum's entrance, hands on their heads. They were flushed with the excitement of combat, but with eyes downcast at their loss. If only they were aware of what their leaders would have taken from them, thought Calgar. He wondered if the deeper lies had set in yet, and how far these boys had been tempted. The promises of Chaos were false. There was no immortality, no freedom from suffering, no easy road to power. Their youth, their health, their vitality – all of it would have been stolen away, replaced with a life-in-death. It began with a sincere desire to do good; it ended with damnation.

He had seen it too many times.

A single Terminator came out behind the boys. Calgar was appalled at how young they were. None were older than twenty, and the youngest looked to be eleven standard years. They were herded down the road and made to kneel in front of the road-block. The auxilia stood to leave their post and aid their masters, but the Terminator held up a hand.

'Stay back!' he said, his armour transforming his voice to a terrific shout that echoed round the pass. 'It is not safe. We have the device. It is biological in nature and unstable.'

The auxilia looked to Calgar. The Lord Defender of Greater Ultramar nodded his head, and they remained on guard.

A few moments later, Julio and his remaining Terminators came out of the building. They escorted nineteen more rebels, these adult, and led them to a space away from the others.

Calgar's vox-bead chimed. He accepted the channel.

'My lord,' voxed Julio. *'The device is a cryo-cask, half a man in height. It is leaking. No one should approach. My sensorium is registering high levels of biological contaminants in the museo. My guess is all these boys are infected. Keep the mortals back until we have secured the area.'*

Calgar cursed under his breath. Even sloppy little insurgencies like this one seemed to have access to biological weapons, gifts of Mortarion.

He turned his anger on Calleduus. 'The building is contaminated. Do you see why I did not want you to go within? Your men would have been exposed. Fortunately, my warriors are completely protected.'

Calleduus stood ramrod straight, his eyes forward. 'I restate my objections, my lord – the Ultramarines should not be involving themselves in police actions.'

Calgar turned aside. Calleduus stuck to his convictions. He was an able man, Calgar reminded himself. One mistake did not make someone a failure.

'This terrorism is part of the war that shakes the realm,' said Calgar. 'The Ultramarines will be seen in every theatre, no matter how small. Next time, make sure the situation does not progress so far, and we will not have to have another conversation like this. You are dismissed, vigilator optimare.'

Calleduus bowed and walked away without a word, his cheeks burning with Calgar's rebuke.

'Ney, relay these orders,' commanded Calgar.

'My lord,' responded the Ancient.

'Summon medicae teams and cleansing units. Decontaminate these misguided young men, and have them transferred to the Massalis penal station for assessment and re-education where possible. Every effort is to be made to preserve them. Send those that test well to the punishment battalions for a single service period. Those who do not recant are to be publicly mindwiped and given over to the tech-adepts for servitors.'

Calgar thought a moment. He looked up at the cliffs either side of the pass, and visualised the sparely populated glens that nestled in the mountains thereabouts. There were not many people in the area, but there were some. All it took was one infected human to kill half a civitas. The Emperor alone knew what was in that flask.

'Evacuate the population for ten miles around this point. Have them all tested. Seal off the district. Station auxilia on all the major roads and place perdition beacons around the boundaries. Second three Land Speeders from the Chapter reserve to assist Vigil Opertii forces in patrolling the area. No one is to enter this part of the mountains until it is safe.' He looked at the Terminator squad. 'Julio, guard these children. Once they are dealt with and you are cleansed, call in a Thunderhawk. Brother-Captain Agemman needs you in the fleet.'

'*My lord*,' voxed Julio.

'What about the road?' said Ney. 'The unitarchs of Illyricon and Testuae are anxious that it is reopened.'

'They shall have to wait,' said Calgar. He seethed still, and was forced to remind himself that Illyria was but one province on one planet, and this highway, though the main link between Magna Macragge Civitas and Illyricon, only one route. 'The risk is too high. We shall reclaim this region when the time is right. Until we have peace, it will have to wait.' Calgar glanced into Macragge's flat grey skies, imagining the embattled fleets in the void and the ongoing siege of Ardium. 'And it may have to wait some time.'

There was a commotion at the rear line. A Techmarine, his helmet bulky with specialised surveillance and comms equipment, came running.

'My lord, my lord!' he shouted. He came to a stop and got down on one knee. 'I have word from the capital. The primarch has sent an astropathic message.'

'Yes?' said Calgar. He experienced a curious mix of dread and elation. He had admitted to himself long ago that ceding all control to the primarch was hard. He did not look forward to doing so again.

'He is at the outer reaches of the system. He is making all speed to Ardium where he intends to break the siege.'

Upon hearing this news, the warriors of Ultramar, both human and transhuman, let out a joyous cheer.

'Call me a transport,' said Calgar. 'I must return. We must make ready to aid him!'

'My lord, the message is explicit – you are to remain here to guard Macragge. Lord Guilliman wishes to prevent opportunistic attacks on the capital world.'

'Does he have enough men?'

'Captain Ventris is with him, and Captain Sicarius,' said the Techmarine. 'He informs us the primarch does not need your aid, my lord. He comes with fifteen thousand Space Marines and three crusade battle groups.'

Again the warriors cheered.

'Mortarion will be surely driven from the system. With our lord Guilliman home, we can take the fight to the enemy!' shouted Calgar. He raised one of the mighty Gauntlets of Ultramar. 'All hail Guilliman, Master of Ultramar!'

His triumphant smile hid the hollowness he felt inside.

Calgar had returned from Vigilus to find his realm wracked with war. Guilliman would soon discover how bad it was himself. Objectively, Calgar had performed no better than Calleduus. Absence was no excuse. He let his hand drop, and bade the Land Raider's doors be opened to him. As he was clambering inside, Julio voxed him.

'What shall I do with the older prisoners, my lord? Mercy or death?'

Calgar paused in the side hatch of the Land Raider, his hands gripping the lip of the hull unnecessarily hard.

'Death,' he said.

Calgar boarded the tank to panicked shouts cut short by the bangs of bolt-rounds annihilating flesh. The sound followed him all the way to the main highway, where faster transport waited.

For the first time in a long time, Marneus Calgar felt like a failure.

CHAPTER EIGHTEEN

ARDIUM

A distinct change to the engine's pitch occurred as they passed into enemy-held territory, and the Overlord's smooth flight turned choppy. The airframe rattled. A sense of wrongness that thickened with every mile they flew upset all minds aboard the transport

'We approach the heart of darkness,' said Donas Maxim. Crystal tracks in his psychic hood glowed as they encountered the increased warp activity. Blue luminescence mingled with the transport bay's red combat lights, painting his helm with neon highlights and making him seem as uncanny as the beasts he was trained to destroy.

'We can all sense it,' said Captain Felix, looking around at his warriors. They had begun to fidget in the way peculiar to Space Marines, looking to their brothers and checking their equipment over and over again.

'Not so strongly as I,' said the Codicier. His words were hard, a shell against the pain. 'The warp taint is far more powerful than we predicted. We must be careful.'

Maxim was the sole original-pattern Space Marine inside the Overlord's twinned hulls. Every other was of the Primaris generation.

Accompanying Maxim was a single other psychic Space Marine, Gerrundium, a Primaris Lexicanium. The pair of them gave off a calming power, a sense of purpose and confidence that infused Felix with a resolve as solid as a neutron star. He was grateful for their presence, for Felix too felt the foreboding radiating so powerfully from their target. It penetrated his armour, provoking a crawling of the flesh. In his mind was a call, an urging to action he would rather not take, the kind that afflicts the insane deep into the night and demands something of violence be done – a dark vitality, a turning-in of agency so that it becomes self-destructive.

'I can feel it well enough. It pains me,' said Felix. He wondered at the sensation, logging it for later consideration. He had not felt anything like it before. 'This is the power that calls the dead from life?'

Gerrundium nodded. 'Disease alone cannot bring back the fallen, nor turn those who live into walking corpses.' He sounded flat and passionless, his own coping mechanism against the corruption they neared. 'That is a physical impossibility, as our Apothecaries and the primarch's magi attest. Sorcery is the root of the disease. Without the warp, there would be no consequence to infection other than death.'

'The Plague Lord delights in the affectation of disease where disease alone is insufficient for his goals,' said Maxim. 'Lies are as great a part of his armoury as contradiction. Untruth is the basis of the actions of the enemy. Nurgle represents the duality of life in death and death in life, confusing states of being and making neither true. As with all things of the warp, his promises are unclean, a trap for the unwary.'

'You include your own abilities.'

The Codicier grunted. His helmet turned within his protective aegis hood. 'Our gifts bring great power, but they spring from the same poisoned well as diseases that rot the soul. To drink from it and remain pure is the greatest challenge we face.'

'We feel this strongly because there is a wicked power at work. It is from the Palace Spire that the corruption comes,' added Gerrundium, 'but we will not know its true nature for certain until we witness it ourselves.'

The Overlord shook, but remained true to its course. Its armour was thick, and its engines powerful. The new craft made Thunderhawks look like toys. As with so much the primarch had commissioned, the Overlord hearkened back to older designs of insertion craft, improved by the boundless creativity of Belisarius Cawl. But its technological power could not shelter its occupants completely from threats either mundane or arcane. An explosion sounded close by, its violence muffled by the thick hull. Smaller vibrations, rapidly pulsed, chased it upwards. The craft slid sideways before levelling out.

'*Captain, there is heavy fire coming from the Palace Spire's mid ranges,*' voxed the pilot. '*We cannot land at the target point.*'

'Get us as close as you can,' responded Felix.

'*There is a skypark cluster twelve hundred feet horizontal, two levels down from the target point, in the next spire.*' The pilot went silent a moment as he consulted his charts. '*The Sighing Spire.*'

The pilot exloaded the position. Felix's cartograph automatically engaged. They headed for a cluster of palaces at the very pinnacle of one of Ardium's great hive cities, their needle points pricking at the belly of the void. Felix saw them as wireframe representations. A psychic overlay provided by the primarch's

Concilia Psykana showed ugly, organic patterns moving sluggishly over the top. The web gathered most densely on a cankerous mass in the tallest tower, once the home of the hive lord.

Gun batteries blinked red around the site. The pilot's alternative flashed up, a domed garden extending on an elegant lever from the adjacent spire's side. Further than Felix would have liked from the target point, but the only practical option in the circumstances.

'Alternative landing zone confirmed. Take us in,' said Felix.

The pilot responded immediately, banking the craft and sending it into a steep dive. The thunder of anti-aircraft fire intensified, becoming a constant rumble. Felix looked over his warriors again. There were forty of them in the craft, and a further eighty in two accompanying Overlords. The Overlords were similar to the Corvus Blackstars used by the Inquisition and the Deathwatch, possessing twin transport bays with their own assault doors, but they were bigger and even more blessed with advanced technologies. Anti-munitions cannons added a rolling burr to the noise from outside, slinging hypervelocity steel balls at incoming shells and missiles. Those enemy rounds that got through exploded on shimmering energy shields, whose hiccuping buzz joined the chorus of the ship's systems.

All the Space Marines apart from Maxim were Ultramarines. At least, they were now – six weeks ago they had been the Unnumbered Sons of Guilliman. They were destined to reinforce the founding Chapter, and the pale-grey chevrons partially obscuring their ultimas had been reverently removed. They had temporary squad markings, and had adopted a light blue for a company colour for this action only.

This would be their first battle as Ultramarines, led by Felix, an eleventh captain where there should only be ten.

Felix pondered how Calgar might feel about the primarch's

unilateral altering of the Codex Astartes. The captain could not help but feel that, in his drive for victory and efficiency, Guilliman had been careless with the feelings of his existing sons. Increasingly, Guilliman looked to the Primaris Space Marines as his first solution. He made no attempt to hide the fact that the days of the firstborn were numbered.

Felix's theorising took his mind away from the coming fight. He refocused his attention on the battle. A mission chrono raced towards zero upon his helm display.

'Stand by for attack!' he ordered.

'Brace for impact,' said the pilot, his voice voxed into every helmet on board.

The ship jinked violently from side to side, accelerating as it did so. Every one of its little voices rose in protest, blending into a raucous machine howl. Explosions boomed from all quarters.

Felix brought up an external vid-feed. A grainy image of an armaglass dome, full of dark shapes, grew rapidly in front of his eyes.

The ship opened fire with its wing-mounted Desolator lascannons. The three-barrelled weapons rotated at blurring speed as they fired, the torque helping offset atmospheric lensing. Banks of melta cannons mounted in the Overlord's nose opened fire a few seconds later.

Molten holes appeared in the armaglass, and the Overlord burst through the weakened dome, sending shards of it scattering inward into the gardens.

'Ready! Now!' yelled Felix.

'We march for Macragge!' roared the Space Marines.

The gunship thumped down hard, throwing Felix forward in his restraints. The ship rocked back on its landing hydraulics. As the Overlord recoiled from the impact, Felix's harness disengaged and shot back into its housing in the ceiling. Simultaneously, the assault doors blew down with crushing force, flattening what-ever was on the other side. An anaemic yellow light flooded the transport bay.

First out were the Aggressors. They wore battleplate of a similar type to Felix's Gravis suit, but even more more massively armoured. They would spearhead the landing.

There were two squads of Aggressors, one for each bay. Two squads of Hellblasters followed, the containment chambers on their plasma incinerators glowing bright as they cycled up to fire. Felix and the two Librarians disembarked next, along with the temporary company's Apothecary. After them came four squads of Intercessors, who fanned out, bolt rifles up.

Ardium was a hive world, a designation synonymous with overcrowding and human misery, but this was Ultramar, and the hive worlds in the star-realm of the Ultramarines were kinder than most. Some provision was made for the wellbeing of their citizens. Ardium had a plethora of domes projecting from its hives, especially on the upper levels, where large-scale bio-habitats recreated those lost from most of the surface. The planet was famed for them, giving the hives the appearance of gargantuan trees.

A forest surrounded Felix's ship, but it was not the healthy place it was supposed to be. Yellow fog raced out through the hole in the dome, sucked away by the differential in air pressure. Flags of it streamed from between blackened branches festooned with slime. At such rare heights, Macragge's sun shone without the impediment of clouds, but though Nurgle's work had not yet poisoned the sky, the strength of the sunlight was stymied soon after entering the hole made by the Overlord, its beams becoming lost amid the vapours poisoning the hive. Winds blew briskly towards the breach, the fog's twists forming screaming faces as it was sucked out into Ardium's troposphere.

Sickly vegetation overran the park's paths. Trees had swollen into giants, their shapes corrupted into menacing silhouettes. People had been overcome by the swift growth and incorporated into their seeping trunks, the change happening so swiftly that it appeared they had no time to flee. Their limbs were trapped in wooden prisons, and their bodies hardened by lignin intrusion. They lived, though only their eyes, moist in skin like bark, had movement, and they were wild and full of madness.

From behind these rotting bowers, bloated Heretic Astartes in filth-brown armour, their plate cracked and dribbling polluted fluids, fired at the emerging Space Marines.

Felix took up station behind a broken statue in the dome's centre. Bolt-fire cracked off the chipped body. A mat of slippery vines carpeted the paving and seats around, blending what had been an open, circular area into the jungle.

'All squads, advance. Secure the landing zone,' he ordered.

The Overlord opened fire with the heavy bolter turrets fixed on its lower wing surfaces. They thundered, the passage of the bolts enough to saw down swathes of diseased plant life. They exploded within wood made soft by overgrowth, spraying sodden pulp everywhere. The dome juddered with the explosions, and Felix looked dubiously at the ground, half expecting it to fail.

Outside the algae-speckled armaglass dome, another Overlord roared past, the backwash of its quintuple engines shaking the entire park. Feed from its auguries came into Felix's helm, and he saw that the fabric of the dome was as corrupted as the plants within it; its metals were rusted, and the armaglass, a substance that could persist for millennia in the most hostile environments, was pitted with corrosion.

'We are going to have to get out of this deathtrap immediately,' Felix voxed to his sergeants and officers. 'The park is close to collapse.'

His warriors voxed back their understanding.

'Overlords *Adriaticus* and *Scion of Ultramar*, find somewhere else to land. This structure is unsound. Overlord *Jove*, take off – we cannot risk losing you. Stand by to extract upon my order.'

'*Affirmative*,' replied the Overlord's pilot. Its lascannons spitting fire still, the ship's engines screeched, pivoted downwards and forced it up and back through the hole it had created in the dome. The park shook, showering the strike team with flakes of rust and stringy, black leaves.

Felix did a rapid scan of the dome. There were twenty or so Death Guard in the park. Bolt-rounds were being traded back and forth between them and the Intercessors, while roaring plasma streams burst from the Hellblasters' guns, to be answered in kind by the Death Guard's own special weapons troopers.

The Aggressors stomped forwards, their armour protecting them from the Death Guard's fire. Plumes of fire roared from their flame gauntlets, drenching everything with burning promethium. The air's oxygen content was low and the wood was wet, but the tenacity of the promethium fire was such that soon tranches of the corrupted woodland were smouldering, helped by the blast-furnace draw of escaping atmosphere, and greasy smoke joined the fog rushing through the breach.

There was a squad of seven Plague Marines holding the exit to the park, sheltered behind a black tree that had fallen over the path. More plants, slippery with decay, coated the block paving. Movement in the woods either side of the main path had Felix bring up his visual filters, revealing more of the enemy attempting to encircle them. One of the Plague Marines was blasted backwards by the combined fire of an Intercessor squad. He remained upright as he was pummelled. A Hellblaster spotted the traitor's survival, and put him down for good.

'Hellblaster squads Flavian and Marcellus – take out designated enemy squads on the flanks,' said Felix, exloading the targeting data to his warriors. 'Intercessor squads, prepare to charge. Aggressor squads, burn out the enemy blocking our egress.'

Away to the right, a ball of brilliant blue lightning burst amid the trees, shaking the failing dome with psychic thunder. Codicier Maxim held up his hand, rotating his fingers, and the thunderball turned with them. As he clenched his fist, the ball lightning collapsed with a second peal of thunder, taking with it all matter that had occupied the space, leaving a perfectly spherical hole in the forest.

'They are falling back,' voxed Hellicus, one of the Intercessor sergeants. Unbidden, Felix's cogitator projected the warrior's name and vital signs across his helm display, highlighting his location on the cartograph, along with status updates on his armour integrity and ammunition count. A combat-effectiveness estimate blinked a steady green at one hundred per cent capability.

'We follow,' said Felix. 'Now!' He ran out from around the statue and drew his power sword.

The Plague Marines opted to retreat, firing as they fell back. Their lumbering movements acquired a certain crispness as they withdrew, an echo of martial training similar to his own, and Felix had a glimpse of the warriors they had once been, perhaps not so very different to himself.

He blinked, and the semblance was gone. The Death Guard were mutated, diseased, far beyond human, deserving only of death. His power sword crackled, echoing his own hunger to strike them down.

Through stands of dying trees the battle raged, the Ultramarines fighting into the teeth of the Death Guard's withdrawal, the wood disintegrating into a vile slop when hit. The Primaris Space Marines were slowed by the terrain, while the Plague Marines did not seem to be, melting back into the mist flowing from within the spire. The entrance to the skypark was ahead, its ornamental brickwork choked with evil-looking creepers and streaked with green tracks of moisture. Beneath the arch, mats of pulsating mushrooms grew, their stalks so woody that they jammed the park's blast doors open, preventing them from closing. The last enemy squad was departing the dome, chased out by burning lines of plasma and swift bolts. They paused a moment, taking shelter behind the columns supporting the archway in order to give out one last volley while their fellows vanished into the murk of the Sighing Spire. Felix saw his chance.

'Charge!' he roared, and ran full tilt through the sickly growths of the park towards the foe.

Bolts burst against his energy field and whined from his pauldrons. The bolts' mass detectors, damaged by the contact, set off in mid-air, so that he ran through a maelstrom of shrapnel. So many explosions so close to his head caused his displays to jump and his auditory suppressors to burr angrily.

The Plague Marines were unbelievably resilient. One was a burning torch, his body fat liquefying in the fire and fuelling the blaze, but he stood firm, blazing away with his gun. Not one of them had weathered this fight unscathed, but still they fought on with cratered flesh and sundered armour. The Hellblaster squads' incinerators were the only sure way to slay the Heretic Astartes. The power of a sun vented as a glaring pike of gas, the plasma shots melted through ancient ceramite and burned the Plague Marines from inside out.

A couple of the last Death Guard fell back, and they were subjected to the concentrated firepower of Felix's half-company as they turned to leave. Though the enemy were quicker than they looked, they were not quick enough.

Felix charged with no thought for support. Tactical consideration was lost beneath a wave of hatred for these beings, who had damned their own species in exchange for false immortality and crumbs of power. A few more bolts came his way, and then the Plague Marines surged in to engage him hand to hand. Suddenly, he was surrounded by things worthy of nightmares: a warrior with the face of a toad, and another with his jaw missing and a long, scabrous tongue whipping back and forth from the hole. Their flesh was riddled with maggot holes, and their armour corroded through to show leprous skin and open sores.

The Death Guard should not have been capable of life, but they fought well, their bodies supported by the power of Chaos, their skills honed by ten millennia of war. A hatred to mirror Felix's own flickered in the yellowed eyes peering at him through cracked eye-lenses. Rusted knives jabbed at Felix, their dull edges blistering the paint of his armour where they scratched. Alarms howled at the pain inflicted upon the machine's spirit. Bolters were thrown down and bolt pistols drawn.

Felix was not destined to die there. He was a Primaris Space Marine; he was a captain. He was armed and armoured with the finest wargear in the Imperium. A potent mix of loyalty and fury suffused him, as efficacious as the adrenal elixirs pumped into his body by his implants and his battleplate. Twin hearts hammering, Felix meted out death to the deathless. His power sword spat with droplets of cooking blood as he cleaved limbs from flabby bodies, and riddled decaying torsos with bolts.

'For Ultramar! For the primarch! For the Emperor!' he roared as he slew. He became one with the moment, every piece of his enhanced mind, body and wargear working perfectly together. He cut and parried with marvellous efficiency, so skilfully that even the prowess of these deadly veterans was no safeguard. Roboute Guilliman might talk of the Adeptus Astartes' potential for peacetime activity, but war was what they were made for. The Emperor's intention for Felix was clearer to him than ever before, and he did not care. If it were his destiny to be a weapon, so be it. He would spill blood until he could fight no more.

A dim awareness of others fighting by his side impinged upon his battle lust; a staff topped with a horned skull smote the last of the Death Guard, and then there were no more foes.

'Do you feel it?' asked Codicier Maxim. 'Do you feel the power in this place?'

Felix panted hard. A tumble of meaningless data rolled down his retinal displays. The Aurora Chapter psyker placed the head of his staff against the centre of Felix's chest. Along its length, the crystalline matrix glowed. Felix's mind cleared.

'Do not fall prey to the power of the warp,' said Maxim. 'It is at work here – so thin the barrier between this place and the empyrean has become, already it corrupts you.'

'I have nothing but hatred for these things,' said Felix, gesturing with his power gauntlet at the fallen Plague Marines. 'I have fought against Chaos many times.' Even as he said the words, he questioned his aggressive tone.

'Then you are very much in danger. The effects of Chaos are unpredictable. Do not expect your seducer to wear the same form as your enemy. The warp will use your mind against you in any way it can. It will turn your sense of duty to evil. More life to kill your enemies, more flesh to withstand pain, so you might kill again, and again, forever. You are a warrior, so the Dark Gods will use your belligerence, your loyalty and your honour against you, no matter which of the four you are unfortunate enough to cross.' Maxim raised his staff and let its base thump into the mess of mutant plants at his feet. At his touch, they shrivelled back, revealing the filthy paving underneath. 'You of the Ultima Founding are mighty warriors, but you still have much to learn. A decade of war is poor preparation for the foes we must face.'

Standing tall again, Felix swallowed. With a trembling thumb he upped the output of his sword's disruptor field to burn off the last of the traitors' gore.

'Then our intelligence is correct,' he said. 'This is the right place. I have not encountered anything like this before.'

Maxim nodded curtly. 'The strength of the device is astounding. We must destroy it. Now.'

Felix shook off his battle fugue. He had never slipped so far from himself. He was on the verge of apology, but Maxim spoke first.

'Be careful,' he said, and strode on. Where the Codicier walked, the stinking mist shrank back.

Felix looked down the hallway linking the skypark to the main body of the spire. It too had a transparent roof, but it was so fouled with slime he might as well have been looking down a tunnel. His wargear's inbuilt short-range auspex probed ahead, seeking foes in the gloom, but found none.

He voxed Apothecary Undine. 'How many casualties?'

'Twelve injured, three seriously. The others can fight on. No dead,' came the efficient response.

Felix switched to company-wide vox-cast. 'Form up,' he ordered his strike force. 'We proceed to mission site alpha.'

They advanced at pace into the Sighing Spire, eager to leave behind the creaking skypark and enter the palace. Similar dereliction awaited them inside. The wind continued to howl upwards, the spire acting like a giant chimney, and the fog thinned. The Sighing Spire had been a masterful display of architectural grandeur, some might say arrogance. The walls were an extravagance of arches all piled one atop the other, nine hundred feet tall, their openings glazed with armaglass, glassaic and other more exotic substances. Within the panes were artful light sculptures, windows that when struck at a particular angle by the sun would project an image with the phantom veracity of a hololith.

None would ever work again. Most were broken or buckled, casting fragments of their embedded imagery in ghastly fashion. Fragments of faces emerged without warning from the dark, and the Primaris Space Marines, battle-hardened and heroic though they were, fired more than a few shots at these unexpected phantasms.

'Spread out,' said Felix. 'This level, level above, level below.' Every command he gave was short and to the point. Verbal communication was inefficient. If his orders were complex, he supplemented his voice with swift-pulsed data exloads. The company noosphere was alive with back-and-forth data-canting, giving Felix a tactical overview.

Walkways bounded the drop every thirty yards. Four die-straight bridges, heavy with thick gothic decoration, crossed over the void at the first, fourth, seventh and uppermost level. Above the highest bridge was a hollow needle, six-sided, its walls pierced by shaped louvres which, in cleaner times, made the high air currents of Ardium into heavenly musics. They had been joined by ragged holes rotted right through the fabric of the hive, and the songs they now sang were as piteous as the lowing of diseased animals. The cybernetic constructs that had tended them hung dead and tattered from wings nailed to the walls.

The spire top oscillated in the winds of the upper atmosphere. Such places were designed to sway with the currents at that altitude and with any tectonic upheaval at the hive root far, far below, but there was a pained lurching to the spire's movement, and stronger gusts were accompanied by the screams of dying machines and the grinding of tortured metal. The floors were out of true, sloping further with each powerful wind-born judder.

Felix watched carefully through the borrowed pict-feeds of helm-lenses as his men ran to the doors to the lesser rooms contained in turrets on the outside of the spire. They deployed expertly at the top and base of the access ramps that wound up between the spread floors, every angle of fire covered with plasma incinerator and bolt rifles. Felix sometimes wished for the tactical flexibility offered by older-style Space Marine squads, desirous of the heavy weapons capability they offered. But single-armament units streamlined tactical choice, which increased battle responsiveness, and the plasma incinerators of the Hellblasters offered a good medium-weight compromise between hitting power and mobility.

'No sign of the enemy, brother-captain,' voxed Sergeant Tevian of the third Intercessor squad.

The middle bridge was their way into the Palace Spire, where their intelligence placed the device of the enemy. An arch greater than all the others spread over the bridge end, forming one end of a tunnel leading out of the Sighing Spire. A statement of power, its grandiosity had become deeply ironic. Its span hung with the shreds of failing phantom artworks, and it beckoned as coldly as a reptilian maw.

Felix glanced at the Codicier and Lexicanium. Reading his actions, Gerrundium spoke.

'It is that way, captain. Close by the feasting hall of the hive governor. If we are to prevail, we must go through.'

Felix attempted contact with the other two subgroups of his strike company, and was rewarded with an earful of sawing static. He cut out his strategic vox, tasking his battleplate's cogitator to reactivate it the minute the lieutenants leading the others made contact.

'Over the bridge,' he ordered. 'Squads Tevian and Hellicus, cover. Hellblaster Squad Flavian behind Aggressors. Move out.'

Felix went close to the front. He would gladly fight at the head of his army, but Codex doctrine ruled placing one's officers at the forefront of an advance as sub-optimal, likely to lead to the rapid elimination of the command cadre. He joined Flavian. The Aggressor squad made an unbreachable shield in front of them.

Empty space yawned on the other side of the bridge's low parapets. Sunlight filtered through corroded holes and the broken light sculptures, revealing the extent of the spire's accelerated decay.

The diversity of Chaos was manifold. Even within the limited purview of each of the fell entities that called themselves gods, there was staggering variety. Where the skypark had been a riot of life, the spire interior was bare of any living thing; instead, its corruption was evidenced in patterns of oxidisation spreading over the walls. Violent oranges, deep greens and vibrant marine turquoises – metal, it seemed, could die as colourfully as flesh.

'Brother-captain, we have contacts moving on our position.'

At the moment Hellicus voxed Felix, he saw the signifiers himself.

'Light aircraft, coming up from below. Forward party, increase speed. The rest of you, cover our advance,' ordered Felix.

The Aggressors broke into a jog that shook the bridge. The Intercessor squads switched their bolt rifles from single-shot to short-burst mode. The greater ammunition expenditure was worthwhile, for it maintained fire efficiency whilst moving at speed, when shots could not be perfectly aimed.

As precise as any Mechanicus machine, the forward party made the other side, turned, and took up position around the guard walls of the spire ramps.

Engines screeched in the spire shaft, jarring with the hideous music – jet turbines, grinding too hard for want of lubricant.

Felix risked a look below. A number of heavy three-engined drones were rising rapidly up the shaft.

'Beware!' called out Codicier Maxim. 'These are daemon engines! I can taste their souls.'

'Destroy them,' said Felix.

Bolts and plasma crossed the shaft, skewering the lead drone from multiple directions as it rose over the parapets. Its armour cracked moistly, like chitin rather than plasteel. An engine blew out, and it whirled down to destruction.

'*More coming in from above!*' voxed Sergeant Brutian of the second Hellblaster squad. Felix glanced up, and saw more of the machines descending.

The dead spire's acoustic design made it a sounding chamber where every noise was amplified massively. Bolts exploded like heavy mortar rounds. Air superheated by plasma streams exploded with the force of tropical storms.

The drones coming from below fired from a poor position. At their angle of attack, the Ultramarines were well sheltered by the ramp and walkway walls. Gouts of sticky, yellow plague liquids splashed against the building's fabric, eating into the metal and causing fleshy boils to sprout and blood to flow around the impact sites in violation of all natural law.

Then those coming from above were in range, and the sprays of infected matter they pumped from their cannons came over the top to wash over the Space Marines. The paint bubbled on their armour, and warriors fell with pained cries as the liquid ate through their softseals and into the flesh beneath. The two Librarians worked together, nullifying hexes and banishing the trapped daemons back into the warp. Three of the drones fell this way, and another two to the concentrated fire of the Space Marines, before the strike force's attention was diverted elsewhere.

'*Captain, I have multiple contacts coming from below on the ramps,*' shouted Hellicus against the crack and boom of battle. '*Some kind of infantry. There are thousands of them.*'

Felix retasked his suit's auto-senses to take a sounding even as he fired his gauntlet bolter, riddling a bloat-drone hovering up before him with explosive rounds. His attack knocked it back through the air. Cratered metal-flesh weeping thin liquids, it dropped out of sight.

Felix's cogitator indicated his scan was done. He rotated his cartograph. The walkways were so crowded with enemy contacts that they were a solid red.

'*More coming from behind,*' voxed Flavian.

Felix looked through the arch leading into the next spire. Movement registered first upon his auto-senses, then upon his vision.

The noble dead of Ardium were marching to war. They shambled forwards, clad in ruined finery. They were propelled by limbs that should not, could not possibly work. Their faces were twisted into rictus grins, but in their eyes was hopeless despair.

'Plague walkers,' he said.

'By the Emperor's light,' said Maxim, 'their souls are trapped within their carcasses. The pain…'

'We shall put them out of their misery.' Felix had to shout to make himself heard. 'Aggressors, turn about. Immolation protocols. Burn them back. All squads, consolidate on our position. We shall fight our way through.'

A drone exploded behind him, showering metal gummed with sticky meat across the walkways. Something inside gave out an inhuman scream as it died – half of pain, half of release.

The Aggressors waded into the dead. The plague zombies' feeble hands and makeshift weapons were no use against the inviolable Gravis plate. They bit at the Space Marines' limbs, shattering their rotten teeth on ceramite. The Aggressors responded with a wash of chemical fire. The dead fought on as they burned.

Four drones remained. Gerrundium speared one with crackling lightning, searing the daemon from its shell. Another took hits from both Hellblaster squads, and was consumed in an actinic ball of energy.

Intercessors gained the bridge. The dead coming from below were slow, but there were so many that Felix's small group could not prevail against them.

'Firing lines! Triple rows,' he said. 'We must clear a way through to the Palace Spire!'

Three squads, all missing a member or two now, lined up. The first threw themselves prone, the second knelt behind them, the third stood.

'Aggressors, back!' Felix ordered. 'Intercessors, prepare to fire. Set weapons to full automatic fire. Release these wretches from their torment, and carve our way out of here.'

The Aggressors stepped aside ponderously. The barrier removed, the burning dead surged forwards, white teeth shining in blackening flesh.

'Fire!' bellowed Felix.

Twelve bolt rifles opened up, sending out a wall of mass-reactive shells that gouged a deep and immediate passage into the crowd. Felix joined his men and fired with them. The dead fell into a thick carpet of twitching limbs, many still on fire.

'Hellblasters, fire!' Felix ordered.

Aside from the squad forming the rearguard, all of the Space Marines were on the same level now, firing into the crowd of dead. Walking corpses exploded, or flash-burst into steam.

'Advance!' bellowed Felix.

His boltstorm gauntlet roaring, he led his men against the damned. His boots crushed corpses flat, the bodies threatening to snag him in traps of broken ribs. He brought his power sword into play, using it like a machete to hack down the foe. He needed none of his considerable skill to kill them. Hundreds fell to Felix and his men, yet no matter how many they slew, they came on in an endless tide.

Foot by foot, the Space Marines forced a way through. Felix raised his sword to strike at a skull-faced warrior, and halted his blow just in time.

The skull was the helm of a Reiver.

'Cease fire!' he commanded.

The last line of the dead fell down. Sparking powerblades were yanked back out of chests.

'Sergeant Lyceus, well met,' said Felix. 'Do you have vox? Ours is not functioning beyond our immediate proximity.'

The Reivers' leader reloaded his pistol. 'The enemy are jamming our communications across the battlezone. Lieutenant Astium ordered us to seek you out. We heard your gunfire, and fought our way to you from the target zone.'

The Reiver squad was armed with oversized combat knives and heavy bolt pistols. Their helms were death's heads, and their left pauldrons enlarged to provide better protection in melee. Their armour was eerily silent, adapted for stealth work.

'Do you have the location of Lieutenant Tobias also?'

'This way, brother-captain,' said Sergeant Lyceus. 'They are together, and under attack close to the mission target. The device is within the chapel off the feasting hall, and the enemy are defending it fiercely.'

'The enemy despise the notion of the Emperor as a god,' said Maxim. 'There is power to be courted by defiling His holy places.'

'The Emperor is not divine, so says our creed,' said Felix, who had heard the sentiment expressed forcefully from the lips of Guilliman himself.

'It does not matter whether He is or not. It is the act that brings the power, not the truth of it. The plague zombies cannot be "true". They are an impossibility. Yet they exist,' said Maxim. 'That is the power of Chaos.'

'Speaking of which, there are thousands more dead coming behind us,' said Felix. 'We must hurry, reach the target, assess its threat level and destroy it.'

Whereas the Sighing Spire had been a rich man's showpiece, the second spire contained the palace proper, and was consequently much larger. Within the walls were a maze of staircases and landings. Elevator shafts plummeted down tens of thousands of storeys to the depths of the hive, their cars nowhere to be seen. Within this outer layer of rooms and passageways, the main body of the palace was a series of giant halls, designed expressly with the display of power in mind. The Ultramarines ruled Ardium, but the office of the planetary governor remained sacrosanct beneath their hand, and there were as many depictions of various historic holders of the title and their heraldic badges as there were of the Ultramarines.

Statues of Ultramarines native to Ardium lined long hallways. Justinian was of that world, Felix recalled, but the creation of the Primaris Space Marines had been a secret, and no monument had been raised to him. Soaring vaulted roofs glittered with mosaics of precious metals, depicting the deeds of ancient heroes. In the silence of the deserted palace, the glittering eyes of the figures in the mosaics gave them a sinister false life. Even so, decay was less prevalent in the Palace Spire than in the Sighing Spire, as if the statues and the devotional images in the palace resisted its progress.

Only echoes held court there, and the hooting wind. There were bloodstains, old and black, and combat damage to the spire itself, but there were no corpses. All the dead walked in the service of Nurgle.

The rumble of battle broke through the funereal wind, and Felix's dwindling force picked up its pace. He had lost seven Space Marines. A dozen more were wounded. His Apothecary's grim silence told him that the gene-seed of the dead had been too polluted to salvage.

'This way,' said Sergeant Lyceus.

Lyceus led the strike force upwards through a series of plain and unadorned service corridors never seen by the lords who inhabited the palace. The sound of rocket fire rushed down the stairs, and they emerged onto a wide mezzanine overlooking the palace's huge feasting hall. A group of Death Guard heavy weapons troopers were firing with impunity down into the combat raging on the main floor. Lyceus held up a finger to his grinning skull mouth. He and his men stole forwards, attacking the Heretic Astartes from behind. Two died, gutted before they could react. Felix had his men shoot down the most troublesome, a purple-faced champion with a clubbed claw for a fist, who took twenty bolt-rounds before he agreed to fall.

The enemy dealt with, Felix's force took their place.

Battle raged. Felix assessed the situation quickly. Lieutenant Astium's forces were heavily depleted; Tobias' squads looked to have arrived later, coming in from outside the hall while Astium was already engaged. The Death Guard fought ferociously, their peculiar specialists choking the air with poison fog and plague spores. Thankfully, the Space Marines' Mark X armour kept this cargo of disease at bay, but the swirling mists made a mockery of their targeting systems.

'A good position,' said Felix.

'Purposefully chosen,' said Lyceus. 'I will rejoin the others. We are more use down there than we are up here.'

Felix nodded, and bade him good fortune, then ordered his warriors to creep forwards, ready to fire down at the enemy.

At his command, they unleashed a torrent of death upon the foe, slaughtering many where they stood. Several took dozens of hits before they fell, but fall they did. Forced to divide their own fire between the two groups in the feasting hall and the new-comers up on the balcony, the Death Guard were hard-pressed.

'Brothers! Victory is with us,' called Felix, amplifying his vox signal to break through the enemy's jamming.

Astium and Tobias hailed him with grim joy. The Death Guard were caught in a crossfire, and the tide began to turn.

But the forces of Nurgle were not bested yet.

A bell tolled, perturbing the poison gases. Unbelievably, the clanging bell shook the Primaris Space Marines. Bolt rifles wavered and dipped. Warriors looked to their brothers in confusion. Felix recoiled as if struck. The bell's note was a poison all its own.

There were promises there among the tolling. *Embrace my misery,* its resonance sang, sinking into the meat of Felix's brain, *and enjoy an end to all future miseries.*

A grossly obese plague lord advanced through the melee, a bronze bell hanging from a crook of black horn suspended over his power pack. The bell swung slowly, and its clapper struck the metal. Another doleful peal rolled out over the battle, invigorating the Death Guard. The effect on the Space Marines was debilitating.

His shots going wide from a hand suddenly weak, Felix reeled back from the mezzanine's edge. Black thoughts filled his head, taking him away from the battle. He was tormented with visions of his own death, his mighty Primaris body undone by disease and age, reduced to a trembling ague-smitten shadow. The world fell away, and he found himself wracked with sickness in a grey place. His armour was corroded and non-functional, a dead weight on his enfeebled frame, and his weapons were breaking in his hands, scorching his nostrils with the harsh chemical reactions of oxidising fyceline and failing energy cells.

There was a flicker of heat in the reactor upon his back, but it too was fading. He tried to stand, but he could not.

He was dying, dying from old age and neglect, and there would be no coterie of heroes to resurrect him as they had Guilliman. The baleful howl of the warp awaited.

The bell tolled again.

There is release from this suffering, the bell sang. *There is joy in pain. Pledge yourself to Father Nurgle and never fear mortality again. Become eternal, become a vector of life. Join the never-ending dance and be merry.*

A light penetrated the dismal world that Felix inhabited. He lifted his head from the ground and saw the glowing figure of Codicier Maxim striding through the grey, his blue armour as pure as sapphire, the green shoulder pad of his Aurora Chapter insignia as bright as virgin forest leaves.

'Stand firm! Pay no heed! It is but a poison of the warp!' bellowed Maxim. His voice strained as he spoke. The crystal rods of his aegis hood glowed with fierce witch-fire.

The bell tolled again. Maxim's image flickered. He approached Felix.

'Captain! You must finish the herald, or we shall fail.'

Felix raised a shaking hand, the last fragments of rusty armour falling from his fingers. Maxim grasped his arm, and suddenly he was armoured again, young and full of the power of the Emperor. The grey world crumbled as if made of dust. He was in the feasting hall.

'Go, now!' said Maxim. 'I shall shield you.'

The bell rang. Felix took the psychic impact with a grunt.

While the Primaris Space Marines were reeling from the bell's dolorous effects, the Death Guard had renewed their attack, regrouping with reinforcements coming up from the lower halls. He had to act now.

Holding aloft his power sword, he leapt over the edge of the balustrade, landing in the middle of his foes. He recovered well and barged past a Traitor Space Marine, desperate to slay the bell-toller before Maxim's protection gave out. Warriors came at him but he smote them down, crushing the chest of one with a blow from his gauntlet, eviscerating a second with a reverse cut of his power sword.

Heart, heart, head – the mantra for combat against other Adeptus Astartes, doubly important when fighting the resilient Death Guard. Despite their toughness, Felix cut them down economically, guarding his attacks against excessive movements that might expose him. A burst from his boltstorm gauntlet mashed the head of a bloated giant whose armour joints sported fringes of tentacles. The traitor fell to his knees, his additional limbs spasming.

The bell-ringer was close. Felix was taller than the traitor, but had far less mass; the bell-ringer was a swollen horror, bloated with disease and fell power. His armour strained to contain his bulk. Horns sprouted from his back. The one the bell hung from was only the greatest, and there were several others crowded together in a keratinous thicket. A filthy tabard hung from his armour, yellowed by smoke pouring from a censer at his waist.

Felix leapt onto the corpse of the tentacled Space Marine, using the backpack as a springboard to launch himself at his foe. The bell-ringer loosed a shot from his plasma pistol. A miniature, globular sun howled past the captain's ear. Felix let fly with his boltstorm gauntlet, the shots ringing the bell, then brought his power sword up and back for a downwards cut. The blade's powered edge sank deep into the traitor's thick battleplate, bringing forth a spray of black blood and a ringing grunt, more bell chime than voice.

The traitor staggered, his motion setting the great bell on his back into another swing. Sound waves pummelled Felix, piercing the psychic protection of Maxim. His auditory dampers burst. The scent of fried electronics filled his mask, and his ears bled.

The traitor held a second, smaller bell in his left hand. He swung it like a weapon at Felix's head. Felix recovered quickly, his Primaris physique, aided by the Codicier's psychic might, purging the great bell's effects from his mind, and he swung his power sword, cleaving the bell-ringer's hand from his body. His plasma pistol fell to the floor. Blood, thick and slow as tar, congealed at the stump. Felix levelled his sword, and rammed it as hard as he could at the traitor's chest. A sparking furrow split the armour as the point scraped across the rounded chestplate, setting the traitor's tabard aflame. It bit near the bell-ringer's armpit, and penetrated the metal to the rotten meat beneath. Felix put all his weight onto the sword, and pushed it through his enemy. Metal squealed on metal. The disruption field cracked and banged. Stinking smoke poured from the wound.

The traitor roared, and flailed once again with his smaller bell. Felix released his sword and punched hard with his gauntlet, caving in the traitor's helmet. As the bell-ringer fell, Felix yanked his sword free and swung, cutting through the bell's supporting horn. It fell with a muted clank, and was silent.

Instantly, the effect of the bell vanished. The Ultramarines recovered their wits and attacked with renewed vigour. Death Guard fell by the dozen, though the cost was high.

'Onward!' shouted Felix. 'Onward! To the chapel!'

Blade and fist swinging, Felix battled his way towards the chapel's high doors. Seeing their leader so far out ahead of them, the Primaris warriors let out a war cry and pressed on, bludgeoning their foes with rifle butt and combat blade when the range became too close to effectively fire.

Cutting the head from a power fist-wielding plague champion, Felix made the chapel doors first. He raised his sword and shouted, 'For Guilliman! For Ultramar! For the Emperor!'

The battle was done soon after.

Felix set a rearguard before going into the chapel with Maxim and Gerrundium. The dead were moving still. Their progress was slow, inexorable, and there were so many that they would eventually overwhelm the strike force. Time was limited.

Maxim solemnly pushed open the door, and together they were confronted by the daemonic mechanism of Mortarion.

All fittings had been stripped from the chapel, leaving it a bare chamber with chipped walls where mosaics had been torn free and murals smashed. Plaster crunched underfoot.

Plinths empty of statues held strange alembics. They bubbled furiously, emitting cool fumes that smelled of sickness. They were arrayed at precise intervals, seven in all, surrounding a huge thing made of brass, wickedness and glass. Its lower part was an immense half-globe, full of dancing black particles that, on closer inspection, proved to be evil-tempered flies. The vapours of the alembics were conveyed to this chamber by funnels of moist leather, though whether this was to feed or to kill the flies could not be discerned.

Towering proudly from the seething mass of bottled flies rose a complicated mechanism of greened bronze and brass. Seven cracked white dials were mounted on the upper parts, their faces divided into seven portions.

As technology, the machine's exterior appeared elegant but primitive, something from a backward world of steam and clockwork. In the centre was a network of fluid circuitry of more sophisticated alien manufacture, though what that held inside was the most esoteric and primitive of all. The xenos circuitry encased a glowing shard of what looked like stone. It had no deliberate shape, appearing natural, or at least created using poorly refined growing processes, but the curve of it – the bladed end and the knotted parts spaced down its length – suggested a monster's finger hacked from a cruel talon. Spiral wires were plugged into crudely drilled holes in several places. Crowning it all was a complicated network of gears that drove three brass orbs round and round, like an orrery representing a sparse star system.

The combination of sciences was bizarre. Such was the mix of technologies employed in the machine's creation, from the most advanced to the lowest, that were it not for the aching green glow coming from it, and the sense of palpable evil, it could have been taken for some dramatist's stage prop.

Clockwork tick-tocked with fussy efficiency. The flies' buzzing set the Space Marines' teeth on edge, but worse was the hum coming from the rotating spheres.

'It is a clock, a monstrous timepiece,' said Maxim. 'A warp thing.'

'Can you discern how it works?' asked Felix.

'In some profane manner, time itself is sickened by this device,' said Gerrundium.

'Can you feel it, my brother?' Maxim asked Gerrundium. 'How it reaches out from here, casting a shade over the planet?'

'I see it as a stain, many-armed and ominous, that embraces all to its darkness,' replied Gerrundium.

'Such evil,' said Maxim. 'And it is not confined only to this room, or even to Ardium alone. Its influence spreads throughout the sector, linking worlds in a dark web.' Maxim's hand traced through the air, pointing out something invisible to Felix. 'It is this that destabilises the star-realm of Ultramar, allowing the leakage of the warp through space and time, returning the dead to unliving life and tempting the faithful from the righteous path.'

'How can a machine do such things?' asked Felix.

'It is not a machine,' said Maxim. 'Not in our sense. It looks like a machine. There is xenos deviltry here besides the machinations of Chaos. Aeldari, perhaps. Those parts are tormented…' He paused. 'Like they are a piece of a device made to function contrary to its intended purpose. But it is mostly warpcraft. This device was certainly built by Mortarion, the fallen primarch. It has the hallmarks of his work.'

'Then Lord Guilliman's information was correct,' said Felix. 'Is it safe for my warriors to enter the room?'

'Safe enough. The device has a perfidious purpose that affects the minds and souls of mortal men. Our warriors should be resistant, so long as they focus and do not lose themselves as you almost did, captain.'

'Then I will call them in and have this thing demolished,' said Felix. 'We have seen enough. The dead are at the doors of the Palace Spire. As soon as this machine is in fragments, we will leave.'

CHAPTER NINETEEN

THE MYCOTA PROFUNDIS

The long-dead builders of the *Endurance* would not have recognised their creation. Ten thousand years had passed since its keel had been laid. But time, even of so long a span, was not responsible for the ship's transformation. The *Endurance* was spoiled by the warp, remade as a small part of Grandfather Nurgle's garden dug up and transplanted into the fertile ground of the mortal world.

Thick, poisonous vapour choked its corridors, growing thicker the higher up the ship's decks one went. At the very tops of its rotten command spires, the gas displaced the air completely, and would kill an unenhanced human in seconds. The cowed tribes who made up the ship's mortal contingent were confined to the lower decks, where the fog clung only to the ceilings of the highest halls. Even so they lived terrible, shortened lives, their lungs rotting from the moment of their first breath.

The fog posed no danger to the daemon primarch Mortarion; rather it sustained him. He strode through its poisons and was invigorated. His robe sent it into a storm of complicated curls where three-lobed sigils and grinning skulls might be seen, though only for a moment. In the high levels where he dwelled, the mist was liquid thick. Glinting droplets beaded the primarch's clothes, armour and flesh. Other parts of the *Endurance* were sweltering as equatorial swamps, but the heights were chill as mountaintops, and here daemonkin, immune to the effects of the toxic air, took the place of wretched humans as crew. Besides, in those quarters the machinery of the vessel required a certain touch. No mortal effort could ensure its smooth running.

Coiled, organic tubing took the place of metal pipes. Taut nerves replaced wiring. Rotting brain matter stood in place of circuitry nexuses, and daemons trapped in warded clay pots did the work of cogitators. A thick plaque of pulsing flesh covered the walls and made the floor soft underfoot. Where it had not been subsumed, the steel and iron of ancient Imperial work was flaked with corrosion. Blackened plastek peeled from wiring. Everywhere was in a state of decay.

The organic parts of the *Endurance* teemed with disease that broke flesh down and digested it as quickly as it grew. Great patches were black with putrescence. Crops of livid cysts throbbed on the walls, trickling oil where they had burst. There were rooms where the growths had died, and there maggots fell as rain, and flies clogged the workings. Whole decks had been overtaken by festering jungles. Others were thick with slime where unnatural ecosystems had succumbed to plague.

It was a vital decay. The *Endurance* quivered vigorously as its ancient engine stacks pushed it free of the Macragge System. The ship still functioned. It still moved through space as it had been made to, but it was not a ship as any sane mortal race would recognise.

Mortarion's personal domain differed from the chaotic

machine-life of the rest of his ship. He came to a door covered with throbbing, vein-like ivy. A pass of his cadaverous hand, and the door opened for him, sending the fog into a swirling dance.

On the far side was nothing but cold, bare metal. The ancient magi who had built the *Endurance* would have recognised these halls. They were rusty, pockmarked by acid burns from the corrosive mists, but they lacked the fleshy vitality of other parts of the ship.

Mortarion emerged into a spire whose floors had been cored out to make a single, towering space. When completed, the alteration had sported decorative gargoyles, and fantastically detailed railings had edged the walkways. That was long ago. The statues were now nubs of iron, the railings dissolved to paper-thin fretting. The fog was at its thickest at the tower's peak, where it formed clouds thick enough to rain. An acidic drizzle fell from on high. Puddles of it sat in concavities it had dissolved in the floor.

With the tower's interior structure removed, the true scale of a Gloriana-class battleship was revealed. Though a minor part of the vessel, this single tower was a hundred yards across, and three hundred high. Mortarion raised his hands and tilted his face upwards. His yellow eyes closed, and he let the rain fall upon his face. It ran in greasy trails around the breathing mask embedded into his flesh.

With a gurgle of pleasure, Mortarion shook out wings that resembled those of a giant fly. After a couple of slow twitches, Mortarion set them into blurring motion, and he rose smoothly from the ground. His wings made a noise as loud as a hundred chainswords revving, but he moved serenely, his long robes trailing after him, dripping with the liquids they had accumulated on his walk through the ship.

He rose to the tower's top, where a pier extended from one

wall. It was so corroded by the fog that it shook as he landed upon it. He folded his wings away. As he walked the pier, it swayed and squealed, letting out a shower of damp rust, but it bore him surely, and he arrived at the door at the far end. Another pass of his hands sent the door grating into the wall. He went through onto a set of wrought-iron stairs that curved up inside the skin of the spire. There were holes in the hull through which shone the steady burn of stars. But the mist was unaffected; the air was unaffected; Mortarion was unaffected. Where decompression winds should rush, there was dank stillness. The *Endurance* no longer obeyed the strictures of reality.

A final door opened into the tower's highest chamber. In ages past it had been the spire's viewing dome. Now it was Mortarion's horarium, his retreat, his sanctuary. A home away from home when he was forced to leave the comforting landscapes of the Plague Planet behind.

He had never thought to depart the Eye of Terror. It amused him that he had, but it was good to be abroad again.

The armaglass dome still covered the top of the tower, though the petal-shaped panes that made it up were broken in several places, and one was missing entirely. This did not affect the poisonous atmosphere, nor the temperature. Rather than the killing cold of space, the dome retained the chill of high mountains: unpleasant, but not deadly.

Past the reality-defying properties of the horarium, there were four other items of note in the chamber. The first was its vast array of clocks. They hung from every part of the walls below the glass of the dome. They stood in ticking ranks upon the floor. Small carriage clocks and giant gilded edifices under glass domes occupied dozens of tables. A new chime went off every second, for the clocks ran asynchronously, marking as they did the time of many layers of reality. Every few minutes, the ringing of bells would coincide, and sound as a single deaf-ening round of mismatched peals.

The largest of the clocks was the second item. Occupying the central portion of the room, and twice the height of the daemon primarch, it had three faces and stood on three legs worked with the tripartite symbol of Nurgle. The legs did not obviously represent any kind of beast, fantastical or otherwise, but were made so that it crouched over the floor, giving the impression the clock was about to strike. Its faces were a yard across, and each had seven hours counted by three hands with pointers made in the shape of flies. The time was approaching the clock's midnight. A massive scythe on a chain served as a pendulum, swishing across the space beneath the clock. Reality sighed as the blade cut into the very stuff of creation, and every tick-tock was the death of something fine.

The third item of note was contained within the great clock. Atop the timepiece was a huge bell jar, covered with arcane symbols. The lower half extended into the space between the triple faces. The upper half made a lesser dome below the greater one of the chamber. There was something inside this glass, a prisoner. Metal tubes were attached to glass valves in the jar. They allowed certain poisons to be introduced, and though meant to harm they were not designed to kill, for the jar was a device of torment.

The thing inside the jar was no longer alive, but it could suffer. Streamers of corposant moved behind the glass. As Mortarion entered the room, they coalesced, becoming a monstrous alien face. Even in death, the soul's psychic potency was great enough to stop a mortal man's heart by sight alone, and then raise up his corpse to serve the creature, but to Mortarion the killing scorn it broadcast was merely amusing.

'*Good day, father,*' he said. The primarch's voice was a ghostly, deep, sighing whisper.

For a thousand years, Mortarion had pursued the soul of his adoptive father through the warp with packs of baying beasts. Over the landscapes of insanity and through the kingdoms of dreams, the pursuit had gone on. Mortarion turned his face entirely from the mortal realm in those years, so bent was he on having his final vengeance upon the xenos creature that had adopted him, used him and been slain by the Emperor when Mortarion had failed to kill him.

Imprisoning his alien father's soul had brought Mortarion a modicum of the peace the Emperor had denied him.

The hunt was long ago, and the novelty of the prisoner had worn off. The Lord of Death paid no heed to his foster father's glowering and went to the clock's pendulum. He caught the scythe by the handle at the apex of its swing, and unhooked it from the chain. Without the scythe, the clock continued to tick, defying the logic of real mechanisms.

Mortarion weighed the scythe in his hand. *'Silence,'* he said, naming the weapon. He ran his hand along the head. His dry hands rasped on the steel. Unlike most other things aboard the *Endurance*, the scythe was free of decay, and sharp as a dying woman's curse.

The fourth and final thing of note in the room was not visible to mortal sight. It had to be summoned. Mortarion stood under the centre of the clock, extended his right arm and opened his hand. He closed his eyes.

'I call upon you, loyal servants of the Great Father. Commune with me, in the name of the sevenfold path.'

The vapours in the room thickened about the spot below the clock's centre. Mortarion stepped back. He rested his hand atop Silence's head, his robes stirring in the stinking wind, and waited. The fog whirled faster and faster until it formed a small vortex of black light. The vortex thickened, taking on the shape of a tall fungus. The flesh of it was ethereal to begin with, but grew more solid with every passing moment. Once fully manifested, the fungus grew unnaturally fast, its rounded tip questing up towards the base of the clock. From the bottom of his prison, Mortarion's father watched it approach, recoiling as it wormed its way within the clock and bumped the base of the glass, smearing it with poison. Black mycelium spread across the floor from the fungus' bulbous volva. They threaded themselves across the floor, swift as serpents and gossamer-fine, rising up and engulfing the clocks of the room in a stringy, slimy mat. Where they encountered Mortarion, they swallowed him to his waist. The daemon primarch closed his eyes, shuddering at their touch in a combination of ecstasy and abhorrence.

Mortarion had never entirely lost his disgust of warpcraft.

The wind dropped. The fungus cap, a pale and narrow thing clasped close to the stalk, pulsed horribly. A musty smell suffused the fog. At once, the clocks went off together, rippling the vapours with a violent carillon, and then they all stopped.

'*Mortarion,*' said a voice.

The daemon primarch opened his eyes. They were shot through with the root systems of the fungus, the whites veined with black threads that extended into the yellow of his irises.

Beneath the clock was an image of Ku'Gath, the Plaguefather, Great Unclean One and first in the favour of Nurgle. It wavered as if seen through a jet of forge heat. There were similarities with an Imperial hololith, but they were entirely superficial. The head looked real, severed as if it had been carved from the body, so that the veins and ways of the organism could be seen around the edges, as if in anatomical cross section.

'*Plaguefather,*' said Mortarion. He bowed his cadaverous head. Ku'Gath respectfully returned the gesture. The ragged skin and exposed fats of his chins creased under his jaw.

'Where is the third? Where is your wayward son?' said the greater daemon.

'I am here, summoned by the Mycota Profundis, as is our bargain,' said a surly voice. A second image materialised, this one of a helmeted Plague Marine, one horn jutting from the brow of his malformed Cataphractii Terminator plate. Layers of diseased flesh, fat and bone, part merged with the being's armour, were visible, again as if cut away. Osseous tubes rose behind his head, and an infernal buzzing accompanied his words that threatened to drown them out.

For all the racket of Typhus' manifestation, his contempt was clear when he spoke.

'Gene-father,' he said.

'My son,' said Mortarion. His tone was coolly indifferent where his son's was provocative. *'We are gathered then, the three champions, followers of the sevenfold path, masters of life and death.'*

'Not yet masters,' said Ku'Gath with a sorrowful shake of his great horned head. *'Unworthy acolytes.'*

'The time of your redemption is at hand,' said Mortarion. *'The way opens. The seven campaigns of this invasion bear fruit ready to rot. Roboute Guilliman has returned to Ultramar.'*

Ku'Gath gave a sly look of delight, almost a smile. Typhus laughed.

'You are foolish, my lord father, if you think this will end well,' said the First Captain. 'We should have finished his realm while he was absent.'

'Typhus, Typhus,' said Mortarion. *'So long you have lived, and so little you have learnt. What use is the destruction of a kingdom without the death of the king?'*

'A king without a kingdom is no king, but a vagabond. His suffering would have been pleasant meat to savour,' said Typhus. 'You court disaster in confronting him. This employment of the

Hand of Darkness is convoluted and foolhardy. Simplicity was the watchword of our Legion – the direct attack, the weathering of pain, not this deviousness. This was not the plan of the Great Father.'

'It is my plan!' said Mortarion, his gloomy voice rising. 'And its success will honour the Great Father. He entrusts us with our will and our initiative. I will use mine. He will be pleased.'

'If you succeed,' said Typhus. He looked around the horarium disdainfully. 'You are blinded by the past as always, my lord. You look to Barbarus and remake it wherever you go. Embrace change fully. Embrace Chaos. Abandon these schemes. Let us drown Ultramar in disease and move on.'

Mortarion flung up his arms and spread his wings. 'I have, and this is my reward! I am remade in terrible image. I am become death!'

'You do not believe. Not truly,' said Typhus. 'You have paid nothing for your power. The false Emperor made you, genefather. Nurgle took you as a prize – you are a trophy, my lord. You would never have found your way to enlightenment without me. Without me, you would have nothing. You would be dead, your soul dispersed into the warp. I fought my way into the Great Father's attention. I became his herald by will and by the dint of my own efforts. What have you done to win his favour?'

'Curb your insolence,' said Mortarion.

'Or what, my lord? I have Nurgle's favour. You would not dare to move against me. You think that you are in control, that your being is separate from the warp and yours to do with as you will. It is not. It is Nurgle's. You must submit to him fully, or Grandfather will have hard lessons for you. This plan of yours, to lead your brother on Nurgle's dance, it is ill-conceived. If we must strike, strike now. We should gather our fleets and cripple his forces while they gather at Macragge. Do not allow him the luxury of time to consult with his warriors, or consolidate his position.'

'*Do not presume to tell me what to do,*' said Mortarion. '*You will work with us in furtherance of our plan.*'

'I will do as I please,' said Typhus. 'If only you would abandon the last of your being to the lord of life, you would see. You have no power over me. You do not truly understand. If you did, then you and I might be reconciled.'

'*Do you level the same criticism against Ku'Gath, First Captain?*' said Mortarion icily. '*You dare speak to him in that way?*'

'He is as flawed as you, in his own way,' said Typhus. 'Maudlin where you are nostalgic.'

Ku'Gath nodded dolefully. '*You are right! I am unworthy. So unworthy. I cannot help it.*'

'All Ku'Gath cares for is setting right the loss his birth caused,' said Typhus. 'He at least desires to honour Nurgle through his efforts, and so can be forgiven. You seek to honour yourself. You do your own work with this fool's errand. Give him a day too many, and Roboute Guilliman will defeat you, and we shall lose all hope of bringing Ultramar within the walls of Nurgle's manse.'

'*You will obey me. You will follow our plan,*' said Mortarion. '*I require your vectorium at Espandor, when the time comes.*'

Typhus snorted. 'You cannot command me as you once did. I am high in the favour of the Plague God – equal to you in his eyes, if not higher. Who was it who delivered him the Death Guard? It was I, not you. You still do not understand the true nature of Chaos. I do. I am following our plan as originally formulated. The blessing of the Great Father was on that strategy, not on this quest for vengeance. You deceived me, Mortarion. You intended to play with your brother all along. This will displease Grandfather, and I will have no part in your folly.'

'If you will not come to Espandor, you will be at Parmenio. The numbers do not lie, my son. It is calculable. Great Nurgle will command it is so. It is preordained.'

'Maybe there is hope for you,' said Typhus. 'More and more you dabble with the warp's true power. Perhaps one day you will master it, and leave your bitterness against your Barbaran father behind you. But you are wrong if you believe that I will fight at your side. You have no real foresight. I will not be there to help you, no matter what your numerology says. And now I go. Be warned, little father – I have the ear of the Great Father himself.' Typhus' image blurred and vanished. The part of the mycelium mat supporting his warp ghost twitched and decayed into putrid slime.

Mortarion stared long and hard at the space where his wayward son had been.

'And you, Ku'Gath,' said Mortarion. *'Are you against me also?'*

'I stand with you, favoured son of the Great Father,' said Ku'Gath. *'You see the chance for revenge, I for redemption. Together we may serve ourselves, and the will of Papa Nurgle.'*

In the main, daemons were beyond the comprehension of men. Many were bizarre things, their motives inexplicable even to Mortarion, who was now more daemon than human himself.

Ku'Gath was different. The misery he wallowed in was something mankind knew only too well, and Mortarion knew misery best of all.

'Your plan is working,' said the daemon. *'The dead walk across the worlds we foul. The peons of Ultramar have had their eyes opened to their slavery and shake their fists at their blue masters. We shall combine forces when the time is right. We shall prevail. I need but a little more time to perfect my new concoction. Every strain of the galaxy's finest diseases contributes their essence to its creation. There has never been anything like it.'* His voice came

close to enthusiasm. *'It will be as devastating as you desire, and more so – the finest plague, enough to slay a demigod! Delay the primarch. Keep him from Iax. Rot his empire, and when he is full of despair, we shall strike, and we shall kill him.'*

Ku'Gath withdrew from the communion. More of the mycelium mat fell into decay. Mortarion pulled himself free of the clinging tendrils, and with a rustle it shrank in on itself, shrivelling up to nothing. His eyes cleared. The fungal spike in the room's centre collapsed into a mouldering heap that rapidly deliquesced into stinking water.

Mortarion walked across the slippery floor and hung Silence again upon its chain. He held the scythe's head in one hand and petted it before drawing it back across the room.

'Soon, Silence, we will reap the greatest prize of all – the death of my brother!' He set it swinging. The great clock restarted. Their king ticking again, so did all the others.

'What do you think of that, father?' said the Lord of Death. The soul in the flask screamed silently at him and raced around its confinement. The machines constraining it buzzed with the additional strain.

'Shhh,' said Mortarion. *'You will need your strength. I have neglected you for too long. I have new stimuli for you to enjoy, new pains and soul-fevers. Such times we will have, you and I, when the hateful Imperium is overthrown. An eternity to explore the rotting of the spirit. The galaxy will be free of stagnation, and there will be a riot of life in its place. The Emperor offers death in life. Nurgle offers the constant renewal of life in death! So many of the Emperor's loyal subjects will join with us when they see how their suffering may be banished. Typhus says I do not understand, father. But I do, I understand far better than him. With Guilliman gone, the Imperium will be doomed. All glory to the generosity of Father Nurgle! It has been foretold, and I shall make it so.'*

Mortarion went to stand by a bank of valves and wheels hidden behind an array of clocks. The workings connected to the tubes that ran into the glass prison. He let his hand hover over them, tormenting the spirit of his xenos father with anticipation of the poisons he might unleash. Under his breathing mask, what remained of Mortarion's mouth smiled. He let his hand drop. Leaving the wheels untouched, he departed the horarium.

The third part of Mortarion's plan was in motion. He would leave Guilliman to his victory at Ardium. On other worlds, in other places, Mortarion would weaken him, poisoning him mind, body and soul, just as he poisoned Guilliman's realm.

And then Mortarion would destroy his brother.

CHAPTER TWENTY

THE COUNCIL OF HERA

The Fortress of Hera had changed greatly since Guilliman's time. The walls had grown outwards, swallowing parts of Magna Macragge Civitas below it and the Hera's Crown mountains behind it. To the west it had spread as far as Hera's Falls. Their foaming rush had exchanged natural beauty for architectural elegance. Where once water had thundered through a steep natural gorge, now it was constrained in a vertical channel of marble. Slippery rocks were replaced with tall statues, the irregular plunge pool by a square lake edged with bronze. The cliffs had been carved back. Statues stood in their stead, and shrines in stacked clusters.

The city was different too. Flat land was at a premium on mountainous Macragge. Like a displaced nation, what Magna Macragge Civitas had lost to the Fortress of Hera's encroachment it had taken from the Pharamis Ocean. The seafront was over a mile further out than it had been ten thousand years ago, and beyond its edge, the water was clustered with floating habitats.

Both fortress and city had lost much of what Guilliman remembered to the vagaries of war. Ultramar had been invaded many times while he slept, and as the capital world, Macragge had been targeted over and again. Tyranids, orks and the minions of Chaos had all left their mark. The grand triumphal arches of the Great Crusade had gone, blasted down in one war or another, and lesser monuments had taken their place. History had a great inertia, and the layout of the streets had resisted change, but every attack had swept away another part of the past in piecemeal destruction. Pale shadows in stone had supplanted old glories.

There were elements that had survived. The Library of Ptolemy was one, and the Temple of Correction another. Other landmarks had been rebuilt several times. One remaining feature was the Plaza of Attendance, a vast space like an inverted ziggurat stamped into the Fortress of Hera's rampart plateau. The walls had advanced from the plaza, leaving the plaza some way from the edge where before it had stood at the brink of man-made cliffs. The side nearest the city, once open, was now walled with a faceless armoury. The halls at the eastern end, where for a brief period the primarch Sanguinius had sat as Emperor, were long ago demolished.

But the plaza remained, and it was upon this familiar ground that Roboute Guilliman elected to land.

It was a windy night, and wet. Every Ultramarine upon Macragge was upon the terraces of the plaza, as were hundreds of dignitaries from many of the worlds in Ultramar and beyond. The humans shivered in squalling gusts that lifted ceremonial robes and exposed bodies to the cold. The Space Marines were still as statues, their armour running with rain. Banners waved damply. Emblems were secrets in the dark. From the city, celebratory fireworks struggled up into the downpour and search beams shone, lighting up the night in a glorious display of colours and turning the beating rain into falling jewels. Snatches of martial music came wavering through the storm.

All eyes were on the sky.

Storm flashes lit the clouds from within. Thunder rumbled. More lightning burst, striking the tallest spires of the fortress. Underground engines whined as they absorbed the unlooked-for power, the humans glancing nervously upwards at the gathering rods glowing with heat.

Through the wind, the roar of a landing cycle made itself known, fading in and out of Macragge's thunder.

Suddenly the primarch's craft was there, emerging from the driving rain, a Thunderhawk gunship chased with gold and heavily decorated with painted battle scenes. Floodlights snapped on beneath it, and the ship came down in a pool of its own radiance at the centre of the Plaza of Attendance.

A clarion blew sonorously. Cyber-cherubs bearing silver instruments and banners flew out of access tunnels, were buffeted by the wind, recovered and flew over the Thunderhawk, where they struggled to stay in place as they proclaimed the arrival of the primarch.

'Lord Guilliman, Lord Guilliman, Master of Ultramar, Lord High Commander of the Imperium, son of the Emperor, Imperial Regent, Lord Roboute Guilliman.'

The door slammed down, and out strode the primarch. With him were five Adeptus Custodes, two high-ranking Sisters of Silence, ten of the Victrix Guard, Captain Sicarius, Captain Ventris and, lost in the shadow of so many mighty warriors, six of his most important civilian aides, a tall Primaris Space Marine following behind them. A human priest in simple robes came out last. He was a man so slight he might have slipped between the cracks of the plaza's worn pavement.

The primarch came to a halt and addressed his people.

'I have returned,' he said. Only that.

Marneus Calgar walked down a sodden carpet to meet his master. The empty presence of the Silent Sisterhood dragged at his soul, but he ignored it. Behind him marched Space Marines carrying the banners of all ten Ultramarines companies, Andron Ney at their head proudly bearing the Chapter standard.

Guilliman halted. Calgar knelt and bowed his head.

'My lord,' he said, speaking loudly over the rising wind. 'We rejoice to see you home again.'

'Rise, lord defender,' said Guilliman.

Calgar raised his face. He wore no helmet. Rain streamed off grey hair and around his bionic eye. He got to his feet, and he and Guilliman clasped their huge gauntlets together. Guilliman looked upon the Chapter Master with genuine paternal affection.

'We can only apologise for the weather,' said Calgar.

'And I can only apologise for the lateness of the hour,' said Guilliman. 'I desired to speak with you all as quickly as I could.' He looked upwards. 'Fear not the storm. This is a cleansing rain, and all Macragge's moods are to be treasured.' He returned his gaze to Calgar's face. 'Ultramar is under threat, and there is much we must do. I believe you know most of my followers here. These others are Sister-Commander Bellas and Sister-Commander Aphone of the Sisters of Silence.' The two women bowed, their proud topknots straggling in the rain, streaks of water running over their shaved scalps. He motioned to a woman and a man in grey uniforms. 'Two of Fleet Primus' chief historitors, Yassilli Sulymanya, Deven Mudire and their attendants. They are colleagues of Fabian Guelphrain. I trust he is well?'

'He is at work now, my lord, in the libraries of Magna Macragge Civitas. He returned with me from Vigilus intact, more or less. He sends his apologies that he is not here to greet you, but he says his work has reached a critical stage.'

'That sounds like him. I am glad to hear he is unharmed,' said Guilliman. He then pointed out a man in a cuirass and tall helm. 'This is Luthian Xhyle, Chiliarch of Rassuneon, representative of the lord commander of the Astra Militarum on the Council Exterra, who attends our council on their behalf. Finally, Stratarchis Tribune Maldovar Colquan leads the delegation from the Adeptus Custodes.'

Calgar bowed. 'It is an honour to stand before someone who personally serves the Emperor.'

'I serve whether I am away from the Imperial Palace or within it,' said the tribune, a retort to an insult that had not been delivered. His voice was unfriendly through his voxmitter.

'This is Captain Decimus Felix, my equerry.' The primarch indicated the tall Primaris Space Marine. He wore the badges of an Ultramarines captain, though there were already ten. It hadn't been the first time Guilliman had ignored the tenets of his Codex Astartes. Calgar thought little of it; he was the primarch and could do as he pleased.

Guilliman finally indicated the priest. 'And this is Militant-Apostolic Mathieu, also serving on the Council Exterra, for the Adeptus Ministorum. He is newly appointed to the role. The incumbent died not long ago,' explained Guilliman. 'He attends to get a feel for his office.'

'Chapter Master,' said the priest. He blinked rain from the corners of his eyes and smiled. 'The blessings of the Emperor be upon you.'

'Militant-apostolic,' said Calgar.

It was curious to Calgar that Guilliman should allow himself to be accompanied by a priest. By all accounts, the primarch had kept his first militant-apostolic as distant from himself as he could. As much as he disapproved of it, the primarch had comprehended the power of the Adeptus Ministorum soon

after he awoke, and the office of militant-apostolic was a recognition of their influence, but the primarch's acceptance had
gone no further than that. He had mistrusted the Ecclesiarchy
from the beginning.

'How goes the war at Vigilus?' Guilliman asked Calgar.

'It goes. There is little sign of it ending. I must go back, I fear,
as soon as matters are dealt with in Ultramar.'

'Then I am grateful you could make it here for this conclave.'

'You summoned, I obeyed. We discuss the fate of Ultramar,
my lord,' said Calgar. 'Vigilus can wait, for a while.'

'Is the hall prepared?' asked Guilliman.

'It is, my lord. We await your council. We have refreshments,
if you would prefer to eat first?'

'Let us be about the meeting. Feasting must wait. I cannot
afford to be away from the fleet long.'

More engines screamed in the storm. All around the plaza,
Thunderhawks descended, and out came all of Guilliman's lords
of war.

'The others are here,' said the primarch. 'We are ready. Let
us begin.'

The Strategia Ultima was insufficiently sized to hold all the
delegates, and so the edification had been arranged in the Hall
of Maxellus, named for the twenty-first Chapter Master of the
Ultramarines. The cold, damp smell of the outdoors came
steaming off the assembled host of politicians and warriors.
Huge heating coils hanging from arches did their best to warm
the company, but succeeded mainly in raising an interior fug
that ran wet on the stonework. A tall statue of Maxellus at the
end of the hall looked on sternly, if benignly. He had been
renowned for his wisdom. Emperor alone knew what he would
have made of Guilliman's return, and the changes that had

befallen the Imperium since his day. Maxellus had lived in a time roughly halfway between Guilliman's death and rebirth. Both the 31st and 41st millennia would have been unrecognisable to him.

Guilliman was afforded the place of honour. A massive bronze chair had been taken from the museum vaults deep under the Fortress of Hera and brought forth for his use after waiting ten thousand years for a lord of a stature that matched its size. Though Calgar had seen the primarch in stasis and was thus long aware of how physically large he was, the primarch's artefacts had always seemed bigger somehow than the being they were made for, as if sized for a titan from a greater age. They were sacred relics all, revered by successive generations of Ultramarines. The Ultramarines did not pray to their primarch, nor venerate him in an overtly religious way. They did not believe either the Emperor or His son divine, but an aura of holiness clung to his effects nonetheless, and it had been the habit of many Chapter Masters to meditate in the museum vaults, looking for inspiration from the things that had known the touch of their gene-sire.

To the primarch, the throne was just another piece of furniture, a possession reclaimed, as Ultramar was. He used it unthinkingly. Even now he was back, his casual attitude towards these ancient relics, although they were his, offended something in Calgar.

It was a ridiculous reaction, and Calgar stamped hard on it.

Present in the hall were the upper echelons of the Imperial command structure within Ultramar, which comprised the Ultramarines' upper leadership, the Chapter Masters of the Howling Griffins, the Novamarines, and the Genesis and Aurora Chapters, as well as the First Captain of the Sons of Orar and the Third Captain of the Mortifactors. The Inquisition were there, as were other, even more secretive organisations. By lithocast, the Chapter Masters of the Silver Eagles and the Libators were also in attendance. News had come that the White Scars were en route in force. Elements of twenty-four other Chapters were either on their way or present in Ultramar. These smaller forces were of varied strengths, ranging from a single squad to a company in size, and they had elected eight further captains from among their number to speak for them at the council. Ultramar's Knightly houses were also well represented, as were its forge worlds, Navy and Astra Militarum forces.

Guilliman had brought numerous groups with him from Fleet Primus, including the heads of various Primaris Chapters founded at Raukos, as well as the three groupmasters accompanying him, who all had their own spokesmen and advisers.

Maldovar Colquan sat at Guilliman's left hand, Calgar at his right. The military leaders occupied the first three tiers of seats around the council table; there were several hundred all told, as varied a gathering, although not as grand, as there had been at the Triumph of Raukos. In the remainder of the seats were diplomats speaking for the governments of dozens of worlds from Ultramar and Greater Ultramar.

A human-sized table, long enough to run the length of the gathering, had been set up down the middle. It was largely symbolic, for there were far too many bodies in the room for anyone to make use of it. Guilliman had expressly ordered that no hololiths or other data-projection devices be present. Instead, the table was heaped with ancient tomes, maps and treaties: symbols of obligation assumed long defunct by many of the dignitaries present.

Calgar thought Guilliman wished to be free of distraction. Less charitably, he thought his gene-father wanted to ensure that he was the sole source of knowledge in the room.

Ever since he had returned from death, Roboute Guilliman had been exerting his authority in a way that Calgar had never truly considered before. As Chapter Master of the Ultramarines, Calgar was no stranger to power, and had on occasion had need for the application of coercion and subterfuge to ensure smooth running of the realm. But it was not his realm any more, and he felt a modicum of disappointment that Roboute Guilliman had to use such tricks, that the primarch seemed so... *autocratic*.

Naturally, Calgar was an autocrat too, a minor emperor in all but name. That he accepted, though it was a burden to have to be so, and he had hoped for better from the primarch. Although in his genius Roboute Guilliman excelled at everything Calgar could imagine, in other ways he was a world away from the idealised figure Calgar had imagined all his life.

Autocracy was the natural order of human society. There was a leader, and the rest followed. So it had always been. The Imperium was predicated on the preservation of this natural hierarchy. The disappointment, then, stemmed not from the fact that Guilliman was capable of such behaviour, and indeed seemed completely at ease with it, but that it was necessary he should have to exert his right to his power.

Calgar had run the theoreticals and practicals of the primarch's awakening through his head many times before Guilliman had come back to them for real. It was indulgent, wishful thinking – daydreaming, even. But who did not wish for a saviour in times of need? Marneus Calgar, who was looked to as a saviour by billions of people, had needed his own idols to put faith in. When he had formulated his versions of Guilliman's miraculous return, as he was sure every Ultramarines Chapter Master since the first had also done, he had not conceived of events playing out as they actually had. He had not foreseen the resistance to the primarch's rule. He had naively expected a primarch to be able to overcome the stagnation of Imperial government by dint of his presence. The primarch would return, and all men would fall into line, and obey him unquestioningly. They would march together to conquer the galaxy, putting the old enemy to the sword and driving out the xenos.

It had not worked so simply. There was dissension, different interpretations of the primarch's edicts – sometimes wilful – and there was disbelief and suspicion. Guilliman's rebirth had caused great rejoicing among the populace, but less so among those leaders who risked losing their influence to his rule. Calgar had relied a great deal on the civilian leaders of Ultramar and beyond. Roboute Guilliman should not need to.

So the disappointment came not from Guilliman's facility with dissembling, coercion, intimidation and threat, but the fact he had to use them. Calgar had more faith than ever in his primarch. To see him living and breathing among them brought a sense of wonder he had never thought to experience as a Space Marine. It had, to some extent, reinvigorated the sense of his own humanity.

But the actions of some people in the face of the primarch's return meant he had less faith than ever in his fellow man. Humanity's short-sightedness and selfishness disgusted him.

Guilliman stood, banishing Calgar's train of thought.

'My lords, my generals, my countrymen,' said the primarch. 'Fellow Imperial citizens, fellow warriors of many worlds, I bid you welcome to this conclave today, at the heart of Ultramar.'

Guilliman's voice rang strong and clear off the stone of the hall. To every man and woman present in the assembly, it was as if he spoke to them personally. Guilliman commanded attention like no other could. His words invited no disagreement. He was forceful and strong, while appearing the epitome of reason.

Marneus Calgar was among the most powerful men in all the

Imperium, and yet awe entered him as he imagined a time when eighteen of these beings had travelled the stars. Being in a room with more than one primarch must have struck men dumb.

'I have summoned you here to discuss the cleansing of Ultramar of my brother's forces,' the primarch said. 'The first stage of the Indomitus Crusade is done. I will soon embark on the second stage. But for now, I come to your aid. When I depart, this realm will be better defended, better organised and more resilient than it has been for many generations.'

Calgar felt the remarks were a criticism directed at him.

'I am saddened that those worlds attacked or overrun within our sphere of influence remain without help while the war grinds on here, seemingly without resolution,' Guilliman continued. He gave the assembly a grave stare. Each person there felt their failings exposed by his regard, and none more so than Marneus Calgar. Failure was a new sensation to him, but he was becoming intimate with it. Under the gaze of the primarch he realised that his failures stretched far back in time. The realisation robbed the glory from all his successes.

'In the days of the Great Crusade, the worlds and realms associated with each Legion provided a solid base for their operations, and a link to the greater whole of the Imperium. Most were paragons to be aspired to, models of good governance and a promise of the peace that would come to compliant worlds. Ultramar was the very best. It was rightly lauded the length and breadth of the galaxy for its fairness – a just place, where every citizen could live free of harm.'

Guilliman got up from his chair and unrolled a star map upon the table. He smoothed it gently with his armoured hands, and stared at it a moment.

'I have read many histories. I recognise and am grateful that Ultramar has continued in the role I intended since the time of my death. I am proud of all that you have done to maintain the traditions of justice this realm represents in an often cruel galaxy. I am thankful for the preservation of the freedoms enjoyed by its people. Circumscribed by the grim state of affairs we find ourselves in as these admirable characteristics may be, Ultramar still remains an example to every other system in the Imperium.'

He took a deep breath, and rested his fists upon the chart. Calgar looked past the armoured hands. The legend on the map read 'Ultramar', but it was not the realm as he recognised it. It included all the original systems of the Five Hundred Worlds, and more besides. The territory was divided into five distinct, coloured blocks.

'However,' said the primarch, and a touch of steel entered his voice, 'I should have done better. By reducing Ultramar to a size that could be protected effectively by one Chapter while the Ultramarines fulfilled their many obligations elsewhere, I reduced Ultramar's effectiveness as an example and as a bastion.' He looked up, a sincere expression on his face. 'I was mistaken.'

Silence greeted these words. To most of the people in the room, he was effectively a god, and gods did not make mistakes.

'Furthermore, my command a decade ago that all treaties of independence were to be immediately rescinded and the ancient Five Hundred Worlds reincorporated into this realm has not been fully enacted. The efforts to reconstitute Greater Ultramar – that is, the ancient Five Hundred Worlds – have not proceeded as well as I would have liked. I am angry with those Imperial commanders who will not submit to Ultramar's rule. I am disappointed with those commanders that pay lip service to my command yet continue to put their own interests above those of greater humanity. Ultramar appears to be coming back into its original form, but it is a sham.'

Several representatives of certain worlds looked very uncomfortable. Guilliman pointed an armoured finger at the star map.

'This is my vision for Greater Ultramar. It will be put into effect immediately. As I cannot rely on the goodwill of local government to do my bidding, I am of today reinstating the ancient offices of the tetrarchy. Four noble members of the Adeptus Astartes, whom I have chosen as much for their acumen as statesmen as for their abilities as warriors, will be installed as sector commanders to oversee the reorganisation of this realm along lines that I and I alone shall decree. They will be provided with all authority to pursue my aims as they see fit, whether diplomatically or militarily.' He let the threat hang on the air. 'They will furthermore be entrusted with the defence of these sectors, and when peace comes, with their rebuilding and further development.'

The people waited for their primarch's word as to who would rule over them, but he gave the map his full attention.

'Under my rule, the tetrarchs governed from the worlds of Iax, Occluda, Saramanth and Konor. Saramanth was devastated some time ago, I understand, while Iax has diminished in relative importance to the systems around it and is currently occupied by the enemy. The seats of the tetrarchs were established early in Ultramar's expansion, and Iax and Konor are both proximate to the capital world. In recognition of these changes in circumstance, I will establish the new tetrarchy upon the following worlds.

'Konor will accept a tetrarch as its lord again. Despite its nearness to Macragge, the situation at Espandor demonstrates that a dedicated defensive strategy must be formulated to guard the northern reaches against further incursions from the Scourge Stars, and, eventually, to push out and cleanse those systems of the Plague God's followers. To this role, I appoint Severus

Agemman, First Captain of the Ultramarines and Regent of Ultramar. You have performed well here while Lord Calgar was absent. Such efforts deserve recognition.'

Agemman stood and knelt. 'My lord,' he said, 'you do me great honour.'

'You will retain your rank and position within the Chapter, tetrarch, though your new duties will be onerous,' said the primarch. 'Rise, Tetrarch of Konor, and take your place among the highest of lords.'

Agemman returned to his seat, his bearing radiating new determination.

'The other worlds that will bear this responsibility are as follows. Andermung shall be the base of the second tetrarch, with responsibility over the southern reach. To this role I appoint Second Captain Portan of the Genesis Chapter.'

Portan stood, his red armour dark in the hall. He held up his hands in confusion. 'My lord, what have I done to deserve this honour? Do you not wish to appoint your own Ultramarines to these positions? I am overwhelmed.'

'I have studied Chapter records of serving Space Marines among all of my sons, not only those of the Ultramarines,' said Guilliman. 'I have selected my tetrarchs according to their ability, no matter their origin. I call upon those who are suitable for the role, without favour to my own Chapter over others. You who have been chosen are worthy in my estimation. Do not forget that although you wear red and carry another Chapter's name, you too bear my gene-seed. That is all that matters to me. Your efforts in rebuilding the Diamat Cluster four centuries ago suggest you have all the qualities the position requires.'

'My lord, thank you,' said Portan.

'You will also retain your title as captain, though I recommend Chapter Master Eorloid promote another to captain your company. The strictures of the Codex shall be waived in this instance.'

'As you command, so shall it be,' said the Genesis Chapter Master.

'Protos in the west will take the third tetrarch. To this role, I have assigned Captain Balthus of the Doom Eagles. I have confirmation that he has been released by his Chapter and is making his way to Macragge.'

Guilliman pressed his finger at the edge of the map. There, his new Ultramar bowed out in a long, curving tail towards the Eastern Fringe, taking in many planets that had not known Macragge's rule for long ages.

'That leaves the eastern marches. This area, under the Sotharan League, remained politically unified until recently, but since the fall of Sotha to the tyranids the League has been without proper guidance, and I hear troubling reports regarding its efficiency. This will change. Vespator, three light years from Sotha, is designated the new seat of authority there, and its tetrarch will rule over the Sotharan League and the eastern shieldworlds besides.' Guilliman looked behind him at his equerry. 'Captain Felix will take command.'

Felix, who was standing to the right of the primarch's throne, looked thunderstruck.

'My lord, I am not qualified!' blurted the equerry.

'You are qualified because I say you are qualified,' said Guilliman matter-of-factly. 'I have been testing you ever since your records were brought to my attention. Why do you think I inducted you fully into the Ultramarines from my Unnumbered Sons? I saw your potential a long time ago, Felix. I have been training you for this role. You have not disappointed me. I need a Primaris tetrarch. All the Space Marines in the eastern quadrant of Ultramar will be of the Primaris type, and many others throughout Ultramar also. I cannot afford any dissension between the two generations of Space Marines.'

Guilliman surveyed the room.

'You may protest that this will never happen,' he continued. 'Archmagos Cawl can assure me that you are made to be loyal. You of the older type may cite your records of sacrifice and devotion, but I know the souls of men. I have heard protestations of loyalty before, and witnessed unintended slights burn them to ash. Where there is difference, there is space for envy, and envy leads to conflict. I will have none of it. Three of the four tetrarchs will be Space Marines of the original type. You will accept this offer, Felix – the books must be balanced. Eighty-six worlds will be yours. Some of them are lost, and you will require all the arts I have taught you to recover them. It shall fall to you, as Tetrarch of Vespator, to govern them all for the good of their peoples, and to be a spokesman for the Primaris Space Marines upon the Council of Greater Ultramar. All of you tetrarchs have similar burdens.'

'My lord!' Felix fell to his knees, his armour banging loudly on the stone.

'You, Lord Marneus Calgar,' said Guilliman, looking to the Ultramarines Chapter Master, 'will continue to rule the central worlds, with the exception of those in the systems of Konor, Veridia and Espandor, which shall fall under the remit of the first tetrarch. In this way, Ultramar will be divided into five parts.'

Guilliman's support of him was sincere enough, but Calgar saw a scolding behind it.

At that moment, the emissary from Occluda spoke up. He was angered, both by his planet being passed over for the tetrarchy and because it should be reincorporated in the first place.

'My lord, what do you mean, that many of the warriors will be Primaris Space Marines?' he asked.

A glance from the primarch had him hurriedly sitting down.

'My concerns that a single Chapter could not protect the Five Hundred Worlds remain valid,' said Guilliman. 'I have therefore decided to station eight new Chapters of Space Marines – created recently at Raukos – within the bounds of Greater Ultramar. Along with the Ultramarines, and the Scythes of the Emperor, whose territories fall within the fourth tetra, there will be henceforth ten full Chapters to defend this realm.'

This provoked a noisy reaction. Guilliman ignored it, and carried on.

'Work will be immediately undertaken to rebuild the Scythes of the Emperor with Primaris Space Marines. They will have responsibility for guarding what is currently the Sotharan League. Here, at Callimachus, we shall base the Avenging Sons Chapter, and at Howsbridge the Praetors of Ultramar shall have their home–'

The murmuring broke out into audible protests.

'You would have your own Legion?' said a female diplomat. 'My lord, what is your intention?'

'You say I have a Legion,' said Guilliman, his tone dangerously low, 'when I myself expressly forbid their formation or use?'

The woman had a choice either to sit down or to press on with her argument. Bravely, she chose the latter. 'You have done this before. Some say the nine brotherhoods of the Unnumbered Sons were Legions in all but name.'

'They were not,' said Guilliman. 'The Unnumbered Sons were organised into Chapters, as are the new defenders of Ultramar.'

'We deal with semantics,' the woman said.

Guilliman scowled, and swept his steely gaze across the crowd again. 'Listen to me. My intention is to save your lives, and the Imperium. Put aside your selfish concerns. Negate the disappointment I have felt in common humanity since awakening.

Show me that my hopes for our species were not unfounded. Impress me with your wisdom.'

'What about the Imperial governors?' said another diplomat. 'What will happen to those of worlds who take tetrarchs?'

'Most of them are loyal,' added another. 'They willingly rejoined the Five Hundred Worlds, and now you will remove them and replace them with Adeptus Astartes?'

Chatter from among the human contingent in the room swelled in volume. The Space Marines remained silent.

'My lord,' said Herodian, the son of the Hierarch of Callimachus. 'The galaxy has changed since your time. The worlds of Space Marine Chapters are often of low worth to the Adeptus Terra. Their tithe grades are set to null. Death worlds and the like, they are recruiting grounds only. Callimachus is a well-developed planet. Howsbridge, though lesser in importance and population, is no backwater either.'

Guilliman was not swayed by the young man's practised tone. 'I am changing things,' he said, and his eyes became cold and hard as cometary ice. 'The Chapters stationed throughout Ultramar will be tasked primarily with the realm's defence. Callimachus and Howsbridge will be governed by their Chapter Masters, as will all other worlds where Chapters will be stationed. Do not mistake me. There will be a need for civilian governors just as there is here on Macragge. The incumbents will be given the opportunity to retire after a period of ten years. During the handover period, they will be commanded to work with their successors to handle the transition. Once completed, their heirs shall be offered the opportunity to serve Ultramar as the administrators of those worlds. They will rule still, only their title will change.'

'They will not be governors!' said Herodian. 'We have served the Imperium faithfully for three thousand years. Is this to be our reward? My father's title was bestowed by the Emperor Himself.'

'The title,' said Guilliman, 'was bestowed by the High Lords of Terra, who were speaking on behalf of the Emperor. I am not speaking on behalf of the Emperor – I am speaking with His full and absolute authority. Unlike the High Lords, I have recently conversed with Him. This is an offer I advise you not to refuse, Herodian.'

Many representatives began shouting then, their questions flying at the primarch. Their own power threatened, they seemed to lose a little of their fear of him.

Power is corrosive, thought Calgar. *It erodes respect. It erodes common sense.* The delegates' reaction strengthened Calgar's conviction that what Guilliman was doing was right.

'My people!' the primarch said. He stood upright. 'My captains, my sons, my loyal citizens, you do not understand. These changes will benefit us all, and in time will aid the Imperium. I intend to make Ultramar a model of what the Imperium can be. Look beyond your own borders – you will see our empire is crumbling! I will shore up the walls and make it great again. With the Five Hundred Worlds secure, we shall become a beacon of reason and hope. From here, the restoration of the Imperium can begin.'

'You do not intend to return then?' said Kenot Friche, Chapter Master of the Howling Griffins.

'No, my son, not for a long time. Perhaps not ever,' said Guilliman. He turned his face upon Marneus Calgar. Calgar struggled to hold eye contact. 'The task of presiding over all the tetrarchs I leave to you, Master Calgar. You remain Lord Defender of Greater Ultramar. You are the ruler here, as you always were. Though you are to return to Vigilus, this realm remains your responsibility. Do not judge yourself by my standards. I am a primarch, you are not. I must lend you the weight of my authority and the warriors to keep Ultramar safe. The Imperium needs Ultramar, but it also needs me. I cannot remain here, but I will leave you in a position of greater strength when I depart. We have lost many warriors here, and three of the realm's six star forts. I will let my attention linger a little on our home, until I am satisfied.'

Another subtle rebuke cloaked in kind words. Calgar bowed his head. Guilliman should not need to do this. Calgar should have managed the realm himself. It did not matter that he was absent these last years. That was no excuse. Having the primarch intervene was humiliating.

'As you command, my lord,' said Calgar.

'And now, to the war,' said Guilliman. 'My brother retreated from Macragge at the first sign of my ships. The siege of Ardium is almost over. I will return there to conclude its relief when we are done here. After the situation is stabilised in the home system, we will counter the actions of the three enemies who dare to invade our realm. We must attack on every front, even if it means defeat within certain theatres. Mortarion's forces must be prevented from reinforcing themselves. They must all be occupied.'

'Cut them off and cut them into pieces,' said Quentus Carmagon, Third Captain of the Knights Cerulean. 'Only you could do this, my lord.'

'My preference is to unite and lead,' said Guilliman grimly. 'But where I turn from peace to war, I shall divide and conquer.' He tapped the map. 'I shall run my brother down, and I shall kill him for all the evil he has done here. If I could slay him a hundred times I would. No suffering is too great for his crimes, the first and greatest of which was his treachery.'

'Where first, my lord?' asked Bardan Dovaro, Chapter Master of the Novamarines.

'Where first indeed.' Guilliman crooked a giant finger. The gates of the hall opened, and a hololith emitter floating on a suspensor field was pushed in by a pair of Chapter-serfs. A quartet of Sisters of Silence bearing tall spears escorted it, each forming the corner of a hollow square around it. The machine was guided to a gentle stop not far from the table.

'Before we came here, I had Tetrarch Felix lead an expedition to the Palace Spire of Hive Creostos on Ardium,' said Guilliman. 'I needed to know how my brother is effecting this plague of the dead, and how his daemonic allies are able to cloak themselves in false flesh so easily in the heart of our kingdom.' He paused. 'There are certain writings that refer to an artefact known as the Hand of Darkness. I believed this device to be the cause.'

'We know of it,' said Calgar. 'It was taken by Abaddon centuries ago, and used by him in the Gothic War. Some learned men say it allowed him to subvert the Blackstone Fortresses in the Gothic Sector. There is little else in our records.'

'It is an ancient device, from aeons before the first age of humanity in the stars,' said Guilliman. 'He who possesses it can direct the energies of the warp easily, and on a massive scale.' He paused again. 'It has come to my knowledge that Mortarion has it – a gift from the Despoiler.'

'From which source do you know this?' asked Calgar.

'The Ynnari of the aeldari. They did not claim the device as theirs, but I suspect it was crafted by their forebears. They have an interest in knowing its whereabouts.'

A murmur passed through the crowd. The aeldari had been instrumental in returning Roboute Guilliman to life, but they were xenos, and could not be trusted.

'Peace, my people. I do not take their word at face value. It was one of many things their envoys revealed to me during my journey to Terra. They insisted that the dead walked at

Abaddon's command across the galaxy because of some sub-version of this device by Mortarion. When tidings of this new plague of the unliving afflicting Ultramar reached me upon my crusade, it added weight to their argument. The rebellions we have been suffering strengthened my conviction. These upris-ings are a madness, and what is madness but a malady of the mind? Observe. Sisters, activate the hololith.'

One of the Sisters of Silence turned the device on. It thrummed powerfully. Loop projectors glowed as the emitter set up a limited-composition stream-cone that glowed silver and white.

'The Sisters stand guard around this thing to shield you from its power,' said Guilliman. 'Even an image of it has the poten-tial to corrupt.'

Combat feed taken by Felix's helm-lenses took shape on the hololith, displaying the strange clock from the Palace Spire chapel.

'Now see,' said Guilliman. At a pass of his hand, a further layer was added to the image, a web of globular strands that overlaid one another and pulsed menacingly. They were such a dark green that they were almost black.

'That does not look like how I imagined the Hand of Dark-ness,' said Calgar. 'I say that is not it.'

'You are correct, Lord Calgar,' said Guilliman. He was distracted, somewhat distant, and in his troubled state he unknowingly spoke down to the Lord of Macragge. 'It is not the Hand of Darkness itself, but a device created by Mortarion using the Hand's power and knowledge he has prised from its workings. This network you see here is psychic in nature. It spreads all over Ardium and beyond, reaching from world to world where similar devices are located, aiding the armies of the Plague God. Codicier Maxim, please.' Guilliman gestured to the Aurora Chapter psyker.

Maxim rose from his position among the assembled Space

Marine leaders. He had come to the meeting bareheaded. Beneath the deep blue of his armoured cowl was an old man who had seen enough evil to last several lifetimes. His snowy hair played host to cables burrowed into his scalp. Power shone in the whites of his eyes. They were trapped by wrinkled skin, topped by a collapsing frown that would never lift.

'I have felt this uncleanness too closely,' said Maxim. 'The touch of it pollutes my mind still. This machine dirtied the psychosphere of Ardium like sepsis in blood. Mortarion has created a psychic weapon that has our people turn against their rulers in the face of all sense, and the dead turn against the living. A net of corruption has been cast about Ultramar by the fallen primarch. Mortarion draws it ever tighter. He sickens the realm in the same way he infects the population with his phages.'

'Lord Tigurius had sensed something of this,' said First Captain Agemman. 'We had no idea of the scale of it.'

'You did not,' said Guilliman neutrally. 'Mortarion's Legion was famed for its commitment to blunt assault and an obsession with staying power in the face of overwhelming enemy fire. They were crude strategies born of pride, and costly. But he is capable of subtlety, and when he chooses the quiet game he is at his most dangerous.'

'It would explain why his movements have appeared so random,' said Captain Torkos of the Howling Griffins. 'If he were planting these devices…'

'Quite,' said Guilliman. 'My once-brother made these things. He is installing them himself. He never did trust others. Consider how your defences have failed in the areas where Mortarion has been seen. The capabilities the devices grant him concern me. If he can draw so upon the empyrean in so many locales, other options might be open to him in addition to the creation of undead hordes and the poisoning of minds. The Cicatrix Maledictum's influence should be weak here in Ultramar, but I find it is not. Mortarion is the cause. The aid of his diseased master is always close to his hand. What is occurring on Iax, for example, gives me great cause for worry. The daemons were brought there, somehow, through this warp network derived from the Hand of Darkness.'

'Then we should go to Iax,' said Calgar.

'Not yet. The creatures there will be too powerful to overcome. First, I shall lead Imperial forces to Espandor. It was there that the war began. It is there that we shall begin the finishing of it.'

The hololith shut off. A collective sigh of relief whispered from the mortal members of the quorum.

'Espandor lies closest to the Scourge Stars,' continued Guilliman. 'It is a corridor for war materiel, and a conduit for the warp. Through that system, Mortarion's armies come, riding fast upon the network of the empyrean's filth that we saw upon Ardium.' Guilliman leaned back from the table, his eyes glinting with the prospect of revenge against his brother. 'By retaking the system, we will cut off Mortarion's ability to resupply his fleets. If we can locate these machines upon Espandor and disable them, the torrent of power sickening the soul of Ultramar can be closed off. His daemon legions will struggle to remain manifest. The dead will not rise so easily.

'Once his mortal forces are isolated from one another, and we can be sure they will not be reinforced by uncanny means, then we might begin their destruction. From what Captain Ventris told me at Raukos, the warriors of Espandor Prime still hold out, but their days are numbered. I say now is the moment to lend them the full strength of our armies and retake the system completely. I name this endeavour the Spear of Espandor. Let it be noted.'

There was no discussion, no semblance of inviting debate. The Imperial Regent stated his intention, and it was accepted. The Space Marines in the hall would follow without question.

Guilliman looked down at the map again. 'I swear it shall be so, for all the people of Ultramar, and the Imperium.'

CHAPTER TWENTY-ONE

ESPANDORIA TERTIO

Espandoria Tertio's spires were tantalising lines on the horizon. Three weeks of fighting had pushed the Imperial advance closer to the city, through minefield and trench network. The city was almost won, and with it the eastern part of the main continent. All that lay between the primarch's forces and victory were the final defences, moated by a sea of mud that was formerly the River Oderia. The river's flow was blocked, causing it to back up and its waters to seep into the earth. The result was an expanse of muck where solid and liquid were indivisible.

Within Espandoria Tertio was the last, and the most powerful, of Mortarion's warp engines on Espandor.

Void shields and defence batteries made an aerial assault impossible. The battle for Espandoria Tertio would be won the way wars had been won since one man had hit another with a rock on the dusty plains of old Afrik – face to face.

'Forward! Forward! Forward!' Felix screamed as loud his as

lungs would allow. His battleplate amplified the cry tenfold, feedback pushing it to the edge of comprehensibility.

A wave of blue, green, gold, red, black and white-armoured Space Marines rose up from the Imperial earthworks and followed the Tetrarch of Vespator in charging headlong at the Plague Marine position. Dozens of Space Marines in the livery of the Ultramarines were around Felix, many of whom had fought with him at Ardium, including Sergeant Hellicus and Sergeant Tevian. The rest were veterans from the initial Ultima Founding reinforcements sent to Ultramar. Among them stomped Malcades, the first Primaris Space Marine to fall in the Plague War, now bound into the massive shell of a Redemptor Dreadnought.

Together the Primaris Space Marines sprinted forwards, outpacing their older counterparts and defying the cratered mudscape to close with their enemy.

Flights of dozens of Land Speeders of many Chapters howled overhead. Their gravitic impellers forced steep Vs of liquid earth to spray skywards, interleaving in patterns of brief beauty. Felix felt the push of their engines as they sped on, and filth rained on him after they had passed. Heavy bolters thunked on the Land Speeders' topsides. As they drew closer to the enemy, these were joined by the whining scream of assault cannon rotary barrels, and the roar of meltaguns and rockets.

A bunker on the far side of the mud sea exploded in a cloud of green-tinged flame. Small-arms fire rose up to meet the Land Speeders and they broke their formation apart, jinking at incredible speed to avoid being downed, but a few were hit. One suffered a violent explosion that took its left engine away. Smoking debris fell from its rear, and it took a steep dive. One of the two crew leapt to safety; the other went down with his craft as it tore into the sodden earth with a dull crump, sending up a column of black smoke.

'Forward!' screamed Felix again. He and his lead phalanx hit the river's edge. The filth he was wading through rose up to his waist. 'Forward!'

The motive systems of his Gravis armour pushed him on against the drag of mud. His part of the advance was driving into the worst of it, and the going became hard. It seemed Espandor itself wished to keep him captive and prevent his victory.

'Forward!' he cried again.

His voice became a growl matching the protests of his armour as he struggled against the drag of the mud. He went over the edge of the riverbank proper, hidden by six feet of liquid soil, and the mud suddenly deepened to his neck. A dead man bobbed to the surface with a sucking belch, his rotting head lolling on his neck. There were many dead there, decaying into the mud sea, their flesh becoming part of it. All were mortal human soldiery. The diseases the enemy spread hit baseline humans hard.

Felix found himself struggling through a reef of bones where liquefied flesh clung to his armour. *Keep your eyes forward. Look at what is to come,* he told himself. *The past is dead, the present nearly so. Only in the future is there life.*

The unknown awaited them. Orbital pict-capture of Espandoria Tertio had been impossible through the thick clouds of flies that masked the city in all weathers. Other auguries met with the same lack of success. Psychic probing yielded only maddening visions for those psykers brave enough to try. Not even Lord Tigurius or Codicier Maxim had had any success. Mortarion's clock would have to be found on foot.

More than a few senior Space Marines had opined that the population was long dead, and that the city should be levelled from the void. Guilliman had told them they were wrong. He had commanded a ground assault to clear the enemy away. He had given a speech condemning any man who would level an Imperial city while its citizens might be alive. Privately, he had confessed to Felix that the others could well be right, but that the city must be taken, in any case, for they must be assured that Mortarion's warp clock was destroyed.

Felix was not sure which factor was the most important to the primarch. Mortarion could withdraw his device anyway if the battle went against him. He was part daemon, so they said, and no longer bound by universal laws. Guilliman had pulled medicae teams from across the sector to treat any of the city's population who might have survived, though Felix was not hopeful that such people still lived. The truth was there was little to choose between either as justifications for the battle, but they were worthy aims, and Guilliman wished to fulfil both.

At that moment, Guilliman awaited in orbit aboard the *Macragge's Honour*, directing the operation and trusting to his ground troops to locate Mortarion's device.

What intrigued Felix was how the primarch explained his actions. Whichever he said was most important to him depended on who he was speaking to. In this way, the primarch directed the energies of his followers according to their own prejudices without actually lying to them. There were almost certainly other factors he kept to himself. This level of layered communication astounded Felix. Though he understood it well enough, he felt he was seeing something that should have been obvious to him months ago. Grappling with the concepts of administration made Felix feel apish in mind, as if his brain were not truly made for it, even though the primarch assured him he was talented in that direction.

Maybe it was a matter of training. He had spent thousands of years preparing for war, and only a few practising statesmanship. If the primarch said the Adeptus Astartes were made for peace as well as war, then it must be true. Even so, Felix had so much to learn. If he could emulate only a tenth of what Guilliman did, then he could count himself worthy of being a tetrarch.

Felix dearly wanted to be the one to find the fallen primarch's machine, and help deliver it to the Avenging Son. Destroying the Ardium clock had been child's play compared to tracking this one down. Stopping it would be an achievement he could understand. Then he might feel worthy of the honour bestowed upon him.

The assault was faltering. All across the front the Space Marines were slowing, caught by the sticky embrace of the river. They had begun their run from the Imperial trench line gleaming, all their colours bright and clean. Now they were caked in filth, a uniform grey-brown. The unspeakable slurry came up to Felix's breathing grille. His armour sealed itself against the mess, increasing the heat generated by his reactor as it could not easily bleed the excess. A chime warned him that his thermal vents were closed, drawing his attention to a pair of bars among a miniaturised display of many indicators. The relevant measure magnified itself, blinking urgently. Slowly but surely, temperature indicators rose. His reactor pack became noticeably warm. All his indicators for the battleplate's fibre-bundle stressing were creeping out of their green segments into amber.

When the charge was mired in the river, the Death Guard opened fire upon the Space Marines. They had no choice but to endure it. Guilliman had sent the Space Marines forwards because mortal men could not cross the sea of mud. Now they must trust to their armour.

The battle cries and war hymns of the assembled brothers became grunts of effort. Bolt-rounds slapped into the thick morass. Only when the bolts reached deep into the mud did their mass fuses trip. The mess blunted their power, and the muted shock waves of their explosions hardly quivered the surface. The huge shells lobbed by the Death Guard's siege tanks were another matter, their watery explosions welling up bubbles and decayed body parts from the riverbed.

Across a battlefront almost seven miles long and in the face of heavy fire, five and a half thousand Space Marines struggled on.

In answer to the firing of the Death Guard, a suppressive bombardment set up from behind Imperial lines. Whirlwind rockets shrieked, heaving up domes of soil from the Plague Marines' trench line. The firing cut out temporarily from one quarter or another, but the trench systems snaked back far towards Espandoria Tertio, and the enemy were quick in bringing up their reserves.

The ground was a trap. The sky was a messy exchange of heavy fire. Warriors died, obliterated by direct hits. Now near the centre of the river, the currents strengthened. Near to Felix, a Space Marine sank below the surface and came bursting out again a score of yards away. Felix's footing became unsure as the flow tugged at his legs. It became irresistible and dragged the assault out of line. After a few more moments, Felix's tactical data-screeds showed his formation becoming hopelessly dispersed.

'Press on!' he said. 'Converge on my position when you can!'

To his left, Malcades forged on unimpeded. He was singled out by the Death Guard, and a blaze of anti-tank fire came his way. Shells deflected from his sloping glacis and lascannons burned molten holes in his armour, but he could not be stopped.

There was no logic to the river flow; it looped back and tugged hard in unnatural eddies, spinning men about and dragging them under. The Space Marines pressed on against the river's hindrance, foot by torturous foot, their squads mingling and separating, but always going forwards.

Felix approached the shore. Mounded banks of earth fronted

the river. Filth-encrusted helmets stuck up from behind the enemy's firing positions, many bearing single spikes. A plasma stream scorched the mud to his right, bringing up a wall of steam. A second shot decapitated an Intercessor nearby that Felix knew to be Brother Cleus, a member of the Second Company of the Ultramarines. Drab brown briefly became arterial red, and he sank from sight into the filth, his gene-seed lost.

Felix raised his foot, put it down and felt nothing beneath. He lost his footing and fell with slow inevitability. The mud closed completely over his eye-lenses. It pressed against him in cold embrace. Not even during his many immersions in stasis had Felix felt such all-consuming claustrophobia. Muted explosions throbbed the liquid earth. A nearby detonation sent him staggering to the side; the stabilisation nozzles on his backpack were closed, the internal gyros of his boots confused by the delayed action of his fall. He stumbled, drifted. Heat alarms screamed in his ears. His position moved across his cartograph, until with a muffled metallic impact he connected with the leg of the mighty Malcades. The collision arrested his progress, and he found solid ground beneath his feet again. He was still submerged in the filth, and was forced to rely on his suit telemetry so he did not get turned about. Using Malcades as a marker, he headed for the shore.

The riverbed rose under him. He felt the grind of a shingle bank beneath his boots. He forced his way out, his backpack emerging first, then his head, then the domes of his pauldrons. He strode forwards the last few yards towards the trench line, the way becoming easier with every step, though he needed to use his auto-senses to see while gritty filth ran from his eye-lenses. The enemy homed in on him quickly, and let fire. Dozens of bolts sped at him. Most exploded on the protective energy field generated by his iron halo. Aggressor armour had been designed with boltguns in mind and the thick battleplate protected him from the worst of the fusillade that got through. His heat vents opened, squirting mud. Air roared from them, and the temperature gauges shrank back to their normal size. Other warnings took their place as his energy field and armour were battered.

'Forward!' he roared again. A wailing machine bellow announced Malcades' emergence. The Dreadnought came out of the river streaming filth from every plane of its armour, its rotary cannon already spinning up to fire.

Without waiting to see if any others were near him, Felix rushed at the enemy line. Bolts crashed. Nine strides – that was the distance. In the second that it took him to cover the ground, he activated the disruption fields around his power sword and boltstorm gauntlet. They crackled spectacularly, the disrupters instantly baking the mud and sending it cascading from his weapons as beads of dirty glass.

'For Ultramar!' he roared. Selecting a target, he levelled the gun built into the back of his gauntlet and opened fire. He drove the enemy back from the lip of the trench with his attack, bolt-rounds blasting divots of soil from the lip and whining off corroded pauldrons. Other guns joined his, in ones and twos and then in hundreds.

'For Guilliman! For Ultramar! For the Emperor!' the Space Marines roared.

Free of the polluted river, they ran into the fray. Thousands of guns replied to their battle cry, felling dozens of them in a firestorm of exploding bolt-rounds. The heroes of Ultramar were riddled with shot and blasted apart. The first rank fell, then the second, but Malcades strode among the warriors of many Chapters and opened fire. His great cannon cut through the defences, hurling the Death Guard into rotten chunks. The Space Marines surged forwards under the cover of his fire, leaping over the trench line and into the foe with the dull crash of power armour slamming into power armour.

As soon as the first lines of loyalists were into the trenches, the Death Guard's fire discipline was interrupted, allowing hundreds more Space Marines to pour into the siege works unharmed.

Their disposition was in chaos. Felix's ad hoc company was scattered across two hundred yards of earthworks. There was not a complete squad in that section. Without their brethren to work alongside or their sergeants to guide them, the Space Marine attack became a war of duellists, individual warriors picking their targets at will.

There was no time to regather his forces, so Felix fought alone. He crashed down onto a pair of hulking Plague Marines and was swallowed in the fierce clouds of flies that surrounded them. The insects rattled off his armour, obscuring his vision, but he saw enough of the enemy's vileness. They were not so tall as him, being of the older gene-stock, but in every other way they were more massive. Monstrous things, bloated beyond the capacity of the human organism to sustain, somehow they remained alive. Their bodies bore other marks of Chaos. One had a slobbering insect's head in place of a human face; the other, tentacles for fingers. The fly-headed warrior went down under Felix. As the foe struggled under the weight of Felix's Gravis armour, the tetrarch punched down, taking the abomination in the face. Felix's gauntleted fist flared. The traitor's mutated head exploded into scraps. The corpse twitched in the mud, the flies falling onto it to consume their erstwhile host as Felix rolled over and opened fire.

Felix drove the tentacled Plague Marine back with a volley of bolt-rounds, but he was hardier, fully armoured head to toe – though his plate was rotted through in places, and punctured with the thick tubes of phage-harvesters, through which the ubiquitous flies crawled like bees in a hive – and he did not fall. The traitor brought his plasma gun up to fire, the charging chamber blazing bright green as his writhing, vermicular fingers wrapped themselves around its trigger. Felix scrambled to his feet and launched himself forwards, the superior systems of his Gravis armour making him preternaturally nimble. He slammed into the hulking traitor, barely rocking him, but got in close enough to punch down and shatter the containment chamber of the gun. Plasma burst outwards. The resulting explosion sent them both reeling.

'One of the Emperor's pretty new sons!' the traitor gurgled. He cast down his broken weapon and pulled out a filthy knife. 'Oh, what rewards would be mine if I could turn you to the primordial truth!'

Felix swung his power sword down in a thrumming arc. He pivoted as he did so, putting all his considerable weight and the power of his armour into the attack.

The Plague Marine laughed. The heretic's size belied his speed, and he deflected Felix's sword with his blade. The shock to Felix's arm was immense. The weapon was small, a combat knife of a type carried by Space Marines since the day the Emperor first set them loose on the galaxy. It was corroded, rusted right through near the hilt. It should have shattered. The power of the impact alone should have sent the Plague Marine staggering back. That was Felix's intention: to come in close, to unbalance and finish the traitor. Somehow, his enemy remained upright, his weapon whole. Unclean power was in the knife and its wielder. Felix's power sword was flung back, a fresh nick in its blade. From this mar a tracery of rust spidered across the metal. The Plague Marine stood firm as old rock.

'I have been fighting the Long War for ten thousand years and more, little soldier,' said the Plague Marine. 'It will take more than a reckless blow like that to fell me.'

The traitor struck. Felix raised his gauntlet, pumping shots into the Plague Marine's torso. Several of the bolts penetrated the crumbling battleplate and exploded in the traitor's swollen chest, but though he coughed and gurgled he did not fall.

The Plague Marine slammed into Felix, and both of them staggered backwards. A hand closed about the tetrarch's throat. The plague knife descended, the dark power infused in it tingling Felix's skin as it pierced the energy field of his iron halo and rushed at his face. With his forearm, Felix smashed the blade aside, and drove the quillion of his power sword through the Plague Marine's left eye-lens. The traitor reared back. Felix followed up with a blow from his gauntlet. The disruption field shattered the traitor's chestplate, and Felix's hand punched deep into his chest. Stinking matter spattered all over him. The traitor hung dead on his gauntlet, but Felix let fire with the gauntlet's built-in bolter to be sure, blasting out the traitor's back and causing his smoking power unit to explode with a crackle of green electricity.

For a second, Felix's eyes and auto-senses were blinded by the insects as they attacked him, seemingly raised to a fury by the Plague Marines' deaths, but they fell twitching shortly, suddenly expiring en masse.

Heavy bolter fire banged out behind him, very close. Felix spun around, ready to fight again, only to see a mud-caked squad of Genesis Chapter Centurions covering his back. Their guns ceased fire. Four Plague Marines were slipping to the ground, multiple holes in their bodies weeping fluid of unhealthy hue. A melta-gun that had been pointed, moments ago, at Felix's back fell into the trench from the hands of the lead traitor.

The sergeant of the Centurion squad saluted Felix, raising his massive powered fist and the underslung heavy weapon to his forehead.

'You have my thanks,' said Felix. 'If you had not intervened, my life would be over.'

'We are all brothers under our colours, lord tetrarch,' said the sergeant. 'Every one of us is a son of the primarch. I would brave the jaws of the warp to secure your life, my lord. In your office, the great days are born again. We stand united against the old enemy.'

Felix scanned the scene. Imperial Space Marines were coming over the edge of the trench all along its length. The Land Speeders had completed their mission further behind enemy lines and had turned back to strafe the front. His view was restricted; Felix could see no further than the nearest bunker. For the first time since he had reached the trench, he paid attention to his tactical displays and called up a cartograph. Felix scanned an overlay of the trench system. Small knots of Plague Marines were holding out nearby.

'Where is your captain?' asked Felix.

'We cannot reach him,' said the sergeant. 'We became separated from our company in the advance. Tracking their locator beacons in this environment is proving hard.'

'Exload your identities to me.'

The sergeant did so.

'You are of the Fifth Company?'

'Yes, my lord.'

Felix pulled up the location of the sergeant's comrades from the welter of tactical data flooding his helm. His own squads had emerged some distance away. There was a knot of enemies closer, and on the other side the Genesis Chapter's Fifth Company.

'I have them,' he said. 'Your brothers are that way.' He pointed. 'Though the enemy lies closer. Perhaps you would join me in their slaughter before you rejoin your brothers, for the glory of Greater Ultramar, and the Imperium of Man?'

They did not hesitate.

'We will come with you, and aid you. Our brothers can wait, tetrarch. We all march for Macragge.'

'As do I.' Malcades' giant frame appeared from the other side of the earthworks. He shifted to retain his balance on the soft ground.

Felix surveyed the core of his little army. Other Space Marines were moving in his direction. He called them to him.

'Onwards,' he said. 'For Ultramar.'

The battle dragged on into the afternoon. Felix and his growing group assailed the bunker nearby, slaughtering the Death Guard within, who were quickly overcome by the Centurions' heavy weapons and Malcades' powerful armaments.

The enemy's resistance was dogged, but doomed. Little more than four Plague Marine companies and auxiliary cultists manned the trenches. Felix expected daemons, or daemon engines, but none came. For all the Plague Marines' hardiness, they were massively outnumbered and quickly bested. The force Guilliman applied was so utterly overwhelming that they stood no chance.

The price, however, was high. Thunderhawks and unarmed lighters came and went over the battlefield, taking the dead and their precious gene-seed away. Many Space Marines had fallen. Felix wondered if any of the progenoid glands of those who had died in the mud could be salvaged without the risk of contamination.

As soon as the last Plague Marine in the trenches was killed, human cleansing teams moved into the complex and began purification by fire. Priests followed when there were transports available, and by late afternoon were chanting prayers over the trenches.

Fighting continued within the city. With the trench network's firepoints and weapons batteries out of action, Imperial aircraft flew over the river in increasing numbers, depositing troops from all arms of the Imperium's forces close in to the city limits. Gunfire soon crackled up from the cathedrum towers of the centre, and Felix pushed on to join the fight there. He bade farewell to the Genesis Chapter, but his small coterie of warriors grew ever larger. Most of his own troops had made the crossing alive and found him as the day wore on. As he reached the edge of the trenches, he joined with a second large group of Ultramarines and lost warriors from other Chapters. They had no officers with them, and deferred to Felix's command.

Beyond the double lines, the earth was less torn up. Espandor's abundant vegetation had been reduced by the poisons of the enemy to a few hardy species scattered on the cracked earth, none of them healthy-looking. Brightly coloured water filled shell craters. Clouds of flies gathered in noisy conclave over these noxious pools, and a chemical tang fouled the air, carried by a thin mist, but that was already lifting. The clouds of flies seemed to vanish when the Death Guard were bested, and as more Plague Marines fell, fewer flies were in evidence. The day cleared, and the sun appeared wanly behind the thinning, toxic clouds.

The further the enemy were driven back, the more the visibility improved. The shattered remains of trees emerged from the departing vapours. Soon Felix could see all the way to the main highway, where Astra Militarum Chimera tanks, caked in mud from their crossing of the river, cut their way across the wasteland, heading with all speed to the centre of Espandoria Tertio. Other Space Marines were landing ahead, deployed from their gunships by the score. Felix urged his men on, eager to re-engage the enemy before they were all dead.

After twenty minutes of marching, they were three-quarters of the way to Espandoria Tertio's compact civitas. The group reached a mound of shattered rockcrete on the edge of a ruined habitation district with clear views out back over the river.

'Wait here,' he commanded his followers. He invited the group's lieutenant and the sergeants to accompany him, and together they set off up the hill.

At the summit, they surveyed the landscape. The roads out of the city were whole, and attracting a growing amount of traffic. On the other side of the sea of mud, teams of Astra Militarum combat engineers had collaborated with tech-adepts to raise a causeway on the site of the Oderia's principal bridge, linking the severed halves of the main highway back together. It had recently opened, and battle tanks were coming over the river in a long column. From their vantage point, the course of the Oderia was apparent as a darker patch in the sea of mud. Heavy earth-moving machines were at work in the distance, clawing at the earth with buckets and shovel hands to clear the obstructions that blocked the flow. Felix imagined that revolting mess suddenly slipping free from the poisoned land, rushing onwards and dirtying the sea.

'Wholesomeness returns,' said Macullus Fides, one of the sergeants. He pointed at the sky. The mud on his armour was drying in the rising breeze, flaking off to reveal his cobalt-blue livery beneath.

Felix followed Fides' finger. A solitary bird winged its way over a ruined exurb. It pumped its wings for ten beats, powering itself forwards, then dropped a little before repeating the exercise.

'This world will be healed,' said Felix. 'The primarch will make it so.' He believed that wholeheartedly.

The group left the rise and pressed on. Shortly afterwards they gained the main highway that fed from the outlying districts into the city proper. The columns of Imperial armour ran nose to tail. Felix had his men form into two files and they broke into a jog, outpacing the gridlocked tanks, Malcades' massive clawed feet making the ground shake.

Soon the centre of Espandoria Tertio was before them.

Espandor was a cardinal world, and therefore its cities were crammed with churches and temples. Felix had still not accepted the way the Emperor was worshipped in this era. It troubled him, though there was no denying the beauty of the buildings raised in His name.

The traitors disagreed far more strongly with the worship of the Emperor than Felix did. All the fine architecture made to honour Him had been brought low. Most of Espandoria Tertio lay in ruins.

Felix had orders to make at once for the central cathedrum, and so he led his company down the main street, rebuffing calls for aid and avoiding entanglement in the localised battles taking place all over the city. Bombardment damage from the invasion was evident in the collapsed buildings and broken roads, but there was a state of advanced decay visible that war alone could not explain.

Plascrete rotted on its reinforcement spars. Evil-looking vines coated buildings whose walls were dangerously tilted on sinking foundations. There were bodies everywhere; Felix and his warriors passed stacks of blackened corpses. It looked like whoever had been gathering the dead had given up some time ago, for there were a great many more bodies in the streets, all bearing signs of sickness. A deadened atmosphere stifled the avenues. Bursts of isolated gunfire echoed down empty thoroughfares. Aircraft and grav-craft raced overhead. Servo-skull probes bobbed in and out of buildings. Together, the noises of machines and the march of feet as tanks and Space Marines came into the city from the west should have been loud and sharp. But the city soundscape was dull. There was a feeling of something malevolent watching them. Several times they started at the sensation of unseen presences. Some of the Space Marines were all for searching the buildings, but Felix disallowed it.

'We are not to be sidetracked. We make for the Cathedrum Magnifica at the centre of the city as fast as possible,' he told his men. 'We must go swiftly. Be on your guard for ambush. Do not engage in any other circumstance.'

Felix soon discovered that there were civilians in Espandoria Tertio.

Amid the filthy ruins of their homes, people survived. They were emaciated where they weren't bloated by disease. There was not a healthy soul among them, but they lived, and they cheered amid their coughs at the warriors who had saved them. Already medicae teams pressed into the centre, ranging ahead of the battle force and putting their lives in danger. Fighting was dying down, and increasingly the sounds of gunfire receded further into the east, changing from those of battle to the single-shot reports of the Emperor's Mercy.

Gaunt faces peered from windows. The civilians were starved and brutalised. But there was defiance in them.

Mankind's spirit inspired Felix. These people had no special gifts, no enhancements, nothing, and yet they lived. These ordinary men and women had suffered the worst the galaxy had to throw at them. It humbled him that he would spend his life in service to them.

They passed through various districts. The Temple Quarter was the largest of all, and surrounded the central square in a thick ward four blocks in depth. Large swathes of the area had been razed, and there was not an untouched building. The streets were half blocked by broken stone effigies and the dented remains of metal statues cast down from their plinths.

As they advanced, Felix's Scouts and Reivers reported that the temples had been defiled with corrupted blood and fetishes put in their place. Always these were made of the vilest substances, mounds of filth and body parts, or bloody bones and the diseased innards of the innocent dead. Felix could not abide to let these things remain, though time was tight. He did not regard the Emperor as divine, but these atrocities were an affront to His majesty, and so Felix diverted some of his men to the destruction of such profanities. Wherever they encountered the marks of the traitors, the Space Marines cast them down. Felix had Eradicator or Hellblaster squads obliterate blasphemous symbols, and when they were done he set the buildings that had housed them alight with his flamers. Materials in the city were wet through and resisted burning, but Felix ordered his warriors to persist, and they left a trail of flaming ruins behind them as they continued towards the centrum.

The Cathedrum Magnifica was five hundred feet tall, and although one of the building's twin towers had collapsed, and the other's steeple was full of holes, it still dominated the city.

The streets were eerily silent. The sensation of being watched grew. As the damaged heights of the cathedrum loomed ever taller over its attendant churches and governmental buildings, the watchfulness became yet more unsettling, the deadening of sound more pronounced. Felix reordered his force, commanding them to circle the cathedrum in mutually supportive fire groups. Together with a Hellblaster squad and a supporting unit of Intercessors, he and Malcades advanced across the open space, the others searching buildings or covering their commander with their weapons.

The state of rot that had hold of the city was most pronounced in the cathedrum. Where the tower had collapsed there was a fan of rubble that stretched halfway across the square. Rotten timbers pointed skywards like black teeth. Diseased plants hung from the crumbling facades. The clouds of flies that devilled the planet had a last stronghold there, and they rose up in droning multitudes from the building, reacting aggressively to the Space Marines' appearance, obliterating themselves on power armour in their desperate need to bite.

The warriors picked their way over the rubble. A mix of religious buildings, departmento offices and commercial premises delineated the square. The majority were reduced to shells. Signs of deliberate destruction were everywhere. Most buildings had carried the Imperial 'I' or the aquila. All these emblems had been torn free or chiselled away, the gougings daubed over with unholy symbols.

The square was impressively sized, but cluttered with the debris of war it looked mournful. Mouldering bodies impaled on stakes were mounted in groups of three and seven, shrinking the scale of the space with the unwelcome intimacies of torment. Ranks of saints stood in niches on the cathedrum's double frontage. All of them were headless and their hands had been hacked off. Beneath the ruined gallery of statues there were three gates, their wood slimy with decay and their metal fittings corroded.

Felix slowed. He held up his hand. The Space Marines readied their weapons.

A second later a rocket streaked down from the intact tower, blasting a Space Marine to pieces. An Intercessor raised his bolt rifle and fired. His aim was true, and the broken remains of a mortal tumbled from on high, landing with a bloody splash on the paving.

'Ware!' shouted Felix.

The Space Marines immediately dispersed, finding cover and bringing their weapons to readiness.

The three gates swung wide. From within the desecrated

cathedrum stormed a screaming mob. They were as diseased and pathetic as their fellow citizens, but their faces were suffused with a hysterical joy and they capered feebly as they ran. They had few weapons, looted lasguns mostly, no real threat against power armour when the crowd used them.

The Space Marines returned fire. Ten seconds of fully automatic bolter fire was all it took to sweep the area clear.

Felix surveyed the resultant carnage. The humans had been blown apart into scraps of meat and cloth. He felt no emotion at their end. They had made their choice. He set his vox-channel to central command.

'This is Tetrarch Decimus Felix,' he voxed. 'Inform the primarch the Cathedrum Square is clear. We shall hold as ordered.'

Felix arrayed his men around the cathedrum perimeter. They waited. The clouds split further, allowing the sun to shine through in its fullness. The day grew muggy, and the thick smell of putrefaction grew worse.

Guilliman arrived half an hour later, escorted by his Victrix Guard, the Adeptus Custodes and ten Sisters of Silence. Codicier Maxim and Lexicanium Gerrundium were among a host of Space Marine psykers that followed, led by Chief Librarian Tigurius of the Ultramarines, summoned back from the southern marches to Espandor. In Guilliman's shadow they seemed small as pages dressed as warriors to honour a visiting lord.

'Tetrarch,' said Guilliman. He dipped his helmet at his one-time equerry. Without slowing, he and his entourage walked through the main gate. 'No one is to enter.'

A pair of Sisters kicked the remains of the traitors away, and closed the door behind the party.

Felix watched the gate a moment. The feeling of a malevolent beast regarding him was so great he had the urge to run. He wished he had gone within, to be at his lord's side, to protect him, as ridiculous as that seemed. Roboute Guilliman needed no protection from anything.

Felix turned his back, facing out into the city. 'Keep watch while the primarch is inside,' he ordered.

'Gladly, tetrarch,' said Macullus Fides, 'though I do not fear for him. There is nothing but ghosts and whispers here now.'

CHAPTER TWENTY-TWO

THEOLOGICA

Guilliman walked under a carved stone motif proclaiming the divinity of his creator and into a space constructed entirely around that belief. The cathedrum enclosed a huge volume to fit the enormousness of the people's faith. The stonework was encrusted with decoration and statuary; it was almost frenzied in its devotion, a plea in stone to be noticed and saved. But like the truth it purported to encompass, the space within the walls was empty.

If only they knew, thought Guilliman. He looked upwards through the roof towards the clearing sky. Beams dangled from decaying ligaments of iron. The floor was slippery with rotting timber and fallen tiles.

The statues were broken, the windows smashed and anything that bore witness to the Emperor's divinity had been damaged, and yet these were the least of the harms done to the building. The desecration of the cathedrum was more fundamental than the mere destruction of art, for the warping effects of Chaos had been forced deeply into its fabric. An unwholesome foetor filled the cathedrum wall to wall. It had similarities to the scent of earth in a forest – a loamy, deep smell, though this had little of renewal to it. The promise of new life it offered up was a lie.

The entourage of Adeptus Custodes, Sisters of Silence and the Victrix Guard fanned out, weapons ready. The Librarians remained at Guilliman's side. Hard sounds clattered through the ruin. There were two major transepts at either end of the long knave. A third minor transept crossed the middle of the church. Like many holy buildings, the cathedrum's plan when viewed from above made the single barred 'I' of the Imperium.

Guilliman surveyed it all disapprovingly. Worship of his creator had become the bedrock of the Imperium. It was as pernicious as the efforts of Chaos, in its way. He did not understand it, but as he looked around this cathedrum, one like many hundreds he had seen all across the Imperium, he doubted his own convictions regarding the Emperor's divinity, and not for the first time.

Theoretical, he thought. *The Emperor is a god and denied His own divinity to protect humanity. Practical, He is a god.*

Or, he continued to himself, *theoretical, the Emperor was not a god, but became one. Practical, He is a god.*

He dismissed the idea. These theoreticals had trooped through his thoughts so often before that he had grown weary of them, but his mind would not stop generating counterarguments to his beliefs.

Theoretical, the Emperor was always a god, but was unaware of it. Practical, He is a god.

No, he thought.

Theoretical, the Emperor became a god to protect humanity. Practical, He is a god.

He is not a god, he thought.

Theoretical, Guilliman thought savagely now, turning his anger against his traitorous mind. *The Emperor was never a god, denied He was a god and has been wrongly elevated by men who see power and mistake it for divinity. Practical, the Emperor is not a god.*

'He is not a god,' said Guilliman out loud. He could not countenance the thought. A being that cold and callous was not worthy of worship.

Why, then, did the question dog him so?

'My lord?' asked Maxim.

'It is nothing,' said Guilliman, coming to his senses. He looked towards the end of the cathedrum where darkness held its secrets close. 'I do not see anything, though the atmosphere suggests all is not well. Where is Mortarion's device?'

'The device is here. It will be at the high altar,' said Tigurius, pointing to the uncertain gloom filling the cathedrum's exedra. 'It hides itself from us in a cloak of bound shadow.'

'There is something there,' said Maxim. 'I can feel it.'

Guilliman looked down the long aisle. Half a mile of marble floor heaped with broken roof tiles was between his party and the altar. His armoured fist flicked a quick signal to the Sisters of Silence in battlemark, their simplified combat language. They bowed and moved quickly, making no sound as they advanced up the cathedrum way, their armour silent and their feet noiseless on the wreckage of the church. Their silver plate vanished into the gloom holding the far transept to ransom.

'Let them go ahead first,' said Guilliman. 'If there is illusion here, their unique gifts will tear it away.'

They waited a while, until a pulsed vox-click came into the primarch's helm. The darkness did not lift. The shadows remained thick, hiding their secrets, the Sisters shrouded now also.

'They have found it,' said Guilliman. 'Come.'

Guilliman's progress up the aisle was far less stealthy than the Sisters'. The shattering of roof tiles under his feet echoed loudly around the ruins. Twenty Librarians of half a dozen Chapters marched in solemn ranks behind him.

They joined the Sisters at the foot of the steps leading up to the altar. They were only feet away, but they could not see it.

'It is here!' gasped a Librarian. The hard emotional pressure of psychic power gathering strength pushed at the hind parts of the primarch's brain as the Librarians of the Adeptus Astartes prepared themselves to fight.

Behold, signed Sister-Commander Bellas. *The weapon of the enemy.*

She went up a single marble step away from Guilliman, closer to the altar. With a sound like the collective death sighs of a dozen old men, the cloak of darkness blurred and fell aside.

Atop the steps, before the grand altar, was a monstrous device, almost as tall as the cathedrum ceiling. A three-legged time-piece of brass and glass and fiendish intention. Throughout its elongated frame, hollow globes held bubbling liquids of no understandable purpose. Three columns of madly spinning clockwork rotated about an axis that, if carefully observed, did not appear to be rooted in the material realm. At the top, three clock faces ran backwards. Each one had its own pendulum, and they swung back and forth in a complicated dance outside of the turning columns, barely missing their neighbours. Their weights were crescent axe heads made of steel sharp as convent whispers. The air screamed faintly as they swung.

Within the open framework of the clock, sinuous dark ener-gies moved, wrapping themselves around crackling cylinders and clockwork that would have seemed commonplace in any other setting. At the very centre, enmeshed in moving gears and impure psychic power, was a triangular menhir, roughly thirty feet high, composed of a greenish mineral. It stood inverted, balanced on its point, the mass of it held up by no more than half an inch's thickness of stone. It throbbed with the intensity of a migraine, a sluggish heartbeat of despair that sank into the soul. Set on red-rusted iron poles around the clock were three cast-bronze representations of Nurgle's tri-lobed sigil. They vibrated with inner power, a shimmering heat haze coming off them.

Where the cathedrum had seemed silent, now it resounded to a rapid triple ticking and the groaning of gears, as if the clock, once noticed, could not hide its corrupting voice and was revealed in totality.

This is an abomination, signed Sister-Commander Bellas. *The servants of Chaos always choose to insult our holy lord where they can.*

Guilliman had made it a priority to re-establish the Sisters of Silence. He had gathered up the broken remnants of their order after arriving back on Terra. As the influence of the Adeptus Astra Telepathica had waxed and waned, their military arm had become less prominent. There had been comparatively many Sisters of Silence during the Great Crusade and the Heresy. Though numerous enough to play a role in the War of the Beast a thousand years after the Heresy, by the 41st millennium they had dwindled towards extinction. Those remaining were occupied aboard the Black Ships, hunting psykers and performing the crucial role of damping the abilities of the cargo. The militant orders of the Emperor's day had been disbanded, diminished or lost to war. The surviving few were scattered around the Imperium, most reduced to a handful of members. They fought on, here and there, but their glory days were a myth at best. They were unremembered by the people they had died to protect.

After thousands of years of obscurity, when Guilliman returned the Sisters of Silence had come back willingly into the light, not because of who he was, but because of what he was. To some of them, he was a living saint. It had shocked Guilliman, that so many of the Sisters of Silence now worshipped his father. Not for the first time, he thought of his brother Lorgar.

The clock loomed over the broken altar like a murderer over his victim. The great slab of exotic stone had been cloven in twain, and the walls behind it were deeply carved with three-ringed symbols. Between them, arcane sigils gleamed with reflected witch-light.

A wooden statue of the Emperor holding out His arms in blessing hung above the altar still, but its head, feet and hands had been hacked off, and the wood was charred all down one side. To the statue's right and left there were small alcoves, each containing representations of the loyal primarchs. For some reason these effigies were untouched. Most looked nothing like their subjects; Guilliman's was laughably idealistic.

With the Sisters standing by Guilliman he was protected from the greater part of the clock's power, but still the sense of evil emanating from it curdled his stomach and made his hands tingle with an urge to violence. It pushed at his mind, voiceless whispers telling him to tear off his armour and abase himself in the squalor of the city's ruin. Were it not for the Sisters forming a circle around it, he would have found it difficult to approach. He pushed back with his own formidable will, refusing to be cowed.

'This is what my brother uses to defile the earth,' he said with cold anger. 'He who was most vocal at Nikaea against the use of psychic power.'

It is the last on Espandor, signed the Sister-Commander. *Such idols weaken the power of your father. Now we have struck down the one in Konor's Reach, and that in the city of Rodosia, this is the sole remaining link to the Scourge Stars. Always, the things of the Plague God come in threes or sevens. If we destroy this, the malady that afflicts this world will be weakened. The daemons will have little power left to remain.*

'Mortarion is not here,' said Guilliman.

'No, my lord,' said Tigurius. 'If he were, we would sense him.'

'Then it is time for me to be away from Espandor.'

Guilliman had dearly wished to face his brother. The chances of meeting Mortarion upon Espandor had been slender, even though the daemon primarch had expended a great deal of effort in investing the cardinal world. He reminded himself he could not be impatient. This was but the first step. He would find his brother, and he would kill him. Patience used to come easier to him.

'This machine will succumb to demolition, as the one on Ardium did,' said Maxim. 'There is a hateful presence here. We must cage it with our minds before the clock can be destroyed.'

'Array your warriors, Tigurius,' said Guilliman. Once the Librarians had arranged themselves around the clock in a loose circle, his hand grasped the hilt of his sword. 'I shall put an end to this personally, with the Emperor's own blade.'

'Guardians of the Emperor, to the Imperial Regent,' ordered Colquan.

The Adeptus Custodes came from every part of the cathedrum to form up around the primarch. The circle of Sisters of Silence turned inwards and they raised their executioner greatblades.

As Guilliman prepared himself to approach the cursed artefact, shouts came from the far end of the church. The door opened a crack.

'What is happening?' the primarch called. His powerful voice echoed clearly down the length of the cathedrum.

'The tetrarch says your priest is here, my lord,' one of the Victrix Guard voxed. *'He insists I let him enter.'*

'Allow him,' said Guilliman. He stepped away from the clock and released his sword grip. 'It is after all his church,' he added.

Militant-Apostolic Mathieu came into the cathedrum with the same air of serenity he exhibited at all times, though he was caked in filth and a long cut marked his cheek under his left eye. Only when he drew closer did Guilliman notice the lines of anger on his face at the sight of the clock. Guilliman was surprised to see he wore no protective garb.

'You are not safe here, militant-apostolic,' the primarch said. 'Disease lingers, and the power of the warp is strong.'

'You are not afraid, my lord.' Mathieu placed his hand on his heart and bowed his head. His plain, undecorated servo-skull buzzed around his head in solemn orbit. 'Why should I be?'

Guilliman looked at him critically. 'I am a primarch, Mathieu. You are not.'

'We are both protected by the Emperor. My faith shields me.'

'Like it protected these people here?' said Guilliman. He gestured at a heap of bones pinned under the fallen roof.

Mathieu smiled. 'Your father cannot be everywhere, my lord, and the faith of some is stronger than others. For the moment, your father protects me.'

'Whether that is true or not,' said Guilliman, 'I would prefer it if you wore an environment suit. See, the Sisters and my Space Marines keep their helms sealed – even Maldovar Colquan and his Adeptus Custodes would not risk being in here without. They are among the closest of all men to the Emperor, and made with great art. If they are cautious, so should you be.'

Very few men would ignore a suggestion like that from the primarch, but Frater Mathieu shook his head.

'I will be well. I have been fighting all day, and I am untouched. I am protected.' He walked around the exedra. He drew dangerously close to the cursed clock. He made the sign of the aquila, but showed no sign of being affected by the malevolence radiating from it.

Guilliman scrutinised the priest, waiting for signs of madness or disease. When Mathieu did not speak for some time,

Guilliman's hand shifted within the Hand of Dominion. He was close to sending the mental command via his battleplate's nerve shunts that would bring it sparking into life. He relaxed when Mathieu knelt in the filth of the floor and bowed his head. There he prayed silently. Several of the Sisters of Silence dipped their helms, as if in communion with him. Guilliman shared a glance with Colquan. The Custodian gave a small shrug that sent his ornate armour into a ripple of gold.

His prayer done, Mathieu stood and genuflected towards the effigy of his god, then he turned to the Emperor's last loyal son.

'Where do they find such hate?' he asked. 'What could make them want to become like this? They have made themselves monsters.'

The question brought a hard expression to Guilliman's face. 'Hatred is in the hearts of all men,' the primarch said. 'It is in my heart. I hate the Death Guard for abandoning reason. I hate my brothers for their betrayal. But I do not blame them. Most hate springs from fear, or shame, or despair. The traitors despair, I am sure. They must feel shame at what they have destroyed, and so they become more extreme in their hatred.'

'You speak mercifully of the heretics,' said Mathieu softly.

'They shall find no mercy from me. They are what they are. But we must not forget that most of them were noble warriors, and were led down this path by others. Words from a beloved leader can twist a man's heart. It was, I believe, the Emperor's fault. If He had not lied…' Guilliman's voice trailed away. He frowned. He questioned himself if that were really true. Maybe nothing could have stopped what had happened. Then he remembered the throne room, and the light, and that vast, inhuman soul touching his.

'Did He really lie?' asked Mathieu into the silence. He was barely breathing, caught up in revelation of his god's words.

'Yes. Yes He did. He knew the true nature of the warp, but kept it to Himself. I deduce He wanted to keep my brothers and I from temptation, but instead ignorance left us vulnerable to it. Horus was a good man before he turned. He was proud and arrogant, that is for sure, but he believed in the Emperor's dream of the Imperium, and the love between them was so strong.' Guilliman looked at Mathieu solemnly. He had once believed that, he truly had. Now he lied just like the Emperor had, because he knew the truth of the Emperor's affection now. 'Chaos found a way to use Horus' love and pervert it. My father made a miscalculation, and it cost us all dearly.'

Mathieu let out the breath he was holding. 'I sometimes forget you walked alongside the holy Emperor Himself, my lord. It is a marvel to hear you speak of Him.'

'I did,' said Guilliman sadly. 'I wish it could be so again.' He had his own reasons for desiring that. He kept them to himself.

Mathieu searched for the right thing to say. 'Gods are not beholden to the same laws as mortal men are, my lord. His reasons for lying are beyond our ken, even yours.'

Guilliman pulled a face at Mathieu.

'Mathieu, you will not convince me that He is a god. He told me this Himself, many times. I spoke with Him like I speak with you now. The Emperor is remarkable, the pinnacle of humanity's evolutionary path, and He has power that you and I cannot comprehend. But He was not and is not a god. He was a man. An exceptional man, but a man nonetheless. As a man, He made mistakes. As a man, He had His flaws.'

'You are His son, my lord,' said Mathieu. 'You have said that you are not a man.'

'I am not a normal man,' said the primarch, 'but I am still human, for all the many gifts the Emperor gave me, and so is the Emperor.'

Mathieu paced around the darkness of the exedra, his sandals plashing in the puddles on the marble as he looked up at the clock.

'If your father has the power of a god, does that not make Him one, whether He believed Himself to be so or not?' he said. 'The Emperor protects us. It is evident in the actions of His holy saints, who are the will of the Emperor made manifest, and the Legion of the Damned, who appear at battle's forlorn hope, and in the Emperor's Tarot, whose readings guide ordinary men day to day.'

Guilliman thought back again to his meeting with the Emperor. He did not like to revisit the occasion; it was as if the memory forced itself on him rather than him actively seeking to recall it. The thing in the cradle of the ancient machines, fed by loathsome technology. And then the golden light, and then the pain...

Guilliman's lips pressed thin. The display had been a form of control. The pain had been a form of control. He was tired of being used.

'He is not a god,' he said.

'He is to me. He is to trillions. Why will you not accept the truth?'

'To me, He was a father.' *A distant, uncaring, heartless, manipulative father,* he thought. 'And a lord. I have died for Him once, and would again. That does not give Him divinity.'

Coldness. That was the defining sensation of his meeting with the Emperor. Infinite, terrible coldness.

He had approached the meeting with dread, fearing what he would find. Would his father be dead? Would He be insane? Would they even be able to talk? When he had been admitted to the throne room and approached the Golden Throne, he had done so as he had approached his foster father Konor's funeral, willing it all to be right, drowning in certain grief. Between the time of the Emperor's ascension to the Throne and Guilliman's own death, the Emperor had spoken to no one. How could anything have persisted for ten thousand years, he had thought. There was the wizened corpse surrounded by banks of groaning machinery. Sorrow suffused everything. The sacrifice required to keep the Emperor alive sickened the primarch, if He were alive. He appeared dead. Guilliman had expected nothing.

But He spoke.

With words of light and fire, the Emperor had spoken to His returned primarch, the last of His finest creations.

A creation. Not a son.

The living Emperor had been a shrewd being, as skilled at hiding His thoughts as He was at reading those of others. What remained of Him was powerful beyond comprehension, but it lacked the subtlety He had had whilst He walked among men. Something was different about Him. Something was very wrong. Being in the presence of the Emperor had been like drawing near to a star. The Emperor's words burned him.

What hurt most deeply was what went unsaid.

The Emperor greeted Guilliman not as a father receives a son, but as a craftsman who rediscovers a favourite tool that he thought lost. He behaved like a prisoner locked in an iron cage who is passed a rasp.

Guilliman had no illusions. He was not the man who brought the rasp; he *was* the rasp.

While the Emperor had walked abroad, He had cloaked His manipulations in love. He had let His primarchs call Him father; He had let them call themselves His sons. He had rarely spoken those words Himself, Guilliman now realised, and when He had He had done so without sincerity. Buffeted by the full might of the Emperor's will unclothed in flesh, a cloak had been ripped from Guilliman's eyes.

The Emperor had allowed them to love Him, and to believe He loved them in return. He had not. His primarchs were weapons, that was all.

Though His power was immense, perhaps greater than it had been before He ascended, the Emperor's humanity was all but gone. He could no longer mask His thoughts with a human face. The Emperor's light was blinding, all-encompassing, but finally – *finally* – Guilliman had seen it as a whole. The being he had thought of as a father could hide nothing from him.

The Emperor did not love His sons. They were things. Guilliman, all his brothers, were nothing but a means to an end.

Mathieu smiled. 'My lord, He is father to us all now. Did your father not speak with you of His divinity when you received your revelation?'

The primarch's scowl was calculated to reveal enough of his anger to shut the priest up, and no more. 'My last militant-apostolic learned very quickly not to ask me what occurred in the throne room when I returned to Terra,' said Guilliman warningly. 'Take this as your lesson. Now, enough of this theological debate. It is time to remove some of the enemy's advantage upon Espandor.'

Guilliman drew his father's sword. Mathieu gasped, though he had seen the Sword of the Emperor drawn on several occasions. Every time, he bore witness to a miracle, for on leaving the scabbard, the blade burst into flame.

Guilliman did not begrudge the priest his awe. There was great warpcraft in the weapon. When the blade had been presented to Guilliman by the captain-general of the Adeptus Custodes after the Emperor's fall, it had somehow fitted his primarch's stature. Guilliman tried to remember how tall the Emperor was, but His living image refused to be caught and examined. In some memories, He was as tall as Guilliman; in others, no bigger than a mortal man.

'I can feel His presence!' said Mathieu. With wide eyes he stared into the flickering shadows made by the fire as if he could see the Emperor looking back at him. 'He is all around us, right now. I can feel His power!'

Guilliman looked at the blade's burning edge. When he held it, he too felt the Emperor close by. There had been places in the past that retained an echo of the Emperor's power long after He had visited. This sword had been his father's own, the blade that had slain Horus and ended the strife of the Heresy.

He hefted the weapon thoughtfully. The firelight danced in his eyes. How it burned was a question of the warp, not of science, for all the machine trappings on the blade and in the hilt. The Emperor had been gifted in both, more so than any other man. The sword resisted all Guilliman's attempts to learn its nature, and he would not release it to any other agency for study.

For similar arts, his brother Magnus had been censured. The retaliation for a warning sent in good faith had created another terrible foe. Another miscalculation on his father's part – only a human could make so many errors.

He is not a god.

Counter to that, no man excelled in so much.

If a man has all the powers of a god, is he not a god? Guilliman asked himself. *That is what Mathieu believes. Theoretical, there is the possibility he is correct. I am not immune to mistake.*

He raised the sword aloft. Its warm, yellow flames beat the darkness back. The scent of incense filtered into the room. The Librarians held up their hands and muttered focusing prayers, the light of their power shining from their eye-lenses and gathering in their hands. The Sisters took a step closer to the clock, suppressing its malevolent power.

'You are not welcome,' Guilliman said, and he did not know

if he was saying it to the stone or to the ghost of his father that seemed to haunt the room. 'Begone to the warp.'

With those simple words he swung.

Whatever its nature, the Sword of the Emperor was anathema to Chaos. It cut through one leg of the clock as easily as if it were butter. The machine lurched, its ticking falling out of time and its pendulums clashing together. Clockwork ground upon the unholy stone in the centre of the device as it took the weight of the mechanism. Sparks sprayed from the rock, but the device did not fall, and the dark energies around it pulsed faster. Guilliman strode to the second of the three legs, drew back his weapon and struck again.

The second leg was cut neatly through. The clock lurched again. All its weight pressed sideways onto the obelisk. It held for a moment, then with the screaming of metal upon stone, the clock collapsed, taking the menhir down with it. The great stone cracked, and its light dimmed. The clock groaned as gears clashed. The mechanism locked, and it was still.

The primarch gestured to the broken device, 'Remove this,' he ordered the Sisters of Silence. 'Make sure all the pieces are gathered.'

They moved forwards. A fusion lance was brought up, and lascutters, and they began to dismember the remains. Guilliman watched them begin work, then turned his back. Mathieu looked at him in adoration.

'I advise you to leave, militant-apostolic,' said the primarch. 'This place is not safe for you. You have been here long enough.'

Mathieu's face changed from rapture. He frowned. 'My lord, I...' He blinked, and pointed.

'Lord regent,' warned Tigurius. 'Something is coming!'

Guilliman looked back at the clock in time to see the first Sister die. A piece of the broken machine shot from the workings she was cutting into, running her through and lifting her into the air on a pillar of brass.

'Daemon!' screamed Maxim.

A pulse of energy boomed out from the wrecked clock, and a foul wind blew in all directions. The carving of the Emperor on the wall rattled and banged against the vandalised stonework, came loose and crashed down to the floor. The Librarians roared with effort, their aegis hoods blazing with psy-amplification.

'We cannot hold it closed – a rift is forming!' one shouted. He fell back, staggering, whips of psychic feedback cracking out and lashing the cathedrum pillars.

The Custodians bowed into the wind, their boots scraping on the floor as they were forced backwards by the unnatural gale. Guilliman planted the Sword of the Emperor in the ground and knelt behind it. Flames streamed from its edges around him, forming a golden shield.

A crack of thunder presaged the opening of a tear in real space, and a heaving, gelatinous presence poured through. Long streams of it wrapped themselves around the clock's workings, its touch turning them green and dull with decay even as it bound them together, remaking them and pulling them into a tall, detestable shape.

A black, oily skin formed over the clockwork and broken stone. The daemon rose up, gathering the stuff of the clock and the menhir into itself, and took on living form. Organs of whirring cogs sank into its chest. Ropey muscle moved under the shining black skin. Where the metal and stone showed in its form, they were corroded: brass and bronze becoming green, fused lumps, and the rock pitting, though it glowed brighter and brighter.

Forearms grew, the fingers becoming long, backward-facing spikes, like the wings of a bat. A short, powerful pair of rear legs burst from the back of the mass. Huge shoulders swelled in seconds, unnatural bones cracking as they grew at pace.

The clock-daemon lurched forwards. For a head, it had the eyeless skull of an equid left long in the forest, green and grey, the honeycomb of its dead marrow showing where the outer layer had failed. It walked hunched over on the knuckles of its elongated fingers, though it had no wing membranes to join them. Indeed, it appeared half finished overall. As it moved its oily surface dulled, becoming leathery, rotting skin. A choking miasma of decay filled the cathedrum.

The wind died.

'Back, daemon!' shouted Guilliman. He raised his sword.

'*I am Qaramar of the Lost Second,*' said a rasping, hideous voice that came from nowhere and everywhere. '*Last Watcher of the Last Moment. Fifth in Nurgle's favour. I cannot be killed. I have seen the end of time. I will be there when the final atomic motion of this hateful realm decays into blessed entropy, and Chaos will be born anew. I am sent here to be your executioner, Anathema's get.*'

'It's a trap!' yelled Tigurius. He raised his hand, and blazed out a fork of warp lightning that stabbed at the daemon's hide.

'Destroy it!' said Colquan.

All at once, the primarch's party attacked. Bolts hammered into the daemon's unnatural body. Psychic power rushed at it.

The daemon marched forwards, its spirit still knitting matter into a false body. The temperature plummeted as it sucked the energy from reality around it. Bolts disappeared like pebbles dropping into water. The thing tossed its head. A stinking mane that looked like rags of seaweed flicked out around its bare skull, and the lightning and fire of the Librarians was turned aside, blasting into the cathedrum. It stomped forwards, growing larger as it moved. Now its skin was full of holes, and ribs gleamed beneath;

a moment later, it was smooth and supple, untouched by time. As it stalked forwards like a dragon from ancient legend, it aged and died, aged and died, over and over, though its mismatched skull remained the same throughout and the stink remained, whether its state was flush with youth or ripe with rot.

Qaramar snickered. *'You cannot harm me. I am the end of time. I am the last moment of decay.'*

It bent its long head low to the ground and drew in a breath that sucked the warriors of the Imperium towards its razor-toothed maw. Then it blew out so hard they were bowled over, and aegis hoods exploded around the heads of a few of the lesser Librarians. They fell, consumed by their own power, their souls burning up as hot white fires stabbed from their eye sockets. Mucus blasted from Qaramar's mouth, a mist filled with gobbets of diseased offal, maggots and all manner of foulness. Where it hit armour, metal rotted, and where it melted its way through to flesh, warriors died. Where it hit stone, it slid and gathered, taking on the shapes of diseased, pot-bellied creatures. All around the cathedrum, plaguebearers rose up, already counting before they had fully materialised.

Qaramar rose onto its muscular hindlimbs, and spread its wing-limbs wide.

'Fear me, for I am the rot-drake, the foul catcher, the master of last moments. I am the death of time!' it said. *'And I am mighty.'*

Qaramar attacked.

The cathedrum became a battlefield. The fog given off by the daemon corroded breathing apparatus, poured down throats and attacked lungs. The enhanced warriors of the Adeptus Astartes and the Adeptus Custodes struggled on, their mighty bodies fighting against the poison, but even their gifts were no guarantee of survival. Several of the Victrix Guard, the cream of Ultramar, fell to Qaramar's pestilence.

The Sisters of Silence attacked it, blades swinging. Their soulless auras perturbed the existence of the daemon, but it swatted them back, or snapped them up in its massive horse's jaws, shearing them in two between scissor teeth. The Custodians charged in, swinging their guardian spears, but they were swept aside by a swipe of the creature's wings, and one of their mighty company died before Guilliman ordered them to disengage.

'Enough! This beast is beyond you. Fall back, I command you! I will fight it!' His sword flaring, Guilliman stepped closer. Qaramar swung its heavy head around to face the primarch.

'You will die. Your bodyguard will die. All things die before Qaramar the Last, the Lifeless, the Never-Living!'

It bounded forwards, the bones of its useless wings clacking against one another. It knocked the Adeptus Custodes down, crushing one underneath a massive hind claw. The power of the enemy was immense. Its very presence scrabbled at Guilliman's soul, threatening to shred the edges and tear pieces away. It roared out a torrent of filth at the primarch; he raised his sword, and its bile evaporated on the blade's fires.

'I have slain many like you,' said Guilliman.

'There are none like me,' said Qaramar.

'There are none like me either.'

Qaramar swung its finger bones likes swords, slashing down hard at the primarch. Guilliman parried one hand, dodging the other. The Sword of the Emperor blazed white hot as it connected with the daemon's skin. But though the sword's touch alone was death to most daemons, it was not enough to harm the Last Watcher. Guilliman was forced back by the dragon-thing's onslaught. The surviving Custodians advanced on it, their weapons swinging in perfect synchronicity with one another. They cut it many times, but the wounds closed as Qaramar aged and grew young in a constant cycle, and the Custodians were always swept away by the blows of the thing's wings, leaving Guilliman to battle it alone. As Qaramar fought, the wing fingers trailed shadow that coalesced into ragged skin. A livid growth of flesh crept up from the base of its equid's skull, cladding it in raw, pulsing muscle.

'With every death, I grow stronger,' it said. *'With every soul I grow greater. At the end of time, I hold all the dead in me, and so none are mightier than I.'*

'This is not the end of time,' said Guilliman. And he struck.

The Sword of the Emperor swung true, flames rushing from its edge like a banner. Qaramar whipped back its materialising wing too slowly. With a crackle of power, the sword cleaved off the tip of Qaramar's littlest elongated finger. Qaramar screeched so loudly part of the cathedrum wall tumbled down, crushing Space Marines and daemons alike. The severed digit-tip skidded up against a pillar, and boiled away to nothing.

Beneath his helmet, Guilliman smiled with savage triumph. 'This is the Emperor's Sword, the great foe of Chaos. It has laid low thousands of your kind. You shall be but an addition to the tally.'

Roaring horribly, Qaramar struck down. Guilliman parried one-handed. Though shaken by the impact, he recovered quickly, raising the Hand of Dominion and raking the side of the creature with bolt-fire. Rotten skin blew out in showers of gore, and when Qaramar cycled back to its youthful state, the wounds remained.

'Impossible!' it hissed.

'I am the light of the Imperium. The Imperial Regent. I was made by the Emperor, and He watches over me now. I shall be your downfall, daemon, not you mine.'

Guilliman swung his sword round overhead, the fires roaring into a perfect circle. He struck again, cutting deep into the forearm of the daemon. Blood and broken clockwork rained down from the injury, and Qaramar roared in anger.

'To the primarch! Let us aid him!' shouted Colquan, dragging himself off the floor, snatching up his dropped spear and eviscerating a plaguebearer with a point-blank shot from its boltcaster.

'*I cannot be killed! I am death!*' cried the daemon.

'There are many that claim that name,' said Guilliman. 'I have killed them all.'

Guilliman pressed his attack, battering at the daemon with a series of lightning blows that filled the space around him with sheets of fire. He carved away the tips of three more wing fingers, and when the creature recoiled, he sliced deep into its right shoulder. It screamed loud enough to interrupt the endless counting of the lesser daemons.

With a bellow almost as terrifying as the daemon's, Guilliman hit its shoulder again, shearing off the whole of its right wing. The limb thrashed about on the floor as it dissolved back into the warp, and the daemon backed away. It attempted its scream again, but a slam of psychic force from the Space Marine Librarians stole its voice and sent it whimpering backwards.

'*I cannot be killed!*' it repeated. '*I am death!*' Brass gears and diseased organs ran from its rotten innards onto the floor.

'Then begone!' shouted Tigurius. Together, he and the other psychic Space Marines bent their will, tearing open the rift the daemon had poured itself through. Purplish light spilled across the ruined cathedrum. Rotting faces gathered there, eager to join their daemonic lord, but the power of the Space Marines held them back, preventing their ingress, and they gnashed their teeth with outrage.

Qaramar skittered back, lurching towards the rift. Bolt-rounds hammered into its side. Sisters and Custodians ran at it and drove their weapons into its flesh, all while Guilliman struck and struck again. The daemon was forced to defend itself, no longer able to attack, its remaining wing batted aside by the Emperor's Sword with every swipe.

Then it stopped, and it laughed.

'You... cannot... kill... me!' it roared, and it reared up. A pulse of power upended the attacking warriors, sending them clattering down the steps of the altar. Dark light flared around it, and its body knitted its wounds, growing its wing anew. It beat both wings, now whole and webbed with patterned flesh. Wafting poisonous air, the daemon rose up over the battling host and spat balls of searing matter down at them.

'Lord Guilliman!' yelled Maxim. 'Force it back! Send it into the warp!'

Guilliman watched Qaramar swoop down the cathedrum aisle, its wings almost brushing the sides. Its long head, now raw and bloody, its sockets filled with rolling eyes, snapped at the warriors of mankind. The doors opened, and Tetrarch Felix came in, his Primaris Space Marines battering at the daemon with a torrent of plasma and bolt-fire. But the daemon laughed, and dived at them, scattering them and slaying three.

'I will end it,' said the primarch. He cast about himself. He spied a set of crumbling stairs within the cathedrum that ended in a broken gallery. They shook as he ran to the top, stone pattering on the ground, and he halted at the edge of the missing floor.

The daemon folded its wings, and turned, nose over tail. It passed down the aisle again, towards the site of the broken clock and the primarch.

'You shall perish, little emperor,' said Qaramar, *'and the Imperium with you.'*

'I think not,' said Guilliman.

Putting all his strength into his legs, Roboute Guilliman waited for Qaramar to come screaming at him; then he leapt. He cleared twenty feet from a standing start, arms and legs wheeling as he fell towards the daemon's back. Qaramar turned its flayed skull around to snap at the Imperial Regent, but he clung on as they both flew towards the portal. Only at the last second did Guilliman reverse the Sword of the Emperor and with both hands drive it down through the beast's back, piercing its mechanical heart.

Qaramar screamed, its wings thrashing. Guilliman leaned back on his sword, making the daemon rear up higher in the air. Power built in the sword, and it glowed incandescently, until light burned in every rent and orifice of the daemon's body.

'Now, my lord, leap!' shouted Tigurius.

Guilliman kicked back off the daemon, jumping sideways as it crashed, body aflame all over, through the tear in space and time.

'Close the rift!' ordered Tigurius.

A shock wave boomed through the cathedrum, blasting out its remaining windows and bringing down another portion of its weakened walls. The remaining lesser warp-born wavered like mirages and disappeared, their droning count fading moments later. The shouts of men calling for aid replaced the sounds of the battle, and more warriors came rushing into the cathedrum.

'It is done,' said the primarch. 'Espandor is free of Mortarion's witchcraft. Its cleansing may begin.'

Guilliman put up and sheathed the sword. The fires went out, plunging the cathedrum back into darkness, but a certain sanctity remained. By the Emperor's own blade, Guilliman had driven back the baleful influence of Chaos. He could not deny the effect. He could not have defeated an enemy like that without the weapon.

Godlike, he thought.

Mathieu sank to his knees. 'Praise be!' he whispered. Tears ran down his face.

'You are still alive?' said Guilliman with mild surprise.

'The Emperor protects. The Emperor protects!' Mathieu said, partway into a religious fugue. 'As you fought and others died, I was unharmed! Praise be, praise be! The Emperor has touched this place.'

'Maybe He has,' said Guilliman. Combat over, he was weary. The emptiness inside him seemed deeper for his encounter with the daemon. His hearts laboured, and his neck scar itched. 'He remains potent, even now.'

'I can feel His love for humanity,' said Mathieu. 'I can feel it all around me!' He hesitated in his rapture. 'Tell me, oh lord regent, truthfully – does the Emperor love us, my lord? Do not say I am wrong!'

The Emperor loves no one man, thought Guilliman. *He cannot afford affection – that is the honest practical for the impossible task that faces the Master of Mankind. He did not love His sons, He does not love men, but He does love mankind. Yet I find it hard to forgive Him. Did His solution have to be built on lies? Lies upon lies?*

Mathieu's question pushed Guilliman deeper into melancholy. More than anything, he yearned to speak with his foster father, Konor, one more time. He had been a noble soul, one who could be trusted. A true father.

Had you not died before the Emperor arrived in Ultramar, would I have abandoned you as quickly as my brothers abandoned their adoptive families? he asked himself.

He knew the answer to that, and it shamed him. No one is immune to the effects of such power, he told himself, but that did not make the truth any more palatable.

He understood. He knew what his father wanted to achieve, and why. Facing things like Qaramar brought it home to him time and again. Knowing what opposed mankind made him see the utility of lies. Could Guilliman honestly say he loved all the men who called themselves his sons? He barely knew them, especially now – Cawl's hordes in particular. They, too, were a means to an end. He and his 'father' had that in common. The mantle of rulership was weighty, and moulded the man that bore it.

I never wanted to be a tyrant, thought the primarch. *Perhaps my father did not wish to be so either. History has roles for us that cannot be denied. We are but pieces on the board of eternity.*

'My lord,' said Mathieu into the primarch's silence. 'Please tell me, does the Emperor love us?'

We are so much more like you than you ever intended, thought Guilliman. *You gave too much of yourself to us. Without realising, in your arrogance, you made yourself a father in truth. We are your sons, in every way. Did you see that?*

'My lord?' said Mathieu

'The Emperor loves us all,' lied Roboute Guilliman. He looked over the broken statue and the few remains of the clock. 'Now leave me be, Mathieu. I must consult with the tribune and the tetrarch.'

Guilliman left Mathieu kneeling in the dust, and went to the gates of the cathedrum where Tribune Colquan, Tetrarch Felix and the rest gathered. Upon the steps outside he unlocked his helmet, revealing his face to Espandoria Tertio's muggy day. He breathed air free of corruption. The Plague God's influence was receding. He closed his eyes, and let the sun dry the sweat on his skin.

'It is done,' said Guilliman. 'We leave Espandor tonight.'

'What are our plans, my lord?' asked Colquan.

'The Genesis Chapter, the Aurora Chapter, the Knights Cerulean, the Mortifactors and sundry other elements are to remain here to purge the daemonic infestation in the far west, and slay the remainder of the Death Guard. The rest of our army will withdraw and redeploy. Mortarion is not here. His web of evil is disrupted. The forces left are a delaying tactic, nothing more. There is no more reason for me to remain.'

'Where do you think he might be?' asked Colquan.

'Parmenio,' said Guilliman without pause. All his careful winnowing of data had suggested either Espandor or Parmenio as Mortarion's base of operations. If Mortarion was not on Espandor, he would be on the other. 'He is on Parmenio.'

'You are sure?' asked Felix.

'I am sure. It is hard to reckon our actions here a victory, but we have taken the first steps to assuring we will win. Let Mortarion feel at ease, and think I cannot find him, nor dislodge him from Ultramar. He is about to be disabused of this misapprehension.'

Guilliman smiled grimly.

'On Parmenio, I will make him see the truth.'

With those words, the primarch passed from the cathedrum and into the ruins of Espandoria Tertio alone, his soul laden with sorrow.

ABOUT THE AUTHOR

Guy Haley is the author of the Siege of Terra novel *The Lost and the Damned*, as well as the Horus Heresy novels *Titandeath*, *Wolfsbane* and *Pharos*, and the Primarchs novels *Konrad Curze: The Night Haunter*, *Corax: Lord of Shadows* and *Perturabo: The Hammer of Olympia*. He has also written many Warhammer 40,000 novels, including the first book in the Dawn of Fire series, *Avenging Son*, as well as *Belisarius Cawl: The Great Work*, *Dark Imperium*, *Dark Imperium: Plague War*, *Dark Imperium: Godblight*, *The Devastation of Baal*, *Dante*, *Darkness in the Blood* and *Astorath: Angel of Mercy*. He has also written stories set in the Age of Sigmar, included in *War Storm*, *Ghal Maraz* and *Call of Archaon*. He lives in Yorkshire with his wife and son.

YOUR
NEXT READ

DARK IMPERIUM: PLAGUE WAR
by Guy Haley

As the Plague Wars rage on, the Emperor's will manifests in Ultramar through miracles that confound the primarch Roboute Guilliman, even as he must rely on them when he faces his traitorous brother Mortarion.